DAUGHTER
OF EARTH

DAUGHTER OF EARTH

A Novel by
AGNES SMEDLEY

Foreword by ALICE WALKER
Afterword by NANCY HOFFMAN

THE FEMINIST PRESS
at The City University of New York
New York

Foreword © 1987 by Alice Walker
Afterword © 1987 by Nancy Hoffman
All rights reserved. Published in 1987 by The Feminist Press at The
City University of New York, 365 Fifth Avenue, New York, NY 10016

11 10 09 08 07 06   13 12 11 10 9 8

Library of Congress Cataloging-in-Publication Data

Smedley, Agnes, 1890–1950.
    Daughter of earth.
    I. Title.
PS3537.M16D3 1987   813'.52   86-33514
ISBN-10 0-935312-68-4 (pbk.:alk. paper)
ISBN-13 978-0-935312-68-3 (pbk.:alk. paper)

The lines from "Song of the Son" from Cane by Jean Toomer are
reprinted by permission of Liveright Publishing Corporation. Copyright
1923 by Boni & Liveright. Copyright renewed 1951 by Jean Toomer.

Printed in USA

Cover photograph of Agnes Smedley (c. 1925) provided by Tillie Olsen.
Cover design by Paula J. Martinac.

Foreword

Another Singing Tree

Pour O pour that parting soul in song,
O pour it in the sawdust glow of night,
Into the velvet pine-smoke air to-night,
And let the valley carry it along.
And let the valley carry it along.
. . . .
O Negro slaves, dark purple ripened plums,
Squeezed, and bursting in the pine-wood air,
Passing, before they stripped the old tree bare
One plum was saved for me, one seed becomes

An everlasting song, a singing tree . . .

JEAN TOOMER, "Song of the Son"

Daughter of Earth is a precious, priceless book. In it
Agnes Smedley lays bare her heart and soul in an
effort to understand and heal her life. In the process,
she—poor, white, nearly slave-class in the "free,"
"democratic" United States where all *whites* at least are
alleged to have an equal chance at "making it"—
connects herself, as if there were no other options, to
all people of her class and vision, regardless of color
or sex. It is a remarkably rare affirmation.

Agnes Smedley was born in the early 1890s in the
"rolling, stony" hills (as she describes them) of north-

1

ern Missouri to parents who, no matter how hard they worked, remained desperately poor. A farmer in Missouri, a miner in the Rockefeller mines of Colorado, a jack-of-all-trades in places unknown, her father, good-looking, part American Indian, romantic—in his youth—worked "like a slave" much of his life, until futility and alcoholism broke him. Agnes's mother, beautiful, with lovely "blue-black" eyes, worked so hard at the washboard cleaning other people's clothing (and deserted for long periods by Agnes's often abusive father) that her hands became large, swollen, "almost black." Agnes's stylish Aunt Helen became a prostitute, feeding and clothing her sister and her sister's children (Agnes among them) from the money she earned on her back.

This is a profoundly harsh story, not for those who want beauty separate from struggle, or who, indeed, feel it is possible. Yet it is the true story (give or take a few minor changes, deletions, or embellishments) of one woman's life. Marie Rogers of *Daughter of Earth* **is** Agnes Smedley, and through her story we glimpse the stories of countless others who could not speak, and who, in any event, were never intended to be heard. Indeed, the people that she writes about with such passionate memory would be surprised, I think, to realize how indelibly their every activity was imprinted on the young writer-to-be, who appears to have recorded every nuance of their personalities as well as her own. This acuteness of perception (similar to that which women experience during the monthly crisis of menstruation, but sustained over dozens of years) is, I am convinced, one of the cruelest products of poverty, for it is in fact an indication of unrelieved

pain, a sign of an extremely loving and sensitive soul—
virtually helpless before the forces destroying all
around it—being tortured to death.

But some of us are given art to save our lives; a skill
or craft with which to throw ourselves a rope. The
creation of this book was certainly one such rope for
Agnes. On it she swung all the way to China and the
second half of a committed, revolutionary life.

Daughter of Earth is another of those "plums" of which
Jean Toomer wrote, just as Agnes represents what
Toomer called "the new race evolving in America: the
American race," by which is meant all of those, black
and white, who choose to acknowledge the full range
of their ancestry, not simply the "black" or the "white."
Agnes Smedley's affirmation of her father's American
Indian ancestry helped her understand better not only
her father, but herself, and she was therefore more
easily able to feel a kinship with all the peoples, colored
and not, of the world. Her presence became a "plum"
and a "seed" among the Indians she befriended (and
on whose behalf she suffered and went to jail) in the
East Indian Freedom movement, as well as to the "red"
Chinese beside whom she joyfully stood in China's
fight for independence.

Hopefully it will be through Agnes's "tree" and
"trees" like it—and not through the U. S. military—
that poor countries around the world will finally know
us. Agnes Smedley never forgot the hungers and
humiliations of her childhood, the oppression of her
parents, the snuffing out of her brothers by the
exploitation of the American capitalist system, or her
own struggle to remember and to affirm them, even
as she fought against falling victim to the poverty that

eradicated them, herself. Everywhere she went she saw herself, her family, her class, her own people's *condition*. Her spirit was darkened at times by all the light in others she saw blotted out. Yet poverty in Chinese or Hindi or black folk speech was recognized as the same language by her; she spoke (and understood) it fluently. This ability then, so far from the capacity of most U. S. white women and men, became for her the gift concealed in the wrappings of pain.

She was a citizen of the planet.

In the cemetery for Chinese revolutionaries outside Beijing where she is buried, "A Friend of the Chinese People" engraved on her tombstone, there are innumerable bright and cheerful hollyhocks. A branch of one had fallen the day I was there in 1982. One pink bloom was left on the ground which I placed on her grave. It was with tears and singing that I did this. It is hard to imagine a more battered, resilient, heroic sister than this woman. Agnes Smedley was a poor white woman who, all her life, continued to think, to act, to write like one. I recognize in her a matriot of my own country.

ALICE WALKER

DAUGHTER OF EARTH

Part 1

Before me stretches a Danish sea. Cold, gray, limitless. There is no horizon. The sea and the gray sky blend and become one. A bird, with outspread wings, takes its way over the depths.

For months I have been here, watching the sea—and writing this story of a human life. What I have written is not a work of beauty, created that someone may spend an hour pleasantly; not a symphony to lift up the spirit, to release it from the dreariness of reality. It is the story of a life, written in desperation, in unhappiness.

I write of the earth on which we all, by some strange circumstance, happen to be living. I write of the joys and sorrows of the lowly. Of loneliness. Of pain. And of love.

The sky before me has been as gray as my spirit these days. There is no horizon—as in my life. For thirty years I have lived, and for these years I have drunk from the wells of bitterness. I have loved, and bitterness left me for that hour. But there are times when love itself is bitter.

Now I stand at the end of one life and on the threshold of another. Contemplating. Weighing. About me lie the ruins of a life. Instead of blind faith,—directness, unbounded energy; and instead of unclearness, I now have the knowledge that comes from experience; work that is limitless in its scope and significance. Is not this enough to weigh against love?

I gaze over the waters and consider. There have been days when it seemed that my path would better lead into the sea. But now I choose otherwise.

I recall a crazy-quilt my mother once had. She made it from the remnants of gay and beautiful cotton materials. She also made a quilt of solid blue. I would stand gazing at the blue quilt for a little time, but the crazy-quilt held me for hours. It was an adventure.

I shall gather up these fragments of my life and make a crazy-quilt of them. Or a mosaic of interesting pattern—unity in diversity. This will be an adventure.

To die would have been beautiful. But I belong to those who do not die for the sake of beauty. I belong to those who die from other causes—exhausted by poverty, victims of wealth and power, fighters in a great cause. A few of us die, desperate from the pain or disillusionment of love, but for most of us "the earthquake but discloseth new fountains." For we are of the earth and our struggle is the struggle of earth.

The first thing I remember of life was a strange feeling of love and secrecy. I was a baby so young that I recall only the feeling—nothing else. My father was holding me close to his huge body in sleep. Was it the dawn of memory . . . or was it a dream!

8

I must have been no more than a year old—for it was much earlier than those beautiful sunny days of my babyhood in the middle 1890's that I spent playing with my older sister Annie under a wide-spreading walnut tree down in the sun-flecked meadows. Above on the hill I heard the voice of my father, the deep beautiful voice, as he labored in the hayfields. My mother came walking down the long path, carrying two pails of water to our tiny log home on the hill. She was barefoot and the wind caught her loose-flowing calico dress and wrapped it close to her slender body.

If you went two steps beyond the well you came to a ditch shadowed by thick bushes and tall elm trees. On the further bank, far back under the clustering bushes, grew flowers so fat and velvety that a ray of sunshine withered them. They grew singly, and the blossoms hung in gentle sprays. Delicate secret thoughts of flowers they were. They were as living beings to my child soul and I talked to them as I talked to the wind in the top of the walnut tree down in the meadows.

We were very poor. But that I did not know. For all the world seemed to be just like our home—at least that world of ours that stretched for some two hundred miles across northern Missouri. The rolling, stony earth that yielded so reluctantly seemed to stretch far beyond the horizon and to touch the sky where the sun set. For us, this world was bounded on one side by the county seat and on the other by the Missouri River. The northern frontier was a town of a few hundred people. The south ended at—well, my father's imagination reached to a mysterious city called St. Joseph on the Missouri River. But then he was a man with the soul and imagination of a vagabond. People listened to his stories, filled with color and adventure, but they did not always believe. For he was not one of them; he was almost a foreigner, in fact. His family was unknown to our world. They were not farmers, and some said they were unsteady, unreliable—a shiftless crew; that was the Indian blood in their veins . . . you never could trust foreigners or Indians.

Later the horizon of our world was extended to Kansas City. That was when the whole countryside was aroused by a young cousin of mine who ran away. In three months he returned—an educated man. He had learned to be a barber . . . and he wore store clothes!

As I sit here I think vaguely of love . . . of fire . . . of the color red. Was it that red bird that came to our cherry tree . . . was it the red cloak I wore as a child . . . now I remember, it was long ago:

I was building a fire—a lovely fire. My stove was made of stones but its back was the wall of our two-room log home. I built the fire on the side near the two tall cedar trees with the swing hanging between them. It burned brilliantly and beautifully, and would have been still more beautiful if my mother had not found it and tapped me on the head with her steel thimble. She was always tapping me with a hard steel thimble that aroused all my hatred. My beautiful fires, my glorious fires that she stamped out when she found them . . . it was like stamping out something within me . . . when the flame flared up it was so warm and friendly! Now I know the spiritual link between fire and the instinct of love. But my mother did not know it. She had gone only to the sixth grade in school. My father did not know—he had gone only through the third: a man didn't need more, he said. Education was only for women and men who were dudes.

I remember my mother's thimble taps, and I remember a tough little switch that cut like a knife into the flesh. Why she whipped me so often I do not know. I doubt if she knew. But she said that I built fires and that I lied. What business that was of hers I was unable to see. As the years of her unhappy married life increased, as more children arrived, she whipped me more and more. At first I did not know that I could sometimes hit back at a person who deliberately struck me; but as time passed I learned that only by virtue of her size she had the power to do what she would with me. I longed to grow up.

She developed a method in her whippings: standing with her switch in her hand, she would order me to come before her. I would plead or cry or run away. But at last I had to come. Without taking hold of me, she forced me to stand in one spot of my own will, while she whipped me on all sides. Afterwards, when I continued to sob as children do, she would order me to stop or she would "stomp me into the ground." I remember once that I could not and with one swoop she was upon me—over the head, down the back, on my bare legs, until in agony and terror I ran from the house screaming for my father. Yet what could I say to my father—I was little and could not explain. And he would not believe.

My mother continued to say that I lied. But I did not know it. I was never clear. What was truth and what was fancy I could not know. To me, the wind in the tree tops really carried stories on its back; the red bird that came to our cherry tree really told me things; the fat, velvety flowers down in the forest laughed and I answered; the little calf in the field held long conversations with me.

But at last I learned to know what a lie was: to induce my mother to stop beating me I would lie—I would say, yes, I had lied and was sorry, and then she would whip me for having withheld the admission so long. As time went on, to avoid a whipping, I learned to tell her only the things I thought she wanted to hear.

"I have but one child who is stubborn and a liar, and that is Marie," she would tell strangers or neighbors. At first I was humiliated to tears; later I became hardened; later still I accepted it as a fact and did not even try to deny it.

It has been one of the greatest struggles in my life to learn to tell the truth. To tell something not quite true became almost an instinct. In pain and tears I have had to unlearn all that my mother beat into my unformed mind. It was difficult for her to beat my need of her love out of me. It took years, for with the least return of kindness in her my love swept back. I see now that she and my father, and the conditions about us, perverted my love and my life. They made me believe I was an evil creature ... I accepted that as I accepted the statement that I lied; for they seemed infallible. Still there are tears I have never forgotten ... childish tears that are said to have no meaning, and pain that children are said to forget. I am weary of memories of tears and pain.

In the west a deep blue cloud was rising and riding on the wind in our direction. It became black and a sinister yellow streak in the center grew and swept onward with it. In terror we watched the yellow streak—my older sister Annie, six, my toddling baby sister Beatrice, and I; for the yellow streak meant danger. A cyclone was coming.

My father and mother were not at home. I had been building another fire behind the house when Annie's cry had interrupted me. She started to drag us across the big cornfield to a farmhouse far away, but suddenly she stood still and screamed with joy. We looked: there, turning a distant curve and sweeping down the long white lane my father and mother came, riding the two snow-white horses of which my father was so proud. Down the lane, faster than the approaching storm they came, and I heard the drum of the horses' flying feet on the hard white road. It grew louder and louder. They swung in at the gate, dashed up to the door, my mother sprang from the saddle and my father, without halting, dashed away with the horses to the stable.

In a few moments we were in the underground cave, my father following with mattresses, feather beds, blankets and an ax. My mother was screaming to him to bring the new sewing machine and the clock—her two most valued possessions—and to bar the door of the house. The wind before the approaching storm had already reached us. My father rushed down the steps, drew the cave door down against the flat earth and bolted it. Then we waited.

The cave was lighted only by a lantern. About us hung the damp odor of earth, of jars of canned fruits, of melons, apples, sweet butter and thick cream in crocks. It was just like going to a picnic to have a cyclone like this and to lie down in the soft warm featherbed and smell and hear and see and feel everything!

There came a great roaring, as of rain and wind, and something fell against the cave door.

"Be quiet," said my father to my mother. "If we're buried, I've got the ax."

"Suppose somethin' falls on the air-hole?" and she glanced up at the little wooden air escape in the middle of the cave roof.

"I'll cut us out, I'm tellin' you. There ain't no need losin' your head until somethin' happens."

I listened to his voice and knew that I could put him up against any cyclone that existed.

The roaring continued. My father's voice came from the passage leading up the steps to the door. "It ain't no cyclone"; and he unlocked the door and peered through the crack. "The house's still standin'. The cedars break the wind." A long silence. "The wind's goin' down. There ain't no danger."

"You never can tell."

"I know. I know the cyclone that struck St. Joe. It sucked up cattle an' horses in it, an' men an' houses an' fences, an' set 'em down miles away. It cut right across country fer sixty miles an' they tried to dynamite it to break it up. You could see it comin' fer miles, a long black funnel . . . it sucked up a smokehouse in one place an' left the house, ten feet away, standin' as clean as a whistle! I think there must 'a' been well nigh a hundert people lost in that there cyclone."

Long afterwards I remember telling a girl friend of mine that once a cyclone swept our smokehouse away, along with the horses and cattle, but left our house, just ten feet away, standing as clean as a whistle! Well nigh a hundred people were lost in that there cyclone, I related, and told her just how houses, fences, men and horses tumbled out of the air around us.

For I was my father's daughter!

Strange men from beyond the hills came to our farm and brought a huge black stallion. The women could not follow the men to the field where our horses ran loose, and we children were told to play behind the house. That was just reason enough for not playing behind the house. My father came to my mother, took money and went back to the field again. Then the men took the stallion away. Mystery hung over everything; and a secrecy of which no one spoke.

A few days before a baby calf had been born and I had seen it. It was I who brought the news of the marvelous event; but then my father and mother forced me to keep out of sight of the field where the mother and calf were, and where I had been but a few moments before. The thing I had seen I dared not talk about or ask about without "deservin' to have my years boxed."

Slowly I was learning of the shame and secrecy of sex. With it I was learning other things—that male animals cost more than female animals and seemed more valuable; that male fowls cost more than females and were chosen with more care. Even when my little brother was about to be born, we children were hurried off to another farmhouse, and secrecy and shame settled like a clammy rag over everything. At sunset, a woman, speaking with much forced joy and in a tone of mystery, asked us if we wanted a little brother. It seems a stork had brought him. But the woman's little girl of ten, very wise to the ways of the world, took us out behind the henhouse and explained the stork story with very horrible details and much imagination.

The next day my father bought a box of cigars from the town and distributed them among men who drove up to congratulate him as if he had achieved something remarkable. They passed a whiskey flask around. A *son* had been born! I felt neglected, and when I ran to my father and threw my arms around one of his pillar-like legs, he shook me off and told me to go away. There seemed something wrong with me . . . something too deep to even cry about.

"Why?" I have asked over and over again, but have received no answer.

Our log home had but two rooms. In one stood our two beds; the other was the kitchen, dining, sewing and workroom all in one. In one bed my father, mother and baby brother slept. In the other, my two sisters and I.

One night I was awakened by some sound and I turned uneasily. It came again. It left me lying, tense with a nameless fear, my eyes closed, yet trembling in terror. An instinct that lies at the root of existence had reared its head in the crudest form in my presence, and on my mind was engraved a picture of terror and revulsion that poisoned the best years of my life. From that moment the mother who was above wrong disappeared, and henceforth I faced another woman. Strange emotions of love and disgust warred within me, and now when she struck my body she aroused only primitive hatred. Only a little later I heard her tell something that was not true, and the perfection I had thought hers, cruel though it was, vanished. For years afterwards she and I gazed at each other across a gulf of hostility. When she came to know that her word or wish had no influence upon me, she began to threaten me with my father. She failed; for he had never struck me and I knew he never would. She was fallible but he was not. His word was enough for me—I obeyed. To be like him, to drive horses as he drove them, to pitch hay as he pitched it, to make him as proud of me as he was of my new baby brother George, was my one desire in life.

There was another day when my mother laughed at little George, sitting flat on the floor of our wagon bed as we all bumped along over a rutty road. His fat cheeks were trembling from the jolting, and when he saw my mother laughing at him, tears rolled down his face.

"That's it, laugh at the boy!" my father shouted bitterly.

Something gripped my heart and I crept up to my baby brother and put my arms around him. He snuggled against me and was comforted. My father glanced at us and said no more and my mother ceased her laughing. From that moment my brother George was dear to me above all things.

My grandmother was a tall, strong woman with stringy gray hair flying about her face, and eyes as black as the night when there is no moon. She went barefoot, smoked a corn-cob pipe, and wore loose-flowing Mother Hubbards. Since my grandfather was slowly dying of consumption, she managed their farm, as well as five grown sons and eight grown daughters. She had brought three daughters and two sons into this marriage; my grandfather had contributed the rest. Mildred, a daughter just my age, had been the fruit of the marriage of these two.

This grandmother of mine was, strangely enough, my aunt as well, for she was my father's elder sister. My grandfather always complained against the worthlessness of her family, against my father in particular. He had not intended to marry her, it seems. It had been an accident. My father and mother had met, fallen in love almost at first sight, and although my mother was but seventeen, had run away to a distant town and were married. My grandfather had raced after them in hot anger, for he was determined that his daughter should not throw herself away on such a man, a man who was part Indian at that! He had found them in this woman's home, she a widow wringing a living from life for herself and her children. Perhaps it was unfortunate that he was a widower and a gentle, pliable soul. For this indomitable woman led him to the altar and married him as quickly and as securely as my father had married my mother. Thus she became in due course of time my grandmother also. The two families became hopelessly mixed up, and I never knew exactly whether I should call her grandmother or aunt, or whether to call her children cousins or aunts and uncles. I compromised by calling her Aunt Mary.

She was a woman with the body and mind of a man. Once married she assumed control of her new husband and all that he possessed. When her word failed with her own or his children, she used her hand. It was a big hand. She milked the cows each morning and night with the sweeping strength and movements of a man. She carried pails of skimmed milk and slopped the hogs; when she kneaded bread for baking, it whistled and snapped under her hands, and her arms worked like steam pistons. She awoke the men at dawn and she told them when to go upstairs to bed at night. She directed the picking of fruit—apples, pears, peaches, berries of every kind, and she taught her girls how to can, preserve, and dry them for the winter. In the autumn she directed the slaughtering of beef and pork, and then smoked the meat in the smokehouse. When the sugar cane ripened in the summer she saw it cut, and superintended the making of molasses in the long, low, sugar cane mill at the foot of the hill.

She extended her managing ability to the love affairs of her daughters. Her sons went courting at other farms where she, unfortunately, could hardly follow. But not so with her daughters. When their beaus called she herself would see that the parlor was in proper order, that the organ was conspicuously open so that the young man might know that this was no house to trifle with. She gave her daughters instructions in private, and when the victim called, she herself locked the parlor door and ordered us children out into the back yard to play. After the young man had called as many times as she thought necessary for any man to make up his mind, she herself went in the parlor and asked him his intentions. No man could look her in the eye and have anything but honorable intentions.

She was like an invading army in a foreign country. And like all invaders, she was a tyrant. On Sundays we were always at her home—no one thought of it as other than *her* home—for dinner. She sat at one end of the table, and my gentle, complaining grandfather at the other. They were almost shouting distances apart; for, along one side sat some eight men and women; along the other as many more, with children wedged in between. I sat near my mother and tried to eat unobtrusively. But one day I found a fly in the piece of blackberry cobbler she had carved and put on my plate. I pushed it aside. She turned her black eyes on me and laid down a law I have never forgotten:

"Flies won't hurt you if they're well cooked!" The table was silent; no one dared speak. All looked at me as if I had sinned. I hesitated, then ate the fly and the blackberries together.

Only two of her children Aunt Mary did not beat. One was Mildred, the daughter of her second marriage, a mean, spoilt child. If this child wanted anything of mine or any other child's, she got it. Her hair was thick and long; mine was thin and hung in one tiny scrawny pig-tail—it was much like Aunt Mary's. But Aunt Mary would stand the two of us together and laugh at me.

"When I grow up I'll have long hair," I would say. But her laughter left deep wounds. Each Sunday she would ask me if my hair had grown.

She gave Mildred lessons on the organ as soon as she was old enough to reach the keys. Music aroused deep feelings in me and I would creep into the parlor alone and try to play softly so that no one might hear. But this woman would appear in the door and tell me to stop strumming or she would "box my years."

The other girl my grandmother never touched was her stepdaughter Helen, a girl of some fifteen years, with deep bronze hair touched here and there with fiery gold. She walked immune through her stepmother's wrath. She feared no one and she openly threatened everyone. She teased me with a strange, gentle humor, and laughed at my tears. She would learn some new, long word, and then use it on me: "You're an insurrection," or "You're a pillage," or "You're an unornamented freckle-faced snicklefritz!" To be called such names! Who would not have wept!

Helen wanted to leave home and work. She asked all the neighboring farmers if they didn't want a hired girl. She was going to earn a lot of money and buy clothes with it! Eventually she found a place and after a number of quarrels with her father, became a hired girl in a far-away farmhouse, earning three dollars a month,— with prospects.

... That was long ago. Since then I have seen her desire for the beautiful, her love of life, walk hand in hand with unloveliness and all that negates life. Why, I ask, must the opposites walk hand in hand? Why should the things that gave distinction to Helen lead her to destruction?

Today a woman passed me and her smile might have been that of a great-aunt of mine. I had an aunt who smiled like that.

Once we sat about her dinner table. She was handsome and long past forty. Near her sat a thin-faced man, a guest whom it was considered an honor to feed because he was a minister of religion. When he spoke everyone listened in respectful silence. His power over others impressed me. Just before we started our dinner I saw him bow his head over his plate and clasp his hands together. Everyone did likewise. With closed eyes they listened while he mumbled some words.

"Mammie!" I cried in a shrill voice, "what's he doin'?"

"Sh-h-h!" Her hand grasped my shoulder and shook me.

I ate in shamed silence, watching the minister in fascination. He ate and ate and ate, and they respectfully pressed him to take more. Then, finished, he pushed his chair back, yawned widely and spread himself in a mighty stretch of satisfaction. The other men also stretched to keep him company. But it was not good bringin' up for women to do so.

Such was my introduction to Christianity, and such was my first encounter with prayer.

This minister came to my great-aunt's house because she was famous throughout the countryside since her husband had been sent to prison for murder. No one passed the white farmhouse perched high on the hill without finding an excuse to stop; it was a glass of water they needed, or they called to ask about the crops; or merely to pass the time of day. Then they went away to gossip over how she looked and what she said. And they retold her story for the thousandth time.

For years she had lived with my great-uncle and had borne him seven children; she had been a good wife and mother. I heard my own mother and other women tell how this great-aunt used to steal away to meet the man she loved—a man named Wolf who had a wife and children. For years they had met and had their love in a little, unused shed at the foot of a wheatfield in a little valley. Wolf was really the father of her twins, now thirteen years of age, although they bore her husband's name. But anyone could see, they said, that yellow hair did not run in the family. As they elaborated and developed the story through the months, I—unnoticed—listened. I saw the big golden wheatfield, and at the foot of it the shed; and in the front of the shed the wheat all broken and beaten flat as if animals had rolled there endlessly! As the story grew, the place rolled flat became greater and greater.

My great-uncle learned in some way of the trysting place. Then he waited for days,—waited and watched. At last Wolf came driving that way to town. My great-uncle saw him coming far over a distant hill; he took his shotgun, loaded for the purpose, and walked down the road to meet him. Some said he told Wolf why he was shooting him; others said, no, he just stepped up and pulled the trigger.

He was given life imprisonment at hard labor. The farmers for miles about drove to the county seat to hear the trial. They went prepared to tell my great-aunt what they thought of her; but, instead, they found that she and her husband clung to each other as if repelling them and the whole world. She comforted him with low words when the sentence was passed, and they heard her tell him that she would secure his pardon even if it took all that they had accumulated through the years.

She carried on her life as usual thereafter, placidly and peacefully, a bit flattered by the attention she received, a bit conscious of her enviable position. Her sons honored her always and labored faithfully in the fields. People came in and tried to catch a glimpse of the twins. She answered their questions frankly and proudly; she was working for her husband's pardon, and he was learning a trade in prison. He wrote her long letters and she replied. He made such fine boots! She was very proud of him and spoke as if he were in a fine establishment in a distant city. Men admired her and women envied her. The minister, who never before thought of stopping at her home, now never failed to come regularly for Sunday dinner; he ate, talked with her grown sons about the crops, and listened with approval to the progress her husband was making in the shoe business. And he watched her with hungry eyes.

She smiled always; some said, no, that wasn't a smile, it was just an expression.

The harvest dance and supper were drawing near, and this year our home was the scene of the great event. For weeks the farmers for miles about—too poor to employ hired hands—had joined in the annual communal labor, going from farm to farm to do the harvesting. Our house was the last to be reached.

While the sky in the east was still a cold, dull gray, they and their wives came driving down the road to our farm. There they found a crowd of farmers and their womenfolk, and although the air was chilly and the grass still cold and wet with dew, their voices were filled with gay expectancy.

Here was the kingdom of the women! Alone before their husbands, these women were complaining, obedient and dull, and the men spoke little; when they did speak it was to assert the age-long rights and privileges of their sex. But here in a crowd! My, how the women ordered the men folks about! And how the men stepped around, calling upon everybody to witness their martyrdom! They stood in groups around a long pine-board table, drinking black coffee and eating crisply fried bacon, fried eggs and doughnuts. Then the women bustled them off to the fields or the forests just as if they wouldn't have thought of going without orders.

All day the men worked in the fields or cut wood in the forests. The faint click of their axes came across the big sunny clearing. The forests were cool and the earth sweet; the trees were beginning to turn. Teams of horses drew high loads of cut wood and piled it in cords against the north side of our house and all along the drive. It was our firewood for winter, serving also as a shelter from the cold north winds.

All day long the women peeled, sliced and canned fruit. By noon the sloping roof of the house was covered with a solid white mass of sliced apples drying in the sun, and by the afternoon long rows of jars of jellies and preserves stood along the kitchen tables. When you looked at them you felt as if you'd really worked and not just enjoyed yourselves. For there are so many things to tell when you have lived alone on a little farm for weeks at a stretch, with no one to talk to but the few neighbors who pass and have only time to stop for a greeting. There was all the news about new scandals; there were recipes for cooking, new dress patterns, and there was the ever-green interest in just who was courtin' who. Occasionally there was a tragedy that deserved a whole morning's discussion. My great-aunt's story was retold. Helen was said to be keepin' company with Sam Walker, the elder son of the family where she worked. That guardian of family honor—the shotgun—had been taken to a young man over the hills; but he married the girl, someone related of another case. Now and then a silence settled over the kitchen while one of the group related an exclusive bit of scandal. At such moments I was sent out of the room. But I hovered near enough once to hear my mother exclaim:

"Forced her! You don't say! Well, I *do* declare!"

Dinnertime came and the men returned to eat. The table was laid out under the tall cedar trees on long boards supported by sawhorses. Something seemed to stir in the blood of the men and women. Bonds of ownership were dropped or openly flouted. Men flirted with other men's wives. Women triumphantly marched off with other women's husbands to eat their dinner, and the men publicly announced their intention of eloping. There was much teasing and laughing, and jealousy would have been considered a very bad breach of etiquette. At home, men might torture their wives by recalling certain words or looks, but here they dared show no resentment. Everyone seemed to hover close to some tantalizing, communal racial memory.

Then work began again and continued, sometimes one day, sometimes two, sometimes three. It was a time filled with happy, cheerful, although hard labor. And with much high excitement when the men and women were together. And then came the eventful night. Outside our house the men had constructed a huge square platform for dancing, over which they scattered candle shavings until it was as smooth as glass.

It was a grand dance—a grand dance! The orchestra consisted of a guitar and a fiddle. I was proud of my father and mother—my mother slender and graceful, and my father standing so finely in his shirt sleeves in the center of the platform and calling:

"Now, folks, choose yer partners fer a round dance!"

Such a father! At his word the fiddler started and my father and mother led off. Around and around in an old-fashioned waltz, my mother bending back slightly, her ruffled skirts flying, and my father swinging her with a right good will. I was so excited that I ran about through the crowd, not knowing whither. Wherever I went I could see my father's head above the crowd of swaying figures on the platform. The big sweeping hat that he always wore with a debonair air down over one eye and that gave him a reputation as a dangerous man with the women, had been thrown aside. For this night was filled with moonlight and music. He held his position as leader during the night as during the day. Even the way he wore his clothing distinguished him: there was his broad leather belt of many colors, with its buckle of real silver. He had bought it in St. Joe, he said. Any other man would have been ashamed to wear so much color. But my father was a colorful man who dared what no one else dared.

As he danced, he sang, and with the first sound of his voice the swaying men and women moved with rhythmical abandon. He was the living, articulate expression of their desires. He knew all the songs he had ever heard and if he didn't remember the music, he composed on the spot.

The music ceased. The silence was the silence that always follows when one has been moved by emotions deeper than the conscious mind. But in a few moments my father again stood on the platform.

"Partners fer a square dance!" he called, for the night was young and the dance only begun. I saw him bow before Helen, my beautiful aunt with the bronze hair. She and Sam Walker, the son of her employer, had driven twelve miles to attend the dance that night. She was "keepin' company with him regular," it was said. To be a hired girl drawing your own money gave you a position of authority and influence in the community. Everyone at the dance knew she earned three dollars a month; you could tell it by her proud bearing and her independent attitude toward her new beau. She commanded! It was but right that a woman of such importance should be my father's choice for the second dance.

"Bow to yer partners!" my father's voice shouted.

The couples bowed low. His voice came intermittently above the dashing music: "All hands around!" "Ladies in the center, gents around!" "Grape-vine twist!" The violin screeched through the strains of "Turkey in the Straw," and someone began to bawl,

Oh-h-h! A monkey settin' in a pile of straw
A-winkin' at his mother-in-law!

and others joined in the chorus:

Turkey in the straw, Haw! Haw! Haw!
Turkey in the straw, Haw! Haw! Haw!
Rake 'em up, scrape 'em up,
Any way at all,
Rake up a tune called the turkey in the straw.

The dancers separated in two lines, and down between the two rows of figures my father and Helen danced, their feet flying, Helen's hair flaming as the light from the swinging lanterns in the trees caught its glow. In the center they met, bowed and danced back again; once more—to the center; once more,—right hand; left hand, and then around. Then down the center once again, their feet as light as the drifting clouds. He caught her by both hands and like a swaying flower she was swung around and around. The men broke into the soft rhythm of clapping as accompaniment.

"Swing yer partners!" came the call again. And in the dance that followed, the driver of a fine pair of sorrels swung his partner high above his head into the air, supporting her under one arm. She braced herself with her hands on his shoulder; around and around he danced, she swinging in mid-air by his side, her face grave and proud at his strength. The people "settin' out" watched in admiration. Another dancer broke loose from his partner and, bending half double, broke into such a clog dance as you have never seen! He knew just how to dance to make the most noise, and the "clickety-click-click, clickety-click-click" of his heels nearly drowned the music.

In my excitement I climbed up on the platform and stood just under the raised arm of the fiddler. Before me surged a sea of swinging legs and skirts. The dance ceased . . . there was a hush . . . from the back I felt my mother pull at me and tell me to come down and get to bed. She rushed me before her through the sea of moving figures. In the bedroom I had to crawl through a mass of baby carriages and stumble over rows and rows of other children lying in sleep on pallets on the floor. I climbed into bed beside my two sisters, but after my mother was gone I sat up, listening to the smothered sound of excited voices, the shrieks of the fiddle, shuffling feet and the calling of the figures in the square dances. A long lull followed . . . then . . . they were eating! Chicken and chocolate cake and mince pie and ice cream and all the good things in the world! It would continue until the east was gray. I wept. Not even my father thought of me . . . oh, to be so little, so little!

The winter snows came, covering the rolling hills and burdening the forests beyond the meadows. The slaughtering and smoking of swine and perhaps a calf had been finished and barrels of pickles, hominy and mincemeat stood in the smokehouse. The mincemeat barrels were just low enough for me to reach all the raisins that lay on top. The cellar was filled with rows of canned fruit; yellow pumpkins filled a corner. Between the smokehouse and cellar lay two soft mounds, as gentle as the breasts of a woman, and if you wanted red apples, you shoveled through the snow at the edge of one of the mounds, through the soft earth beneath until you struck layers of them, separated by layers of yellow straw. Or, if you wanted cabbage or potatoes, you dug into the other mound. The crib in the barn was heaped with corn that slipped between your fingers in a rain of yellow gold. Above, the hayloft was stuffed to the roof with sweet-smelling, dusty hay. Up there it was always soft as twilight, and one could dream strange, formless dreams.

There was knitting to be done through the long winter months, and my mother now had a big loom for weaving carpets and rugs. On pleasant afternoons women from near-by farms would sometimes drive to a "carpet tacking." Gathered in our kitchen, they tore or cut into narrow strips all the old clean colored cloth and rags to be found, sewed the ends together after color schemes of their own, and then wound them into big balls. Later, when my mother wove carpets during lulls in her other work, I wound shuttles for her from these balls. While the women tacked rags, the men husked corn for winter feed. At other times sewing bees were held, women gathering at various homes to help sew or knit the necessary winter clothing. The men chopped the cord-wood into kindling or, on pleasanter days, mended fences.

You always knew, weeks in advance, of a molasses pulling, and for this all the young couples of dancing age prepared. When the day arrived you hitched a team or two to a big bobsled, filled the bed with hay, threw in hot bricks or stones along the center to keep the feet warm, and then quilts to cover you up to the chin. Then the bobsled glided off into the moonlit night, collecting couples as it went. It met other bobsleds, or single sleighs, greeted them with merry shouts and swept onward. Everybody sang, and the sleigh bells jingled in tuneless medley. You were at last dumped into somebody's big clean kitchen, which was gayly decked with four or five lamps, branches of cedar and red berries. Logs blazed in the fireplace and the kitchen stove was steaming in readiness.

The pop corn poppers were brought out—mesh wire cages on long handles. You threw in a handful of pop corn and locked down the mesh lid. A row of men and women stood before the fireplace, shaking the cages back and forth over the coals until the corn burst into flakes as white as snow. Other women boiled black molasses over the kitchen stove and you could eat your pop corn as you wished: with salt and melted butter poured over it; or in balls as round and white as snow-balls, held together with the hot molasses.

At last the boiled and tested molasses was poured into deep plates to cool. Then men and women alike put on big long aprons and with screams of laughter at the transformation, buttoned each other up the back. They chose partners, greased their hands with butter, and rolled the cooled molasses out into their hands. Facing each other they pulled the soft candy, standing farther apart as it became cooler and tougher, and throwing the ends back and forth to each other. They pulled and laughed and gossiped and flirted. When their candy was tough, they laid it out on buttered plates or along the greased kitchen tables, scoured to virgin whiteness, and worked it into dozens of designs—curled sticks, corkscrews, animals and men, towers, figures, and hearts with bleeding arrows.

Then they made ready for the dance. Between numbers there were cries for a song from my father. Once he sang "Sweet Marie." I remember it well—for was not my name Marie?

> There's a secret in my heart, sweet Marie
> A tale I would impart, love, to thee,
> Every daisy in the dell
> Knows my secret,
> Knows it well,
> And yet I dare not tell
>   Sweet Marie.
>
> Come to me, sweet Marie;
> Sweet Marie, come to me!
> Not because thy face is fair,
> Love, to see.
> But because thou art pure and sweet,
> Makes my happiness complete,
> Makes me falter at thy feet,
>   Sweet Marie.

Strange it is, yet I remember his voice, his face, every tone that fell from his lips when he sang. I remember every note of it, the way his voice lingered over the last word in each stanza; and I remember that I felt embarrassed.

After the songs, the dance continued. The dancers stopped at midnight and at two or three for coffee and cake. The stars went out, the moon faded, but still they danced. Only when the dawn came creeping from the east did they cease. Then they harnessed the horses, brought in the stones or bricks from the sleds, heated them and bundled in for the long drive home. The sleds glided silently over the beaten snow and the sleigh bells jingled in loneliness. For the east was gray and the dancers slept.

My father and mother were quarreling. Such a quarrel it was that it struck terror into my heart. My father cursed and my mother wept. It was the beginning of many terrible quarrels that blackened my child life.

My father wanted to make money, he said—a *lot* of money—and he could make it now if we went away somewhere. He wanted to break away from the farm with its endless pettiness. Our life there had indeed been poor, but as I see it now, it had been healthy and securely rooted in the soil. My mother was satisfied to work ceaselessly and to save a few pennies a year, but for my father such an existence was death, and he had stood it as long as he could. There were but three or four festivals a year. The rest of the time he had to follow the lone plow over badly yielding, stony soil, stumbling over the clods with his bare feet. He wanted to wear shoes all the year, but my mother thought if she could carry two buckets of water at a time from the well a mile away—and in *her* bare feet; if she could, as she put it, "work like a dog," he had nothing to complain of. No, he replied, he wasn't a Garfield, like her folks—satisfied, stingy like the whole family! He was a *Rogers!* Yes, indeed, he was a Rogers, my mother replied—he was a Rogers every bit of him, and all that her father had said against him was true—he was never able to stick to anything more than a year! Always wanting to change, always complaining, always telling stories that weren't true and singing songs instead of working; and thinking hard-working people couldn't see through him!

That touched my father to the quick. He said he'd leave her and never come back. "Come here, Marie!" he commanded, and then, "Come here, George!"

He was going to take George and me with him!

My mother sank into a kitchen chair and began to weep. My father ordered me to come to him again, telling my mother that she treated George and me as if we were dogs! But there was something about my mother that made me disobey the father that night. I ran to my mother and placed my hand on her knee and her tears fell on it.

My father did not go away, and I thought it was because I would not go with him. But he won at last, for we all went away. And from that moment our roots were torn from the soil and we began a life of wandering, searching for success and happiness and riches that always lay just beyond—where we were not. Only since then I have heard the old saying: "Where I am not, there is happiness."

We went by covered wagon for a long distance, traveling for days. In the wagon were two beds and a cooking stove, together with boxes of food and clothing. At night one bed was removed from on top of the other and put under the wagon. There my father and mother slept. We children slept in the wagon. We reached a forest and stopped; a tent was pitched, bedsteads were made and erected, and a table constructed from white pine. My father began to cut trees for a man who lived in a white house on the hill. The man sometimes came down to our tent and my mother called him "Sir" and insisted upon his sitting down while she made him a cup of coffee. When he was gone she cried and quarreled with my father again.

The forest smelled of a thousand sweet things. We built fires at night from its pine branches. All day long I played where it was deeply silent and dusky, and the earth was soft and yielding to my feet. And since we lived in a tent in the open and had our meals out under the sky a fascinating transitoriness hovered over our lives; there was talk of distant prospects; and the road swept over hills into magical distances. At times I stood at a crossroad and watched the white ribbon of a highway stretching to the further end of the world. Sometimes a handsome woman rode by on a black horse. Her hair and her eyes were black and she wore a black riding costume. Beneath her black hat her cheek was fair and soft. My mother came to know the wives of other woodchoppers and they talked about the beautiful woman. She was very rich, they said, but she had been attacked by a tramp down by the bridge over the river. That was a few years ago and that was the reason she had reached the advanced age of twenty-two and no man would marry her!

After I heard that I watched for the woman often. Strange! She didn't seem at all unhappy that no one would marry her! Her lovely face was dignified and calm. Calmer than my mother's.

With the first heavy fall of snow we left the silent

forest and returned to our little farm where the soil was so gray and hard. My father and mother hardly spoke to each other, and she wept much. Then once more he left us and went away and we did not see him again for many months. Our house was cold and lonely and my mother's eyes were often red with weeping. My grandfather brought sacks of food for us; he would stand in the kitchen and talk with my mother. His face was thin and very pale with a fugitive beauty seldom seen in men; his beard was black and he wore a black hat with a wide brim. And his eyes, so like my mother's, were hard and bitter as he talked. She stood in her loose faded calico wrapper, her hands clasped before her, her head bowed, and she cried very softly.

Her tears . . . they embittered my life!

That winter I went to school. The road was long and the one-room, unpainted board schoolhouse stood on a hill that was slimy and slippery with yellow clay. At the end of the schoolroom was a blackboard and I learned that when I sat facing it, that was north, while south was back over my shoulder. East was on my right side and west on my left. Even now, after twenty-five years, I think north is always in front of me and south over my shoulder and if I wish to be correct I must turn around until the little school building seems before me. Figures, too, were strange little creatures. Number one stood on the lowest rung of a tall ladder, and number one hundred sat high up on the top rung almost hidden in the clouds. When compelled to add a big figure to a little one I had to run all the way up the ladder, find him and carry him down and sit him beside the little one. It was very tiring work and took me a long, long time, and my teacher scolded me for my stupidity.

I learned words from a yellow spelling book that was so much alive and smelled so new that I took it to bed with me at night. It has been many years, yet even now the smell from the crisp leaves comes through the years.

That teacher, thin and cruel and fearful! He played games with the older boys in the forest and girls could not go there. Once I crept under a bush and watched. The cries rang through the woods, and boys chased each other wildly. The teacher fled past, in full pursuit of a boy, his face tense and his eyes staring. He caught the boy . . . I crouched under the bush in dumb terror, fearful even to breathe. Later the teacher was discharged, but people liked to talk in low, shocked voices of him.

I learned another very important thing that winter: it was when I fell and broke my arm and the older school boys carried me home. My mother cared for me for weeks, talking tenderly as I lay in bed, and people called to ask how I was. It was very depressing and cheerless to get well again, and to find that people ceased noticing me. So I complained of my broken arm long after it was healed. Thus I learned that if you are sick or injured, people love you; if you are well they do not. Another paradox impressed itself upon my being,—that the way to love lies through suffering. And throughout my child life I was known as a sickly child.

One evening at sunset as I stood watching the hard, white, dusky lane, a carriage turned the curve. It was drawn by two snow-white horses traveling with sweeping ease and swiftness. In the carriage sat two dark figures. They came soundlessly as a dream comes, the horses tossing their heads against the painted sky. The click of hoofs grew clearer, then the carriage rolled in at our gate and my father leaped over the wheel. The other man followed slowly and carefully and I saw that he had white hair. Both he and my father were dressed in store clothes. My father's broad-brimmed soft hat was pulled down over his left eye and he wore a black tie that flew in the wind. As he turned I saw the shining buckle of his many-colored belt.

So it was that my father returned after more than seven months of absence. And he returned to find that another baby boy—Dannie—had been added to our household. He had gone to St. Joseph with his horses and in some way or other entered the service of an eye specialist. He drove for the doctor and said he was learning to be a doctor himself. In those days in the Middle West, doctors were often made, not by university training, but by practical work.

My father brought my mother black silk for a dress and she stood in her loose calico wrapper and bare feet, with her hands folded, gazing at it sadly.

"Now you can't say any more that I ain't done nothin' fer you!" he said to her.

"Ain't you even got a kind word?" he continued bitterly, when she made no answer.

"It's awful purty," she answered, and her tears began to fall on the gleaming silk.

He turned and tramped into the kitchen and sat down with the white-haired doctor. They passed the whiskey bottle to each other.

The next day I heard the sound of angry voices and weeping from the kitchen. With dread I crept in at the door, drawn to something that I knew would torture me. My father stood near the door, accusing my mother of having drunk whiskey with the doctor. He accused her of other mysterious things . . . she was first angry and then wept. He kept shouting at her something about "carryin' on with other men." Small as I was, I knew instinctively by some loose expression about his mouth that he was lying and knew that he was lying. He was making a deliberate effort to keep his voice convincingly angry, and I felt ashamed . . . as if I myself had done something.

My mother accused him of saying things he knew were not true. He said he would teach her to call him a liar! He turned and went to the stable, and in a few minutes returned with the horses hitched to the carriage. The doctor came down the lane and my father went to meet him. Then he returned to the kitchen.

"Go out an' shake hands with the doctor an' say goodby! It's a nice way my wife treats my company!"

My mother fell on her knees and cried in uncontrolled anguish: "Don't go, John! Don't go! Think of me an' the children!"

But he turned and left the house. My mother lay prostrate on the floor, crying with hard, dry sobs. I ran to the door. The carriage was going down the hard white lane, and the snow-white horses were traveling with sweeping ease and swiftness. Occasionally they tossed their heads proudly, in clear outline against the sky.

40

In the autumn of the next year my grandfather moved us away from the farm to a little village, on whose outskirts stood an old, abandoned, two-room board house. It had no plaster on the inside and there was no ceiling. You could stand in the room and look straight up to the roof where there were holes that let the sky in. That I liked. Outside the house the earth was packed hard, as if baked, and no grass, trees or flowers grew there. That also I liked, for it was different.

My mother now talked to me as if we were friends. She always did that when my father was not there. Together we put up her loom and she began to weave rag carpets and rugs. The village people not only gave her work to do, but they brought us bundles of newspapers and with these we papered the house. We made big pans of paste from flour and water; I spread out the newspapers on the floor and my mother smeared the mixture over them. Then we pasted them on the walls, layer upon layer, for they would keep out the cold of the winter. We talked of plaster as we worked, and my imagination, that always swept beyond the bonds of reality, now dwelt in the realm of plaster. I dreamed dreams: my mother was away and she returned to find I had plastered the two rooms with lovely plaster! She stood in the center of the front room with its single window in the corner, and exclaimed:

"Well, I *do declare!* Who plastered the house?"

Then I would look at her slender figure and beautiful eyes and proudly reply: "I did!"

So the dream ended—no dream of mine ever came nearer to reality than that. Even now—sometimes I wonder what is real and what phantasy; even now I think, sometimes, that perhaps these past years will fade and I shall know that I was only dreaming; for it is difficult to know what is lasting.

After my mother and I had papered our house—I hardly remember my brothers and sisters—we tried to dig up the packed earth around the house to plant sweet-peas there in the spring. But the soil was too hard and poor. It needed manure, my mother said longingly. So I took a bucket and a shovel and walked along the road collecting manure, dreaming of fragrant flower beds.

We were town people now and that was something to boast of; not everybody lived in towns. Our village had a main street with a board walk down one side of it. The girls walked back and forth there on Sundays and flirted with the men lolling against the stores. There was a schoolhouse where I went to school and a little church which my mother called the Christian Church. Now that we lived in town she thought we ought not "act like tramps"; so one Sunday she made us wash our feet very clean and follow her across the vacant lot to the Christian Church. There a woman gave each of us a little card with a picture on it. This picture showed a man in a long red robe talking to a little girl. It was Jesus, but who Jesus was I had never heard. My attention was riveted on the packet of colored cards which the woman held in her hand and I waited for the moment when she would lay them down for a second and forget them. For in my imagination I saw our house papered with them—long rows of gorgeous red pictures. But that dream remained unrealized also, for the woman kept the cards in her hand!

It was a few days later that my father returned to us. He came walking along the railroad track, and asked someone for our house. Now he spoke no more of his dreams of becoming a doctor, of earning much money quickly, nor of dressing my mother in silk. Instead, he was shorn of all his glory. His fine clothes had been replaced by a soiled shirt and a pair of blue overalls. His white horses that traveled with such swiftness, were gone—where he would not say. But to me he was unchanged. He may have forgotten his dreams of becoming a doctor—but I did not. There were many times, even in my adult years, when someone asked me the profession of my father, that I involuntarily replied, "He was a doctor." Then when I suddenly recalled that he was not I was swept with a strange doubt—was he, or was he not; had I had a dream that still left its imprint upon me? And I wondered again what was reality and what a dream.

My father had been with us but a few minutes when, in a mysterious voice, he told my mother he had killed a man and must leave the country or get caught and be "hung" or sent to the "Pen" for life! And again I saw that loose expression about his mouth that made me feel ashamed and embarrassed. My mother was now hard and silent and did not weep. He became angry and accused her of not believing him—her own husband! She turned her back to him and gazed out of the door at the vacant lot beyond covered with ugly, tough jimpson weeds.

"Y' ought to be ashamed of yerself, tellin' such things before th' children," was all she said, and then with a flash of wrath: "If you want to run away and leave us like you've already done, jist go; don't come tellin' me stories fer an excuse!"

He was taken aback that she could see through his tales. He talked to her back; he could make a lot of money in the West; he would send for her and us children! She turned swiftly and looked at his mouth. He gazed at her standing there in her old calico wrapper, at her face, once so delicate and now scarred with wrinkles. Even the wrinkles could not hide the wistfulness and longing; the eyes were still young, a beautiful blue-black with long silky lashes; and her hair was as black, as smooth and glossy, as a raven's wing. She looked so frail, standing before him.

My father's lips could become thin and firm and his jaw square—as now. With a movement so quick that I hardly saw it, my mother was in his arms and sobbing as if her heart were breaking, her wet face hidden in his neck just where the shirt flared open at the front.

I had never seen affection between them before. I ran out into the back yard and lay down behind the henhouse and cried. Why, I did not know, and I was ashamed, afraid that someone would see me and laugh. As the tears ceased to flow I began to make up a story in case anyone should see my red eyes: I would say I was just walking down the road and fell down and hurt my leg! Or that I was sick with the measles again! But to avoid even that eventuality I arose and, keeping the henhouse between me and the kitchen door, slipped out into the jimpson weeds in the vacant lot. I lay down flat on the earth for a long time. Above me were waving weeds and sunflowers, and beyond, the blue sky covered with softly sailing baby clouds, pushed by some wind carrying stories on its back. Of course there were stories up there . . . who wouldn't ride on the back of the wind if he got the chance!

. . . The next day my father left us again. He went away on a railroad hand-car. A number of men sat around the edge. We all stood on the track and watched and my mother's face was very wistful. Sometimes my father waved his hand. When he was afar off he waved his hat. We watched until he was a black speck in the distance. Even then we strained our eyes to catch the last glimpse of him. Yes, there he was . . . then he was no more . . . surely that was a black speck . . . then he was gone. The shining railway tracks stretched to the horizon, melted together, and plunged over the edge of the world . . . and over there my father had gone . . . into the distance where happiness was.

Part 2

The sea is gray and colorless today, and the sun is hidden behind these cold northern mists. So was my life in those long years that followed: gray, colorless, groping, unachieving. With many things begun and none finished; or if finished, failures. There was but one thing on which I could depend—poverty and uncertainty.

Our tent, as mud-colored as the packed earth on which it stood, was near the banks of the Purgatory River. My father had pitched it on the low land lying between the railway tracks and the back yards of a row of little two- and three-room houses on the outskirts of the town of Trinidad. The railway had been built on an embankment of stone, slate and slag from the coal fields. Each day Beatrice and I and our two little brothers dragged gunny sacks along the tracks and filled them with coal that had fallen from the passing engines. And when the trains came rumbling by, we rushed to the side and waved at the fine people framed in the flashing windows.

If you looked across the river, beyond the row of

little houses, you saw the gray-purple hills that guarded the approaches to the mountain peak beyond. These were the foothills of the Rockies. The mountain peak— Fisher's Peak—was over a mile and a half high, my father told us proudly, and it was just as if he had said:

"Look at my mountain that I have found for you."

"In the fall," he continued, I'll take you campin' there and I'll shoot deer and we'll eat venison."

Everything was new and wonderful about us. Inside our tent three beds were wedged nicely along one side. The other side was almost a parlor, for there stood the treasured sewing machine and the clock my mother had brought with her, and there was also a rocking-chair. A rocking-chair, a clock, a sewing machine, a mountain, and venison . . . I enumerated our luxuries proudly.

My father built a board shed in front of the door to serve as the kitchen. There my mother worked while he was away earning three dollars a day. He had his own team and wagon and he hauled sand from the river bed to some place or other. Sometimes he hauled bricks. I would stand on the bridge that stretched over the river and watch him drive by, and in the evening I would run to meet him. He would seat me astride one of his horses and I trotted proudly homeward, hoping all the neighbors would see.

My mother was in a state of quiet, suppressed excitement all the time and she was humble and modest before my father now. For he was really making tremendous money. He talked in much bigger terms than formerly . . . he was going to be real rich. My mother kept her silence again.

After a time, lured by enthusiastic letters from my mother, Aunt Helen came, flaming and vital, to join us. She had grown even more beautiful; no rose petal was silkier than her skin. No queen had more confidence than she. And her laugh! When she laughed everyone laughed too, even when they didn't know why. Awkward, ugly girls who might easily have hated her for her beauty, stood gossiping with her over the back fence, and when she came darting in at their back doors their eyes were wistful and hungry. She helped them make lotions to soften and bleach their skins, she shampooed their hair with eggs to make it grow and glisten, she cut dress patterns for them, and when they had company on Sunday evenings she did up their hair in puffs and sometimes even loaned them a skirt or a blouse. She could well afford to be generous to others, for she had more than her share of beauty!

She considered what work was worthy of her—for she knew her value. The neighboring girls argued for the laundry. She hesitated: what did it pay? They must remember she had been a hired girl making six dollars a month, with keep, the last years where she worked! And—with a shade of pink mounting to her cheeks—the eldest son of the family had been her beau and she was still engaged to him.

My mother and father urged her to go out again as a hired girl, for girls in the laundry "went bad." She flashed. She was not afraid of hard work, but she could take care of herself anywhere! They must remember that the laundry offered more money and only ten hours of work a day, instead of the sunrise-to-sunset or midnight work in a private home. After much arguing and consulting all the neighbors she decided on the laundry, starting on the mangle at seven dollars a week, with her goal as the stiff shirt machine that paid eleven a week.

From the first she placed her weekly wages before my mother, and only under protest would she keep two dollars for herself.

"I've got nice things, Elly; you an' the kids hain't. You can't live like tramps all the time. When you've got nice things I'll keep more."

She loved colors and beautiful things, and what it must have cost her to sacrifice them like this no one ever knew. Yet for years it was her money—earned in one way or another—that furnished us with most of the colorful and good clothing we had. When Helen began to draw weekly wages she took an equal place with my father in our home. She was as valuable and she was as respected as he. The two of them talked to each other as equals; they laughed or they quarreled as equals. My mother would listen wistfully, her hands folded across her stomach, and when one of us children interrupted, she would scold:

"Don't you see your father an' Aunt Helen are talkin'?"

When my father quarreled with my mother, Helen would invariably step in and meet him halfway. For she loved her sister. Her hair would shake loose when she tossed her head and her voice would rise high in excitement.

"You can't talk like that to *me*, John Rogers! An'

you can't boss me around like you boss Elly, for I pay my room and board here!"

So it was! She paid for her room and board and no man had the right to "boss her around." My mother did not; she could never toss her head proudly and freely and say, "I'm payin' for my keep here!"

My father was never quite certain of his ground with Helen when she was angry. For beneath her beauty lay a wild, untamed spirit and she had never been "broke in to the bridle," as men spoke of broken wives. She often threatened to "scratch his eyes out," and she meant every word of it. She was capable of attacking him even if he were fully three times her size. Sometimes her anger was so deep that speech failed her; at such times she would resort to a primitive and vulgar insult that seemed almost instinctive, it was so far removed from the daintiness of her usual behavior. She would whirl with a rapid movement and, just before flinging out of the room would, with a flash of her hands, hoist her skirts to the waist in the back. My father was left speechless with rage. There seemed no answer to such an insult!

We were now city people. Trinidad had fully five thousand inhabitants, but claimed ten. It had a grade school building, and a high school building reared its head among trees on the hill across the river; over there rich people lived. The high school and riches seemed to go together. Anyway we, who lived beyond the tracks, knew that we could never dream of going to high school.

The grade school building stood on the other side of the town, on a hill directly facing the old historic Santa Fé Trail that had first been traveled by the Indians, then by the early Spaniards, and later by the white pioneers to the great Southwest. It wound near the foot of a jutting peak on top of which slept one of the earliest pioneers of the West. The school was the first grade school I had ever seen. Each day I took my little brother George by the hand and guided him there and we knew that we were treading holy ground, for my mother constantly spoke of it as such. The teachers were clean and seemed smoothly ironed; they wore tailored suits and white waists and spoke a language that I could at first hardly understand. My mother had explained to one of them on the first day that I was near ten years old and had been in the "third reader" in my last school. The teacher had gazed at her for a long time, her eyes traveling down over the calico dress, over the hands so big-veined and worn that they were almost black, and then to the wistful, tired face lit up by the beautiful blue-black eyes. The eyes were young—but the hands might have belonged to a scrubwoman of fifty.

"Yes," the teacher had remarked at last, "I understand."

She was a kind, young teacher. When I read before her in a trembling voice she smiled encouragingly at my eagerness and at my attempt to forget the room filled with well-dressed little boys and girls. Then she sent me to the board and dictated figures. The fear of being sent to a lower grade drove me forward. Yet I was terror-stricken. Figures always were my enemies. I put down numbers at random . . . a certain native cunning coming to my aid—I knew she would think I had only made a mistake. And so it was.

"How can you make such a mistake!" she protested. I gazed at her blankly but did not reply. She took the chalk and worked out the simple problem. I watched her hand so intently that even now, nearly twenty years later, I see exactly the figures she wrote and her long white hand with a gold ring on the third finger.

For weeks she continued this method. I memorized what she said and wrote, but I never understood. A row of figures held before my eyes was, and remains, like a row of soldiers standing before me ready to shoot when the top one gives the command, "Fire!"

I felt very shy and humble in that school. In the front seat on the outside row sat a little girl. Her skin was white, her hair was thick and nearly white, and her dresses, shoes and stockings were always white. When the teacher had asked about her father, she had replied, "My father is a doctor!" and I had stared at her fascinated. She sat very straight in her seat and the teacher always took her copy book and held it up for the class to see. The handwriting was as prim and clean as she was; the margins were broad and even; there was not one mistake. One day after school my fascination led me to follow her home; she lived in a large, low brick bungalow surrounded by a lawn with many flowers. The grass was cut as smooth as a window pane, everything was peaceful, orderly and quiet. Even the fence and gate were painted white.

On Mother's Day the white girl's mother came and sat

near the teacher and didn't associate with the other women. My mother had put on a new calico dress with a belt, and I had walked proudly by her side to the school. She stood in the back of the room, apart from the well-dressed women, and her frightened eyes watched as they talked so easily with each other. After that she never went again. Yet to her the school remained a sacred place to which it was an honor to send her children.

One day our teacher stepped aside while another one entered and read to us from a book on Manners. I learned about eating with a fork and keeping the mouth closed when you chew. Then she read something about washing the teeth, but I had never heard of that before except that my mother sometimes put yellow soap on her finger and washed her teeth with it. But I would have been ashamed to ask her to actually buy a brush for me to use only on my teeth! The teacher read about bathing daily. How that could be done I could not imagine. For my mother washed clothes only on Monday and we children had to bathe in the last, clean rinsing water; the oldest one bathed first and the youngest one last.

Then the teacher read a chapter about sleeplessness. If unable to sleep, one should get up and take a walk; or one should have two beds in a room and change from one to the other; the fresh sheets produced sleep! I had never seen sheets on a bed; we used only blankets. And to what bed I should change was a puzzle! For we only had four beds for eight people. Of course, I reflected, rich people like the little white girl did that. I pictured her arising in the middle of the night and crawling into another bed. Rich people perhaps could not sleep at night; it was aristocratic to be unable to sleep. I watched the little white girl, and she seemed to understand everything that was read.

But for all her perfection, victory was mine that year. The school year was not half finished before I sat in the back seat on the far outside row—and she only sat in the front seat. The back seat was the seat of honor! The child who sat there was the best in the room and needed little help or correction from the teacher. When all other children failed to answer a question the teacher would turn with confidence to the seat of honor with the word—

"Marie?"

With eyes that never left her face I arose and answered. The whole schoolroom watched and listened, waiting for a mistake. I, for all my faded dresses and stringy ugly hair, who had never seen a toothbrush or a bathtub, who had never slept between sheets or in a nightgown, stood with my hands glued to my sides and replied without one falter or one mistake! And the little white girl whose father was a doctor had to listen! Then it was that the little white girl invited me to her birthday party. My mother objected to buying bananas as a present, but after I had cried and said everyone else was taking things, she grudgingly bought three.

"They are rich people," she protested bitterly, looking at the precious bananas, "an' there's no use givin' 'em any more."

When I arrived at the little girl's home I saw that other children had brought presents of books, silver pieces, handkerchiefs and lovely things such as I had never seen in my life. Fairy tales mentioned them but I never thought they really existed. They were all laid out on a table covered with a cloth shot through with gold. I had to walk up before them all and place my three bananas there, covertly touching the cloth shot through with gold. Then I made my way to a chair against the wall and sat down, trying to hide my feet and wishing that I had never come.

The other little girls and boys were quite at ease,— they had been at parties before. They were not afraid to talk or laugh and their throats didn't become whispery and hoarse when anyone asked them a question. I became more and more miserable with each passing moment. In my own world I could reply and even lead, and down beyond the tracks no boy dared touch me or my brother George. If he did he faced me with a jimpson weed as a weapon. But this was a new kind of hurt. In school I had not felt like this before the little white girl: there I had learned an invaluable lesson—that she was clean and orderly, but that I could *do* and learn things that she couldn't. Because of that and because of my teacher's protecting attitude toward me, she had been ashamed not to invite me to her party.

"Of course, if you're too busy to come, you must not feel that you ought, just because I've invited you," she had said. She was not much over ten, yet she had been well trained. I felt vaguely that something was wrong, yet I looked gratefully at her and replied:

"I'll come. I ain't got nothin' to do!"

Now here I was in a gorgeous party where I wasn't wanted. I had brought three bananas at a great sacrifice only to find that no other child would have dreamed of such a cheap present. My dress, that seemed so elegant when I left home, was shamefully shabby here. I was disturbed in my isolation by a number of mothers who called us into another room and seated us at a long table covered with a white tablecloth, marvelous cakes and fruit such as made my heart sink when I compared them with my three bananas. Only my desire to tell my mother all about it, and my desire to know everything in the world even if it hurt, kept me from slipping out of the door when no one was looking, and rushing home. I was seated next to a little boy at the table.

"What street do you live on?" he asked, trying to start a polite conversation.

"Beyond th' tracks."

He looked at me in surprise. "Beyond the tracks! Only tough kids live there!"

I stared back trying to think of something to say, but failed. He sought other avenues of conversation.

"My papa's a lawyer—what's yours?"

"Hauls bricks."

He again stared at me. That made me long to get him over beyond the tracks—he with his eye-glasses and store-made clothes! We used our sling-shots on such sissies. He was stuck-up, that was what he was! But what about I couldn't see.

"*My* papa don't haul bricks!" he informed me, as if to rub it in. Wherein the insult lay I couldn't see, yet I knew one was meant. So I insulted back.

"My papa can lick your papa I bet!" I informed him, just as a pleasant elegant mother bent over us with huge plates of yellow ice cream in her hands.

"Well, Clarence, and what are you talking about?" she asked affectionately.

"Her father hauls bricks and she lives beyond the tracks and she says her father can lick my father!" Clarence piped.

"That doesn't matter, dear, that doesn't matter! Now, now, just eat your ice cream." But I saw her eyes rest disapprovingly on me and I knew it did matter.

Clarence plunged his spoon into his ice cream and henceforth ignored me. I picked up my spoon, but it clattered against the plate. A dainty little girl in blue, with flaring white silk ribbons on her braid of hair, glanced at me primly. I did not touch the spoon again, but sat with my hands under me watching the others eating in perfect self-possession and without noise. I knew I could never eat like that and if I tried to swallow, the whole table would hear. The mother returned and urged me to eat, but I said I didn't like ice cream or cake! She offered me fruit and I took it, thinking I could eat it at home. But when the children left the table I saw that they carried no fruit. So I left mine beside the precious ice cream and cake.

In the next room little boys and girls were choosing partners for a game, and the little white girl was actually sitting at the piano ready to play. My eyes were glued on her—to think of being able to play the piano! Everyone was chosen for the game but me. No little boy bowed to me and asked:

"Will you be my partner, please?" I saw them avoid me deliberately . . . some of them the same little boys who were so stupid in school!

The mother of my little hostess tried to be kind:

57

"Are you sick, Marie?" she asked. "Would you like to go home?"

"Yes, mam." My voice was hoarse and whispery.

She took me to the door and smiled kindly, saying she hoped I had had a nice time.

"Yes, mam," my hoarse voice replied.

The door closed behind me. The game had started inside and the voices of the children were shouting in laughter. In case anyone should be looking out of the window and think I cared, I turned my head and gazed sternly at a house across the street as I walked rapidly away.

And in case anyone I knew saw me with tears in my eyes I would say . . .

The springtime came, first to the plains and foothills and then up to the mountain snows. In Trinidad the cottonwood trees put on a fuzzy greenness and the Purgatory River rose higher and higher, swelled by the melting snows. Each day we stood on its banks and watched it eat nearer to the row of little houses in front of our tent. It rushed against the iron and cement piling of the railroad bridge and people fearfully recalled the time ten years before when spring floods had torn out the great steel structure and cut a new riverbed through the town. Each night we went to bed with the roar of the rushing water in our ears and at intervals throughout the night men arose to listen; they wandered restlessly to and fro near the river bank, talking in low tones.

It was in the gray of an early morning that my mother's terrified voice awoke us. My father insisted that there was time to dress, but when he looked out once more his voice was filled with fear.

"Grab yer things an' come," he commanded. Trembling with the cold, we followed him out of the tent and along a ridge between two ditches leading toward the railway tracks. The river had broken its banks and was filling ditches and all low places, rushing through weeds and willows with a sound of danger. It was a terrible sound . . . mad waters rushing and rising . . . elemental forces speaking in a voice of finality.

Through the semi-darkness we heard the screaming and shouting of men and women escaping from the little houses. We reached a ditch between us and the railway tracks. It was already filled with water . . . we were hemmed in!

"It's not deep, Elly," I heard my father say, "don't git scared."

He reached down, picked up George and Dan, one under each arm, and waded into the flood. I cried out . . . how could he take George and leave me here . . . George could not be alone over there! We saw his dim figure struggling to reach the other bank, then scrambling up the slag embankment. He was back again and carried Annie across; once more he returned and each time the water crept nearer his hips. I felt him feel with his feet and fight the pushing waters with his legs as he carried me and Beatrice. I ran to George and his little hands clung to mine.

Voices came from across the ditch.

"You go first, Helen," my mother was saying, and Helen was replying:

"No, Elly, you go and leave me; I'd jist as leave stay! . . ." Just as if it were a Sunday afternoon walk she was talking about! And not a rising flood that might wash her away any minute.

My father's voice boomed. "Don't argy!"

He lifted my mother in his arms and stumbled with her across the flood. Helen was now a dark, slender outline on a little piece of dry land across the waters. Then in a minute she also stood by us on the railroad track, with my father soaked to the waist.

Down the tracks on higher land stood the big house of the section-master. There lights were burning; everybody was up; everybody was listening to the voice in the flood. We hurried toward the light. Yes, the section-master said, we could stay on the front porch. His wife came out; we need not be frightened, she assured us, for although the water was rising, yet the section-house was built on high ground and would not be swept away. Even if the water surrounded it, still it would stand. She was a pious Catholic and had been praying all night and she put her faith in God against the might of the flood. She smiled continually, as one sometimes whistles when walking up a dark canyon at night. We ought to pray also, she suggested; at such a time as this one should not hesitate. My mother drew back; something in her was hostile to Catholics, as to foreigners. My father did not reply; he would have prayed, still unbelieving, for the picturesque effect of it . . . a warm room, burning candles, a lighted shrine, perhaps incense, the sound of sweeping waters carrying danger on their bosom. Only something hard and cold in my mother's manner prevented him from taking advantage of such a dramatic situation.

The pious woman smiled and when she walked it was softly and languidly, like an animal that has eaten until sated. Occasionally she would come out to say a few words to us, then retire to her bedroom to pray. Her whole manner showed that although God had permitted the river to surround all the other houses on this side of the tracks, He was protecting the section-house.

My mother and Helen resented the woman's manner; the night air was cold on the veranda, my father was wet to the waist, and we were all but half dressed. Yet the woman did not ask us into the warm house. She asked us to pray—but my mother was not a person to pray under compulsion; she was too honest for that.

The water continued to rise with the growing dawn and from the end of the veranda my mother and Helen watched the now dim outline of our tent. It was half covered with water.

"The machine is ruined, an' the featherbeds!" they told each other in voices burdened with despair.

"John, John! It's goin'! It's goin'!"

We all ran to the edge of the veranda. Across the seething, rolling waters was the dim outline of the tent, swaying from side to side, turning half round and slowly sailing away. The wooden poles and the board floor to which it was nailed kept it upright. It caught on the willow trees and hung for a moment, sailed further, caught again, careened around and then sailed out of sight. My mother watched it, with a face of desperation, until the corner of the section-house hid it from view.

"Everything we've got in the world is gone . . . my featherbeds, th' machine, th' clock, Helen's clothes . . . we've got nothin' but th' clothes on our backs!"

My father put his arm around her shoulder. "Don't take on like that, Elly! It'll catch in th' willows an' we'll find it in th' mornin'." But his voice was also heavy with dull hopelessness. She leaned limply against him. No tears came, for she had long since lost the ability to weep.

The morning came. Then the pious woman came from the house and smiled reassuringly at us shivering on the veranda. The flood was rapidly receding, she announced. The mercy of God and the power of prayer were proved—God had saved the section-house.

Today is Sunday, and my mind once more recalls those who were of my flesh and blood, and once more I live through the little drama of our lives, the little drama of the lowly.

There were many attempts and many failures as my father and mother pitted the strength of their bodies against brutal reality. They were naive folk who believed that a harvest followed hard labor; that those who work the hardest earn the most.

I remember one place where defeat came in a setting of unparalleled beauty. After our tent had been carried away in the flood, my father signed an agreement to haul coal for a mine-owner. The mine lay far back in the mountains; the coal had to be hauled from a dark canyon, and he told me stories when I sat by his side. That big mound of stones up the canyon, he said, was a burial mound of Indians who once fought a great battle there.

"They come from down th' canyon, some naked an' some in blankets an' skins, an' some layin' down on their horses, hangin' from th' mane with one hand an' from a foot, an' here they met an' fit an' fit an' fit until not one was left alive to tell th' tale."

How he heard the tale, if no one was left to tell it, he failed to relate. It did not matter—to him, as to me, fancy was as real as sticks and stones. To him, the foreign miners who worked up the canyon and lived at our house were romantic characters; in their strange tongue lay color and untold adventure. The dark forests on the distant mountain range called to him mysteriously—there mountain lions and wild cats prowled and the earth smelled of wildness. Our adobe house, built with walls three feet thick, like all Mexican or Indian houses, was not just a house, but a fortification against attack and against soft-footed night animals.

To my mother, the mound of stones up the canyon was nothing but a den of rattle-snakes; how the stones came to be piled up like that in a peak she also didn't say—she never believed in imaginin' things. To her, the foreign miners were nothing but men who had lice that forced her to hang a lump of asafoetide in a little bag around the neck of each of us. Lice don't like asafoetide. The lazy clouds above . . . yes . . . no, she hated lazy things! The dark forests beyond merely meant that we lived far from the town where we children should have been in school long ago. Yet . . . I wonder . . . her eyes were wistful. Perhaps she did not dare let herself see the clouds and dark forests, or the ripening berries on the mountain-side . . . the workers cannot afford to take their eyes off the earth.

She seemed to live only for the moment when the owner of the mine would come from the city and "settle up" that we might have money enough to return to Trinidad.

It was November before the mine-owner came. He was a little man with a black mustache and a derby hat. My mother cooked and baked and was much excited. She had not cooked such food for years.

"Now, Mr. Turner, jist set down an' help yerself!" she told him proudly. Mr. Turner took off his derby hat and sat down. He ate alone and we watched, my father sitting at one end of the table and talking grandly to him as men talk to each other, my mother waiting on table and urging him to eat more. We children sat against the wall and watched each bite he took: there wasn't enough of the good food to go around. When he was gone we could get bacon and beans again . . . bacon and beans endlessly.

With the evening I returned from play and paused at the door of the house to hear my father shouting:

"An' my wife's worked like a dog an' now we ain't got enough to buy her a shirt!"

The polite voice of Mr. Turner replied, "Look at the contract, Mr. Rogers, look at the contract!"

Again my father's voice: "God, man, I've worked since May an' I've had my own team an' wagon an' I've been up at daylight an' come home at dark."

The quiet little voice of the prim little man: "You

seem able to afford good food here . . . you're not starving!"

"We never can eat such things, sir, I made it only fer you," my mother was crying.

Mr. Turner had seen many angry men and weeping women in his day . . . men and women who knew nothing of legal phrases in the contracts they signed; he owned many little mines hidden back in the foothills. To my mother he replied, just as if she were a piece of wood:

"I'm only holding to our contract, Mrs. Rogers . . . here's your husband's signature."

The signature was a scrawl, for my father could hardly write. When he saw his own awkward pencil-marks that mocked at his ignorance and defenselessness, something seemed to break in him. "God damn you! . . . So we're to work to buy silk dresses fer yer wife an' send yer kids to high school! I've got a wife an' five kids. Look at my wife . . . she's thirty an' she looks fifty. Think of it, man! An' you come here an' show me a piece of paper. I trusted yer word . . . I come from a place where a man's *word* is his honor an' he don't need no paper . . . I didn't know you was a God damned thief stealin' bread out of the mouths of women an' children . . . you . . . !"

He reached out and clawed into Mr. Turner's neck, shaking him as a bull-dog shakes a rat. The little man was screaming: "I'll have you, arrested, John Rogers, if you don't let me go! Let me go! Let me go!"

My mother was struggling with my father and crying, "Don't, John, don't . . . think of the 'Pen'!"

Then the little man was gone, looking as if he had passed through a riot. Our house was very still and the atmosphere was heavy. My mother threw herself on the bed and lay without a sound. Father went out without his hat and only returned late from the hills. He lay down on the bed without undressing and without speaking. The next day we packed our few household things, loaded them onto the wagon, and started down the long road to Trinidad. All we had in the world was the little money my mother had saved from the boarders.

Hope and disappointment—once more the counterparts—walked hand in hand. My mother was joyous with hope now that we lived within the shadow of the school again. When my father found work in a distant mining town she had rented the "Tin Can Boarding House" beyond the tracks. I was very proud of it and of the new gingham dress Helen had made for me. When my teacher in school asked for my address I replied in a loud voice laden with enthusiasm:

"The Tin Can Boardin' House!"

"What is that?" she asked, and her eyes seemed to open just a bit wide.

What a question! Everybody surely knew where the magnificent Tin Can Boarding House was that had two stories and looked like brick from a distance! I proudly answered:

"Beyond th' tracks!"

Having made an impression, I set to work to make up the school work I had missed by entering late. A boy sat in the seat of honor. . . . I needed three months . . . he wouldn't sit there after that! At home there were no quarrels now and my mother hustled me into the "settin' room"—we had a settin' room now—to study, while she literally flew about the house.

Two months passed . . . I was gaining on the boy in the seat of honor. And he knew it! Sometimes when I glanced his way I saw him just raising his eyes to look at me—then we both dived into our books again.

Then things began to go wrong at home. My mother was losing money. The boarders would not pay, they made demands too heavy for her to meet and make money. My father came home again and my mother and Helen told him the wearisome, depressing story. The next morning he sat at the breakfast table and watched the boarders come in, dissatisfied, complaining. A fat woman followed by her husband dropped into her chair with a weary sigh. An old man glanced over the table bitterly.

"Jist help yerselves, folks," my father said grimly, "fer it's yer last meal in this here house!"

"Whatdye mean?" the old man barked.

"What I say!" my father bawled.

"The week's not up," the fat woman announced haughtily.

"You'll jist pay fer the days you've et here and git out!"

After breakfast he went upstairs and knocked on one door after the other, collecting money. I knew by his voice and manner that this was one of the great moments in his life. He had dreamed things just like this—when he, with all power in his hands, cleared everything before him. It wasn't a battle-field exactly, but in time it would grow into something like one. He would go back to his work and spin it out into a yarn worth hearing.

That I knew, for I had heard a tale grow under his treatment until it lost all semblance to its starting point. The story was simple. A man had been drowned in the flood which had washed away our tent months before, and his body had been found after a party of men had searched for it a number of days. That was the beginning and the end of the story.

My father, having heard it in the saloon, came home and told how he and a party of men walked down the Purgatory River searching for the lost man. With some gruesome details he related just how it was discovered. About a month later I heard him tell a group of people the same story again, but this time he and only one other man found the corpse alone, dug it out of the sand, and carried it to the morgue.

Much later I heard him tell the story to two miners. After the flood, he began impressively, he had walked down the banks of the Purgatory, for he had heard that a man had been drowned and he thought he ought to look around. He walked for miles, turning up first this log and that one, for some of them might 'a' been corpses. He lingered a bit over the details. Then . . . what was that sticking out of the mud? Another log! No, by God! He drew near. It was an arm—sticking straight up in the air as if the man were signaling to him: "Here I am, John Rogers!"

He dug with his bare hands; unearthed a shoulder, a side, a leg, and then a whole body! By God! He washed it in the Purgatory to see if perhaps it was a friend of his—strange, it looked like a friend! He looked it in the bloated face to see—his listeners gasped with horror. Then he picked it up in his arms—he, by himself—and carried it to the morgue; it was a damned heavy corpse if he did say it himself, soaked with water—here half of his audience arose and walked away to the stables; but the other man stayed until the dead man was bathed and laid to rest in the grave.

This was the story as I last heard it.

Upstairs the fat woman was now arguing with my father about the rent. The eggs yesterday morning hadn't been fit for a dog to eat!

"Mis' What's-yer-name, ye're a fee-male; but you'll pay up or I'll not leave a grease spot of yer old man!"

The husband paid up.

Helen stood at the foot of the stairs and listened in satisfaction, not without laughter. She had lost money also, but she was unmarried and could afford a few losses. But my mother sat in the kitchen, her face dull and heavy. Once more she had given the strength of her frail, willing body—and lost.

An unutterable loneliness filled my soul. There was no warmth about me—not even interest in my existence. I was "kitchen help" to a family that lived near the school. After school I washed dishes and took care of the baby. The baby screamed as I listlessly rocked it.

After my mother had failed to make a living in the

69

boarding-house venture she had come here and talked with this woman. They had argued about hours and payment; the woman—the wife of a railway fireman—stood very stiff and, to show that she knew how to deal with hired help, very briefly and coldly enumerated my duties. At last I was turned over to her. I got food on a plate and ate it on an old kitchen table overlooking the back yard, and the woman seemed to think me a part of the kitchen furniture. I was the first "help" she had ever had and she wanted no mistake made about the difference in our positions. I still remember how I tried to love her, and how cold her response was. It was a very difficult thing to learn that I was not a child, but just a "hired girl."

George and Dan and Beatrice were in school each day with me but they no longer seemed to belong to me. Annie had gone to work as a mangle girl in the laundry. Helen, who had worked up to the stiff shirt machine at last, used her influence to get her in. After school George would often slip his little hand into mine and walk to the corner of the street where we separated, he to go home, I to go to work.

The school work was a burden now, and my dreams of capturing the seat of honor faded into nothingness. The little white girl, as perfect as ever, seemed to have forgotten that I existed. My new teacher's eyes passed over me without interest. I cried a great deal over the dishes as I washed them, and over the screeching baby. Then I began to get sick. The woman asked me where I was sick . . . I didn't know. I had broken my arm once, I told her, and it was aching again! The woman complained to my mother at last and I was discharged. My illness disappeared with my discharge.

At home I found many changes. We now lived in a little frame house of four rooms. Helen and Annie occupied one of these alone because they worked and paid for their board and room. Annie pretended to be very grown-up; she refused to work in the house or to respect the opinions of my father or mother, and Helen was taking on the ways and speech of a city girl. She stopped saying "ain't" and used "have" or "have not." As sensitive as a photographic plate, she was taking on new manners. She bought sheets, and she slept in thin nightgowns instead of in her underwear like the rest of us. My mother respected her mightily and seemed to identify herself with her in all she did; perhaps through Helen she was living all that was denied her in her own life. On Saturday nights I would often hear the two of them arguing:

"You just take it, Elly. I've got nice things now and you ain't—haven't."

My mother would reply, protestingly and tenderly: "I don't feel like takin' all yer wages, Helen. You don't keep nothin' fer yerself a tall."

"Now you just take it, Elly, and shut up! You needn't think I don't know John's not bringin' his money home." It took Helen a long time to learn to put "g's" on her words.

My mother's eyes would travel along a crack in the floor and Helen would go out of the room, leaving her week's wages behind.

After school hours, on Saturdays and on holidays, I

helped neighboring women wash dishes or clothes, ran errands, and carried firewood or coal. For this they paid my mother. At night I could go home. In one place I worked for a woman who was newly married. She had been a laundry girl working with Helen and earning money; but once married, her husband said no wife of his could work! He forced her out of her active, independent life into a three-room house where most of the work was done by me after school. All day long she lay on the bed and often did not dress until the afternoon.

"Catch me gettin' married and layin' around like Gladys does!" Helen once said with a proud toss of her head.

After the first few weeks of Gladys' married life she and her husband began their quarrels. Neighboring women listened from behind drawn blinds. When she complained to them, as women beyond the tracks did, they all seemed to agree that a woman had to "mind" her husband. Something within me revolted at this and I hated and despised them all.

"Fer Christ's sake, what are you always fussin' about?" her husband one day broke out.

"I want to go back to work. You're gone all day and I jist set at home."

"What! Go to work and have people sayin' I can't support my wife! I don't know what you want! You've got duds enough and you don't hardly have to put your hands in water."

"I want to go back to work."

"An' gad about the streets and stick your money

under my nose? If you go to work you leave *my* house!"

So Gladys did not go back to work. Months passed and the neighbors smiled . . . for now it was said she was "expectin'." And the quarrels with her husband continued. The words that passed between them are still carved into my memory as if a dagger had made its ruthless way there.

"Give me back the clothes I bought you!" he bellowed at her one day.

"Damn it, kid, you know I love you!" she begged through her tears—for now she could not go back to work even if she wished.

Two other women in the next yard heard the words through the window and they laughed. She couldn't be so uppish any more, they said. I did not laugh. There was something in the words so heart-corroding that I could not even repeat them at home; only once since in my life have I been able to repeat them, and that once when I was trying to find the source of my hatred of marriage and my disgust for women who are wives. Those two sentences sum up, in my mind, the true position of the husband and wife in the marriage relationship.

"To him that hath shall be given, and from him that hath not shall be taken away!" Thus the minister was preaching. What he was saying I already knew. We belonged to the class who have nothing and from whom everything is always taken away.

The church was lofty, and the sun streamed in

through painted windows. The voice of the minister was harsh and accusing. I thought of the new green gingham dress I had bought. My dream was to buy a green hat, green stockings and green shoes and gloves, just as the woman I now worked for had. She was so beautiful that everyone stopped and looked at her as she passed.

The words of the minister beat in upon me. God gives to those who have and takes from those who have not. God seemed an unseen and unfair foe. When we, beyond the tracks, fought, we did it in the open and the other fellow had a chance also. Once my father had carried me home, bleeding and half-conscious, after he had separated me and the meanest boy beyond the tracks. I never understood the idea of God that they tried to teach me in that church. I had come to Sunday School and church three times and they kept telling me to love and fear God. How was that possible—there was my father; how could I love him if I were afraid of him at the same time. Then I was supposed to be afraid of the devil. God and the devil became all mixed up in my mind and the fear I was told to have for both was just the same. The whole thing was silly.

The church was a great disappointment. Yet it had started so beautifully; the three revival ministers had come down from Canada to convert the United States to Christianity. I was a part of the United States and they converted me—at least for three weeks. They were slender, young and very handsome. They stood in the corridor of our school and sang "The Maple Leaves Forever"; I saw yellow and gold maple leaves trembling in the sunlight and there was a wind in the tree tops

74

carrying stories on its back. The ministers had gone to this church and I had followed them there. After they had sung again and again, one of them asked the audience in a very soft voice:

"Is there anyone here who would like to come like a lamb to the arms of Christ?"

It was a bit funny to put it that way, but I nevertheless arose and walked up the aisle before him and before the whole congregation. A flashing fear that someone I knew might be in the audience and laugh disturbed me for a second, but I went on. If any kid from beyond the tracks laughed at me we could settle it in all due time!

"Will you always be a lamb of Christ?" the man asked me. His eyes were very blue and his hair fair.

"Yes, sir!" I had replied with tears in my eyes, for his voice was deep and his eyes beautiful.

Thus I had become a Christian. Now here I was in this church trying to keep it up. But each Sunday I had a sneaking feeling within that I would not remain a Christian for long. The whole thing was too dull since the blue-eyed minister went away.

The church stood on Commercial Street, the main thoroughfare that twisted its way like a snake through the city. It was also a part of the ancient Santa Fé Trail. The church and the saloon were the two landmarks on Commercial Street. The saloon was across the street from the church and a little way up the hill. There I could find my father at all times when he was not at work. It was a small, one-story building with swinging doors and behind these doors men gambled, drank and "swopped yarns." Next to it stood the cigar store in front of which men lounged, smoked and spat all day long, exchanging obscenities and blasphemies.

Across the bridge at the foot of Commercial Street, beyond the railway station that was the boast of the city, stood the boarding house where I now worked. From school I went directly there. Its owner, Mrs. Hampton, was a young widow whose beauty and cooking made it possible for her to charge such high prices for board and room that only firemen or engineers on the railway could afford to live there. She had a parlor with an organ in it. Her bedroom was big and sunny and was connected with it, for she was a luxurious lady who demanded the best for herself.

One night, from the couch in the parlor where I slept, I heard voices from her room. I listened—surely my name had been mentioned! Yes . . . she . . . she was talking with that engineer. She was saying:

"I think she drinks some of the milk each morning before I get up."

"Why don't you fire her?" The engineer's voice was authoritative and complaining, like that of a husband.

"Yes . . . but she does such a lot of work—as much almost as a regular hired girl."

". . . but if she's not honest!"

I heard no more. For hours I lay awake. The charge against me was true—I took a sip of her milk each morning when I brought it in from the back steps. Often I was hungry, for I got only what the boarders did not eat. Mrs. Hampton was an important woman and she sat at the head of the table herself with her boarders. She was a kind woman and I did not feel lonely in her house; but she did not always notice if there was food enough left over for me. She had no time for the female sex. I ate up what was left as I stacked and washed the dishes in the kitchen.

To wipe out my crime I arose very early the next morning, boiled water and washed out dish cloths, hand towels and pillow cases. By the time she was up, the clothing was flapping on the line and the milk bottle was standing on the table in all its pristine fullness. At the end of the day I secretly took a pail from the kitchen and went down across the tracks. For my mother had been taking in washing for some time and, together with help from Helen, had saved enough to buy a cow. Although she sold the milk, I would tell her the truth and ask her to give me a pailful of milk to pay back my debt to Mrs. Hampton. Then I would tell Mrs. Hampton I was sorry—my crime would be wiped out. I even contemplated returning to the church as a punishment.

With a light conscience I approached our house. But at the gate I stopped. My father was cursing and dragging my sister Annie into the house by her hair. Annie was screaming and struggling.

"I'll maul hell out of you if you're twenty-five years old an' as big as th' side of a house!" he was shouting.

My mother's voice was filled with anguish. "Oh, Annie, tell me if you was in a roomin' house last night!"

Annie was coarse and vulgar. "Have I got to tell you a hundred times I went to a dance an' stayed all night with Millie? Go an' ask her ma if I didn't!"

"You're lyin'!"—but my father's voice was cooling.

"I'm lyin', am I? Then whatdye ask me for?"

"Well, I'll let you go this time, but th' next time I hear of you goin' to that ornery low-down dance hall an' dancin' with pimps an' stayin' out all night, I'll maul hell out of you!"

"You look out fer yourself, Pa, and I'll take care of myself! You're always in the saloon . . . you ain't got nothin' to say to me! . . . I'm makin' my own money now!"

Annie was fifteen and a woman of the world. And, by the standards of our world, a woman who earned her own money was a free woman. Only married women had to take orders. By touching Annie my father had violated the code of honor beyond the tracks. He was bellowing back at Annie in a voice loud enough for all the neighbors to hear:

"Yes, you earn yer own money, an' it's a lot o' good it does us! Helen gives yer mother her money but you spend yours on duds fer gaddin' about the streets!"

"Why don't you give Ma *yer* money, I'd like to know, instead of spendin' it in th' saloon?"

"No back talk from you, missy! You do as I say, not as I do, or I'll maul hell out of you if yer're twenty-five years . . ."

The back door slammed violently. . . . Annie had replied contemptuously and left in the middle of his threat.

There I stood at the gate with a pail in my hand. A thousand emotions had swept over me as I listened to the quarrel in the house—hateful, bitter emotions. Memories rushed to consciousness, forming an indistinct, vague picture of repulsion. "Annie in a rooming house all night"...that meant sex. My father and mother on the verge of beating her for it...what right had they...they were liars and hypocrites themselves! I had heard them in the middle of the night...and now *they* were shocked! What liars grown-up people are! How dishonest! And that Annie...growing up...with fat breasts and hips, and proud of them! How disgusting! I did not like to be near her...nausea almost overcame me. Growing up and doing what all other grown-up people did—wallowing in sex!

On the one hand stretched my world of fairy tales, the song of "The Maple Leaves Forever," the tales of good little girls being kind to animals, of color, dancing, music, with happiness in the end even if things were not all right now. On the other hand stood—a little house with a rag pasted over a broken window-pane; a lone struggling morning-glory trying to live in the baked soil before the porch; Annie being dragged by her tousled streaming hair; my father, once so straight and handsome, now a round-shouldered man with tobacco juice showing at the corners of his mouth.

Turning, I retraced my steps without even opening the old gate leading into the yard. Along the banks of the Purgatory, over the tracks, across the arroyo flowing into the river, past the round-house back to Mrs. Hampton's. I crept into the kitchen and replaced the pail on the shelf. Then I went to bed and waited.

Mrs. Hampton was saying:

"Marie, I think I can do my own work alone from now on. I don't need you any more."

I looked through the back door into the yard beyond where washing was flapping in the wind. So I was being discharged for having taken a sip of her milk. I thought she had forgotten. I had worked so hard for the past few days and had tried to make up for things. It did not seem possible for her to do it . . . no, it must be that engineer who made her do it; she was going to marry him. He was going to make her a "respectable" married woman now, with standards such as Christians have. And she would have to obey him.

"Can't I stay another month fer nothin'? You won't have to pay me nothin'." My chest felt as tight as a skin stretched over a drumhead.

She thought that over for some time. "No. I can do my own work!" Her voice was sad, but it was final.

It took me hours to reach home. I sat down under a cottonwood tree near the big round-house for a time, then when it was darker, under a weeping willow hanging sadly over the arroyo. I knew I had either to make up a story or get a whipping from my mother. She would scream that she would "stomp me into the ground" if she ever caught me stealing again. Or that she would whip me "until the blood ran down my back." I had to have time to think and to get rid of the weight in my chest. Perhaps it would be best to jump in the river and drown; then Mrs. Hampton and my mother would be sorry. The river rolled on mercilessly, dark and troubled against the gleam of the gray sand bank beyond. It was talking to itself . . . how strange that voice . . . it was like the night of the flood when it rushed upon us. This was one thing that you could not make love you . . . it was worse than an animal. That voice . . . fear held me back. . . . I could not trust a thing with no feeling in it.

It was late and very dark . . . it must have been hours since I left Mrs. Hampton's . . . it must be nearing midnight now. I dragged my feet homeward, up to the kitchen door, and pushed it open. I didn't care about telling a lie now.

But what was wrong? Helen and Annie were standing together near a corner where it was darkest. My mother was sitting on a chair, her head in her arms, her body shaking with sobs. Like a bull ready to charge, my father stood near the door. They all looked up as I came in. My father saw that my eyes were on my mother, and he perhaps remembered that I could never endure her weeping. Perhaps he felt in a weak position, as if he were author of this misery, for he shouted at me:

"Lookie, Marie, at your . . . your Aunt Helen. . . . I caught her layin' in the corner of the porch with that Dago beau of hers! Payin' fer that there brooch on her dress an' fer her fine duds! That's what she's been doin'!"

"John . . . what in God's name do you mean talkin' to a child like that!" my mother gasped in horror.

"She's got to know what kind of sister her mother's got . . . that's what!"

There was silence. Within my skull it seemed that a brush had made one complete sweep. . . . I could hear it as it made the circle. We all stood where we were. Helen's face was filled with white bitterness.

"You, John Rogers, to talk like that! You treat Elly

like a dog! You've got nothin' to say to me when you spend all your money in the saloon."

"God . . . ! You that's a whore to . . ."

Helen rushed at him with a wild scream. Like a flash of lightning her hand struck and left a bloody streak down one side of his face. Then he caught her arms and held them savagely, high in the air. She, frail as she was, struggled viciously, kicking at his stomach, trying to reach him with her teeth. Only by the most violent effort could he hold her from him. My mother arose and in terror ran to them; she put her arms around the writhing Helen, stroking her hair and clinging to her. "Let her go, John! Helen . . . Helen . . . little sister . . . come here to me!"

She separated them and dragged Helen, white and panting, to the other side of the room.

"Takin' the part of a whore agin yer own husband!"

Helen made another lunge, but my mother's arms were around her and the weight of her body stayed the rush. "Elly"—Helen was panting like an animal—"let me go! let me go, Elly!" She and my mother rocked with the struggle, but my mother clung fast. Over her shoulder Helen turned her white face to my father.

"If you call me that agin . . . you low-down dog . . . I'll choke you to death with my own hands, an' Elly can't stop me!" My mother's trembling voice tried to soothe her, stroking her lovely bronze hair and her white cheek. But Helen's voice came, low and passionate.

"An' if I *was* a whore, John Rogers, I want to know who made me one! *You*, John Rogers! You! Elly ain't

82

had enough money to buy grub and duds for herself and the kids. I've give her my wages each pay-day. Yes, an' you know it! If 'twasn't for my money, she'd have starved to death. You in the saloon ... you comin' home on Saturday night when every cent's gone, then lyin' or threatenin' if she complained. How d'ye think she was to live? ... Washin'? ... damn you! You're an ornery low-down dog! *You* to call me names! You! Where did you think I could git money for my duds. ... I *won't* go in rags. ... I *won't* get married and let some man boss me around and whip me and let me starve! *I've* a right to things. If I'm a whore ... *you* made me one, you, John Rogers, ... you ... you ... you!"

"You pack up yer duds an' march, an' don't you ever dare darken my door agin!" My father was livid with rage. Helen had spoken the truth. "Git out now ... to yer Dago pimp! Yer're not fit fer a dog!"

"And you *are* I suppose! And you call this *your* house, do you ... you don't even pay the rent. You don't bring in *nothin'!*"

"Git out of my house or I'll throw you out!"

My mother had her arms about Helen. "If she goes out in this night, John, I go with her."

"Yer're a nice wife to talk of goin' out in the streets with a woman like that! You let her go an' come here!"

My mother stood, straight and slender, her face ashen-colored like the face of a wounded coal miner I had seen long ago, a few minutes before he died. Her blue-black eyes glistened ... where had I seen such horrible eyes before. ... I remembered ... why ... long ago . . . I must have been no more than four . . . I killed a kitten . . . clodded it to death in the road because it was strange and I pretended it was dangerous . . . its eyes in its death agony looked like those of my mother, now.

"Come here!!" my father bellowed at my mother.

But she stood with her arms about Helen.

"You come here or I'll break all the furniture in this God damned house!"

My mother continued standing in icy silence, her eyes glistening. With a grunt my father flung out of the back door and we heard him fumbling in the dark. Helen's voice was tense with passion and misery.

"I'll go alone, Elly. I'll go now. John'll break up everything you've got . . . an' then he might kill you."

"*He* can go . . . not you."

"He won't go . . . he'll kill us all first."

"Then let him break up everythin'. And I'd rather be dead than alive anyway!"

"Don't, Elly. I'll go. I'll send you money an' things fer the kids. No! Stay here, I'm goin' alone. Stay here, I say! Think of the kids! What'll they do without you! Wait until I'm makin' enough for all of us . . . just wait!"

Helen pushed my mother away from her and backed into the room where she and Annie slept. Annie crept in after her, and the key turned in the lock. There were fumbling noises, quick steps, fugitive whispers from behind the door. My mother had sunk to the floor in a heap and lay, face downward, with her head in her arms. Her breath came in hard gasps. The back door opened and my father tramped in with an ax in his hands. His eyes fell on my mother on the floor. He stood listening . . . from behind the bedroom door hasty steps were moving about. He lowered the ax to the floor and waited . . . waited.

There was the sound of an outside door opening and closing . . . two steps on the porch outside, one step downward onto the hard earth, three steps more to the street. The old gate, hanging on one hinge, squeaked and flapped to with a dull rotten sound as if a spirit had passed that way. The rag pasted over the broken window-pane bulged inward from a wind that swept down the canyons in late autumn. My father breathed heavily, turned without a word, and slammed the kitchen door behind him. The click of his steps crossed a ditch leading toward the railway tracks . . . the tracks that wound through the city within a few steps of the saloon. The silence of the kitchen was broken only by the beat of my mother's sobs as if they had always been and would always be.

Weeks passed and then the sword fell. My father carried out his oft-repeated threat and left home. He knew my mother was too frail to support us all. No word had come from Helen.

After my mother had defied him about Helen and showed with each passing day that she no longer cared for life, he had become more and more violent. At night I heard hard, bitter weeping, but the door leading into their bedroom was locked. The horror of uncertainty hung over everything.

That year women were given the vote in our State. My mother's chin raised itself just a bit but she held her peace. She was not a talking woman.

"Howrye goin' to vote?" my father asked her.

She did not reply. Quarrels followed . . . he did the quarreling. At last a weapon had been put into her hands. At least she felt it so. He threatened her, but still she would not answer. On election day he threatened to leave home if she didn't tell him. But, without answering, she walked out of the house as if he did not exist. That night he asked a question that was a command:

"D'ye mean to tell me how you voted or not?"

"I don't mean to!"

The next morning she stood on the kitchen porch and he sat on his wagon outside, holding the reins, ready to drive away. My heart was heavy and I felt sick. He asked one more question, but she just stood quietly with her hands folded, and did not answer. Then he went. My mother's frail body braced itself anew. She decided it was better to go out to wash instead of taking washing in at home, for when she went out she got coffee and dinner; it saved food. Each morning she crossed the Purgatory to the comfortable homes bordering regular streets, with the high school rearing its head amidst them. She knocked at back doors and informed women that she did very excellent washing and ironing. Thus she became a regular washerwoman. Each morning she left home at seven, and she returned at eight at night. Her charges were one dollar and thirty cents a day. Yes, she said, she was frail, but she washed things white—all people had to do was to just give her a trial. The women looked at her eyes and wistful face and shook their heads; but then they saw her hands, big-veined and almost black from heavy work. That convinced them.

She washed all that winter. At night she was, as she herself admitted, "tired as a dog," but never too tired to relate in detail just the kind and quality of food she had had for dinner. It was sent to the wash kitchen on a plate to her. She sometimes had meat. She lingered over the memory, and was so thankful for such good treatment that she offered to wash extra things or stay half an hour later. The only thing that worried her was the neuralgia pains that tortured her in the face and head.

Annie went daily to the laundry and refused to help at home—she was "workin'." My task was to help do the housework and get my brothers and Beatrice ready to take to school. Then I locked the door and we trudged away through the snow.

There were days when my mother did washing at home. She started with the dawn and the kitchen was filled with steam and soapsuds. In the afternoon her face was thin and drawn and she complained of pains in her back. I wrung and hung out clothes or carried water from the hydrant outside. She and I were now friends and comrades, planning to buy a washing machine as we worked. We charged thirty cents a dozen pieces for washing and ironing, but the women always gave us their biggest pieces—sheets, tablecloths, overalls, shirts, and generally they threw in the thirteenth piece just for good measure. Thirteen is unlucky, but for washerwomen it is supposed to be lucky—at least they thought so.

Our house was one mass of steaming sheets, under-wear and shirts, and to get from one room to the other we had to crawl on the floor. We stretched lines in all but one sleeping room and we could afford a fire only in the kitchen stove. Each day Beatrice and I, beating our hands to keep them warm, ran along the railway track picking up coal that had fallen from the passing engines, and after it was dark we "snitched" as much wood as we could carry from a near-by lumber yard. At night my mother and I prepared a dinner of potatoes and a gravy made from flour and water, and sometimes flour and milk. We still had our cow, but we sold all the milk. We ate in silence about the kitchen table, and the air was laden with the smell of soapsuds. We never ceased dreaming of a washing machine to save her back from so much pain. But there were always shoes to buy, and there were school books. Unable to make any headway we decided that I must also get work and she must wash alone.

I found work in a small cigar shop, owned by a short, dark-faced Jew. From school I went directly there and worked until eight in the evening. With three or four other girls, I sat in a dark back room and carefully stripped the central vein out of big, soft, brown tobacco leaves. These leaves we piled beside us to be taken to the adjoining room where men sat in a row before a long table rolling cigars. Their room was light and clean; ours was filled with tobacco dust. The men could laugh and talk; we could not. At five o'clock a bell rang and they arose, whipped off their aprons, and left. On Saturdays they left at one. I learned they were union men and dared do this. Our employer respected them, but not us in the back room. Strange, I thought, those who are strong and do not need it are respected; those who need it do not get it. Christianity was that, also; to him that hath shall be given and from him that hath not shall be taken away. Strange it is, this religion and this society of revenge!

One of the cigar rollers was young and very handsome. As I stripped I watched his brown head in the light of the other room . . . perhaps, I dreamed, he would see me sitting here one day, and, like a prince in a fairy story, ask me to marry him! I pictured myself sitting by his side rolling cigars. One day I deliberately placed my box of stripped leaves directly in the way. He had to stop as he passed out; he saw me, indeed; but he asked me why in the devil I stuck things before people like that!

I wept over the tobacco leaves. Eight o'clock seemed never to come. There was no love in this place. . . . I was a piece of wood, it seemed. Time and again my employer would come back and scold me for my slowness.

"You're always dreaming," he said kindly at first, "you must wake up and strip faster; look—like this." When his voice was kind and he sat near me I stripped very fast; but then he went away and it was dark and cold and dusty in the room.

"What do you do at night when you go home?" he asked once, sitting by my side. I thought he was interested in me and I beamed. His presence seemed so warm and friendly.

"I read books from the library."

"What books?"

"All kinds of books."

"You oughtn't to read; that's the reason you dream instead of working. I warn you, Marie . . . if you don't do better, I'll have to let you go."

How ashamed and miserable I felt. That night I cried, stuffing the blanket in my mouth so that no one could hear. They might laugh—for in our world no one was supposed to show affection or pain. Only weaklings and women did that.

One day my employer gave me my week's wages—one dollar and a half—with the words:

"You need not come back here any more."

I walked out without a word, and when I reached the lumber yard beyond the tracks I stopped between two piles of lumber and wept. At home I took my place by the side of the wash tub again and my mother seemed almost too dull to notice my return. All feeling was being washed out of her. In school I was unspeakably miserable and was one of the worst children in my class. Time and again I answered questions, certain that I had learned them aright, only to find that my teacher considered them all wrong. On the playground I herded with the "tough girls" from beyond the tracks and they talked of the kissing parties they held in their homes; in secret places they exchanged confidences about life's mysteries. At night I was sometimes permitted to go to their parties, where all the games called for kissing.

Then I took my place as one of the leaders of the "toughest kids beyond the tracks." In school I let nothing hurt me—no reprimand of my teacher, no look or word. Swearing had always come easily and naturally with me, for my father had been a very good teacher. He even separated his words to insert curses: he would say "the very i-God-damned-dea!" I fought boys and girls alike in the alleys beyond the tracks, and my brothers hovered proudly under my protecting wing.

When my mother would send me to the store to buy a spool of thread, a sack of salt, or a cake of soap, I made good use of my time. The clerk would turn his back to fill the order, and I would, with a quick movement, take the things that we needed at home, and slip them into my pockets or under my coat. It was a box of macaroni here, a can of peas there, and at all times any fruit that was within reach. My face was innocent and peaceful when the clerk returned. Many boys and girls beyond the tracks stole, but of them all I was one of the most successful. Perhaps I possessed more native cunning than they. . . . I went uptown to buy my cakes of soap! No one suspected you in the big stores where rich people from the big houses where my mother washed clothes, bought things. There, behind the unsuspecting backs of the clerks, I loaded myself and I came to regard almost everything I saw from the viewpoint of its stealing possibilities; just how I could manage it, just how I could get out of the store, just how it would look at home. I seldom came home empty-handed now. At first I lied to my mother and said someone had given me things; or that I found them.

My mother was dull now; she scolded but in a passive, kindly way. I watched her mouth and saw an expression there that told me she was glad to have the food; for the winter was cold and we were hungry. When once I had seen that look I became bolder and stole in larger and larger quantities, going directly from school uptown, taking a can of peas here, condensed milk there, honey from another place. I avoided eggs in case of detection when I would have to run. Sometimes I brought in more than my mother did, and our diet of potatoes and gravy, made with flour and water, was enriched by all sorts of canned food and by real butter—by everything that could fit into a big coat pocket or be carried under the arm next to the dress. Only one thing I paid for—her washing soap; but it took me two or three hours to buy two or three cakes, for I had to walk from store to store.

Both George and Dan sometimes wore warm woolen stockings now—stockings can also be carried inside a coat pocket. In the late winter I was able to enrich their supply of clothing by securing work in a store holding a bargain sale. I accepted the very low wages they paid, and worked like a slave. My mother looked severely at me when I brought home warm flannel shirts for my brothers. I said I bought them with my money. She was silent at that. She never had the time nor the desire to go uptown and inquire if what I told was true or not. Even had she done so she would have learned that I was one of the most obedient and trustworthy clerks in the bargain store!

Part 3

The spring brought hope to the forests and mountains and the distant mountain sides changed imperceptibly from a dark purple to a dull gray-green. But to us beyond the tracks the spring brought defeat.

Two or three times during the winter my father had driven up to our kitchen door and, from the seat on his wagon, asked my mother if she was ready to tell him how she had voted. She stood, her arms and hands steaming with soapsuds, and replied: "I ain't got nothin' to say." Her figure straightened itself when she said that, and there was a dignity about her that caused me to walk to her side and raise my chin just a bit also. I always expected my father to lift his whip and slash her across the face. Something made me think that, had I not been standing by her, he would have done it. Once she informed him, in a very quiet tone of voice, that she was "thinkin' of gettin' a divorce." He was scandalized.

"That's a nice thing fer a respectable married woman to say—talkin' of gettin' a divorce from her own husband!"

"I know you're livin' with that woman cook out in Ludlow, so don't you go talkin' to me!" she had replied.

"God damn it! This is a nice to-do!" he cursed, as she turned and reëntered the kitchen, closing the door firmly behind her.

But spring came. Youth beyond the tracks dreamed of vague, restless things that sent it prowling along the river banks at night when the moon was high, standing in groups, or sinking under clumps of tough brush; there was soft laughter through the night, low voices, tormenting things, and the wind was very soft against young cheeks and throats. But my mother never ceased her washing, and at night she entered the dark little bedroom and sank in exhaustion upon the bed. Life was difficult in the spring, for many women who during the winter months had given out their washing could now have it done at home. My mother reduced her prices to one dollar a dozen, with an extra piece thrown in, and then to ninety cents.

"It don't pay us, Mrs. Rogers, now that with a little help at home we can do it ourselves," some of the women told her. My mother's face was thin and haunted, and her back, she said, "jist seemed as if it couldn't hold out." Her teeth tortured her and she had them pulled out one by one. It was cheaper that way and now she had but one tooth on one side of her jaw.

There came a morning when she wanted to "lay jist a little longer in bed," and I stayed home from school and started the washing. She got up later but pains and dizziness in her head forced her back into bed. She lay sick for days. Doctors are only for the rich and it never occurred to any of us to call a doctor. We always just waited to get over a sickness. I heated hot bricks all day long and kept them against her back and the side of her head. And each day I cooked potatoes and made a flour-and-water gravy for us all.

Then my father drove up before the kitchen door for the last time. He didn't go away. When the right of women to vote was ever mentioned in the presence of my mother after that her eyes sought a crack in the floor and followed it back and forth in silence. And her silence was heavy with bitterness.

My mother was well again and we were going to leave the city and go to the mining camp Delagua, where my father had a contract for hauling and excavating. My mother was to "board the men" and I was to wait tables. The children were to be taken from school again—it could not be helped; we had starved long enough. But Annie was not going with us. The spring had touched her also. She was only sixteen, but she was going to be married.

A vague feeling of disgust seized me when she announced her intention. She was no friend of mine, she so fat and selfish! When I looked at her, a thousand memories flooded my brain; all ugly memories; once she had awakened me in the middle of the night pressing her body against mine; another time, when the revivalists had told me to become a Christian and pray, I had prayed; when all were asleep I had crept from bed, knelt down, and prayed to the God I was supposed to fear, to forgive me for everything. Just as I knelt waiting to see what would happen, Annie had turned over and exclaimed:

"Uh-huh! You think I don't hear you! I'm goin' to tell on you tomorrow." She did not tell, but she used that secret against me for months.

Now she was going to be married. Her mouth was loose when she talked about it. But my dislike of her was almost swallowed up in the mystery surrounding it. For her betrothed was a man from "back home," the elder son of the family where Helen had been a hired girl earning six dollars a month; he was her betrothed then, and when no reply came to his letters he had come in search of her.

I was sent out of the room. When I returned later Helen's letters lay on my mother's lap. Sam was crying and my mother was trying to soothe him; then he had gone away—to get Helen, my mother said. He returned two months later—but alone; and before another month had passed he and Annie were engaged to be married, and Annie was very proud of it.

The marriage took place a few days before we left for Delagua. Sam had shaken hands with my mother after the ceremony and said he would be a good husband to Annie. It seemed to be a pledge between two people who had tasted the dregs of suffering, and in the years that followed, Sam kept the pledge he gave my mother. Perhaps it is easier to forgive faults in a person you do not love than in one from whom you expect the noblest and most beautiful that life has to offer. Perhaps he would not have forgiven the same faults in Helen.

Years later I saw Helen, when a decade of suffering

lay between her and Sam. Still the mystery about the two of them and about my sister tormented me.

"I couldn't marry him," she had jerked out at last to stop my questions. "Of course I saw him—do you think I'm blind? Why didn't I marry him? Why, in God's name, should I marry him? . . . That's none of your business . . . Anyway it would of been all right at first but when a woman gets married and can't make her own livin', a man starts remindin' her of her past."

I followed the trail of mystery ruthlessly. She denied and admitted in the same breath.

"Of course that was why I wouldn't marry him. There was Tony at first and then he brought others. . . . I can't have a baby any more . . . you're a nosey thing, Marie! . . . What business is that of yours? Why, I can't have a baby because I've had two operations. . . . I have to go down to the Springs ever' year fer treatment. Now, in God's name, are you satisfied!"

At that time I was still a bit blind. I thought of "the Springs" as a fine summer resort where rich people went. Helen certainly dressed like a rich woman at that time. Later I learned why she went to the Springs, and what the disease was that she tried to cure. I am sorry that I knew so much . . . a young tree can not grow tall and straight and beautiful if its roots are always watered with acids.

Sam and Annie went down into western Oklahoma and took up a homestead, built a house and worked on the land that stretched, desolate and dreary, to the horizon. Annie was of the clay of which good wives are

97

made: a physical animal who would quarrel violently with her husband, but submit to superior force in the end. Such women follow their husbands to the grave, untroubled by ideas or principles. She was too physical for ideas or principles. Sam took her from her numerous girl friends, from the streets and dance halls and the bright parties, where she had dressed as well as the rest, and made of her a pioneer woman who wore loose calico wrappers, went barefoot and rolled her hair into a little knot at the back of her head. She endured the life for two years and then went into the silence where all pioneer women have gone before her. As she died she expressed the regret that I had always seemed to hate her. My mother repeated those words to me and watched me longingly, her eyes searching my face for a glimmer of tenderness. Tenderness did not come. I was a savage beast and I harbored injuries and hatreds in my heart. Right or wrong, it is true. It is. The ways of life had taught me no tenderness.

So went my sister into the darkness. And I remained behind in what is called light.

When Annie and Sam left Trinidad for their homestead, we remained in the city to wait for the conclusion of one of the first strikes in the coal fields of the Colorado Fuel & Iron Company. For three weeks the town of Trinidad had been occupied by the state militia. They "kept order." Camped on the sloping hill on the other side of the Purgatory River opposite our house, they drank, and settled their quarrels with guns. Flying bullets struck terror into the hearts of the mothers on our side of the river. Children had to play in the back yards behind the houses. With each setting sun fathers began to look for their daughters. If a girl worked in the laundry, as did many from beyond the tracks, some one waited to bring her home. Once the news spread like wildfire that a girl had been beaten half to death by her father who had found her talking with a soldier along the railway track. The soldier had smirked and swaggered off—he wore the uniform of the United States and no father dared touch him. A few days later a man two doors from our house had not gone for his daughter, and when she did not return home as usual he set out in search of her. He found her in the possession of two soldiers, away down between piles of lumber in the lumber yard. One standing on watch had warned the other and the shouts of the father had not led to their capture. The lumber yard was isolated and, anyway, no one would have dared touch a "uniform of the United States."

News travels by air beyond the tracks, and before the father and his daughter had passed a dozen houses along the street, men and women emerged from their doors or stood in groups watching. It was a silent march those two made, with heads bent and eyes that did not see, the girl's blouse torn from her and her eyes red and swollen from weeping. The man walked with a slouch, his fingers moving stiffly and then closing into a hard fist. Had there been a murder of a soldier, and had the jury been chosen from our side of the tracks, no father would have been convicted, and no man or woman would have appeared as a witness against him. When at last "order" was restored, the miners forced back to their holes in the ground, and the blue-uniformed guardians of the law removed, the town beyond the tracks drew a deep sigh of relief.

When the air was still thick with hostility, we reached the mining town of Delagua. This was one of the larger camps, lying at the junction of three or four canyons, barren and stony. The black mouths of mines, with tipples thrust far out over slag dumps, choked the canyons. A long, low row of coke ovens, glowing dull red at night, lay back of a line of miners' houses, and a network of narrow railway lines connected it with the mines.

The Company owned all the mines and all the country for miles about. We rented our house from the Company—there were no other houses. The one store from which we bought food and clothing was the Company store—no other was permitted to exist. We paid the high Company prices or we went without. The school building belonged to the Company and the teacher was chosen by Company officials; the saloon where the men gathered and spent their money was leased to a saloon keeper by the Company, and this saloon keeper had to be in "good standing" with the Company. The minister who passed through the town once a month had to preach of God and heaven and not of this earth. The railways leading to the town were Company railways. This Almighty Power issued its own money—script—and all miners and workers were paid with it instead of in American money; the banks in Trinidad cashed it at a 10% discount. A man was told he would be paid two dollars a day, but he was paid in script. When he objected to the high prices for food at the Company store, he was told it was necessary because he was paying in script, and script was discounted in the city.

Before the crooked rows of two- and three-room houses where the miners lived, stood groups of big-shouldered men. They met on the front porch of the saloon and before the Company store, speaking in many different languages—Polish, Czechish, German, mingled with English. The atmosphere was a cloud of stifling discontent and hatred, filled with curses about the weigh boss, the long hours, the bad pay, the dangerous conditions in the mines. I learned that the miners labored far back in the dark tunnels, loaded their coal on cars, and mules dragged it to the mouth of the mines. There it was run over the scales and a Company official weighed it. The miners knew, from years of experience, how much they had dug; but always they were credited with less than they dug. A few pounds deducted on each car made a big hole in their pay envelope on Saturday night. It was the end of the month, the strike had been broken, and their bills at the Company store had risen extraordinarily. The bills were always more than they earned, men charged bitterly—a blanket added here and there that they had not bought, all kinds of things added that they had never seen, and they were told they had bought them and should pay or get no more credit. They had to pay or lose their jobs.

"Ignorant, lousy foreigners," the officials in the town called them. "Dangerous customers," others said when they heard them speaking a tongue they could not understand. For to the American all things he does not understand are dangerous.

"Pay or get out" was the motto of the Company store. The miners paid. To leave the town meant money. To go to another meant going to the same conditions; even if they left and went to another town, they found their names on the black list and they could get no work. They were tied hand and foot. In all directions lay the lands and the towns of the Company, and to the north lay other towns of other Companies with conditions just the same.

I walked fearfully along the dirty winding streets and looked into the homes of the miners. Bare little rooms with a table, a chair or two, a few pots and pans—and a musical instrument. Sometimes books. In the evening many of them sat outside their houses and played melancholy folk music. As I passed, they greeted me courteously in a foreign tongue; for I did not belong to a family of the official class, although we were native Americans. There were times when no woman dared go on the streets. Outbursts threatened when men were killed in the mines and their bodies were carried through the streets. They would pass our house, carrying their wounded or dead on a board, and a crowd would gather and follow. Insufficient props in the mines, I learned, time and again; or gas explosions from the open lamps.

When a man took his pick and shovel and disappeared into the blackness of the mine, neither he nor his family knew if he would come out dead or alive. All native American working men feared the mines. When my father contemplated martyrdom because my mother, as he said, treated him badly, he threatened to become a miner. My mother's silence would drive him into the mines yet, he let us all know. I came to fear the mines and all American working men feared that one day they would be in such desperate straits that they would have to put on a cap with an open lamp and take their places on the cars that hauled the miners into the darkness.

Native American men worked for my father, for his work was in the open. He now had eight or ten teams of horses and wagons. How he came into possession of such property is a mystery. Some twenty men were working for him, dynamiting and shoveling earth away for the construction of new buildings for the Company. They came pouring into our house for their meals and my mother and I worked ceaselessly. When the dishes were washed we began preparing for another meal. My mother's hopes were again soaring and she forced her frail body without stint. I think she once had hopes of some comfort for herself while her youth lasted; she was still young in years, but old in body and spirit and her teeth were almost gone. She now dreamed about me—I was to learn to play the piano; for didn't I try to play every musical instrument I could get my hands on? A piano meant an "edjication" to her and I was to have it. She urged me to coax my father for a piano; he could afford it, she argued, for he bought fine harness for his horses and everything he needed outside in his work. But when I coaxed him, he laughed at my wild ideas. Instead, he put up what he called "a proposition" to me. He was making money now and he was going to "keep books." He would see this time that nobody cheated him "as that son of a bitch Turner did.". . . He would just write everything down in a book and if there was ever any dispute, he would just show the "figgers." His confidence in "figgers" and books was remarkable, for all his scorn of education. One day he brought home a ledger and a day book and placed them before me on the kitchen table.

"You've got an edjication; now, open the books!" he commanded.

I glanced at him, then reached down and lay the books open before him.

He became very sarcastic: "You've got to the eighth grade, but yer Dad knows mor'n you! When you open books you have to write in 'em! Here, now, set down an' take that there pencil."

He began to dictate figures and I made a long row on one side of the ledger.

"Now add 'em up!"

I added and re-added . . . but got a different total each time. He stood smiling down at me . . . me with an "edjication" and unable to add figures! With a flourish to shame me he took the book and pencil and started to add. He got a different result still; he added again, moving his lips, mumbling and making dots on the page—a different number still was the result! He was angry that I stood watching, but for the sake of his own dignity he dared not send me away; and for the sake of mine I wouldn't go. "Elly!" he bawled into the kitchen, "come here an' add this. Here you've got a datter that's been to the eighth grade an' can't add." He called me *her* daughter now; when I did something he liked, he generally said I was a "datter of her old dad."

That was a proud moment for my mother! She just wiped her hands on her apron and sat down. She added aloud so that we could hear: "two an' five's seven, seven an' eight's fifteen, fifteen an' eight's twenty-three, twenty-three an' nine's thirty-two". . . and then finally the result. My father stood above her, listening and watching, his eyes filled with the unwavering faith and confidence of a child. From that moment onward his intellectual life lay in my mother's hands. I have seen that look in other eyes—my brother George always looked at me like that; the man I loved and who loved me gazed at me like that, and I knew that to him I could do no wrong. It is a terrible thing, that expression; for it means that the individual is lost, submerged in another, whether he wills it or not.

When mother had finished the column of figures, she arose and stood looking at my father. He was very humble.

"I'd like you t'do the books ever' night, Elly. I want it so's if there's trouble like with that Turner dog, I can show the figgers."

Each night thereafter they sat over the table, he dictating items and figures, she writing. He would bring out a book from his pocket with long rows of awkward figures that no one but himself could read. They were his daily expenditure and his estimates—he used the word "estimates" and glanced at me without explaining its meaning. How he arrived at any estimates is a secret of the gods. When contracting for work he would look at a piece of ground, think and mumble to himself, scratch his ear, and scribble in his book. Then he would go before the Company officials in the town and bid for the job against other contractors. Some of the others turned in typewritten offers, but my father stood in his shirt sleeves and high-laced boots and bid verbally. He had a bit of contempt for men who could not do anything without paper and a typewriter. He would contract to excavate, furnish the cement and stone foundations, workmen, teams, wagons and tools. He mentioned a round sum, he to be paid in two installments, one at the beginning of the job, the other when it was finished.

The officials would look at him standing in his shirt sleeves, bidding against the offers of other men. In the end they often gave him the job. It must have been his personality, the way he talked that convinced them, for he had a way with him, and his speech and his manner were colorful. He could barely write, and I never saw him read a line of printed matter in his life. His world lay not within the two covers of a book, but within himself and the world about him. There was nothing in a book for him; but even a hole in the ground became filled with romance. He kept his eyes, not upon the stars, but upon the earth; he was of the earth and it of him. He dug in the earth, he hugged the earth, he thought in terms of the earth.

I would often stand on the edge of an excavation and watch him through the cloud of dust below. He was deaf to all things but this work; had I gone close to him, he would not have seen me. His mind was working in great circles—I knew that back deep it was sweeping over the horizon of his life, far beyond. . . . He was digging not just a hole in the ground, but uncovering marvelous things, all that lies in the earth. That I knew because I knew him, for I was my father's daughter.

He was a lean, lanky cowboy of twenty-eight and he worked for my father. He had left his ranch in New Mexico for a time to go out and see the world. He, like many of the men who worked for my father, tired of one place or one kind of work and then moved on to the next. They were men who as a rule carried all their worldly possessions with them: a gun or two, a fine belt, a pair of marvelous spurs and boots, perhaps an unusual hat band, a Mexican quirt and gloves. They nearly always owned a horse, a saddle that was far from ordinary, and sometimes a bit and bridle to match, and that set them apart as men of taste. They came from the cattle ranches beyond the Divide. They were silent, picturesque men, much mixed with the clay. Courageous, kindly, trusting—and foul-mouthed. When they received their wages they spent it in one night in Trinidad, "on the hill" where women sold themselves to men's desires. When they married, which was indeed rare, they married only virgins. Women had nothing but virginity to trade for a bed and food for the rest of their days. Fathers protected the virginity of their daughters as men guard their bank accounts; with a gun slung at the hips and a gleam of warning in the eye. But now I was growing up and my father let all men know that I was not to be trifled with.

Yet I was a friend of all the men. I admired and envied them. Many of them lived about us for years, and

107

in the end I knew as little of their intimate lives as when they came. They perhaps knew as little of each other. Anything stirring the emotions was never touched upon. They alone knew if they had mothers or sisters. If they had ever loved was a secret locked in their own breasts. If the majesty of the mountains or the dark starry nights left their hearts lonely and their souls humble before Infinity, it was a secret shared by them with no man.

The lean, lanky cowboy who worked for my father was one of these. Jim was his name and, like the other men, the only one he gave. But a day came when he gave my father his last name,—Watson. That was becoming intimate and the other men exchanged glances. Big Buck, who always sat at the end of the table at dinner, glanced from Jim to me and his eyes, often filled with suspicious humor, gleamed with some hidden merriment.

"Please pass 'Mr. Watson' the spuds, Marie," Big Buck remarked, and the table stirred with smothered laughter. For women were scarce in the West even in those days and it wasn't an easy thing to get a wife. Jim Watson had a ranch, and a ranch needed a female on it. I was a female.

Jim next presented me with a gold chain that made my neck black if I wore it too long at a time; he rode with me to dances, and I slipped the chain in my pocket until I reached the dance-hall. Big Buck, nearly thrice my age and size, laughed to himself, and one day gave me a revolver—it might come in handy, he said. He wasn't the sort of man to give dinky little chains and things!

One Sunday afternoon I borrowed Big Buck's pony

to ride up a canyon for squirrels. Jim called to me; he would go along. Big Buck was leaning against the fence resting his head on his arms, and he laughed under his breath. Jim had decked himself out in a white shirt. About his waist was a broad, silver-inlay belt and his great gray hat was decorated with a hat-band quite as fine as his belt. He wasn't handsome, but he was elegant, and it wasn't every man that wore a white shirt. He rode in an easy, slouching gallop just as if it didn't matter much to him which way the horse went or what it did. We passed through a canyon filled with goldenrod, quaking aspen and pines. Jim swung one long leg over his saddle-horn and rolled a cigarette while he told me about his cattle ranch in New Mexico.

"Whatdye think of it?" he asked at last.

"It sounds great."

"Whatdye think about gettin' married to me . . . then it would be half yours; and you can have this horse I'm ridin' and I'll give you a .45 instead of that play-thing you're carryin' around your waist now."

Well! So this was a proposal! Of course it wasn't like a book, but it was a proposal. Marriage . . . . that was a strange, distant thing; but to be engaged . . . a gun . . . a pony of my own . . . . a ranch!

Jim was asking: "Well, whatdye say to gettin' married?"

"Sure!" I replied.

"Honest Injun?"

"Sure!"

He decided, as he said, to "clinch the bargain on the spot."

"This here pony's yours now an' as soon as I can git

into town I'll git you a regular .45, and gloves, and a quirt. Then you can give Buck back that gun he give you."

"Not by a long shot I don't! What's wrong with this gun?"

"It's give to you by another man, an' when you're goin' to marry me . . ."

"You just take a run and jump at yerself! There ain't nothin' wrong with this here gun!"

He saw he was treading dangerous ground. So he laughed.

"I was jist joshin'," he said, "jist to see what you'd do! When I give you a gun you'll have two . . . it ain't every girl that's got two guns."

I said no more than "thank you" and looked down the canyon at the dull green and yellow that was stealing over the land. Too bad it wasn't a little more exciting, this engagement, more like it is in books.

"Ain't you goin' to kiss me?" Jim's horse was close to mine and his voice was low.

I continued gazing down the canyon. To look at him would spoil it all. He seemed very old, and he had a mustache . . . heroes in books weren't like that. He was very close to me and was bending over from his saddle. His lips touched mine and I tried not to notice the smell of tobacco and perspiration . . . perhaps one had to expect such things with men . . . and it wouldn't be half bad to have someone love me really. The idea caught in my blood, as a hook catches on a snag in a stream.

We rode back home. It never occurred to me that marriage for myself meant what it did for other people

. . . ordinary marriage was something too awful even to think about. But when we reached home, Jim went into the kitchen and I was filled with foreboding . . . he might be blabbing . . . the long-legged fool . . . couldn't he keep his face shut for a few minutes!

I was laying the table for supper when my father and mother appeared in the door. "Marie!" my father said, and I felt I could sink into the earth with fear and shame. "Marie," he repeated, "Jim's told us he an' you is goin' to git married . . . You're too young to git married!"

"Yes, Marie," from my mother, standing sadly with her hands claspēd before her.

"I'm near fifteen, an' Annie was married at sixteen."

"That's too young . . . but Annie was more grown up than you are. Yer're not of age till yer eighteen. Then," his voice became hesitant and embarrassed as he continued, "an' there's things in marriage you don't know nothin' about . . . there is dooties . . ."

"Dooties!" I exclaimed angrily. "I won't have nothin' t'do with dooties!" I looked at them both standing there, and a wave of shame and revulsion swept through me. "Dooties be damned!" I flashed, "dooties be damned, dooties be damned! Some things make me sick, some things make me sick! . . . dooties be—!" I hated everything . . . the two of them standing there . . . that long-legged, lanky, mustached jackass fool of a Jim Watson! I turned and fled from the house.

I didn't wait tables that night. Instead, I found the little gold chain Jim had given me, and I called Beatrice and asked her to return it to him.

111

"Tell him I don't want no gun and no horse from him!" I instructed.

The next day Jim left town. The men stood along the fence and smiled as he rode away.

Once more we lived beyond the tracks in Trinidad. My mother was very bitter. One year wasted, she said. All the money we had made gone. Only one team left. Our home was a nest of daily quarrels. But she refused to leave the town again.

"An' take the children away from a decent school agin?" she asked my father accusingly when he demanded that she go with him to cook for his men in another mining camp.

One day angry voices came from the back yard. I hurried to the kitchen door. My mother was standing with her hands in a tub of wet washing, her face as ashen as it had been when Helen went out into the night. She seemed unable to even lift her hands out of the water. My father stood near her with a short, doubled-up rope in her hands. They heard me and looked up.

"Marie, he's goin' to hit me with that rope!" Her voice was lifeless.

It was as if she had turned to me for help against him. I saw him standing there, broad-shouldered, twice her size, the tobacco juice showing at the corners of his mouth. He was going to beat her . . . he had of late spoken admiringly of men who beat their wives. Still he had not carried out the hidden threat. Something held him back; he had had to curse and accuse much to whip himself up to this point. As I stood watching him I felt that I knew everything he had ever done or would do—he and I knew each other so well. And I hated him . . . hated him for his cowardice in attacking someone weaker than himself . . . hated him for attacking a woman because she was his wife and the law gave him the right . . . hated him so deeply, so elementally, that I wanted to kill . . . why hadn't I brought my revolver from my trunk!

My mother's eyes were still on me.

"Marie . . . if he hits me, I'll drop dead!"

"You! . . ." I spoke to my father.

It was too late to get the gun . . . but I didn't need a gun! I was suddenly by my mother's side, facing my father, keeping her behind me.

"Do that if you dare, you! If you dare!"

I felt my mother's frail body against me at the back. My father's eyes were glistening and hard and his breath reeked with liquor. I wondered if he would strike me, and my mind was panic-stricken . . . if he did I would . . . yes, I would get at his throat with my teeth! . . .

We stood staring into each other's eyes, enemies. Then the rope fell from his hand and curled snake-like about his feet. Turning without a word, he walked heavily through the alley-gate, his big shoulders round and stooped . . . so stooped . . . his shirt ragged and dirty . . . he stumbled along the railway track. That I should ever have been born!

How long it took him to vanish around the bend! When he had disappeared, I found my mother lying prostrate across her bed. I stood close beside her and

113

stared at the faded blue calcimined wall. To touch her would have been impossible. Perhaps when I was a baby I had touched her in affection. But that was years ago and I had forgotten. Now I could not. I turned in silence and went back to the yard. When she came out again, I had nearly finished the washing, and darkness had come.

"No, I'd just as leave finish it . . . there ain't much more," I protested when she came near.

A bond had at last been welded between us two . . . a bond of misery that was never broken.

There was a man . . . but that was not love. Bob was his name. He was twenty-one and a barber. I had slipped away from home one night and went to a public dance-hall; there I had met him and his elegance had made a deep impression upon me. When my mother learned of him she timidly protested. He was a soft-handed city man, she said—soft hands, sly tongue and slick ways. He was a high-class man, I argued, not like the men who were rough and worked with my father. It would be better for him if he were, she replied, for the men who worked with my father were honest, hard-working men who protect a girl and do not take advantage of her.

"Protect!" I screamed. "*I* don't need no protection from any man! I can take care of myself!"

Defiantly I went to meet Bob that evening, and my mother was too cowed to have her way. It was moon-light, and Bob waited for me across the bridge with a buggy.

It was beautiful to sweep along the gleaming road in

the silver moonlight, so warm and caressing. The team leapt forward like swiftly running water. Bob's arm crept around me and it felt very comforting. The horses sped onward . . . down a long slope, up another, down another . . . then slowly around a corner and under a dark bridge. They halted at Bob's jerk. Bob's other arm encircled me and I felt his hot lips search for mine, softly and slowly his hand crept downward over my breast . . . what a fool I had been to come with him!

"Stop it, you . . . please!"

"I won't hurt you. Come here!"

"Get away, I say!" I struggled to free myself from his arms. His lips . . . yes . . . liquid silver. Something weak was creeping through my blood and overpowering me. Panic seized me. His hands tightened on me, convulsively—and I remembered my father and mother, Helen, Annie . . . the married woman pleading, "Damn it, kid, you know I love you!" Memories! . . .

Blindly I tore at him. His hands were soft . . . mine were not. A primitive fear was in me and I struck with all my might . . . there was hot flesh and something warm and sickening ran between my teeth.

"God damn you! You ——— !" I felt his hand against my breast, and there was a wrench when I caught at the wheel in falling.

I lay on the soft earth, dizzy with terror. Bob climbed out and stood beside me on the road. One side of his mouth was dark with blood. We faced each other like two animals in the night.

"Get in! I'll leave you at the bridge and no further!" he said.

"I'll walk home!"

"What'll people say if they see you!"

"That's none of your business! I'll walk home!"

"Then walk, damn you! An' I never want to see yer ugly face again!"

Slowly I started down the dreary gray road toward the town. The moonlight was cold and hard now, like ice on a windy lake in winter. Loneliness mingled with my misery and tears.

Never had I known such a lonely place. Our tiny frame house crouched, as if about to spring, against the side of a canyon covered with pines and aspens, and the delicately purple Colorado columbine. Up the canyon to the west lay gaping, gas-reeking mines, abandoned after an explosion that had killed nearly a hundred men and burned the mines out. Beyond these stretched a primeval wilderness of wooded hills and mountains. At night wild animals cried there. Rattlesnakes, as big as a man's arm, coiled around jagged stones or lay stretched on sunny slopes.

When you rode down the canyon you passed the empty houses of the former town. The mouth of the canyon opened upon a broad level plain,—"the flats" we called it—golden in autumn, with a short, tough prairie grass. Far to the east slept a low range of hills, and beyond them still the tops of others. To the northwest the plain crept along the earth until it reached the foothills guarding a range of the Rocky Mountains, gleaming white in summer and winter with everlasting snow. "*Sangre de Cristo*"—the Blood of Christ—they

were called, perhaps because the snow glowed softly like warm blood long after the setting sun had cast all the canyons and plains in darkness.

When the moon shone on the still, white flats, we could hear from the depths of our dark canyon the yip-yipping of packs of coyotes that had left their hiding places and met on the plains. There seemed to be thousands of them. When the air was filled with their high sharp yapping, our dog crept far back under the house and lay shivering.

If you rode across the flat to the southeast you passed a prairie dog village. On the tops of their thousands of little mounds the small fat animals sat on their haunches and gazed upon a sunny world. Beyond the village lay soft rolling hills, and beyond these the world: first, an adobe Catholic church attended once a month by Mexicans, when the priest—a harmless old Sin-hound, my father called him—made his rounds to minister to souls. Further on stood the saloon—the sign that Rockefeller civilization lay near. It was my father's halting station when he went down the canyon. Beyond the saloon stood the schoolhouse on the borders of Tercio, a Colorado Fuel & Iron Company mining camp.

Over Tercio brooded the same atmosphere as in Delagua,—smoldering discontent and hatred. Here were the same complaints about the weigh boss, the hours, wages, insufficient props and other precautions against falls, the high prices and dishonesty of the Company store, the payment of script instead of American money. The miners dragged themselves to the holes in the mountain-side each morning, and, black with coal smut, dragged themselves home at night. Their children—boys of ten onward—worked around the mines until they were strong enough to become miners themselves. To these miners, as to us, existence meant only working, sleeping, eating what or when you could, and breeding. For amusement there was the saloon for the men; for the women, nothing. A book was a curiosity; we had one in our family, a "Speaker" it was called; a newspaper was a rarity; to read was a recreation of the rich. A few children of the miners actually finished the public school; the majority did not. The children of the higher Company officials went away to high school and later to college.

When the next strike spread through the Company camps, none of us dared go into Tercio. Rumors ran like a forest fire. The sheriff was ruler of the little camp; he was an American who carried a Colt .45 on his hip and let every miner know that he was paid for doing his "dootie," and was going to do it.

"For less than a nickel he would fill a damned furriner full of lead," he said. Or he was ready to "put the fear of Christ" in one of them.

Hatred and hunger walked hand in hand through all the camps. There was no food except in the Company store and the store could not give credit. The school was closed, the streets deserted. The State militia was again encamped in Trinidad and in all the larger mining camps along the canyons. Strike-breakers were herded in, and the soldiers guarded them as they went to and from the mines.

Then after weeks of bitter struggle and hunger, the

strike came to an end. Nagging women and crying children helped send the men back to the mines, defeated.

My mother listened to all the news from the camp during the strike. She said little, especially when my father or the men who worked for him were about. I remember her instinctive and unhesitating sympathy for the miners. She hated rich or powerful people or institutions. Through the years she had been transformed from a poor farming woman into an unskilled proletarian. But my father was less clear. As a native American himself, with hopes of becoming an employer, he tried to identify himself with the sheriff and the officials of the camp against the strikers, who were foreigners. Still he was unclear; he had men working for him and yet he was an ignorant working man himself, and however hard he worked he seemed to remain miserably poor. He was too unknowing to understand how or why it all happened. But he, like my mother, had certainly come to know that those who work the most do not make the most money. It was the fault of the rich, it seemed, but just how he did not know. He drowned his unclearness and disappointment in drink; or let poker absorb his resentment.

The men who worked for my father were no clearer. They did not seem to care much one way or the other, because they were not married and did not have a brood of children depending upon them. Still they were not happy, and they also drank much. During strikes, their sympathies seemed whole-heartedly with the miners, but as ex-cowboys they were individualists and did not understand the struggle. In all the arguments and debates that took place outside our kitchen door in the evenings, I cannot recall one idea that gave me knowledge of what the strikes were about. The fault seemed to lie with some distant group of men,—the Company officials who came on inspection tours once a year or so. During these tours the men always wondered if anyone of the big bosses would be shot—but they never were. Resentful everybody was, but we bowed our heads and waited for the strikes to pass, and in the end we obeyed those who paid us wages and thereby gave us the right to live. We said "Yes, sir!" and "Thank you, sir," for we knew that this was necessary.

Too many years have flown since those days, too many storms have swept over my own personal life, for me to recall fully the depths of non-knowing that was ours. Often in later years I heard men and women say that "people get what they deserve," and always my mind has swept back to our canyon-like existence. "Deserve" is the word which the possessors use as a weapon against those they dispossess. The darkness of not-knowing—who can realize what that means unless he has lived through it! Those who speak of "deserving people" are the most ignorant of all. Because the world of knowledge was far removed from us, we in our canyon reacted instead of thinking.

There was my mother, with silence settling more and more about her. Since my father had attempted to beat her, and then had forced her to take her children from school again and come to this canyon, she was more crushed than ever. Her existence was isolated, for we were the only English-speaking people for miles about. She never spoke of her unhappiness to her children; and my father was not her friend. He worked for the Company, and she and I cooked and washed the clothing for the ten men who worked for him. Our food was of the coarsest. A new pair of shoes was an event. Sometimes packages of clothing came from Helen, and my mother and I remade them. For herself she made nothing. She said:

"I don't need nothin'. I don't go nowhere and I don't see nobody."

When these occasional packages came, my father attempted to break her silence by reminding her of the life her sister led. She would wince, as if struck across the face, but then turn her back, and without a word, continue cooking.

"By God, this is a nice to-do!" he would curse, and fling out of the house.

There were Sundays when the Mexicans for miles around would gather on the rolling hills surrounding the flats at the foot of the canyon, while competing teams, stripped to their underwear, played "shinney." We all sat with them on the hills that formed a vast amphitheater and watched.

There were also evenings when the weather was fine and the men would remain outside our kitchen door after supper, talking and singing, and when I hurried with the dishes to join them. One of the men would sing a song and others would follow: songs of the West that are long since dead; songs with dozens of verses, all sung in the same tune, low and melancholy, unrolling stories of adventure, of the joys and sorrows of cattle men, of dying cowboys, of disaster, range songs and songs of love.

Sometimes one of the men would take out a "French harp" and begin to play. Another would get up and dance. Once it was a man, young and slender, with whom I was in love—but so secretly that no one but myself knew it. His blue shirt was open at the throat. He bent over and danced, swaying his body and arms; he stood in one spot on the hard earth and danced until the heels of his boots sounded like pistol shots on the hard, packed earth. He stood tall and straight, his hands on his hips, his face turned upwards to the moon, and the moonlight ran in little shining rivulets up and down the legs of his black boots.

At last the music ceased. There was silence, broken only by the wind rustling gently through the tree tops. The dancer wiped his forehead with a big red handkerchief. He drew his belt in another notch. Big Buck, his boots in the moonlight, his head lost in the shadow of the house, began to tell of another dancer he had seen down in the Texas Panhandle . . . or was it on the Rio Grande? He used to dance around the range fires . . . that must 'a' been fifteen years ago . . . no, well-nigh twenty, come to think of it . . .

Part 4

Had it not been for the wanderlust in my blood—my father's gift to me—and had I not inherited his refusal to accept my lot as ordained by a God, I might have remained in the mining towns all my life, married some working man, borne him a dozen children to wander the face of the earth, and died in my early thirties. Such was the fate of all women about me. But settled things were enemies to me and soon lost their newness and color. The unknown called.

Within a year after we moved to Tercio, I found myself a school teacher—I, who had not finished the grammar school, who could not add one figure to another without mistakes, who could not remember one rule in grammar. And I was teaching children of six and boys of my own age: far out in New Mexico, on top of one of the purple-green-red mesas that suddenly rear themselves from the great plains and plateaus, a broad, flat mesa above the timber-line, surrounded by perpendicular rim-rocks that caught the lightning in the fierce storms sweeping over the mountain ranges.

123

There, out near the edge of the rim-rock, I lived in isolation in a two-room school house, the front room serving as my class-room, the back room as my living-room where I slept, cooked my food and corrected my school papers. It was May when I arrived, but at night the snow still flew before the wind and beat the rope hanging from the school bell against the side of the house: a dull, ghostly sound mingling with the hoarse wailing of the wind and the creaking of the bell above.

From the broad sweeping mesa, little boys and girls came to school; from the deep canyons below, Mexicans and half-breed Indians came; from the plains that stretched as far as eye could reach to the south, a few boys and girls from the ranches came riding on cow-ponies. I was ignorant, yes, but I was learned compared with those about me. And I possessed a native cunning. When a smaller child could not do a problem in arithmetic, and I saw that I also could not do it, I called upon one of the older boys to demonstrate his knowledge before the classroom. He did it proudly, and all of us learned something.

I was "teacher," and it was considered an honor to have me in a ranch house. Children brought me food as presents, a horse was always at my disposal, and I rode through a rough but kindly land—and I rode safely, as all women rode safely, for it was a land not only where strong men lived, but it was a land where women were strong also; or, if not, where the gun slung at their sides could answer their needs. But neither physical force nor guns were necessary. I recall now the years of my girlhood and youth amongst the men of the far West—

unlettered, rough working-men who had tasted the worst of life: and with but one exception—that of a barber in a small town—I had never suffered insult and not one man had tried to lay a hand on me in violence. Perhaps I was too young or too ignorant. I had many suitors for marriage, for there were few women in that land. But I was wiser than most girls about me. My intellect, rough and unshod as it was, was wiser than my emotions. All girls married, and I did not know how I would escape, but escape I determined to. I remember that almost without words, my mother supported me in this.

There in New Mexico I rode with men far and wide, singly and in groups, at midday, or to and from dances at night. I danced with them in ranch houses down in the dark canyons or on the plains. They were honorable men, and I was safer with them than are girls within convent walls—far safer. Of sex I thought not at all, for not only was I little more than a child, but I was too busy. There were so many other things to think about; and then, I had no intention of marrying.

I now recall with joy those hearty, rough, hairy-chested, unshaven men. I recall the rougher, unhappy men in the mining camps, and their silent, unhappy wives. It is with a feeling of sadness and of affection that I think of them now. But there were years when, in search of what I thought were better, nobler things, I denied these, my people, and my family. I forgot the songs they sung—and most of those songs are now dead; I erased their dialect from my tongue; I was ashamed of them and their ways of life. But now—yes, I love them;

they are a part of my blood; they, with all their virtues and their faults, played a great part in forming my way of looking at life.

Back in Tercio I had, by the purest chance, met the camp school teacher, a woman from a normal school. At first I was resentful and suspicious of her because she was an educated woman. At last we became friends. We borrowed horses from the camp and rode and hunted together in the hills. She had urged me to study with her, take the county teachers' examination, and become a teacher. Before the year was finished she had loaned me one of her blouses and skirts, and I rode across the Divide to a New Mexico town where the teachers' examination was held.

"Say you are eighteen," she warned. "Lie—it won't hurt anybody."

"I'm not afraid of lyin'," I replied.

"Lie!" Big Buck later exclaimed when I told him of it. "Why, you can lie quicker'n a jackrabbit can jump!"

In fear and trembling I sat among older, better-educated women and took the examination. Two days passed and the County Superintendent of Schools sent for me. He was a tall, lean, black-eyed Mexican, intelligent and kindly.

"You have low grades in arithmetic, and grammar, and school law, and a few more things," he announced, "but if you can speak a little Mexican, here is a school. It is lonely. It is so cold that school is held only in the summer. It is rough and far from town. You will have to cook your own food and wash your own clothes. The life is rough . . . cattle men, you know!"

I didn't understand, but wisdom taught me to listen and look intelligent; it was news to me that there were people who did not cook their own food; and I thought that everybody except rich people washed their own clothing. Then "rough people" . . . what could he mean, I wondered . . . he must mean people who hang around saloons . . . yet that was not possible, for he said it was a lonely place. I would just wait and see; it never occurred to me that I myself belonged to just such rough people as he referred to.

So it was that I became a teacher. I had no fear of loneliness or the cold or wild animals . . . and as for roughness . . . well, I waited to see what it would be like. I never saw any of it. Everybody acted just like I did. Even when, up there on the mesa, I was stunned by lightning that struck the rim-rock a short distance from my house, and I was left lying stretched unconscious across my doorway for hours, it really never occurred to me to be either afraid or give up the school. I merely dragged myself into my room, crept to bed, and waited to get better. The school was the best thing I had ever known. I was making forty dollars a month and sending part of it to my mother. And she, delicate and gentle, proudly made shirts and skirts and sent them to her school-teacher daughter! She had always known I would become "edjicated." Now, when she met the wife of the Superintendent of the camp at Tercio, she did not try to hide her big-veined hands and pass by without being seen; she raised her head proudly and said:

"Howdye do, Mis' Richards . . . it's a nice day t'day, ain't it?"

Up there on the mesa I found a cheap, monthly, housewife's magazine that contained continued love stories, patterns for dresses, recipes for cooking, beauty hints, and odds and ends of a thousand kinds. There was also a list of names and addresses of men and women who wished to exchange picture post cards. From this list I chose the name of a man—the most beautiful name there—a Robert Hampton, whose address was Columbus, Ohio. That was a city far back East, and I had great ideas of the beauty and learning and culture of cities. I sent him a post card. He replied, and as the summer wore on one card gave way to two, then to four in an envelope. He wrote that he was finishing high school—a learned man, in my eyes! He began sending me his old books to read—history, literature, botany—and I studied them, even the things that were dry and uninteresting. Then I sent them on to my mother; for I wanted her to study also. When the school closed and I went home in the autumn, I found my mother sitting by the kitchen window patiently studying one of the books. It had taken her weeks and she was not yet half finished. It was so very new and difficult for her, yet she, as I, felt that it was necessary to know these things.

That was a great home-coming for me ... I, the triumphant, conquering daughter of sixteen! I was now one of the chief supports of our family. My father was working on a far-away ranch. He came to Tercio, where my mother now lived, while I was there. I still remember how he came. My mother was sitting by the window, her face enthusiastic as I told of my teaching and of the new school I was to have during the winter. I told her of Robert Hampton, who had sent me a picture of himself—how he was handsome and learned like the men in books. She replied nothing; perhaps she thought it best that I fell in love with a distant hero rather than a near-by reality. As we talked, her eyes wandered to the hillside beyond and I saw her face become suddenly miserable. I noticed how gray her hair had become, although she was but in her late thirties. My eyes followed her, and there from beyond the Company store came my father, walking heavily, his big shoulders stooped, his head down, his hands moving as if talking to some imaginary person.

I went almost immediately to my other school. It lay in a canyon far back of Primero, another of the C. F. & I. Company camps. There, for four months, I heard no English except that spoken in my school; even my students talked to me in Mexican. At night I went to my room in a Mexican adobe house. The man of the house was a Mexican on the school board and he felt it his right, as a man and as an official, to talk at length with the most intellectual woman in the countryside. And that woman was I! His wife was a broad, good-natured Mexican with no ambitions and no ideas. He always ate his supper with me and she waited table, moving back and forth from the kitchen to the room which was the dining-room, the living-room, and my bedroom, all in one. Later, she and her child ate their supper in the kitchen. Her husband spoke a remarkable jargon that was half Mexican and half English, although he led her to believe that he spoke perfect and fluent

English. His contempt for her was great and he was always trying to let me see how humiliating it was for a man of his position and intelligence to be married to such a woman. I dared show no sympathy with the woman . . . such would have been a deadly insult to the man and perhaps I would have lost my position.

. I wearied of his talk. But he thought a woman should always listen to a man and improve her intellect . . . a woman always knew less than a man; it mattered not who or what she was. I longed for the comfort of silence in which I could read the new book and the letter that had come from Robert Hampton in the East. Those letters were the most important things in my life; they were written in a handwriting that was perfect. While I was in my school the Mexican read them, without my permission, then questioned me about their contents. He understood little, but he knew the handwriting was incomparable and he respected me more for having learned friends. At night I sat for hours with them propped before me, trying to learn to write like that, and to this day my handwriting bears a similarity to them. I knew that if I could ever learn to write so beautifully my education would be complete.

My distant correspondent became the ideal who guided my life. He must have felt like a god, he, sitting back there reading the humble, groping, scrawling letters from a lonely canyon in the Rocky Mountains. Over my little table stood his picture and on the table his old books; if my emotions ever wandered to some dark, handsome Mexican-Indian boy in the neighborhood—as they often did, for I was a wanderer in all things—I fought them, and felt ashamed of myself at night when I went home. But it was not easy. There was an Indian boy just my age in school; he watched me with worshipful eyes, not daring to approach so learned a person as I. His homage to me was the discipline he exercised over all the other pupils—a blink of an eyelash against me from one of them and he escorted them to the edge of the forest at recess time!

One day as I was standing before my classroom and trying to induce my school to talk to me in English—my chief occupation—the door opened and my Mexican host appeared. A telephone call had come from beyond the hills, from Tercio; my mother was sick and I must go home. I stood staring at him, as if he were a messenger of death. He repeated the message. I turned without a word, took my hat and coat hanging in the corner and left the school building. It never occurred to me to dismiss the school. I only knew that my mother was dying . . . had I not dreamed it the night before?

The man caught up with me at his house. He would drive me over the hills tomorrow, he said, for now his team was up in the timber hauling props for the mines. Only one train a day came up the canyons from Trinidad and stopped at all the coal camps. It would reach Primero at two in the afternoon and Tercio in another hour. It was now eleven. I said I would walk to Primero. No, he protested, the snow was deep in the canyons and it was freezing cold. . . . It was dangerous. I hardly heard him. I went into my room, strapped my gun tightly about my waist beneath my coat, and started. He and his wife stood in the door watching in amazement as I started up the canyon road and turned to take the short-cut across the Divide. The snow was heavy, but a herd of sheep had been driven that way and had beaten it down. I climbed the slippery slope, pulling myself up here and there with the tough scrub oak that fastened itself in the frozen ground. If I could only reach the top of the Divide, the rest would be easy, for there I would reach the road. The cold, the possibility of meeting wild animals, the danger of slipping and falling and lying with a broken leg—nothing came to my mind except the top of the hills. Thinking nothing, feeling nothing, seeing nothing, I climbed.

At last I reached it. It had been swept clear of snow by a fierce wind, and was rutty and frozen. I hid my head in my coat collar for a second to warm my lungs. Then I began a slow, easy, steady trot that makes it possible to cover long distances and still not be too exhausted. My mind watched my body as if the two were separate units. My body was tough and strong—as tough as the mountain oak. My mind knew that when the body was so exhausted that it seemed unable to go further, a new energy would flow through it—the "second wind" would come. My mind was I, down that long hard road with the wind lashing my back—my body was a foreign thing. I—my mind—as clear as the winter air, was concentrated on one point—to reach the mining camp by two o'clock; my body was a foreign thing that must be coaxed and humored into doing it. The chief thing, I assured myself over and over again, was to keep the legs steady until the second wind came. There was a time when my legs trembled, weak and faltering. I turned a bend and there, far beyond and below, I saw the smoke of Primero. I lifted my chin—a new warm energy was coursing through my blood, and down the slope, my mouth buried in the neck of my coat to warm the air entering my lungs, my hands free to catch myself in case I should fall, I swung along, running in that slow, steady trot.

I reached the outskirts of Primero, turned to run past the Company store and take the road, black with coal dust, leading to the station. But I was not the only one running—other people, with horror-stricken faces, were rushing through the streets, and I saw that the windows in the Company store were shattered into bits . . . across the street the windows of other houses were also broken. A woman with a plaid shawl over her head stumbled by, weeping in wild terror and crying out in some foreign tongue.

Without faltering in my trot, I turned the corner of the store to pass the mouth of a mine on the hillside that lay before the station. The road was filled with people. Two working men met and ran toward the mine, one shouting at the other:

"They're shuttin' the air-shafts, the God damned . . ."

The mine was belching black smoke, like some primeval Fafnir. Men were drawing ropes around the base of the slag dump and were trying to beat back the struggling women, who fought with the savageness of wild beasts. Their men were penned in the mines, I heard . . . the air-shafts were being closed to save the coal . . . but the fumes would smother the men to death. Such was the burden of their cries. Coal was dear . . . life was cheap.

I ran on. I stumbled onto the station platform and up

133

the steps of the train without even thinking of a ticket. I threw myself face downward on a seat. My lungs were tight and cold. Beyond . . . miles beyond the other side of the humming . . . humming . . . came the scream of a woman.

For three days and nights I watched by her bedside. A movement would awaken me as I dozed. Her blue-black eyes were tender as they followed me back and forth. The doctor who made his weekly rounds from mining town to mining town was out of patience . . . there seemed nothing wrong with her as he could see. Yes—pains in the stomach, of course . . . that was from bad food and from too little . . . what else could you expect, he said, if she insisted on living on potatoes and flour-and-water gravy! She must have better food . . . she was under-nourished. I wondered what "under-nourished" could mean. No, he answered my question, even if she wanted it, she could have no more bicarbonate of soda to ease the pain.

During the first two days she talked with me. Annie had died two weeks before . . . that she had written me. She had gone to her, away down on the desolate plain of western Oklahoma where Annie and Sam worked like animals on their homestead. Annie had left the baby . . . a tiny thing, lying in the next room. I warmed milk and fed it, and it watched me with wistful blue eyes; strange it was that its coming should have caused my sister's death.

My mother was very happy as I sat by her. But I think she knew that death was near, for she said strange things to me—things touching the emotions that she would never have dared say otherwise, for affection between parents and children was never shown among my people. She called me "my daughter"—a thing she had never said before in her life.

"I don't know how I could of lived till now if it hadn't been fer you," she said once, as if the words were wrung from her.

Once in the middle of the night she woke me to say: "Promise me you'll go on an' git a better edjication." Her hand closed upon mine, steady and strong, as if asking for a pledge. A wave of unfamiliar emotion swept over me. I clasped her hand.

When the doctor came the next day I said, "Please give her somethin'...she's goin' to die." He was disgusted...he had a lot to do and was sick of my telephoning down for him to come all the way up there when there was nothing wrong with my mother except that she needed decent food for a while, he said.

I watched him go. Then, standing by my mother's bedside, I realized that we faced death alone...and that I was helpless. She pleaded for the forbidden bicarbonate of soda. I would not give it. But she pleaded again and again and the look in her eyes appalled me. Then, in my ignorance, I gave it. But when I did it, I turned and ran up the alley to the school building, burst into the schoolroom and, without thinking, called aloud to Beatrice, George and Dan.

When we reached her bedside, my father, who had come home that morning, was there. He had fallen on his knees and had buried his face in the covers. My mother's eyes were large and glistening, and she turned them on me in an appeal beyond all speech. I bent over the bed and, for the first time in my life, took her in my arms and held her close to my trembling body. "Marie!" My name was the last word she ever uttered.

The lids closed down over the glistening eyes. The body grew limp. I tore back the covering and listened to her breast, so flat, so thin, so poor. The heart throbbed twice, stopped . . . throbbed once more. I listened an eternity . . . intensely yearning . . . but no sound came. My father pulled me to my feet. With difficulty I could stand on my feet. But there were no tears in me. I only knew that I stood by the body of the woman who had given me life. I understood nothing except that this thing I could not understand. In my mind a brilliant light ran in circles, then contracted until it was a tiny black spot, then became lost in nothingness, and nothingness throbbed in beats, like the waves of a sea against a cliff.

Helen came. She and my father touched hands in the room where my mother's body lay in a white pine-board coffin. Her hair was still a burnished bronze with flashes of dull gold. Her cheeks and lips were painted. She wore a fur coat of great beauty. Her eyes traveled about the room—to the cold, bare floor, the rickety old bureau in the corner, the little rusty stove, the cheap white curtain at the window. Then she turned back the sheet from my mother's body and gazed at the worn, wrinkled face, wistful in death as in life; at the rough, big-veined hands almost black from work, clasped across the thin breast;

at the hair, almost gray, although my mother was still young. Turning away to hide her face from us, she stepped into the sleeping room at the side, removed her cloak and stood watching the tiny bit of kicking baby on the bed—the baby that belonged to Sam, the first and perhaps the only love in her life.

We were to take my mother's body to Oklahoma to bury it beside Annie. We had waited only for Helen's coming. In the afternoon the pine coffin was put into the baggage car of the train, and we began our journey.

We left the train at a station on the plains of western Oklahoma where Sam met us in a big rough wagon. When he caught sight of Helen he walked away, but turned back to grasp her hand and look at his baby lying in her arms.

It was January and the earth was hard and cold, swept almost clean by a bitter wind that rushed across the plains. A lonely clump of trees stood here and there, but apart from these the plains stretched endlessly, freezing and bare, the road a rutty, winding trail across the waste. After a long time we reached a gaunt, frame house where Sam and Annie had lived, and where Sam now lived alone. The coffin was placed in the bare front room.

By the next morning crude board benches and a few chairs stood in rows before the coffin. A number of men and women had gathered from farmhouses, together with the ignorant minister who was to preach the sermon. This minister now stood on the other side of my mother's coffin and talked to us. He was illiterate, crude and vulgar, even more than we. He said things that had nothing to do with my mother's body lying there, or with the poverty and unhappiness that had killed her. He looked squarely at Helen, sitting there in her fur coat . . . he looked at my father sitting with his head bent, chewing a cud of tobacco, his shoulders round and stooped. He looked accusingly at us all, one by one, and spoke to us without calling our individual names. We were not Christians, he said,—and dared touch the coffin of my mother! He warned us that we were going the way of sin . . . some of us the way of scarlet sin . . . his eyes swooped upon Helen as a vulture swoops upon its prey; God had punished us by taking my mother from us, but He would punish us still more!

My father arose and went up to the preacher and knelt down, the imprint of a bottle in his hip pocket showing through his coat as he bent. The preacher reached down and laid his hand piously on his head—one soul saved! He turned to Helen and his lips parted for speech. But with a gasp of disgust and anger, Helen arose and walked out of the room, deliberately and with quiet dignity. I followed her, and the mourners and the preacher stared in scandalized silence.

The funeral ceremony came to an end, lamely and unimpressively, and amidst a shocked silence Helen and I joined the small group to proceed to the cemetery. We drove a long distance and entered a graveyard by a fence made of one single barbed wire stretched on crazy posts leaning in every direction. Perhaps twelve mounds were in the lot, all with one straight piece of board at the head and one smaller one at the foot. On these had once been written the names of the dead, but the wind and rain and snow had long since eradicated them. The name of my sister was still readable, and near her grave lay the mound of fresh earth that had been thrown up for the grave of my mother. We stood among the graves and listened once more to the preacher calling down the blessing of God upon my mother and a warning upon those who failed to heed him.

Then we were told to look at my mother's face for the last time. I did not weep. Helen did not weep . . . her face was filled with a hard white misery as she gazed down on the sister she had so dearly loved . . . for "greater love hath no woman than she who will sell her body for the sister she loves."

For months I followed the road that I had marked out for myself. With resolve I determined to care for my brothers and sister and my dead sister's baby. So I gave up my school and came back to Tercio, to cooking, washing, ironing and sewing. My father returned home. I tried to make things homelike—it seemed to me that if my mother had perhaps done that, my father would not have drunk himself into stupidity all the time. I bought a carpet and new window curtains, a round brown table, a few pictures for the wall—pictures of children with angel's wings—and I bought white spreads for the beds.

But the daily housework and worry of our little house bore heavily upon me and I thought ceaselessly of my mother. I was succeeding no better with my father than she had. To think of years and years of living like this, as she had done! My conflicts with him became frequent and my desire to go away grew stronger and tormented me. The transient atmosphere that had always been a part of our life had become a part of me, and I was restless, unhappy, resentful.

One day my father returned home drunk. Dan had done something to displease him, and the boy watched him in terror, for my father had a long horsewhip in his hand. He reached for Dan, who rushed behind me and threw his arms about my waist, keeping me between him and my father. I held the little hands tightly about me . . . my father cursed and ordered him into the center of the room where he would "teach him a lesson." Then my father lunged toward him, but I kept my body between them. He made a dive around me, but with all my might I pushed him back. Not a word was spoken between us . . . I felt him grasp my shoulder to throw me out of the way, and without thinking I hurled myself upon him, striking with my clenched fists, blow upon blow.

Then he was standing motionless. He and I stood looking at each other. He turned and picked up the whip from the floor. I watched like an animal, ready to spring, for he should never use it! He looked at the whip, then turned and slowly passed out of the door, the whip dragging along the floor behind him.

Part 5

Helen and I sat in my room in Denver. Sam's baby lay asleep against her bosom. It seemed to have become tangled in the folds of her silk dress, as a bee might, had it fallen there; one chubby hand had caught in the opening at the neck and a foot had disappeared altogether. Helen had been talking to it as one might talk to a grownup person, and had laughed herself into tears at its solemnity. I watched her, thinking of Sam who had followed her and Tony to Denver, but had failed to induce her to leave this man and marry him because—as she said—when a woman marries a man and can no longer make her own living, he begins reminding her of her past.

I was young, but Helen needed someone close to her, and she was glad I had come. I learned that she had tried to make a living for herself and Tony, but that it had not been sufficient. "Then I was always trying to send your mother things, and you kids needed clothes," she said—as if that must be taken for granted. At last when she lay ill in a hospital, Tony disappeared with a healthier girl.

141

The baby that now lay against her bosom seemed almost like the fulfillment of a desire that had long been dead. She would keep it with her, and she exulted when she thought of it. The Helens of the world are said to be hard and without desire for children. The Helen who was my aunt was not. I was proud of Helen. To me her profession seemed as honorable as that of any married woman—she made her living in the same way as they made theirs, except that she made a better living and had more rights over her body and soul. No man dared mistreat her, although Tony had once beaten her just as if she were his wife. If any man told her to "give back the clothes he bought her," she could order him out of her house—no wife could do that; if any man struck her, she could call the police—no wife could do that. She was pledged to obey no man. By such things I judged decency and self-respect, and such a life seemed preferable to marriage. But for me—I wanted neither that life, nor marriage.

We talked for hours. She could not understand why I had just picked up the baby and, after but a few words with my father, left home. Neither could I understand it. She listened in questioning silence to the clumsy explanations that were no explanations. I would go back some time, I interposed, feeling awkward and superficial, for down deep was the conviction that I would never go back. Impatience, restlessness and resentment welled up in me and hardened my manner and my speech. Love, tenderness and duty belonged to women and to weaklings in general; I would have none of them!

142

"But Beatrice and the boys?" she asked.

Beatrice, I explained, was soon to have gone to a family on a ranch in New Mexico, and now she could go sooner—was already there. As for George and Dan, they were being taken by my father to western Oklahoma where they would grow to manhood—they call it that in books—on the plains. We both sat without speaking after that, for we thought of the two graves there. Perhaps she was thinking of Sam in that gaunt house. My father would go there, too, my voice continued, and would live with Sam—as if that made it any better.

For a long time we watched the flat face of the building opposite my window. Life was strange. I couldn't understand why some things were and others were not. How did it happen that we had always been poor, for instance. I resented everything, hating myself most of all for having been born a woman, and Helen for her silence that made me feel guilty; hated my brothers and sister because they existed and loaded me with a responsibility I refused to carry; hated my father and mother for bringing me into a world when I didn't ask to come. Why couldn't they have left me alone there in nothingness!

I now began a process of reasoning that I kept up for years—I drew a dark curtain before my conscious memory and began to forget that I had a family at all. What were they all to me, I argued, any more than any other people? But . . . there were George's eyes following me, eyes filled with trust . . . what would he do without me . . . his frail hands had always rested in mine.

"What are you going to do?" Helen had asked her question for the second time.

"I want to study."

"To study! Study what?"

"I don't know . . . just study."

To us both "study" meant some vague luxury—that we did not know; something connected with reading and doing nothing. Only rich girls or girls who were frail and could do nothing else would indulge in such a luxury; others always "got their ears boxed" for wasting their time. I had known an educated man once, but he had tuberculosis. Robert Hampton was also educated, but perhaps he was rich or sick or something.

"You ought to study something to make a good living," Helen debated. "I've got enough money to help you for a time—but not for long."

We discussed the subject and decided I should study to become a stenographer. So the very next day I went to a small town south of Denver to learn my profession. Helen would not permit me to remain in the city.

Those months of study were among the most miserable I have ever endured. The girls in the school often smiled and said things to each other as I passed. I was awkward and crude. I spoke badly—perhaps they smiled at that. Or perhaps it was my clothing . . . I felt silly in the dainty blouses Helen had given me, and had discarded them for my old comfortable shirts and ties.

To return to Helen in Denver was like going from a dark land into a land of sunshine, but I found her very unhappy. Sam had come the week before and had taken his baby from her. Gradually I pieced together the

144

miserable story, for she did not like to talk of Sam. She had told him she would like to keep the baby, that she would send it away to some school as soon as it was old enough. He had replied, saying harsh things about her way of life,—then, in the midst of it all, had turned suddenly, thrown his arm up against the wall and buried his face in it. Once more he had asked her to marry him, and once more she had refused. But her arms were empty since he had taken the child and gone and sometimes she walked the floor and cried. Her voice was dull when she said she could not see how she was going to stand the loneliness.

She and I were often together in those days, although I lived in a little room apart from her. I heard her telephone conversations, and a man now and then joined us for lunch. She introduced me to one, an elderly man with gray hair who stuttered when he talked; he was the editor of a magazine and agreed to employ me in his office. I now started to work. As I typed I dreamed—beyond the horizon of reality as usual—of the money I could save, of sending clothing to my brothers and to Beatrice. I dreamed of this nice old editor who would treat me as a daughter and help me get an education. One day when he asked me to stay late and do some extra work, I was very flattered, for he had chosen me instead of one of the expert typists.

"S-s-s-sit down!" he said, when I offered him my finished work across his desk. He pointed to a couch against the wall. There was something subtly wrong somewhere, but I was working for him and he was educated and old. Then, without explaining, he brought a book of photographs and sat by my side. I looked at the pictures; they began to be blurred . . . perhaps I had an evil mind . . . he was a nice old man and so educated. Still everything became mixed up when he put his arm around me—it crept around like a snake—the pictures, the arm, the typewriting all became confused.

My arms stiffened . . . they were still strong and I was not yet too ladylike and too civilized to use them. And he was a soft man, for all his education and his magazine! I reached the door, half blind from fright and shame, then turned to look. He was lying half sprawled across the couch. His high white collar was torn away in front . . . Yes, that dark blotch on the side of his neck . . . I must have bitten him. It was strange that a man's dignity should disappear with his collar and that when one's teeth sink into flesh, the flesh feels like rubber . . .

The brown editor was different. He not only gave me things to type, but he was very jolly, and reminded me of Big Buck. Twice he took my photograph, standing me against an Indian rug hanging in the corner of his office.

"Look serious!" he commanded. "Think of God! Lord . . . but that's no way to look! Pretend you're going to write a story for my magazine. Now, then again . . . bring those braids of hair around on your shoulders . . . that's good . . . look at me . . . dreamy-like . . . dre-e-emmy-like . . . as if I were your best beau . . . now, one, two, *three!*"

He was a jolly man and he was a friend of Helen's

also. After Helen had heard what had happened with the other man she talked with the brown editor. He had stood with his hands in his pockets and looked me over carefully. His smile had seemed very warm and honest.

"You just give me a try," I pleaded. "I can't type quick, but I'll learn."

"Quick*ly*," he corrected.

"Quick*ly*," I repeated.

His eyes were brown and always held the threat of a laugh in them, especially when I was in deadly earnest or told him what I intended to do before I had finished with life. It would have been better if he had laughed outright and given me a chance. But he didn't. The suits he wore were always brown, his ties and shoes were brown, and his hair was brown.

"When I look at you I always think of fuzz," I told him one day.

"You look at your typewriter instead of at me," he replied.

After a few weeks we became real friends. He took me to lunch and we drove in his automobile to all the places I wanted to see. He laughed a fuzzy laugh when I invited him to the moving pictures. He was the only friend I had, for in the evenings Helen usually refused to see me. Even Robert Hampton ceased sending books because his father had died and he had left school and started to work. So there was nothing for me to read and nothing to study; in the evenings when I stayed at home my eyes traced the figures on the wall paper in my little room until I felt like screaming; then I would go out and walk through the lighted streets looking in at the shop windows or watching the streams of people flow by.

My friendship with the brown editor changed all this. He induced me to write little things for his magazine, then he rewrote them until not one original line was left, and published them under my name. But still he would not introduce me to his daughter who once came to the office. I learned that she was in a university and did no work.

"Now what's wrong?" he asked after she had gone.

"Why don't you introduce me to your daughter? Why don't you take me to your home? What have I done to you? Ain't I good enough?"

"Am I not good enough," he corrected.

"Am I not good enough," I repeated.

Then he explained. His daughter was a snob, he replied, and was in a university in another city. He and his wife were not friends . . . they did not even speak to each other . . . he could not take me to his home.

"Oh, then, why didn't you say so at first?"

A number of men worked for him also . . . out "on the road" they called it, soliciting subscriptions and advertisements. It was foolish of me, they told me, to sit in an office for five dollars a week. Out on the road you not only made money, but you saw the fastest places going.

"Come with me, peachy," one of them said, "and I'll show you the world."

The brown editor frowned when I talked about going "on the road." I should stay right at my desk and not listen to all the junk those men put into my head, he said. I had a much better chance right in his office.

"Your idea of seeing the world, and their idea about it, are two different things," he added.

There was the evening when he and I drove out of the city in his car. The air rushed past our faces as swift and soundless as thought. The stars came out in splendor. On a mountain road we came to a halt and gazed at the distant twinkling lights of the city. I turned and caught his eyes fastened on my face.

"Now what have I done to you?" I laughed.

He released the brake impatiently and we glided downward toward the city. He pulled the machine in at a very well-known, expensive restaurant. I felt very insignificant as we walked up the thickly carpeted stairs ... restaurants with tiled floors and marble-topped tables seemed more natural to me.

We entered a room with a single table in it; a couch stood in the corner,—all couches seemed suspicious to me now, this one also. A door in the back of the room was slightly ajar ... perhaps leading into a restaurant. I peeped through it—it was a private wash-room. There was a soft movement at the corridor door and a waiter entered. His face was of uncanny blankness as he took the brown editor's order. Quickly he laid the table, keeping his back toward me, then still with his back to me he disappeared through the door, closing it softly behind him. A restless and shameful fear gripped me. Yes, I admitted to the brown editor, I was afraid of this place ... oh, everything about it ... yes, perhaps I was a little fool, but I would rather go home.

He was frank about it all: of course he was a gentleman; he did not know that I disliked him. . . . I had a wrong idea about everything and I didn't know what I was doing. But I must know that he was willing to be a real friend, through everything and everything amen, which meant helping me to study if I wanted to. In the university, too, yes, if I wanted . . . in fact he thought I could learn to write for his magazine also. Oh . . . it was nice of him, was it? Then why should I be afraid of love . . . yes, of love? His voice was as soft and fuzzy as his coat. If . . . perhaps it was children I was afraid of, I need have no fear! So delicate he was! He had become very, very fond of me . . . perhaps he was a crazy old fool, but it was so. He was not? Then what was I afraid of. Oh . . . I was afraid of . . . sex . . . itself? So! So-o-o! he laughed a low laugh. What nonsense—it was just like taking a pill! Didn't I have any wish to be loved at all? He took my chin in his hand and raised it gently to his face.

"Now! Now! What is all this crying about—I didn't know you were such a baby!" He was so surprised that he stopped talking and, putting one arm around me, pressed my face to his shoulder.

"Come, come!" his voice came heavily. "Don't cry. I am sorry. Come, we will go as friends, and we can think it over."

We descended the stairs without speaking, but my face was flaming hot and I could not look up. I did not hate him nor even dislike him. But why had his voice become so disinterested now. Was I only a female? How I hated that . . . hated it with all the hardness in my heart. Hated myself . . . for I had come here and

150

somewhere down deep I had known that something like this was going to happen . . . the stars and his long gaze on the mountainside had told me that. Yet I had come!

The Unknown, the wind, and I, became companions again. The brown editor tried to dissuade me, and Helen tried. But the things I yearned for lay just beyond somewhere. To go "on the road" was no work for a woman, the brown editor had argued—then I knew that that in itself was sufficient reason why I should go. At last he had reluctantly given his permission and his circulation manager turned over to me a bundle of magazines and a box of cheap fountain pens—each subscriber was to receive a fountain pen free of charge.

"I am doing for you what I do for no one else," he told me at last, pressing in my hand an envelope. I opened it and saw a free pass on all the trains in the state. The pass was not only for going, but for returning; in case I changed my mind and wished to come back! He lifted my chin in his hand quickly and tenderly, and kissed me lingeringly, as if expecting to awaken a response at the last moment . . . "something to remember and come back to," his soft voice said in my ear. But I turned and ran. Out on the street I shook my head savagely and tried to think of other things.

I went on and on, from town to town, soliciting subscriptions. At first I ran up the steps of private homes and smiled at the women who came to the door. They heard what I had to say, then slammed the door in my face; sometimes they would talk curiously for a second, staring suspiciously.

My heart began to shrink within me when I saw a row

of neat, smug homes, or when I approached one of them, and gradually I began to approach business offices where I could meet only men. The men received me, many of them kindly, and there was no personal animosity even when they did not subscribe. Many said they did not have any interest . . . no, but just to please me they would take a look. They turned the pen over in their hands and laughed a little when I tried to defend it. They subscribed in the end, and they sent me on to friends; one would give me a card or a letter, or sometimes an address, and I found myself introduced from office to office. Many of them subscribed, but told me to keep the pen and with it to write them a nice tender letter. When I stepped into the presence of men I began to feel a confidence and a mastery such as I had never felt before, as if something were saying to me, "Here is your world!" I never went to a private home again and when I thought of respectable women I shivered. My bank was an envelope pinned inside my shirt where I kept the money I was saving. At night I did not remove the shirt and I always slept with my gun or with a little dagger that I carried, beneath my pillow.

Out of pure curiosity I stopped at Trinidad . . . the scene of my childhood. It was the early gray dawn of morning. I walked slowly down Commercial Street toward a little lodging house; later I would go over beyond the tracks and let some of my old friends see what it meant to be a successful lady! The street was silent and deserted except for one man who stumbled out of a saloon just in front of me and started down the street, reeling now and then. I watched him and remembered how my father had, years ago, gone in and out of

152

this very saloon; but, thank heavens, my father was in Oklahoma now and far away from any saloon. Over there on the other side of the street was the red brick church that I had attended three times . . . it didn't seem at all majestic now . . . at least not to one of my broad, worldly experience! In fact, contemptuously small.

The man before me stumbled on. There was something almost familiar about his rounded, stooped shoulders—yet all working men were like that. He wore a black vest, a dirty blue shirt and no coat. His overalls were dirty with grease and dust. A broad gray slouch hat was pulled in a rakish manner down over one eye. I was gaining on him and watching. As I came nearer . . . I saw . . . he was gesturing with his hands . . . as if talking to some imaginary person! My heart throbbed so fiercely that I could hear it. I hurried faster and faster, drawn toward something I did not want to see, until I was walking by his side. His head was bent, his drink-blurred eyes fastened on the pavement . . . the tobacco juice ran from the corners of his mouth!

I will never forget. It was my father. We walked side by side in silence, and he did not look up. He mumbled, cursing, waving his hands in the air. Before us stretched the gray, winding street, and beyond it the barren mountain. As he turned a corner he glanced up and saw me. He stopped and braced himself against the building for some moments.

"Where're you goin'?"

"Where's Dan and George?" The black, thick curtain I had drawn down over my memory was now torn asunder.

He wiped his mouth on his sleeve and started down the street. I walked by his side.

"Where's Dan and George?"

"Here! With me!"

We turned a corner leading into a dirty alley, and climbed the rickety stairs of a dilapidated building. He climbed the first flight, then the second, then the third, then a narrow ladderlike stairway to a single room up under the roof. He pushed open the door and entered. I looked about: the room was very small, calcimined with some undefined color that had fallen off in spots as the hair falls off a mangy dog. The floor was rough and bare, and dirt from many decades had settled in the gaping cracks. There was one chair in the room. George stood with his foot propped up on it, trying to lace onto his small feet a pair of worn-out shoes of my father's. He wore thin, faded, blue overalls, a washed-out shirt and no coat. Dan stood by his side watching, the upper part of his body lost in a dirty colored coat of my father's . . . the sleeves hung half way to the floor. Both boys were dirty and disheveled. They glanced up and saw me behind my father, and they stood staring blankly to see what I intended to do.

My eyes were riveted on the old boots and the coat and my mind began fighting to defend itself against unbearable pain; then hardness and hatred of all things rushed to the rescue and I turned on my father.

"I thought you'd taken them to Oklahoma!"

George's voice answered me: "We're goin' next week!" . . . he, whose slender hands had always rested against my heart . . . he was defending my father against me. I had become a stranger.

We all stood, saying nothing . . . there was nothing to say . . . we who had come to this, we four. George's questioning eyes were on me; Dan's lips were quivering. My gaze traveled along the gaping cracks in the floor and I fought with my emotions. I believed only in money, not in love or tenderness. Love and tenderness meant only pain and suffering and defeat. I would not let it ruin me as it ruined others! I would speak only with money, hard money. Even now I had power—for I had over eighty dollars pinned inside my shirt . . . a tremendous sum!

Before the day was spent I had less than ten dollars in the envelope beneath my shirt . . . the rest I spent on warm clothing for my brothers. So it was that I tried to buy off my guilty conscience. I could not and would not give love and care. I would make it all back by subscriptions in Trinidad. But something was lacking when I tried it—I had no success whatever. Men looked at me as they might have looked at anyone else, remarking that they had no interest, and my air of conqueror was gone. I did not have the spirit to press them. Outside, George and Dan stood waiting, exactly where I had left them. They watched me now with an expression of those who place their lives in your hands . . . they who loved and trusted me . . . and my mind warred against the love that tried to conquer. My father sobered up and tried to make himself clean while I was there; there was confidence in his eyes also. . . . I tossed in bed at night and assured myself that women were weaklings and fools, they all got married, had a dozen children, and let men order them about. I would not be a woman . . . I would not. I would make money,

money, money, and only with money would I speak. It would not take long, for I was making so much before. I had failed in Trinidad—something was wrong . . . but just beyond. . . .

Thus I deserted them a second time and strangled the emotion that tried to convince me that I should not. I would come back, I told myself, knowing I never would, but unable to face a definite fact. My mind had dragged me up the steps of the train as a chain would drag a dog. I looked back and saw their faces, the two of them . . . how thin and lonely . . . faces that questioned and trusted and yearned . . . George's lips were trembling and he held Dan by the hand.

It was early dawn and I know that somewhere a cock was crowing . . . once . . . twice . . . thrice.

But a black curtain descended softly and erased from my memory the faces of those I loved. So deeply did I love them that I even forgot them . . . except for the dreams that awoke me at night and sent me further and further away, where I did not know . . . where I often did not care. But the curtain was thick and my hardness called itself principle. I threw up fortifications to protect myself from the love and tenderness that menace the freedom of women; I did not know then that one builds fortifications only where there is weakness.

Down over the plains of Texas, where an occasional mirage arose before me . . . broad stretches of water with palm trees on the shores. I walked through little settlements, barely making my bread. My railway pass had become useless now and railway fare cost money. The money I had left over was not sufficient for food. I still met and associated only with men, for women were cruel and fearful creatures. A big cattle man with black eyes and a broad gray felt hat invited me to live on his ranch—it was not a proposal of marriage, but the invitation was given in a friendly manner and my refusal was taken in a manner no less friendly. After that he settled down heavily in his seat, gazed out of the window and remarked that this was a hell of a life.

The landlord in a cheap rooming house in a little town where I stopped one night came in and suggested that he spend the night in my room. My refusal so wounded his dignity that he ordered me to leave his place. There was but one hotel in the town—an expensive one. I slept on the wooden bench in the station waiting room, turning over and over to ease my aching hips.

At one straggling town where I changed trains at night the white, soft-handed clerk in the cheap hotel where I stopped smiled at me. I was alone, hungry and tired. It was three in the morning when a low tapping awakened me; the lock on my door was broken, but I had propped a chair under the handle. I lit the lamp just in time to see the chair grating backward and the clerk entering. He closed the door swiftly behind him. Instinctively I reached under my pillow and grasped the cold pearl handle of my little dagger.

"I've come t' ask you if you'd like a drink of whiskey!" he smirked, looking at me as if he and I knew each other only too well. I backed to the open window behind the bed, trembling, the dagger held behind me. A terror had welled up and closed my throat.

There was a sickly smile around the clerk's face as he slowly moved toward me. My body trembled and I felt sick and weak. He was within arm's reach and I feared I would faint in a moment,—if I waited. Quickly and with the strength of desperation I reached out and struck, not knowing where. It seemed to go wrong, but when I looked again I saw it had not; the knife had torn down his sleeve, ripping it from shoulder to wrist . . . in terror I looked at the knife in my hand and saw a thin trace of blood on the blade.

The smile was gone from the man's face and he was a sickly white.

"You God damned whore!" his voice came from far away. The white face shimmered before my eyes, but with his words my cold fingers gripped the knife and raised it again. Horrified, he rapidly retreated to the door, and the dark corridor swallowed him up.

I stumbled to the wash table and dashed water over my face and hair; the water was cold and I was already trembling with cold. Desperately I pulled on some clothing, fastening nothing. Then with my gun strapped close to my body beneath my coat, I groped my way along the dark hall and down the creaking stairs. Once my suitcase banged against a corner and I stopped dead still in the dark and waited. No sound answered. I felt cautiously with my hands and feet, then crept forward, down the stairs, from step to step like a thief. The faint glow from the clerk's corner threw the desk in light . . . the place was empty!

158

I sped into the night. Through the darkness loomed the form of freight cars, and beyond them the station light. I stumbled toward the light, crossing the network of tracks. Hearing a noise, an old station master came out and regarded me in surprise:

"Well, well, what's all this!"

"I . . . I . . . isn't there a train due here soon?"

"Nothin' but the one fer New Mexico that comes in an hour. Aire you waitin' fer that one?"

"Yes . . . where do the other trains go to?"

"Well-l-l! Don't you know where you want to go to? . . . No. 7 due fer Dallas come at eight in the mornin'."

I wanted to go to Dallas . . . it was a large town . . . I could make money there. But to wait until eight in the morning . . . suppose the clerk had me arrested! People were a pack of wolves . . . how could I explain where I was going and why, when I didn't know myself. What was it all about, this whole thing! The old telegrapher stood watching me with a suspicious expression . . . he also belonged to the wolves.

"I . . . I . . . didn't know I was so early for the New Mexico train . . . and I didn't have a watch or clock."

The suspicion vanished from his face. "Yes, yer a little too early . . . but just come in and set close to th' stove . . . here in my office's a rockin' cheer."

I dropped into the chair, closed my eyes and tried to compose myself. But my thoughts tumbled one on top of the other . . . where in the name of God was I going . . . there was nothing in New Mexico except a waste!

It was a little town of ambitious name—Carlsbad. The "news butch," as the man who sold newspapers on the train was called, spoke of it with pride, for it had a hotel that charged prices beyond his fondest dreams, where people stayed while being cured of various diseases. It was a sprawling little town set on a flat New Mexico plain. I took a room in a two-story hotel near the station and began to solicit subscriptions at private homes. As I again ascended the steps of smug little bungalows my courage almost failed me, and when I descended them again my heart was always filled with humiliation. I walked back and forth before the high-priced hotel but could never find courage to go in and approach the guests there. I had no money left, and the one restaurant in the town told me they needed no help of any kind and could not give credit.

My last two pennies I used to write to Helen for money—just enough to pay my way to a mining town in Arizona where Big Buck was living and where I was certain I could get work. For he had written me even in Denver and told me I could be a stenographer there if I wanted to. Four days passed and I did not eat, and for weeks before that I had half starved. The last loaf of bread I had bought was gone; the crumbs had remained in the paper wrapper. I wet my finger in a glass of water and picked up each crumb, ate it, then reluctantly threw away the wrapper. The hunger during the four or five days that followed was savage and I thought of nothing else . . . in every word uttered about me I sought some way to food. Over a garden wall hung the branch of a peach tree, laden with green fruit. Just as I reached up to get one, two men turned the corner. They passed me, glancing at one another. One was the thin, sharp-faced young man, the beloved of my landlady—so gossip in the little hotel had it. He was the bartender in the saloon on the corner that I had to pass each day on my way to the postoffice.

Each day after that he stood in the door of the saloon.

"Ain't you lonely, kid?" he asked one day, and I hurried by.

One evening on the Plaza, where a Spanish string orchestra played each evening, he sat down on a bench beside me.

"Fine night, ain't it?" the bartender asked.

"Yes."

"Ain't you lonely?"

He slid over to my side and an arm crept about my shoulder. Then he was sitting alone in the night and I hurrying through the dark. A subtle fear of offending him held me ... I feared that he and others might learn that I had not eaten ... feared he would tell my landlady and she would demand the rent for my room.

At the end of the week my landlady indeed came for the rent. I explained that I had an aunt to whom I had written for money and I was waiting for it. What was my business and my age, she asked? Well, she didn't believe I was eighteen ... I looked thirty if I looked a day; and then "travelin' women ain't always what they're cracked up to be."

Nine days and nights passed and I hungered. Hunger-pains no longer tortured me ... there was only a growing weakness. Each morning I awoke and wondered if I could stand on my feet, if I could reach the postoffice and return. Death was still but a name . . . I thought of it as I sat in the window and listened to the wind through the tree outside, but the consciousness of it did not penetrate my spirit. Some secret fate had always helped me at the last moment, and I still trusted in that.

Each morning I sat up in bed slowly, grasped the bedpost to draw myself upright, and stood regarding my reflection in the mirror. "So that is how white a person looks when he is starving," I thought, watching the reflection curiously. And how old! The black dress I wore to save washing made me look still paler and older. I wondered about comfortable people in the smug houses . . . they had enough to eat. I feared them—they regarded poor or hungry people as suspicious characters and their only solution of such problems is to call the police.

A woman arrived in town and took the room at the head of the stairs across from mine. I saw a frail, dark figure through the door. During the night I was awakened by running footsteps, by cries and loud voices. I lay as in a daze and listened, and after some minutes the sounds subsided and the last hurrying footsteps had died on the stairs. The next morning the town was scandalized. During the night, the Negro porter who cleaned my room related, the woman across the hall had heard a gentle tapping at her door.

"Who's there?" she had answered.

"The porter," a voice had replied. "Do you want ice water?"

"Yes."

She had opened the door, three men had entered, overpowered, and outraged her. She had recognized one of the men—the bartender! He had been arrested, released on bail, and would be tried for assault when the next Court sat. He had given an excuse: he was drunk . . . dead drunk; he and his two friends had gone to the hotel to visit a travelin' woman who was staying there! They were so drunk that when they came to the head of the stairs, they had knocked at the wrong door! They had thought it was my door! Who I was they did not know . . . they only knew the "news butch" had brought me in one night! When I heard that, I recalled the news boy on the train who had told me Carlsbad was a large town, and had offered to carry my suitcase to a hotel for me. I had never seen him since.

"Youse liable to be arrested too, missy," the Negro porter assured me.

The day after the scandal I was not only too weak to walk to the post office, but I feared to go on the streets. My landlady had entered my room violently in the morning, called me a "street-walker," and gave me until the next morning to pay my bill and leave her hotel! My mind was very light and if I stood up I became dizzy. Her voice came from far away, dream-like. I was sick, I told her. I was not sick, she said. I was a low-down "street-walker."

She went away. My mind was so ethereal that it was almost pleasant . . . and there was hunger in my body. So this was perhaps death . . . it would not be so painful as I had always feared . . . perhaps I would go to sleep and not wake up.

That night I could not walk to my door to lock it and

the next morning the Negro porter found me when he came to clean the room. I had lifted myself by the bedpost . . . my reflection in the mirror had been very white and shimmering . . . dancing and blending with the air. The wind in the tree outside my window was very gentle and I turned toward it. Then I had fallen and lain unconscious on the floor.

The Negro porter brought whiskey from the corner saloon—and the bartender accompanied him. They poured it down my throat and everything vanished again, then danced and shimmered, appearing and disappearing before my eyes. A part of my brain sat far back and watched with a calm, impersonal interest— being and non-being. It did not seem to care. The other part struggled . . . there was the Negro porter and the bartender talking together, and there was fire in my brain and in my blood. The consciousness far back recorded all things, but without decision or judgment. It recorded that the bartender had brought hot soup and poured it down my throat, that a nausea and dizziness overcame my body and it lost consciousness and had then awakened again. Each time the bartender left the room and reëntered it, the struggling brain thought: "Now it is the end . . . it does not matter," but the other consciousness concerned itself with no such things as fears or joys. For it, things just were, nothing more.

Long afterwards the room became clearer and steadier and the bartender came and went during long intervals. The following day I lay with my eyes toward the mirror and without turning watched the door open and close. The bartender stood there and through my mind flashed the thought: "It does not matter . . . I shall die anyway." For days after he brought soup as usual, and then a piece of meat. When he was gone I wrapped a piece of paper around the meat and slipped it under the pillow. I could not eat it now, but I would eat it tomorrow or next day or next week! It never occurred to me that I could not keep it so long. In the late afternoons the bartender often came and stood looking at me. One day he fumbled in his pocket and then dropped something on my bosom.

"Here's my month's wages," his voice came from above, "I guess you can use it as good as me."

For a long time I thought it over—what did one do in such cases. My mind forced my hands to reach out and gather up the crisp bills and hide them under the pillow close to where I had hidden the meat. The meat was gone! The porter, I thought, when he had prepared my bed . . .

Nothing was strange . . . everything just was.

When my landlady entered my room a few days later she had not relaxed in her hostility. I paid my rent without a word and told her I would leave as soon as I could walk.

Through the long hours I sat in a big chair near the window and the Negro porter came and went.

"You jist call me, missy, when you wants somethin' . . . don't you be afeared of me." And I wasn't. He was the kindest person I met in Carlsbad, and his hands were as skillful as those of any nurse.

The soft southern breeze caressed my face and the tree outside rustled in the wind—the wind that always followed me. One night a bird sang in the tree and I crept close to the window and listened . . . somewhere I had read of the nightingale—could this be that sweet singer of the night? A strain of liquid music poured out of the darkness—love must be like that,—and like the wind.

The days were long and lonely. My legs trembled when I stood, my mind was a confused mass of wishes, fears and desires. Restless. Yearning. Sometimes in the evenings the bartender sat in the window and talked with me. How humble he seemed now! We talked of things of which we knew . . . our families, daily petty things, of the men who came to his saloon and of the things they said and his replies, of my plans to leave Carlsbad very soon and go to Arizona. We did not speak of his arrest. And that great world where intellectual things are spoken of, that world where waves of thought sweep onward, was unknown to us, for the depths and darkness of not-knowing are abysmal. We, he and I, knew of work and food, and we knew that some men work for a living and some don't. We knew that love exists—or passion. The few things I knew from books could be exhausted in a few hours' discussion: one can't sit talking of dates in history, of school law, of typing or how to spell words.

"I've been a school teacher," I told him.

"Why don't you be one now?"

"My certificate only lasted two years. I never took another examination."

"You think you'll find work in Clifton?"

"Yes."

"Have you ever thought of gettin' married?"

"No."

"Well, what do you say to thinkin' about it now—you and me, I mean?

"You see," he continued, as if explaining this weakness in himself, "I thought you was just pretendin' to be straight . . . I know girls like that . . . I thought you'd been there before!"

That revolved around and around in my mind. Because I had never "been there before" I was being proposed to! That seemed unjust and shameful . . . to be judged by my body. I had nearly starved to death; in the end I found that I had merely demonstrated my fitness to marry a man! A vague resentment filled me; this man who had lived with the landlady downstairs—that other woman across the hall—what had he done to deserve the right to marry me? He had given me money . . . yes. My mind traveled further,—I saw that men and women were like that . . . the girls had to be virgins, the men had to have money. Something about it was vile but what it was I did not know. Anyway, it was a trade and I wouldn't trade like that. I would pay him back his money . . . I would go down to Big Buck at once and ask him to pay it back until I could earn enough money. I would make my own money and then we would see who had the right to marry me!

He was waiting for me to answer his question. No, I said, sharply, I didn't believe in marriage. I would *never* marry.

He came next day at dusk and sat in the window again. I suddenly became aware that I had been waiting for his coming. His hands were gentle as he reached over and picked up the pillow that had fallen to the floor, and arranged it behind my head. Nice it was to have someone do that, flashed through my mind . . . tenderness . . . Love and gentleness always. And rest. Outside the wind was whispering through the tree tops. The bird sounded its first trill and I bent out to watch it. He caught me suddenly as I leaned forward and I nearly forgot . . . nearly. It was not love, but it was the desire for love. His arms were unyielding, but his lips were humble and tender, ever so gentle. I remembered and pulled myself from his arms and he left suddenly without a word. When he was gone, his touch still lingered on my throat. My body and mind were filled with loneliness.

By the time the dawn had come, and the matter-of-fact day, I had remembered all things—weeping, nagging wives and husbands who cursed them. Women begging for clothing, shamelessly. "Damn it kid, you know I love you!" Food . . . I would buy my own food. Virginity . . . I would let no man judge me by that as if I had nothing else but my body! I would never marry . . . I would never have children . . . I would never be so weak as to love!

I packed my suitcase before it was light and then lay down to wait. It would be an hour before the first train to the south came through. In a few minutes I arose, carefully descended the stairs, and knocked on the Negro porter's door. When I told him I could not carry my suitcase, he hurriedly closed the door and, after a few minutes, joined me. We went to the station together, my arm through his to support myself; the eastern sky was graying in the early dawn.

The memory of Big Buck is dear to me. He always had to stoop when passing under a door. Colossal in height and bearing, he was a man whose silence was but the shield of a proud spirit. Was there ever a man closer to the spirit of the West than he, I wonder: a strain of ironic humor in all he did; generous in all material things he possessed or earned, very remote in thought and spirit; stubbornly convinced of the inferiority of Mexicans, Indians, Mormons and men frail of body. He had known me since I wore short dresses, had taught me shooting, lassoing, and tricks with the jack-knife; had tried to blast out of me everything feminine. That I belonged to the female persuasion never induced him to show any leniency, and he showed me on more than one occasion that I had to face the consequences of my acts every bit as much as a man. When, in a burst of rage, I had hit him or thrown something at him, he sent me twirling with a thud from the paw he called his hand.

He was taller than my father, but younger and, as he himself modestly admitted, his mustache was long enough to wrap around his ears. Perhaps he had worn a coat in cold climates, but when I met him this time in the blazing sun of Arizona, his colossal figure was decked in his customary costume: a blue shirt and handsome vest, brown trousers tucked in at the top of knee boots; and a high gray slouch hat that he wore tipped forward to shade his eyes from the blinding glare. He had once been a cowboy, but the West was passing and the cattle men were coming into the towns and cities. He was now a mechanic in the copper works of Clifton—had worked himself up he said, and was still following the trail.

When we met he looked me over seriously. Time had added to my stature and placed the seal of womanhood upon my body. But he merely remarked dryly:

"Well, yer're just about two fingers wide!"

After I had told him all that had happened, he made no reply or comment; my story was confused and disconnected, but he caught the main outlines. He took a room for me in a hotel where he lived with his friend "Blackie," and he introduced me to "Ma," the owner, a round, jolly woman who was perhaps thirty-five, but looked fifty. She addressed me as "Miss Buck."

"There ain't no use in your a-puttin' your back up because she calls you Miss Buck," he told me later, "for this joint ain't none too lady-like. When you wrote you was a-comin', I told her my sister was comin' . . . nobody but Blackie knows different and you'd better let it stand as put."

My room was on the second floor overlooking the back alley through which men tramped to and from the saloon and pool room next door. Fights were continually spilling over into the alley and I often hung out of my window and watched them. Buck told me that the "Chink" restaurant across the way had its orders to feed me up. All his treat, he said,—room, grub, everything, until I carried out my threat and found work; but if I asked him, his opinion was that I ought to laze around for a month or so and put a little beef on my bones.

The town lay in a canyon cut in two by a flowing river, though where the river came from is beyond my imagination. On one side arose a wall of almost solid stone, on the other a steep, barren mountainside on which no tree could grow. During the day the blistering mid-day sun heated the stone wall and it was long past midnight before the air cooled. Our hotel boasted the only sidewalk in the town—a board walk that stopped when the hotel stopped. Down the street stood a rambling shed—the Chinese laundry where I learned to swear in Chinese and to sprinkle clothing by squirting water from my mouth,—both no easy accomplishments. Up the street and along one side of the river lay a row of little, unpainted one-story houses. Beyond, blocking the canyon, towered the dark buildings of the copper works and further beyond, the mines. Above, on top of the mountain ridge, lay a part of the trail where the warriors of Geronimo, the Apache chief, had once guarded this pass against white invaders. Beyond the trail stretched an endless series of brooding, rugged hills, devoid of all life, and to the north a range of black, forbidding mountains. A world deserted by man, inhabited by rattlesnakes, lizards and gila monsters. The sun beat down on the black stony hills until they were frying hot. Hell must be such a place as this. Buck and I rode along the trail one day and the sun was so fierce that it aroused his humor. He repeated an old story of a man from Arizona who, in the natural course of events, went to hell, but to the chagrin of the Devil, caught a severe cold and demanded blankets at night. The story was as old as this waste itself, I replied; my hat-band was limp from perspiration and furthermore this was no time for a joke. We both watched a man, sitting in his saddle as if he were a lump of melting butter, come riding down the trail and turn to take the path leading into the canyon below; his skin was burned to the color of leather and his horse's head hung until it nearly touched the ground. He just managed to raise his hand in greeting.

"He looks like the man who's come back for his blanket," Buck remarked casually, his eyes smiling under his hat brim. "But he ain't; he's only the forest ranger."

"The *forest* ranger. Is that another joke?"

"No. There's a tree or two over yonder. There's a ranch there too and this Mormon comes to Clifton once a week fer the mail."

"Why do you call him a Mormon?"

"Look at the way he rides! I can tell a Mormon as far as I can see one . . . they look ashamed of themselves."

"Ashamed! What have they to be ashamed about?"

"How should *I* know! . . . I ain't no Mormon!"

That angered me. The heat angered me. Everything angered me. And later in the town when I met the Mormon I stopped and talked to him.

Each week after that I met him. He was a young but an extremely lean man, long-legged and very tall. With him I rode along the old Geronimo trails, searching for arrow-heads, and he took me far up the canyon where the trees began to grow again and where ruins of ancient cliff dwellings hung in the side of canyon walls. Buck became more and more disgusted. The man was a *Mormon*, he said! He began calling him "Billiard Cue"; he looked like one except that a billiard cue had a backbone, he added. He expressed his opinion very frankly as we were riding down the canyon to a dance one memorable evening.

"You're always a-fallin' in love with someone," he said; and when I protested vigorously, he interrupted with determination. "An' the men you choose is a sight! First it was Jim that you turned down . . . you remember . . . a few minutes after you'd promised to marry him as a trade for a six-shooter and a horse. Then it was a saloon keeper and now it's a Mormon! There's that Indian that's made you that bracelet and ring with them Geronimo arrerheads in it . . . I suppose you've got your eye on him too! It's a sight! Why don't you fall in love with someone respectable . . . with me, fer instincts?"

"With you! You're too old!"

"I'm too old, am I! I'm only forty-two, an' that Mormon's after thirty if he's a day."

There seemed no reply to that. But he continued. "I look old because of my mustache . . . I can shave that off an' look as young as the best of 'em."

The darkness swallowed up his resentment for a few seconds. "I'm older'n you," his voice came across to me, "but I'd treat you right, which is more'n can be said fer Mormons or saloon keepers. That Billiard Cue's got two mothers and before he's finished he'll have a dozen wives."

Buck knew the Billiard Cue would be at the dance we were riding to, and women were scarce in those parts. The Billiard Cue danced—he didn't. He was too big and too dignified to dance even on this all-memorable occasion. Arizona had just become a state and had entered the Union; this was the great day of celebration—the last Territory Day. It had been a holiday and in the early morning Buck and I had ridden along the ridge trail, up and down canyons until we reached Morenci. The town was ablaze with decorations; flags, bunting, Chinese lanterns strung across the streets, green boughs were hanging everywhere. There was to be great dancing that night, and the street was also to be a dance hall. We rode back over the hills before it was dark. We wouldn't be so fine, perhaps, where we were going, but men were coming from the big ranch up on the plateau where Buck had once been a cowboy; Mormons were coming from scattered settlements down the canyons; all the men from the works were coming. And I was one of the few women . . . not altogether an inconsiderable object in that territory at the time.

Our conversation through the dark had ended with Buck's outburst about marriage. His speech had been unusually long and had left me astounded but untouched. There seemed nothing to say, and the silence remained unbroken until we rode up to a dance hall and hitched our horses in silence. The hall was a big pool room and the tables had been shoved back against the wall. Chinese lanterns were strung along the beams above, lighting up the flags and bright bunting. Green boughs were banked in the corners and over the windows. A billiard table had been separated from the others and placed at the end of the room; boards were stretched across the top for the orchestra—two fiddles, a banjo, a guitar and an accordion. Buck and I sat on a pool table against the wall, swinging our legs and watching the dance.

"Some crowd of dames, eh, Blackie?" he asked his friend.

Blackie nodded knowingly and rolled a cigarette, his eyes traveling from one woman to the other. Many of them were heavy, with painted faces, and had come here for business. Then there were some girls from the town and a few from the ranches beyond. Blackie and I entered a square dance. Painted women danced on either side and beyond was the fair girl who had come with the Billiard Cue. Most of the men were without coats, wearing new hats, brilliant vests and belts, and fine boots.

After the dance I crowded my way to the side of the fair girl.

"Fine dance, ain't it?" I remarked, to start the conversation.

"Yes, but it's better up above ... we didn't go up there though, for I have to leave for school on the morning train."

She spoke with a slow, soft drawl, as the forest ranger himself spoke. Where was her school, I asked, like a flash. A school for teachers over by Phoenix. I tried to hide any display of arrogance, but I replied:

"I've been a teacher. And I've studied and become a stenographer. I finished my education long ago!"

Her reply was couched in the tones of a woman who is trying to hide her superiority. She couldn't see how that was possible, for in the school where *she* was studying, one had to study for over six years ... through the high school and the normal!

That took the wind out of my sails—six years!

We made our way to the pool table beside Buck. He listened in silence to our conversation. I heard little of the squeaking fiddles or the strumming of the guitar as the couples weaved past. My imagination had swept beyond to a school where one could learn the things the fair girl was talking about . . . to study . . . what I didn't know . . . just study. It took a long time to finish, but perhaps I could finish sooner . . . for didn't I know more than most people! If this girl needed six years, I could do it in two! My returned health had by no means brought humility.

"Will you dance?" The Billiard Cue bowed before me, handsome as the day.

We swung into the sea of swaying dancers. The room was just a pool room . . . but was it now . . . or was it not the gleaming hall of a great school and my partner the handsomest, most graceful man on earth; was I not dancing as never before, down those long gleaming halls, the seductive swing of the accordion and the low, primitive thump of the banjo lifting my feet on magical wings and beating a passage, a long glimmering passage, with soft music and clear air and a night filled with stars. . . .

The early morning had come before the dance ended, and many of the women had long since disappeared with their partners into the night. Buck and three other men had played poker in the corner for hours; Buck had won so much money that he was excited and did not want to go home. At last he, the Billiard Cue, the fair girl and I rode homeward. They called *adios* to us and turned to cross a bridge.

"Well, you want to go to that school, I see," Buck remarked as we stopped before the hotel.

"Yes."

His voice was tired and a bit proud. "All right, I'll help you out fer six months till you find somethin' to do. I don't make enough to pay everything all the time, but I'll help an' if you ever want to come back I'm here. . . . An' what I said about a-gettin' married stands if you want to think about it. I don't like ignorant females any more'n you do . . . wouldn't waste myself on one of 'em!"

His shadow was dark and huge across from me and I felt embarrassed.

"If you'll help me out maybe I can pay it back sometime . . . when I finish . . . I don't think it'll take long . . . maybe no more'n a year." I could not think in terms of longer than a year, and even that seemed a long time. "I . . . I . . . don't know as I want to get married. I'll think it over . . ."

There it was again—saying a thing that, down deep in my heart I knew was untrue. He made no reply; perhaps he knew also—he knew me so well.

I remember him sitting tall and straight in the saddle, riding away into the gray of the morning, without speaking again or looking back. As dreams go.

One afternoon a few days later, just as the sun was beginning to set, I stood before the row of red brick buildings of the school near Phoenix. It, and the little town to one side, clinging to the banks of a river, sprang out of the desert like a mirage that one often sees when riding across a plain shimmering and prostrate in the heat. Once on a New Mexico plateau I had seen just such a town as this in the distance; my horse had reared his head and swung along eagerly. But when we descended into an arroyo and came up on the other side, the mirage had disappeared and we searched in vain for it through an atmosphere so thin that the eyes could see for hundreds of miles.

This town, however, did not vanish, but lay at rest as if it had waited for my coming! Beyond, on every side, stretched the desert, gray and sinister, covered with sagebrush and cacti. During the day the sun beat down mercilessly, but in the dusk a soft opalescent veil began to settle over the land. The nights came suddenly and were cold, and the deep sky flaunted untold myriads of stars, hard and brilliant. On white moonlit nights the desert became flooded with cold silver and countless giant cacti stood like grim sentinels against the sky, their spiked arms flung up and outward.

Far beyond the desert to the east a range of red and blue-gray mountains thrust themselves from the earth, barren and forbidding. There stood Spirit Mountain where the wind, rushing and sobbing through the desolate caves, was said to be the spirits of the dead haunting the scene where once a battle had taken place between tribes of Navajos from the north and Apaches from the south. I often gazed at the mountain, then at the arrowhead ring on my finger and the bracelet set with an arrowhead on my arm; arrowheads that I had found along the old Geronimo Trail and had had set in silver by an Indian silversmith near Clifton. Arizona penetrated my spirit and I felt no friendship for the American soldiers who had hunted and fought the Apache leader Geronimo until they had captured him and sent him and his warriors to the swamps of Florida, most of them to die. I understood why Geronimo had fought for so long to hold the land he loved. The deserts were indeed gray and sinister wastes where only the cacti, the sage brush, the rattlesnake and gila monster seemed able to live; yes, but it lay there, calling you to come on and on . . . just beyond was something still more beautiful in the moonlight. And if you kept going, sometimes you heard through the crystal-clear air the sad, monotonous singing from a camp of Indians who had wandered over from Mexico. The singing seemed a part of the desert, and could only have found birth there. Wistfulness. Yearning. Desolation.

The Arizona desert came closer to my spirit than has any place I have ever known. I came gradually to resent the river that was fed from the colossal Roosevelt Dam in the mountains; and I resented the towns—Mormon settlements—that had sprung up along the irrigated country, gradually transforming the contemplative desert into fat, well-fed little ant-heaps of human beings.

The officials of the school did not know what to do with me. I had no preparatory training.

"Your family?" they asked.

"They are all dead!"

"All dead!"

"I have an aunt."

"Her name and address?" And I gave it.

"Both your father and mother are dead?"

"Yes."

"What was your father's profession?"

"He was a doctor."

More than this they did not learn. They gave me an examination and after a long conversation admitted me as an irregular student. For three months after that I did nothing but study as I had never studied before. And I learned much: I learned that I possessed but little grace and charm; that my speech was crude and my manner rough and uncultivated; that the well-dressed girls whose homes were in Phoenix disliked me for the hatred I expressed for women, marriage and children.

But I learned other things in that school—remarkable things: in an atmosphere of study, and under the sympathetic interest of teachers, my mind began to work, freshly and vigorously. One professor of zoölogy made me his laboratory assistant and paid me a small monthly salary. And I worked—how I worked! It was strange really to watch ideas and thoughts take form in my mind—never had I dreamed that learning could be like this. Before five months had passed, I was elected the editor of the weekly school newspaper. I bowed my head and worked harder—did I not say I would be able to do more than others!

Other things I learned, and a conviction was planted in my mind,—a primitive, elemental and bitter conviction this time. The girls, now that I was editor of the school paper, sometimes walked with me to and from classes, embarrassing me with a politeness to which I did not know how to respond. Politeness hides such a world of sins. Young men students sometimes came into the little editorial office and talked with me. Also politely, very politely. That I liked less. I began to see that a girl could be beautiful, or she could command respect by intellectual ability, a show of power, a victory. But intellectual ability, a show of power, and victory, are dry, tasteless things. It was a tragic lesson to learn. I yearned for beauty, grace and love.

Sometimes my rôle as an intellectual person, scornful of frivolous things, was a hard one to play. There was one evening when the girls prepared for the school ball. In exquisite evening gowns they flitted down the dormitory corridors and entered the reception room to greet their young men escorts. Their light feet passed my door, and later their steps passed into the night to share in the beauty of life. One girl tapped on my door and peeped in.

"Aren't you coming?"

"Oh, no, I have to write an editorial," I replied indifferently, as if dances were beneath me!

My heart was heavy with longing and misery, and when the dormitory had settled down to silence, I sat before my table and tried to think of the beauty of intellectual things. But the Arizona air is thin and clear and sound travels far at night; from the campus came the low, seductive strains of throbbing music. Unable to write, I crept out of the window and made my way across the grass. Other windows in the dormitory were lighted: above was the light of a fat, ugly Mormon girl; near-by that of the poor girl who washed dishes in the restaurant. How I hated to be among them—we, the unbeautiful ones!

From the shadow of the hedge enclosing the rose garden I watched the ball through the broad open windows of the reception hall. Beauty, music, rhythm. An occasional couple wandered out into the cool air and paced slowly back and forth among the rose clumps. Once it was a fairy-like Mormon girl and her escort; she had eyes of violet blue that at night became shadowy pools. She was clad in a gown of clinging yellow. I shrank further into the shadow lest she shame me by finding me there.

When she had returned to the hall I took the broad road leading into the desert. Occasionally halting, I heard from afar the strains of music. At last the road blended with the desert, the desert where nothing matters. Into it, farther and farther, we wandered, my friend the wind and I, and a night-bird that called in the loneliness. For just one hour of careless, untrammeled happiness, for just one short hour of beauty and love!

The desert is never-ending and at night the imprint of oblivious ages lies upon it, ages that have swallowed up all things human—passion, hope and high resolve. The stars that hang in endless space with such complete finality strip the soul of all earthly passion and leave but a burden of wonder and an all-pervading unrest.

She was a Scandinavian goddess, an unusually tall, dignified goddess with golden hair, blue eyes and the hint of an accent in her speech. When she came into my room I saw that she limped . . . such women exist in books . . . tall, pale, of natural gentility and dignity. And they often limped, if I remembered rightly, and some were rich.

This goddess was named Karin Larsen and she had come to our school to hear a State debating contest on woman suffrage. Her eyes traveled about my room. To the gloves, riding hat and Mexican quirt hanging on the wall; to my revolver in a leather belt and holster, slung over the bed-post; to the dagger that served me as a paper-knife, lying on my study-table. Then we both stood in the center of the room and looked each other up and down, around and around, slowly and curiously.

"So-o-o!" she uttered at last, taking me in.

"So-o-o!" I thought, taking her in, wondering if my voice could be as soft as hers.

"I am from the East," she said, "but I teach in Phoenix just now. Where are you from?"

"Oh . . . I'm from everywhere I guess."

She had come out West to be near her brother and to see a little of life, she continued. It seemed to be a funny place to come to, yet one never knew about such people. She was a funny person—a teacher with no respect for teaching, who said she was made to teach things she knew nothing about. Educational institutions in general seemed to be "antiquated, reactionary and uncreative—static also"; and to my terror she asked me what I thought. It had never occurred to me that there could be anything wrong with a school of any kind. She spoke of "society," and I learned that she didn't mean fashionable society people, but everybody, including myself.

Then he came—Knut Larsen, her brother. He was in his early twenties and looked much like his sister, except that his eyes were deeper and bluer, and they smiled when he shook my hand. There was the same suspicion of a foreign accent in his speech, and his manner was so cultivated, so courteous, that I was embarrassed. His gaze, turned often to me, sent the blood to my cheeks, and I became conscious of my crudeness and ugliness. . . .

The month passed, but he, Karin and I, were often together. One evening we waited under a pepper tree on the campus, discussing the Easter dance of the Yaqui Indians that we were going to drive to see. He and Karin made me feel very ignorant, and when we reached the Yaqui village on the desert, they seemed to see beyond physical appearances and to be watching what I did not understand. The Yaqui village was just a group of huts, many of them only roofs held up by posts. Everywhere the short, dark little Indians were selling Mexican tortillas and hot tamales. We squatted down under a roof with a crowd of Indian women dressed in loose, faded calico wrappers. In the center was a cleared space; near the edge sat the musicians. One was tapping on a crude drum and the other had a long empty yellow gourd filled with peas or pebbles that made a soft shuffling noise as he beat it against the earth. The men were naked except for a loin cloth, and the heads of the animals over their own heads.

In the center stood the dancer, a fat Indian, dressed like the musicians. The string holding his loin cloth in place was lost in rolls of fat about his waist. He danced around and around, across and back. The women clapped or hummed a low monotonous tune; sometimes they showed their appreciation for some particularly graceful step by laughing or exclaiming in approbation.

We moved to another roof, long and low, under which two rows of men, clad only in loin cloths, danced, facing each other. It was an endurance dance of some sort and many of them had been already dancing for twelve or fourteen hours. Now and then one would drop out, exhausted. On the central post supporting the roof hung a little image of the Virgin Mary, and above it a cross. Before this the men danced, the rows advancing and retreating, crossing over and changing places. These Indians were Catholics, and this was their Easter celebration; the dance before us lasted until the last dancer had either fallen exhausted or had withdrawn. Only men danced—for was not religion the instrument of men? Outside stood rows of Indian women and girls, bobbing up and down to the rhythm of the weird music, accompanying their movements with a low singing without words.

"It is just as sensible as our own religion," Karin was telling Knut, "and it's odd to see the Virgin Mary and the cross hanging in the center."

Knut's gold tooth showed as he laughed. "Well, I'd just as soon dance like this as kneel . . . this is healthier and has much more joy in it."

I stood at the back and watched them take notes and talk of those things to which I was a stranger. The love, the comradeship and understanding between them was very deep and beautiful . . . Could love really be beautiful and free, I wondered . . . Could human beings be tender and still not weak? Could there really be love free from danger and subjection for a woman?

Light . . . ideas . . . thought. And still my own way was obstructed. I returned to the school to stare steadily at that hemmed-in road of my life. I would break all obstacles . . . work, money, study!

Over six months had passed since I had become a

student and I had won honors coveted in vain by students who had been in the school for years. Then Big Buck ceased sending money; the six months had passed during which he had promised help, he wrote, and he hoped I could get along alone; he also understood from my letters that I was not returning to Clifton again. So he and Blackie had decided to go into Mexico and help in the revolution; if he lived he would write . . . if not, *adios!*

The silence that closed around him has never yet been broken.

I floundered in an attempt to study and make my living at the same time—typing, sweeping floors in the dormitory, doing anything I could find to do. My studies could be attended to only late at night, and then I was weary and dull. Work as I might, my expenses could not be covered.

The school year was within a month of closing, but my hopes went the way of much hope in the desert, and I left to find work in Phoenix. Karin and Knut heard my story and laughed at my unhappiness; school did not necessarily teach one anything, they held—often it perverted and destroyed intelligence. But their words carried no meaning to me . . . their feet were planted firmly on sound knowledge, and from the heights they could afford to be critical.

I found work, but a gnawing discontent tortured me night and day. There was no prospect of a continuation of study in the future. Knut and Karin were leaving for San Francisco, not to return. The glimmering light was becoming dimmer and my loneliness greater.

On a still moonlight night before they left, Knut rode

by my side over the bridge, down through the outskirts of the town, and along the white hard road leading through the desert. Something maddened my horse, and it took the bit in its teeth and tore through the cold night air. When I felt the peculiar fierce movements of its body beneath me I remembered that down deep somewhere I had always feared horses—feared them even as I rode them, and that now blind fear was seizing me. Desperately I turned my head and called to Knut; the horse perhaps sensed my fear, for it dashed ahead more fiercely still. Knut's face was desperate as he answered my call; he spurred his horse savagely to reach my bridle bit. Neck to neck we rode, the wind sweeping his hair back from a high white forehead. He was bending far out over his horse's neck, then his hand caught my bridle and with a terrific jerk he brought my horse under control. With the animal rearing and whirling, white, lathering, mad, I leaped to the earth. My legs trembled from exhaustion and I sank into the shadow of a clump of sage-brush. Knut's voice came from a distance where he was soothing the animals and fastening them to the brush. In a few moments his steps came rapidly toward me. He bent down and I reached up to grasp his arm. . . . A tremor swept through his muscles! He dropped on his knees by my side, his arms were around me and I felt the quivering heart-beats through his soft white shirt. He was whispering as if the lonely desert might hear him . . . elemental things, ecstatic things. A great peace swept through my body and mind in the all-embracing gentleness of his touch . . . and his lips were as caressingly tender as the moonlight falling on a quiet sheet of water.

Part 6

What was love? I considered it: a confused, colorful mingling of the fairy tales I had read as a child and novels I had read later on; a very lovely but forbidden thing. Still it was not connected with that other forbidden expression,—sex. Sex had no place in love. Sex meant violence, marriage or prostitution, and marriage meant children, weeping nagging women and complaining men; it meant unhappiness, and all the things that I feared and dreaded and intended to avoid.

Since I had known Knut such thoughts had often passed through my mind. I was ashamed of the desire for love, tenderness and companionship that existed beneath my rough and defiant manner. I was nearly nineteen, undeveloped in emotions and not fully developed in body. I had thought little but acted much. My fear of sex expression had grown with the years. Yet I resented virginity, and the so-called "purity" of woman, and reacted violently to any suggestion about it. It had always shamed me that men judged women by such a standard.

In my hatred of marriage, I thought that I would rather be a prostitute than a married woman. I could then protect, feed, and respect myself, and maintain some right over my own body. Prostitutes did not have children, I contemplated; men did not dare beat them; they did not have to obey. The "respectability" of married women seemed to rest in their acceptance of servitude and inferiority. Men don't like free, intelligent women. I considered that before marriage men have relations with women, and nobody thought it wrong—they were but "sowing their wild oats." Nobody spoke of "fallen men" or men who had "gone wrong" or been "ruined." Then why did they speak so of women? I found the reason! Women had to depend upon men for a living; a woman who made her own living, and would always do so, could be as independent as men. That was why people did not condemn men.

I was alone in Phoenix when I considered all these things. Knut and Karin had gone to San Francisco. They made me feel very humble—they were so educated and beautiful and intelligent. They had no anxiety about making a living, and hunger would have been quite an adventure for them. Knut wrote me, asking me to join them in San Francisco. He wrote of love, and also of marriage, but what he wrote was different from all I thought marriage could be.

"I have no money," his letters read, "but I love you. If you marry me we will be poor. But we are both young and we can work and study."

I saw that I could have companionship in marriage and yet make my own living. Love. . . . I did not know what love was. I was lonely, yes, and I feared uncertainty and ignorance. Knut spoke of love, of work and of study. All the things I longed for were combined in him. The fear of sex and of children still barred the way. But I decided to go to him and Karin and see what the future would be. Even if we did not marry, to be with him and Karin would be a great thing, for, through them, I could learn of another world. They incorporated the only independent thought I had ever known, and this thought did not come from books. It seemed to me that they just sort of manufactured their thoughts as they went along, and that was indeed a remarkable thing. I recalled my wonderment when they took me in Phoenix to see the first drama of ideas I had ever seen. It was "The Twelve Pound Look," and we sat in the gallery. Knut and Karin were absorbed in the play. I was bored to death. Only the fact that they listened intently made me realize that what was going on was of importance. I did not understand anything on a stage that did not have a lot going on: clog dancing, loud music and laughter, rough jokes, gaudy clothing and very extravagant acting. To see people acting *naturally* and just talking *ideas* was strange. The play seemed to be about a married woman who saved up money until she could buy a typewriter and by it earn her own living. Such a silly thing to write a play about! The idea in itself was not sufficient to keep me fully awake. I saw that Karin and Knut lived in this world of ideas, but such ideas seemed to me so natural that I did not understand why a play should be written about them.

I was packing my trunk to go to San Francisco to join them when a letter came from my brother George.

When I read it my heart sank within me and the veil of forgetfulness that I had so carefully constructed fell apart. George had written me only once since we parted in Trinidad. And the letter that now lay outspread in my hand might have been an indictment against me. I read it once, then twice, for I did not want to believe it. It charged me: my father had, one year before, put the two boys on a farm in Oklahoma to grow up. It charged me: they had been turned over to a brutal farmer to do with as he wished. It charged me: they did not go to school, but worked like animals from dawn to darkness. It charged me: the man had beaten Dan until the skin had been broken on his body and blood had run down his back.

Thus read the indictment against me, I who was considering a better life in San Francisco!

It has been many years now since that letter came. But time can never heal a memory like that. The desert, and not the Christian God, was my solace and my refuge, and I sought it now. I took the still white road down which Knut and I had ridden on that clear night when he had told me he loved me. The hours walked and I walked with them. There is a misery so deep that it is calm. Nothing moved on the desert, not even the little gray bird that calls in its loneliness; not the wind that touches the sagebrush; not the stars that bent low. But always before me in the desert walked my wounded brother—his shirt torn off and his back a bleeding wound. I looked across the desert to the right—he moved there before me; I turned my eyes to a giant cactus rearing its arms toward the sky—he moved in that direction. So I walked, and he walked before me. He became a bloody gash in the night; he became a gash in my heart; he has remained a gash in my memory through all the years. Even the desert that buries all passion, all pain and all desire cannot bury that.

The night dragged on and I turned to retrace my steps. I reached home in the early morning. Which road should I follow—to the East or to the West? How could I spend my life in that gaunt house on the plains, accepting food from a father I hated? What did the future hold for me if I did it—I would become old, and lose hope and the desire to study; I would help feed and clothe my brothers—but on whose money? . . . I could not earn money out there and they also could not earn money. I would be but another mouth to feed.

I took out Knut's letter and laid it beside the one from George. Life is hard and life had taught me hard lessons. I would not go back where I had come from—I would study never-endingly until I could make enough money to bring my brothers to me and send them to school.

Then I wrote three letters: one to my father, accusing him of all that he had done, demanding that he take my brothers and care for them and send them to school; one to George, enclosing all the money I had, and telling him to take Dan and go away to my father; and then one to the man—a torrent of murderous hatred. He had beaten my brother until the blood ran from his little body, I wrote; he was using my brothers like animals. I could not come, I did not have the money—but time was with me and one day I would come. I would never forget, and even though an old woman, still the time would come when I would kill him with my own hands.

I went out and posted the three letters, and down the long, straight road to the east the first breath of light was appearing over the desert. The little gray bird was calling in the dawn—down there somewhere.

The leaves on the mountain oak were turning red when I met Knut and Karin in San Francisco. We took an apartment together and all found work. Knut and I discussed marriage.

"I don't want any children, Knut."

"Nor do I—not for a long time anyway."

"I don't want any at all—there are enough children in the world. Then I have to think of my brothers and my sister."

"Good—we agree on that point."

"I don't want a home either, no cooking, washing, scrubbing. I want to earn my own living and you earn yours."

"We agree there too. I want to earn enough money to get out of this work and take up something else—I hate this work."

This marriage would not be like other marriages, I thought. But Knut did not know how deep the poison was within me. I really thought marriage without sex was possible—a sort of a romantic friendship, two people working together and remaining friends! We hesitated until Knut was informed that he must leave the city and go into the desert to the south to carry on work for many months. The day he was to leave he called in at the office where I worked and we decided to have lunch together and then I would go with him to the station. We passed the city hall on our way and he turned to me:

"Suppose we go in and get our marriage license now!"

It took two minutes and cost two dollars. I insisted upon paying half. We laughed at this daredevil thing we were doing; it would be such a surprise for Karin. Once on the street outside, Knut stopped suddenly:

"And I say, why don't we go on up and get married right now?"

The elevator boy looked us up and down and stopped without a word at the first floor. "Third to the right," he directed, cynically. For a moment we both felt insulted that he had recognized our purpose—did we look as guilty as that? We stepped in at the third door to the right, rather timidly. A little, round, perspiring man was sitting in his shirt sleeves laboring over books of some sort.

"Just a minute," he said, glancing up, not waiting for us to state our purpose. In a moment he was ready. "Oh, I guess we need a witness!" and he opened an inside door and bawled at someone at the top of his voice. In a few seconds another little man, also fat, round and perspiring, appeared. He was likewise in his shirt sleeves.

"I guess I ought to put on my coat," he exclaimed, taking in the situation. The little official guessed that he ought to do the same, and slipped into an old black shiny alpaca hanging on a nail over his desk.

We all stood there—the little witness trying to stand straight and look dignified, the official with a glistening face. The official examined our marriage license.

"Now," he said, without ceremony, looking at Knut, "aire you willin' to take this woman as yer wedded wife?"

Knut and I stared at each other in amazement—it came so suddenly. We didn't think it was going to be like this!

"What's wrong?" the official asked in surprise.

"It's rather sudden," Knut explained.

"Sudden! Don't you know whether you want to get married or not?"

"Oh, yes, but you go at it a little bit too suddenly."

"Lord, man, what do you want me to do—do the hula-hula?"

Knut laughed: "The idea's not half bad!"

Knut became more serious and the little fat man asked the question again:

"Aire you willin' to take this here woman as yer wedded wife?"

"Yes!" but there was a funny little sound in Knut's throat.

The little man turned to me, solemnly. "Aire you willin' to take this here man fer yer wedded husband?"

Well, what a question to ask me! Suddenly I wondered if I was! What a silly position to be in! Always before I had been in bad situations but knew that right around the corner I could slide out of them—I had never been completely discouraged. Here was a blank wall with no corners! All my decision to get married vanished and I faced a finality that seemed akin to the finality of my mother's death.

"Say yes," Knut was urging in my ear. "All you've got to do is say yes and then we'll get out of this."

The perspiring little man continued looking solemnly at me: "Ain't no use gettin' scared," he said, "people go through this all day long. Now—aire you willin' to take this here man fer yer wedded husband?"

"Yes, I guess so."—Was that my voice marrying me like this!

The little man seemed to think that the dignity of the occasion should be further impressed upon our minds, although the only ceremony required by law had been completed. Knut's voice and face carried a suspicion of the desire to laugh and he did not like it. He was a romantic man. Or perhaps he decided to rub it in. So he turned to Knut to ask another question—I know now it was of his own manufacture; but just then it made a deep impression upon me:

"Aire you willin' to support this woman through all the viscissitoodes of life, through sunshine and rain, through storm and stress?"

He thought that would hold us!

"Yes," came from Knut, trying to control his voice. Why he felt inclined to laugh I couldn't understand; it seemed a most serious question—especially that word "viscissitoodes," which I had heard for the first time and which had a most suspicious ring about it—as if it had something to do with sex.

"And—aire you willin' to support this man through all the viscissitoodes of life, through sunshine and rain, through storm and stress?"

That word used at me also! Anyway I had an agreement with Knut that we would have no children, so it didn't matter what I said here. So I agreed.

"Have you got a ring?"

"No, we don't believe in rings!" My chin tilted with pride when I heard Knut defy an official right to his face like that.

"All right then, that's all. Five dollars please."

Knut paid half and I paid half—I was going to start right, from the very start. He couldn't pay for my marriage as if I belonged to him. He laughed at the two dollars and a half he had saved.

"I'll have a good dinner on the train with it," he said, while the little official watched the transaction between us with horrified disapproval.

We signed our names and addresses, the little witness signed, and the official ripped off his alpaca coat, hung it on the nail above his desk again, and went back to his books. We'd get our papers from Sacramento in about a month, like everybody else, he remarked, glancing up wearily.

"And the next time you come here," he said to Knut, "come prepared! Marriage is a serious business."

"He looked like a toad," I cried, when Knut and I got on the street and stood staring at each other.

"Easy way he has of making money—five dollars a fling!" Knut replied. "He got me all balled up at first."

"I feel like going back and asking for our money back and making him cancel our names."

"We can't do that—it's legal now."

"So we are married fast! I feel a little funny about it, don't you? It doesn't seem natural at all."

"We'll feel more natural after we have a feed . . . come, a place with music, and then I'll rush my train."

We went to a restaurant with music. I objected because the music sounded like church music. Nonsense, Knut said—that was the "Pilgrim's Chorus" from Wagner. What Wagner was and who the pilgrim chorus was, was a mystery to me, but I trusted Knut because he was an educated man, and we entered the restaurant, as he said, to have a feed.

Karin, a man friend of hers named Bob, and I went to a Socialist picnic. Bob was a lawyer and a Socialist. He was black-eyed and black-haired, fiery in temperament and ruthless when it came to his principles.

We went into a forest outside of San Francisco. There in a big open space a merry-go-round had been erected. There was a shooting gallery, a few booths for the sale of cheap gee-gaws and a rough dancing floor. As we walked through the crowds of men and women, boys and girls and children, I was revolted. They were so unbeautiful, so dull and dreary looking, so cheaply dressed—just like the things I had always known and hated. The merry-go-round was blaring out some tin-pan air, and near-by a speaker in shirt sleeves was standing on a platform haranguing a crowd of men and women who munched peanuts and popcorn as they listened. Sometimes his voice drowned the merry-go-round, sometimes the merry-go-round drowned his.

"Why did you bring us here?" I protested to Bob. "Just look at them! They are so cheap and ugly."

Bob turned on me with flashing eyes: "Yes, they're

cheap and ugly! But *what* made them like this? Stop and think—*what made them like this?*"

"Well, what did?" I replied.

"The system!"

I did not answer. I did not know exactly what he meant by the system. His words, "What made them like this?" expressed with such vehemence, were indelibly written on my mind, returning to me countless times in after years.

Knut returned to San Francisco before going to the deserts of the south where an All-American canal from the Colorado River was being constructed. I did not want to go—it seemed that one could make more money and be nearer to schools in a city. Karin had left for New York City, but before going had given me a large and generous piece of her mind; I was not only an idiot, it seemed, but was doing her brother an injury by being married to him and not living as his wife. That aroused my resentment: Knut and I had agreed before marriage, I informed her, that we would have no children. She was astounded at my ignorance. Furthermore, I said, if Knut wanted to be married like other people, he could get a divorce. Love, she insisted, meant following a man even into a desert. Love which meant that, I replied, was an enemy of woman and most certainly of mine. My aim in life was to study; not to follow a man around. I knew nothing of love, she told me. "Thank God I don't!" was my reply.

When Knut came, after over eight months of absence, I coldly laid the controversy before him and said I had no desire to be married if it meant what Karin said. Of course, of course, he exclaimed, I was perfectly right—our life was *our* life and we had the right to live as we wished. My hostility to him began to vanish as he defended me even against the sister he so dearly loved. Suddenly it seemed that he and I were very close to each other.

"Knut—is there any chance of making enough money to go back to school down there?"

His arm went around me. There was a town on the desert, he said, and we could perhaps both make money enough, after one year, to return to school. More than in San Francisco. I could work in the town while he went into the desert, he said.

I went with him, he who was so gentle and tender, who had never dreamed that men could treat women other than as equals; he who had known only good things. And yet it was the fate of such a man to reap the bitter harvest that a harsh and distorted society had sown within me. Often, in the following months of our life together, he stood in shocked, amazed pain before me. For, down there in the south, it began—the sex relationship that I had always feared. Knut was very young and as ignorant as I. There was no beauty in it all—at least not for me—and over my head hung the fear of children and poverty and then—no opportunity to study. Beatrice and George—what should I do with them if I ever had children!

There were times when I hated Knut. Why I didn't know. People called me "Mrs. Larsen," just as if I, Marie Rogers, had sunk into the earth, or at best had become an appendage of Knut. The word was like a taunt to me. Everything about me intensified this. There was the young married couple next door in our apartment house. She stopped work when she married, and sat at home all day long waiting for her husband to return. They lived a purely sex existence. In two or three months eruptions began to show upon her mouth and on her face—the entire house knew what the disease was. She was heavy with child also, but syphilis within marriage is respectable. So I said to Knut.

"Now," I warned him—he who so devotedly tried to take the sting out of life for me, "now he will soon beat her. She can't make her own living any more and no one would marry her because of the disease. She is his wife and he will beat her!"

Knut stood gazing out of the window, his face twisted in pain. As the days passed I saw that he listened nervously when there was a noise from the next apartment.

He was not at home when it happened. Through the partition I heard the woman scream, there were two or three thuds and an overturned chair or table. The weeping of women who are wives—what is more bitter?

When he struck her two days later she ran out into the hall weeping. I told Knut of it when he returned. No one dared interfere—she was the man's wife. Sometimes I did not know what I did, so violent was my reaction against men and marriage, and against Knut and my own marriage. When I heard the man and woman next door, something blinded me. My emotions struck out in short, violent thrusts within me.

"Marie!" Knut cried out one day, "one day I shall kill myself if you say a thing like that again!"

Still I said just such things again. Once he dropped to the floor, striking his head on a chair. In terror I picked him up and placed him on the bed.

"You are a hard, cruel girl and I want to die!"

"Why don't you divorce me then—I shall not object."

"Because . . . I love you."

"Love! That's no excuse. That's weakness!"

"In the name of God, Marie . . . don't!"

Why did I hurt him so! he who was so innately good, so innately noble? I don't know. Something within me had been touched down deep,—something as hard as steel and as sharp as a knife. This alone I know now: it was not against Knut that I struggled, suffering far more than I made him suffer. There was a merciless war being waged within my own spirit, a war between my need and desire of love, and the perverted idea of love and sex that had been ground into my being from my first breath.

Knut went far into the sandy desert at last, to be gone for months. I was left in the little town of El Centro that had just sprung up on the edge of the desert. There were about a hundred houses, and men were pouring in to take up land along the canal route. Frame boarding houses were lifted in one night and rents became fantastic. The land was rich—a great desert stretch, lying below sea level which in ages long past had been the bottom of a mighty lake or sea. All it needed was water, and the water was coming. But it was hot—unbearably hot there below sea level, sometimes one hundred and twenty in the shade,—and no shade! A blistering heat blew from the desert, and the Sierras to the west shut off the winds and the rains from the sea.

I became a public stenographer in the one hotel in the town, sitting out in the waiting room and typing business letters for the land speculators who poured in from Los Angeles,—fat, bloated vultures who bought up large tracts of land and held them until poor men who needed land mortgaged their lives to buy. The vultures dictated their letters to me, shouting before a crowd of spectators that ten cents was too much to be charged for a single typed letter. But I had countless opportunities to make more than ten cents on letters. One bay-windowed vulture, with a long cigar tipped heavenward, sat down heavily by my desk one day, shoved his bowler back from his perspiring dollar-like face and, without removing his hands from his pockets, made a "proposition."

"What's yer price?" he asked finally, irritated by my monosyllabic replies, "but you needn't pitch it too high just because you've got the monopoly. I never pay more'n five dollars a night. My room's number nine. If the price suits you, I'll be waitin' for you."

Another land speculator, connected with a Los Angeles newspaper, adopted the attitude of a philanthropist. He was willing to make me the correspondent for his newspaper—for a consideration.

"You can't have somethin' for nothin'," he informed me with what he considered a benevolent and tantalizing grin. It was an opportunity for making money and it appealed to my ambition. We bargained.

203

"No 'consideration,' " I said, "but you can take a percentage of what I earn by my writing"—for I had learned to bargain in percentages also. He defended his viewpoint:

"You're a married woman and your husband's not here; I'm a married man and my wife's not here. It's not as if you'd never been there before,—when you consider it all the way round, you'd get more out of it than I would."

A few days later he broached the subject again. "My terms remain as put," I told him. "No 'consideration' but a percentage. I've nothing more to say."

We closed at that—he to receive twenty percent of the income from anything I wrote, he to see my accounts; no crookedness on my part, he warned, or he would see that I lost the job!

Thus I was initiated into the newspaper world. He gave me tips about stories here and there, but not without remarking that he was doing it free, of course, and I wondered if he kept an account of the free tips he gave for which he got nothing.

"Work, money, school—work, money, school!" ran through my head like the leitmotif of a symphony. Half of my time only was spent in the hotel, and my charges per letter went up to twenty cents.

"Damned swindle," the vultures said.

"I don't beg you for work," I told them.

Knut returned for a week, brown and leathery, then left once more. I had saved money and the future was opening up to us. In a year we would have enough money to leave the desert and go someplace to school.

Then I knew something was wrong—something that drowned the music of "work, money, school." I complained to my landlady of a sickness each morning. She laughed coarsely. Sex and birth were huge indecent jokes to her.

"Yer goin' to have a baby!"

I turned and left the room when she said that. Fear, bitterness, hatred, gone from me for weeks, swept through me again like a hurricane. Everything that was hopeful vanished—I saw myself plunged back into the hell from which I was struggling—the hell of nagging, weeping women, depending for food and clothing upon my husband, with study but a dream. I looked upon my baby with concentrated hatred.

"I won't have a baby!" I announced to my landlady as if it were her fault. "I won't. I'll kill myself first . . . tell me what to do."

I rode along the desert roads, madly, alighted and ran until exhausted. Wept and hated, wept and hated. Still the sickness came each morning. I stopped eating, thinking in my ignorance that the enemy within me would stop growing. The doctor who had his office above the pool room told me that he could do nothing to help me—it was illegal; I could go to a drug store and get something. He instructed me verbally. If things went wrong, he said, I could call him and he would have the legal right to finish the operation.

"How much will it cost?"

"I'll make a special price for you of one hundred dollars."

All the money I had saved! Still it would be cheaper.

I paid his consultation fee of ten dollars, and stopped at the drug store. But I did not even know how my own body was constructed. In secret and in blind terror I tried to learn. I could not—my mind was unclear, terror-stricken. I had not the least idea of the nature or workings of my body, of the conception or nature of growing life.

"This is your fault," I wrote at last to Knut. "Come and get me out of this or I shall kill myself."

Days passed and no reply came. One night I lay face downward in the bath tub, but could not hold myself under the water. My landlady, hearing the splashing and choking, ran in and pulled me out.

But Knut came—he had traveled for days. He went to the doctor. "You either operate or we go to the city and have it done," he told him. "My wife will kill herself within a week if something is not done."

The doctor gravely examined my lungs and heart and said it was as he suspected—I had tuberculosis and the operation was necessary! Childbirth would be most dangerous.

When I came back to consciousness Knut was sitting by my bedside, smiling. I lay gazing at him and hating the smile—hating it, hating it, hating it! How dared he smile when my body was an open wound, when I had stood before eternity . . . how dared he smile when a child had been taken from my body, and now my body and mind called for it . . . how dared he smile when I felt alone in space . . . how dared he . . . he a man who knew nothing, nothing, nothing!

All my money was gone and Knut had returned to the desert. I would not let him pay for the operation . . . it was my body and I would let no man pay for it, I said. He had become very pale at that.

Then I learned of a normal school beyond the mountains and I wrote to ask if I could not work my way through. The answer came after a month, and it said yes, I could make some money but not enough. I wrote Knut a letter and said, "Now I am going and I am not coming back . . . if you ever want to see me you must come where I am."

I spent three years in that school and they were unhappy years. They asked me my name. Marie Rogers, I replied. Father a doctor, yes. Dead, yes. Husband's name Knut Larsen.

"Oh, your name is Larsen then!" they exclaimed.

"My name's Marie Rogers!"

"You're married, you say?"

"Yes, but Rogers is the name I was born with and it is the name I will die with."

"Sorry, Mrs. Larsen, but your name is Larsen."

This poisoned my three years of study.

Once an elderly woman teacher pitied me: "It is really a shame that you, a married woman, should have to make your own living when you should have a home and children!"

I turned on her quickly, and she and I looked at each other across a gulf separating two worlds. She knew then that I must be a bad woman! But I knew that I was a woman not yet broken in to slavery.

Another teacher asked me if I could not do something to make myself look neater: she offered me five cents for my carfare if I would come to her home and accept a dress. I turned quickly and she and I also looked at each other across a gulf that could not be bridged.

The teachers watched me—disturbed and curious. It wasn't right, they felt. A graceless, thankless, hard girl. They tolerated me because I worked hard. For I worked with the fear of desperation, burdened with mental and spiritual conflicts that were more devastating than pain or hunger. I typed for hours, pausing only to run to classes. In my boarding house I waited tables to earn my food and room. At night I buried my head in books and studied until my brain whirled and the night took my youth, my health, all sweetness and gentleness—all spontaneity that belongs to youth. Before me was the possibility of a diploma from the school; and then I could help Beatrice and George.

In the midst of it the city became disturbed. A woman named Emma Goldman was announced to speak on the social drama. The business men of the city refused to permit a lecture. Who was she, I asked. A very terrible sort, I learned, a free-for-all public character with a long and dangerous tongue. I paused to hear a discussion in a bookstore. The speakers were the woman who owned the store, a young physician, a musician who had once played at our school, and a young minister who was a Socialist. From them I learned that Emma Goldman was a noted woman speaker and writer, a fighter for social justice, for freedom. They were in the midst of the struggle over her right to speak.

For days after the suppression of her lectures, the public fight raged. The business men hurled themselves and the police against the crowds of working men and women who demanded the right of free speech. I knew little of theory of any kind, but I listened. The opponents of free speech were like the land speculators I had known. The things the working men and the Socialists said expressed my own feelings and convictions. Then, when the police and the business men were turned loose upon them, I also was moved to action, and I helped break their shock. The jails were filled with working men, Socialists, I.W.W. who came in by each train, and with a number of the intelligentsia. The free speech fight that raged for months in California, led by the I.W.W., had begun here. I took part where I could, convinced that we were right. I heard my friends called unspeakable names, saw them imprisoned and beaten, and streams of water from fire hoses turned upon their street meetings. I escaped arrest, but the fight released much of the energy damned up within me. Of the deeper issues at stake, I knew little. For I was always a person who felt and acted first and thought afterward.

It was in this struggle that I felt the touch of a policeman for the first time. Before me in a small group, two policemen walked deliberately pushing against a working man who walked peacefully with his hands in his pockets. One of the policemen shoved him until he was hurled against the other policeman; the second policeman then grasped him by the collar and, shouting that he was attacking an officer of the law, knocked him to the pavement.

"That's a lie!" I screamed, horrified, thinking they

would listen to me. "That policeman shoved him. . . . I saw him . . . the man had his hands in his pockets."

The policemen were already upon the man. Blow after blow they beat into his upturned face, and in horror I saw the blood spurt from his eyes. Crowds of working men closed in and I with them. With a spring I was on the back of one of the policemen, tearing at him. There were shouts and running feet. Around the corner came a squad of policemen, running. A blue, ape-like arm encircled me from the back and I was flung through the air. The arm hurled me fully ten feet into the street, but a button from a policeman's coat was clutched between my fingers. Two working men picked me up and ran. From the hall of a printing press we watched the policemen clear the streets with their clubs, haul blinded and bleeding working men to their feet and drag them off to the police station—for "attacking officers of the law"!

Beatrice, my sister, came, as I had come before her, out of the wilderness. I had finished the school and was working as a teacher. With my first month's salary I had sent for Beatrice. When she came I saw that she was more of the mountains and deserts than I had ever been—not of their grandeur, not of their majesty that can lift one to heights greater than they, but of their rugged, forbidding life that ruins the body and spirit. Her eyes had to be treated and fitted with glasses, her teeth worked upon for months, her spine treated for an old injury.

It had been over four years since I had seen her, and

now she came, a woman and a stranger, silent, suspicious, hostile, her skin as brown as the earth she had lived on. A tall dark girl with black hair stretched back severely from a beautiful forehead, lips that were made for laughter instead of the pain she had known; and beautiful eyes that carried in their dark depths so much of our mother lying in her desolate grave.

Beatrice resented my more cultivated speech as an attempt to "show off," for I had tried to correct my accent and dialect. Her resentment expressed itself in a scornful silence. When she undressed I saw big brown muscular arms, a back welted with muscles that glided under the skin. She removed her stockings and I gazed in astonishment. Years before, when she was a long, thin-legged little girl in short dresses, Big Buck had once remarked in his most solemn manner:

"Bee, you ought to be a very good singer when you grow up."

"Why?" she had asked, expecting flattery.

"Because you've got legs like a nightingale," he had replied.

But the legs were no longer those of a nightingale. They were brown and scarred from hip to ankle. Down one side the flesh had been torn away. Black skin alone hid the bone. She had once been riding a horse, she told me, and it had thrown her into a barbed wire fence which had torn the flesh from her leg. Blood-poison had set in and they—away out on that ranch where there is much majesty but no doctors—had cut it out themselves and then cauterized it! Her entire body was welted and scarred. Her hands were scarred and rough from heavy work—washing shirts and overalls. She had always been tired. She only wanted to forget ranch life.

Knut left his work and came over to see us. He and Beatrice had looked each other up and down critically. He reached over and lightly dented in her arm with his finger, asking: "Do you suppose you are as strong as you look?" With a quick movement she caught his hand and they had measured her strength once and for all. In a few moments he was lying full length on the floor and she was sitting on his stomach giving him friendly advice:

"Never try to set on a band wagon if you can't toot a horn," she was advising.

When I mentioned the advisability of study to Beatrice, she glanced at me forbiddingly. She had no intention of studying. If she became lonely, I suggested, there was a workshop across the way where the men and a few girls from the school made furniture and musical instruments. Her lips curled in scorn . . . musical instruments! . . . but she glanced covertly across the road.

She became restless as the days passed. Were there no horses in this joint, she asked? Yes, there were horses, but they cost money to hire. Then, knowing her, for I knew myself, I said:

"Bee, I receive a monthly salary. At the end of each month you and I will divide it exactly in half. We each pay half of our living expenses and do with the rest what we wish. Then you can ride all the horses in town to death if you want; or you can use the money and go back to the ranch—just as you wish."

When we divided our first money, I waited with

interest. But she did not spend her share on horses nor did she buy a ticket to leave. One day she wandered over to the school workshop and looked about. The machinery and tools she examined or twirled about.

"That is a plane," the teacher explained to her.

"Oh, is it now," she scornfully retorted. "I was brought up on a plane!"

He attempted to explain nothing further to her.

She tested the Mexican mahogany wood on which the students worked, and contemptuously watched them as they sawed or hammered. That was no way to handle tools!

Then she began to work. "I think I'll just take a shot at a few things over there," she informed me. She began making furniture for a little bungalow we rented. She made tables and bookcases and chairs and coat-hangers and footstools. Her long brown arms sawed and planed and sandpapered and varnished. She hammered as she thought a person not afraid of a tool should hammer— not female-like! Her hammering gave much satisfaction to herself and it did not matter in the least if the ears of others were too delicate for it.

One day she enrolled in a class in English, and then said she "guessed she'd just take a little mathematics and geometry to help her in her wood-work." A little later still she "guessed she'd just take a fling of literature and history and perhaps learn to weave baskets and do some modeling." At the end of a few months she said: "Looky here! I guess I'll just take a run and jump at the whole darned sheebang!"

She learned to love the school and the teachers.

Through the months she developed into an elegant girl student clad in white sports costumes. But she retained the attitude that ability and worth could, in the final test, be decided by physical strength; and when challenged, she often offered to settle disputes or moot questions "on a chamois skin, with one hand tied behind her."

Still she and I remained strangers . . . the years had done that, and nature. She disliked me as a person. To her, my associates had "no class." Nothing could induce her to set her foot in a Socialist hall. And much later, when War convulsed the world, she saw in it a splendid pageant of military music, handsome young men who could "whip the world with one hand tied behind them," and her regret was that women could not help "clean up."

Beatrice had been with me for one year when the University of California opened its doors to me as a student. The term would be brief and precious—three short summer months. Knut wrote that he was joining us within a few days. In the summer Bee and I passed through the great iron gates and stood upon the university campus. It was like opening the pages of a fairy-tale. So many years and so much pain! I was obsessed with a feeling that it was all a dream. I, a student in a university!

At last the card that enrolled me as a student lay in my hand. Beatrice was admitted as a special student. We left the registration hall and hurried through the crowd of men and women, and a weak impulse to cry almost overcame me. We made our way through the pine forest up to the Greek Theater, deserted and brooding. Above, the pines sighed as if troubled. But they could not be more troubled than I. It was the thought of George that troubled me . . . perhaps I could make enough money the next year to bring him. Of what Beatrice thought I do not know—her silence always covered a depth of feeling that I suspected, but of the nature of which I knew nothing.

As the weeks passed we both worked with unabating intensity, and I often caught glimpses of her dark head as she hurried along campus paths. Time seemed to be at our heels, but new energy welled up and drove me onward and forward. Knut came and joined us, sharing our common flat. Freed from the suppressed atmosphere of the school where I had taught, freed from heavy work, my mind became crystal-clear and strong and I felt as if borne forward on wings of light.

Still, even in that pleasant, sympathetic atmosphere, I could not avoid conflict. There was the dread of having children that hovered, like a bird of prey, over my head. And there was the tendency to rebellion that could not be lulled to sleep. It began one day in a class in anthropology when a student denied that there are no scientific proofs of the inferiority of the Negro. Men of color were by nature inferior, he said—all you have to do was to look at them to know it! Behind him was the face of a thin, dark man from India; a Negro girl was not far from me, and there was an American Indian in the back of the hall. I arose and challenged the student to prove his statement.

215

The Professor found such conflicts amusing and interesting, and he listened without interruption.

"Would you marry a Negro?" the student demanded.

"I'd rather marry some Negroes than some white men I know!" was my pointed reply.

"Here! Here!" the Professor exclaimed, "let us discuss this scientifically!"

Knut and the student continued the discussion outside, Knut politely, the student dogmatically, his mind long since petrified. I flung along the campus feeling as if I could tear the trees from the earth by their roots. Then I went home and wrote my first essay on Asia—an essay on the contribution the Chinese made to civilization when the white race was savage!

My university work had been going so magnificently ... when again a nausea began to overcome me each morning. The shadow of dark wings came oftener and oftener across my mind. It seemed so deeply unjust that a woman alone has to bear this burden; that men go free and happy through it all.

I cast about for some way out. Perhaps, I suggested to Knut, I could be operated upon so that I could never have a child. He opposed it ... it affected the mind, he said. To me that seemed better than having to struggle and fear like this. No doctor would help—it was illegal, they said. I lost weight and my studies became a burden. I began to say harsh things to Knut—as if he were more responsible than I! He, so pale and miserable!

We learned of a doctor whose trade was secret operations. Knut feared, but in desperation we went.

The house stood on a broad, respectable street in San Francisco where such men ply their practice and make fortunes. We waited for two hours in a reception room filled with other women,—respectable women, young and middle-aged, wives and mothers. Well-dressed women—only women with money could afford such an operation. About every fifteen minutes one would be called. The door was always opening and closing and others were coming in or going out. My heart was sick and I clung close to Knut.

Then my turn came. We were ushered into a back room.

Knut carried me to the taxi. "Walk!" the nurse commanded angrily, "or people will suspect this house!" But I could not walk. We drove to the ferry and there I made a superhuman effort and walked. On the other side we could find no taxi, and had to take a street-car. I climbed up the steps, not knowing just how much longer I could endure the pain. The cold perspiration poured from my forehead. I lay down on a seat and reached for Knut's hand.

"Sit up! People are looking at you—do you want to make a scene in public?" His voice was harsh and angry.

The shock sent me upright. I closed my eyes and rested my head against the window. Knut was angry. He was a cultured man and could not endure "scenes in public."

"Sit up!" ran through my head and mingled with the pain. "Sit up . . . sit up . . ." how rhythmically it beat! Then I climbed the endless flight of stairs to our apartment and flung myself on the bed . . . "sit up . . .

sit up . . ." coursed through my hot brain, keeping time with the blood beats.

Knut became tender again. But I turned my head to the wall. I did not need his kindness now. Not after he had ordered me to sit up like that.

That was the end. I, who had been so cruel to him, could not forget the one cruel thing he did to me. It had been as the command of a husband to a wife—and I would be owned or ordered about by no man. That he was excited at the time, made no difference.

When I returned to my school, Knut remained in the University. By friendly letters we agreed to a divorce. It was better, I said, in case he ever wished to marry again, that the responsibility fall on me. There was no one whom I could hurt, and I would never marry again.

"I take the blame," my letter continued, "and I *am* to blame. I do not want to be married; marriage is too terrible and I should never have entered it. I was wrong—for you loved me and I do not know what love means. I want my name back, also."

So he brought proceedings against me for desertion, objecting as he did it, for he loved me. I returned to him the presents of silver that had been a gift of his family to us. Two weeks passed and I received the gentlest of all letters from him. It read:

"We are now divorced and you are again Marie Rogers. As I sit here with these red and gold autumn leaves falling about me, I am very sad. I have loved you dearly. You were the first love in my life and I think you will perhaps be the last. Our marriage has been a failure, some way or other such a useless failure. There were always things between us that I did not understand. Perhaps I was too ignorant. Now perhaps we can be friends, and at all times I shall be ready to help you. If you are in need, let me know and I shall help you."

I did not like to read the letter. I glanced over it quickly, that it might not awaken something in my heart, that I might not wish for love. For love is an enemy of woman. . . . I knew what it meant—the end of everything if I went on, the end of the education of Beatrice, of George. No! I would not listen!

Then my mind that worked so tyranically over my spirit began to draw that veil of suppression and forgetfulness down over the desire for love and the need for tenderness between man and woman. Somewhere there was loneliness, uncertainty, sadness. Yet I tossed my head—such things are for the weak. I was a free person again, my name was Marie Rogers, the world was my home and the wind my companion.

A Hindu came to our school to lecture about his country. Two men of English birth were on the Board of Trustees and when they heard of the proposed lecture, they objected. Why, I wondered, and learned for the first time that India was under British rule. The Indian would be permitted to lecture provided his ideas were first presented to the Faculty and the Board of Trustees, and found satisfactory.

The Indian came—a tall, dark, elderly man with a thin face and earnest eyes. He passed me as I stood on the steps of the main entrance. Something about him made me feel very sad. Perhaps it was that he was a man of color in a land that judges men by color. Or that he belonged to the subjected, and was being humiliated.

An hour later the doors of the Conference room swung open again. A young teacher and one of the English trustees came out, engaged in heated argument.

"The man is a seditionist!" the trustee was exclaiming angrily, his face red with excitement.

"He is only speaking for the freedom of his country," the young teacher replied. "We do the same for ours . . . in fact we fight for it and call ourselves patriots!"

"He is a traitor! A traitor!"

"A traitor!" the teacher asked in surprise. "A traitor to whom? To the British—but not to his own people!"

So! The Indian had spoken for the freedom of his country! then he must be right. The doors swung open again and he walked out, alone. No one accompanied him as they did other speakers; no one shook hands with him—for the trustees held power over the teachers. His face was set in a peculiar expression, and again I felt very sad. He passed me and descended the steps. Like a shadow I followed . . . if I spoke he might misunderstand . . . yet we were at the foot of the steps and he would be gone in a second. Quickly I stepped to his side.

"They wouldn't let me in to hear your lecture, but I heard a teacher say you spoke for the freedom of your country. I am sorry I could not hear."

When he looked at me I saw that I was, in his eyes, only one of my countrymen—a strange American girl saying rather stupid things. He replied briefly, formally, but his voice struck me by its wistfulness.

"Give me your name and address and I will send you something to read if you are interested."

I wrote down my name and address just as steps descended the stairs and reached my side. I turned and saw the English trustee. He glanced at us both, at the address book in which I was writing, and passed without even a greeting.

The President of the school was very definite and dignified. "You understand, of course," he was saying, "that you cannot stay in this school any longer. Your ideas, your attitude, your actions, are not suitable for the young men and women here. You must look for another position—the sooner the better for us!"

The Dean of Women stood by, trying to be as stern as her innate gentleness would permit. She also was definite. "Permit me to say that for the sake of your sister it is best that you go to another place . . . do not feel badly, but . . . you are a bad influence on her."

I learned that there were many things wrong with me. They had learned that I was a Socialist; that I was seen with men in the city; that I permitted other girls in the school to read books that were not proper—Ellen Key's "Love and Marriage" and such things, they said.

"My dear," the Dean of Women pleaded, "don't you know that if you really study the Socialist movement you will find that they believe in . . . in . . . free love?"

"They may believe it, but the Republicans and Democrats practice it!"—I had learned quick answers downtown!

"Enough!" interrupted the President, who was a Republican.

I went away and wept in blind abandon. What was

wrong with me I did not know. A bad influence on the sister I loved! Yet even Bee condemned me, condemned me by her silence. Perhaps it did not matter! Perhaps somewhere else . . . just beyond . . . it would be better.

Slowly the train drew up to the station platform in Denver and I descended. Helen came toward me, a slender figure in a black fur coat and fur hat. I kissed the painted cheeks and heard her birdlike laugh and teasing voice. Back of her stood another woman, watching. I stared in astonishment, for the woman might have been myself; my face, my eyes, mouth and skin, and beneath a fur hat, my hair . . . and just my height! She moved forward . . . and she walked as I walked! It was as if another Me had arisen from the platform; with but one exception—the woman was handsomely dressed, and her cheeks and lips were painted.

It had been nearly fifteen years since I had seen my cousin-aunt, Mildred, just my age, and then she was a bad, spoiled little girl. We now gazed at each other curiously, and seemed to like each other no better than we had in our childhood. Her voice was husky. Something about her made me feel apologetic. Her chin tilted itself a bit defiantly.

We reached the house where they lived. Helen had put up an extra couch in her room for me. It was a room hung with sentimental pictures, of men and women in affectionate poses, of angels with wings. Carved wood pieces hung against the wall, carved and painted boxes rested on her dressing table . . . hand-carved, some imperfectly done, but some fine and intricate.

222

"I made them," Helen's voice behind me remarked, with a shade of timidity in it, when she saw me examining the wood.

"You!"

"Yes. I've learned from a carpenter. When I'm lonely it's something to pass the time! I bought this chair and carved it . . . and the bedstead I done too!"

I ran my fingers over the carved designs and patterns on the chair and bed. Then I turned and watched her, she so much older than when I had last seen her, the wrinkles showing in her forehead and about the eyes and mouth, the paint painfully obvious. There was a birdlike timidity about her as she drew out other pieces of carved wood from a box beneath the window.

"You see, that's not so good!" she said.

"But I think it's wonderful! . . . why, it's as nice as anything Bee has done, except that you do fine work and she does big sweeping things."

Her face flushed naturally now. "Yes, I thought it was nice myself, but I didn't think you'd like it!"

"What else have you done?"

"Here's something . . . it's not very nice."

"But it is! Why do you say such things!"

"I'm not working today because you were coming," she was telling me, and in her manner was an echo of the pride she had felt years before when she had mastered the shirt-machine in the laundry. She was explaining: "I work in a factory with about a hundred other girls,"—she still spoke of herself as a girl—"making pennants for colleges. Mildred and I both work there. Some of the girls here in the house work there."

In the afternoon she took me to see the factory.

Rows of girls sat at sewing machines making felt pennants to decorate the rooms of college and university students. Helen earned the highest salary—seven dollars a week. Then we returned to that house where the "girls" lived. I began to understand. Helen was growing old and men like younger women. With the factory she was able to pull along without touching her small bank account. For there would come a time when she could find no "friends" at all.

Mildred was younger and more successful. Unscrupulous, and spending all she earned on clothing. Men were sources of money to her—nothing else. Some of the girls down the hall were like Helen—older women with an uncertain future. Some were rough and coarse, like Mildred, knowing that life was a beast of a thing and that they must grab while they had a chance.

I was with Helen for many days, but no man came to see her during that time. It was perhaps because she had taken a vacation in my honor. One night she and I lay awake for hours, she on her bed on one side of the room and I on the couch on the other. As on former nights, the outside door opened and closed for hours; steps climbed the stairs, halted on our corridor, or went further up. Men's voices sounded here and there, and sometimes the laughter of women. Heavy feet descended the stairs and the outside door opened and shut again . . . the respectable men of the city were going home to their wives and daughters and sisters and mothers.

Helen and I talked across the darkness as we lay there.

"I couldn't stand this life, Helen," I said, "and I don't see how you can."

"Beggars can't be choosers." Then she added. "Tell me what I can do."

I had nothing to tell her.

After a time she asked again: "Why are you going to New York?"

"I'm going to get work to support myself and Bee, and then I'm going to try and study in a university. I've a friend who lives there and she says I can work in the daytime and go to the university at night."

"To a . . . college? . . . You've not finished studying yet?"

"No. I want to study a lot of things—history, literature, economics, and I want to learn to write."

"But I thought you'd finished your education and knew all those things."

"No. There's always a lot more to learn. Every time you read a new book you find that you know less and less."

She was silent for a time. "I guess no one can read all the books in the world, can they? But I suppose it's nice to know a lot as you will." Her voice continued: "I suppose you'll make a lot of money."

"I don't know—I guess not much. I don't seem to know how to make much money."

"Then what's the use of gettin' more educated?"

"Because I like to learn more things."

A silence fell between us again. We both lay staring into the darkness. Then her voice came over the room.

"You've been . . . married . . . only once?"

225

"Yes."

"Why didn't you marry a rich man? . . . you've got an education."

I thought this over. "I didn't know any rich man. And I don't know if I could have married one had I known him. I am sorry I got married at all. I don't want to have anything to do with men any more . . . if they are rich or poor it is all the same to me."

She listened, then timidly, as if not wanting to hurt my feelings: "But if you get *very* educated, Marie, you might marry a rich man. What's the use of saving yourself? You'll be getting old some day."

"I'm not saving myself, Helen! Anyway, not for any man. If I'm ever rich, it will be money I've made myself."

Then I was ashamed . . . over there she lay and she might think I was passing judgment on her. She, so gentle and kind, she who had sent me to school for six months. The room was heavy with darkness, and outside the city hummed. "I didn't mean to say that, Helen . . . but I think that if I learn a lot I can make a lot of money of my own."

"Yes, that would be nice."

I turned restlessly. It was awful . . . the night punctuated by slamming doors and passing feet. Outside the city settling down to a listening silence. I felt miserable before the awfulness of this brief existence. Such useless pain . . . so useless . . . so useless.

Helen's voice interrupted my meditations. She was speaking confidentially: "You see, I'm learning something new, too. The factory wears me out . . . I'm not as strong as I used to be. So I'm learning to shake dice . . . it takes a lot of time to know how to, real nice. Then I'm going to get work in a cigar store . . . you know how men come in and shake for cigars? Well, if I can get a good job there it won't be such hard work, and then you meet nice men there."

I covered my head with the blanket and when the faint sound of her voice died away I uncovered it again and lay staring through the window, watching the stars that twinkled far up in the vaulted heavens . . . nothing seemed good or bad . . . everything just was . . . all was an experience to be endured. I fell into a heavy slumber. Helen hovered through my dreams—a large indistinct figure, surrounded by a light more brilliant than anything I had ever seen. I awoke, but the feeling of the dream remained for hours, and I lay staring at the stars that never changed their course.

When I left Denver, that puritanical city, for New York, Helen accompanied me to the train. There were tears in her eyes when she kissed my cheeks; on her face was an entreaty . . . there was something she was unable to express. A depression hung over me . . . it seemed a betrayal to go away and leave her. There was nothing I could do if I remained . . . still it was almost like leaving my own mother. What else could I do but go . . . there was Beatrice; there was George, and time was at my heels. Helen . . . there seemed nothing I could do until later . . . then she would be an old woman.

A thought flashed through my mind. I would not go on directly to New York, but would take a southern route to see Robert Hampton, a man whom I had never seen. It was this man who, for years, had sent me his old high school books and made it possible for me to study and later to pass examinations and enter schools. His letters had encouraged me to study, his photograph had hung over my study-table for years, and his old books were still my treasures.

It had been over two years since I had heard from him. A few years before his letters had become irregular, uninteresting and even dull. His father's death had forced him from high school into work in a little town in the South. His salary, I had learned, was used to support his mother and unmarried sister. But what his work was I did not know—perhaps something of importance.

In my mind he was still the distant hero,—surely the tall, dark man who smiled grimly, if at all, as all heroes smile,—a learned man, silent and stern before chattering frivolity. A man who, when he saw me, would gaze down from his noble heights and, without speaking, wait for me to speak! So stern, so wise, and yet condescending to sit in my presence, understand my tongue-tied silence or listen to my flustered speech!

When I had married Knut, something told me that I had betrayed this man.

It seemed presumptuous of me to send a telegram to that little southern town and wait in Chicago for an answer. But when the reply came my suitcase was packed and I was ready to start. It was nine o'clock at night when the train rolled up to the little station platform. A few travelers made ready to descend. I waited until everyone had gone first but even then I hesitated, trying to compose myself. Then slowly I descended the steps and stood looking about. No one was in sight . . . no one except a little man at a distance, a little man with a black derby hat and a long-sleeved coat that looked as if it might slide off his sloping shoulders any minute. Robert Hampton had not met the train . . . and yet what could I expect! Perhaps he was a very busy man. It was a relief after all.

The little man now standing at a distance watched me as men watch women who descend at small railway stations at night. He was smirking. I picked up my suitcase to fling past him, noticing that a button on his old black coat was hanging from a thread and twirling in the wind. There were two big dusty grease spots on the coat, cast in vivid relief under the gas light. He stepped forward as I brushed past . . . perhaps to take my suitcase; but I walked hurriedly by as if I had not seen him. Then his voice called after me:

"Marie Rogers!"

I turned and stared . . . he came up and I looked down into his face shining under the light. The top of his head just reached my shoulder. The derby was big and rested on his ears. He removed it with a gallant gesture.

"Why, Marie! Don't you know me? I would have known you any place, for you look just like your picture . . . taller . . . but that don't matter to me! Didn't you know me?" he beamed up into my face, proud of the surprise he had given me.

"Yes-s-s . . . I thought I knew you!"

"Now come and I will find a good hotel for you . . . How long are you going to stay?"

"I am not going to stay. . . . I must be in New York as soon as possible. I will take the next train . . . Is there a check-room here?"

He was miserably disappointed when the ticket agent told us that the next train left just after midnight. He was saying that he would take me to a restaurant. We tramped through the slush, I shortening my steps to keep pace with him. His derby rubbed against my shoulder now and then as he chattered enthusiastically in a thin, eager voice. He would take me to a good restaurant where he ate each day. I was glad . . . perhaps tables laid with white linen and silver and crystal—where had I seen such a table? Oh, yes, in that cheap little magazine in which I had found his name and address years before; there were square-jawed, handsome men in black evening suits, women in deep *décolleté*. Perhaps we could go to a place where we could talk . . . he might be very learned after all. Why should I feel badly because he only reached to my shoulder and his voice was high and thin—one cannot judge men by that. Napoleon was not a big man!

We turned down a little street. He led the way into a lunch room with chairs standing in rows against the wall. In the center of the room was a large, round, high, marble-topped table, and men were standing about it eating. We passed down the center of the blue and white tiled floor to a long table of food. Robert took a tray and asked me to do the same. We walked along and selected the food we wished. . . . I wanted nothing and was still so dazed that he himself felt it necessary to fill my tray. He protested:

"Now you just eat! I've invited you and *I'm* going to pay!"

His voice was proud as he said that. We sat down and rested our trays across the big arms of our chairs. All the other men in the place kept their hats on while they ate, but Robert removed his in my honor. I do not remember what we talked about. His thin voice ran on and on. Sometimes it seemed suspicious of my silence . . . suspicious and hurt, and then I insisted that I was indeed interested but that I was tired.

"Tell me something about your life," I requested, to support my statement.

He lived in the Y.M.C.A., high up on the top floor in the back, he said. It was nice and cheap there and the fellows treated you right. He had been in this town since his father died, keeping books in a big grocery concern and the owner said he didn't know what he would do without him, for when the other clerks failed to do a thing right, *he* was called and he did it . . . just like that! He snapped his fingers to show me how quick. No, there were no theaters in the town, but he didn't know if he approved of theaters anyway; there were church socials in the basement of the Presbyterian Church twice a month. The women were nice and the older ones liked him—they knew the right sort when they met one! Yes, he read a lot—the *Saturday Evening Post*, a good, clean magazine with no nonsense in it, and good live stories. Did I ever read any of those stories? . . . Did I know how much one advertisement in the *Post* costs? Did I know how many million circulation it had? No! I saw that he was proud to be a reader of a magazine with such a circulation and with such expensive advertisements.

He asked me questions. His voice was plaintive when he heard I was not a Christian. Why should I be a Christian? Why, he had never heard such a question in his life! It tore his heart out that I did not pray.

"Pray—what for?" I asked. "Could prayer have saved my mother or my brother, or prevented my father from drinking, or saved my aunt from prostitution?"

He turned his head away—I had mentioned prostitution—and in connection with my aunt!

"Pray!" I continued. "Why should I pray? To get rest for myself? Why should I have rest? Why should the world have rest? Why should *you* have rest? I am not interested in rest today—not until things are different!"

"Prayer and belief in God would make them different."

"People have prayed and believed in God always—and see where we are!"

"I hope you don't believe in Socialism, Marie. You talk so hard."

"I am a Socialist—or was. Now I'm thinking of joining the I.W.W. I met some men in Chicago who are members and I met some in California before that. They told me what they believe."

"Did they tell you they are bums, too? They are! I.W.W. means 'I Won't Work.' I'll bet they didn't tell you that!"

"Well, if it means that, why don't rich men belong to it?—they don't work."

He turned his head away, as he spoke:

"Socialism and the I.W.W. would destroy the home and the purity of women."

"Well, it didn't destroy our home, nor the 'purity' of my aunt. Yet they were destroyed. Now you tell me who did that!"

I continued talking to the back of his head: "What is purity, anyway, I'd like to know! It means you don't live with a man. Then are all the married women impure? . . . This I'll tell you—I'm not going to let any man judge whether I'm pure or not! Your kind of purity doesn't mean anything."

"Do you mean you wish you were not pure?" he began, turning to me miserably.

"I mean I won't let any man judge me by my body!"

There was silence between us. "I thought you'd be different," he began, after a time.

"There's plenty of girls that are different."

I felt sorry, for his face was so miserable.

"I'm sorry," I began awkwardly. "You maybe like to pray—but I don't. It would not help me in anything."

He saw I had changed. "I could explain to you," he began. "I could really explain if you stayed a day or two. We could walk along a river near here, under the trees, and talk; I've thought it all out—just walk along arm in arm and talk. I think a lot, but I've got nobody here to talk to. I thought too that you'd be—well different . . . you understand I'm not saying anything against you. . . ."

It was past midnight and he had not ceased talking. His hope lay in Christianity. It was indeed too short a time in which to save a soul, but he did his best with me. He still talked as we stood waiting on the station platform for the train. He lifted my suitcase up the steps and I turned to say good-by.

"Marie . . . you will be studying in a university maybe. Would you remember to send me your old books when you've finished with them? I could read and keep up with things . . . down here a fellow gets stuck in the mud. It wouldn't cost anything if you'd send them after you don't want them any more."

I stumbled up the steps as the train rolled away. My old books! I looked back. He was standing under the gas light and his shabby coat seemed ready to slide off his shoulders. A loose button hung by a thread, and when the wind caught it, it twirled and twirled.

New York was a new and strange world. Vast, impersonal, merciless. I felt its mercilessness from the night Karin met me at the Grand Central Station and took me by taxi along Park Avenue. The night lights glinted on the pavement as on a mirror. I stared out at the pavement and at the stone buildings rising from the streets on either side, without even a touch of green to soften them. What sort of people lived in them, I wondered, where things seemed so gray and cold—were they like the buildings they created? I felt lonely and little and very weak. This feeling remained with me through the months that followed. Always before I had felt like a person, an individual, hopeful that I could mold my life according to some desire of my own. But here in New York I was ignorant, insignificant, unimportant—one in millions whose destiny concerned no one.

New York did not even know of my existence. Nor did it care.

I had to find work at once, for my sister was dependent upon me, and I had to make my own living. At Karin's suggestion I searched the "Want Ads." of the newspapers and magazines and at last found that *The Graphic Magazine* needed two stenographers. The next day I applied for one of the positions, and after an examination, was employed. In the mornings I took dictation from the Book Review Editor, and during the afternoons typed, sitting in a room with many other girls. The Book Review Editor was an Englishman who had but recently come to America. He was a liberal and a patriotic Englishman who considered himself destined to destroy the impression that America was a "melting pot." The English, it seems, melted with nobody or nothing at any time. He was a missionary for everything English and he was a ceaseless advocate of America's entry into the World War. In him was an antagonism against American things, and he always made me feel on the defensive—as if I had committed some wrong by having been born American. A defensive hostility against him developed in me, but out of fear of losing my position I remained silent. I hoped to be transferred to one of the other editors, most of whom seemed very friendly, kindly and liberal-minded men. Perhaps it was because of my need of coming closer to people, to still my loneliness, that I felt closer to them. Their friendly greetings, their occasional conversations with me when we met in the halls, their interest, however passing, in my life and thoughts, made my work tolerable.

I had been on the magazine for a number of weeks when I summoned up enough courage to request the Book Review Editor for permission to review a book myself. I saw many books passing through his hands to others. The book I asked to review dealt with the American Indian. It was small and not of great importance, and because of this the editor finally agreed to let me try. I read and re-read the book, then wrote to the Secretary of an association of American Indians, about whose work I had read, telling him what I thought of it and asking him if I was right in opposing it. His reply supported me, and he gave me much information against the Indian Bureau in Washington, sending me also the magazines of his association. I read the magazines and incorporated his views and my new knowledge in the review. Then I gave it to the editor. He was opposed to it from the first, for he was one of those liberals who instinctively support an institution or a thing just because it exists, perhaps desiring to patch it up here and there. He challenged my statements, and only when I had shown the letter and magazines I had used, was he willing to publish what I had written—but with sweeping deletions.

This incident deepened my antagonism. Later I hesitatingly suggested that he have someone review two new books that had come, one the history of the nationalist movement in India, one an economic study showing what England had gained from India in wealth during the past two centuries. He refused with devastating finality, saying:

"The titles alone are sufficient to show that they are of no value and deserve no mention."

"I live with a friend who is a teacher in the high schools, and she says they are very valuable," I argued.

"The titles alone show that they are not scientific," he replied coldly.

"Scientific . . . *what* is scientific?" I protested. "You have not even looked at the books. You get books with all kinds of strange titles."

He turned his swivel chair until his back was to me, and said: "Please have my letters here by four this afternoon."

I went back to my room where dozens of stenographers did their work without question, without presuming to think that they knew what a magazine should contain. For a long time I sat at my desk, humiliated and resentful, hating my work, hating the necessity of spending my days taking down the thoughts of such a man when I wished to learn to have and express thoughts of my own. I glanced about at the girls working in the din of typewriters—efficient, seemingly contented girls earning their twenty to twenty-five dollars a week as I was doing, year in and year out taking down the thoughts of men and then typing them on pages. Why could I not be happy and contented with such an existence—why did I resent girls who accepted it—why did I wish the Book Review Editor would suddenly fall dead in his office?

From my work I went to Karin's apartment on Washington Square, where I slept on a couch in her large, studio-like living room. There was a grand piano in the room and on it was often a low bowl of yellow flowers. Frequently they were narcissus blossoms—Karin was like a narcissus herself, tall, golden, her head slightly bent. She was delicate and ethereal. She was like her house—the grand piano, the bowl of blossoms, the plain dark blue carpet, the delicate water-colors in narrow frames. I felt the beauty that belonged to her and her home, but it was not a part of me. It was years before I could understand or appreciate such beauty. I could not appreciate paintings that seemed to have no meaning. A picture that showed a man or woman actively doing something, I could understand. So it was with literature or music: folk songs told a story, but classical music, such as Karin played in the evenings, was beyond my comprehension. From her I learned that there had been European composers named Chopin, Beethoven, Mozart and others. She often played their compositions that I might learn the difference. They all sounded alike to me. She often played one composition of Chopin and I gradually came to recognize it and to love it. As with music, so with literature: I read for the story, knowing nothing of style, of form or of authors. Poetry had always been foreign to me, for I could not understand why people did not write as they spoke, naturally, and not in verse. Karin had books of verse and, sometimes, standing near her piano on which some of them lay, she read from them. I simply could not appreciate them. Only if they told a story of endeavor, of struggle, could I understand their purpose.

It was in this world of good taste, and often of abstract thought and beauty, that I went when my office closed at five o'clock. Yet it contained more than abstraction. Karin was not only a teacher interested in modern education; she was also a Socialist. There were many people who climbed the long flights of stairs to her apartment in the evenings. They lay on the broad couch, sat on the floor about the room or occupied the chairs, as pleased their fancy, smoking and discussing the life of New York City: the theater, Socialism, Anarchism, art, new writers, love, psychoanalysis, philosophy, death. They seemed to be searching out social themes in the life about them. Very many of them spoke of grave things in that light manner that is American, apparently never permitting their feelings to be too deeply touched. They skimmed the surface only—perhaps too wise to be drawn beyond their depths, for it is so easy to be drawn beyond your depth in New York City.

I do not know if they were superficial,—or if they were wise. In any case, they and their ways were strange to me. Their quick, humorous repartee left me silent—wondering how they could think of clever things so quickly. Sometimes they smiled or laughed when I spoke. Once I said a certain man I had met was a "statiktician"—so I pronounced it. One of them protested to those who laughed: "Do not laugh—there are so few delightful things left in life." Only when they were gone did Karin tell me how to pronounce the word—but the laughter had left a bitter feeling in my heart. With these people day by day I learned that the purely formal, purely dry knowledge I had gained in schools was of little value and even seemed out of place here. These people did not repeat what they read in books—they expressed the life about them, and they used books critically, skeptically, comparatively.

Karin sometimes took me with her to the Socialist Local to which so many of the intellectuals belonged, and I sat in beaten wonderment and confusion amongst them. When I was introduced to them they automatically extended a hand, but their eyes were on someone else and they were speaking to others. I might have been one of the chairs they were gripping in passing. I came and went in their meetings, hoping to learn something, and I made no more impression upon them and their world than a stone makes when thrown into a lake. They left in me a feeling of confusion, of impotence, of humility, and even of resentment. I did not know how to learn the things they knew, and they had no time or interest to tell me how. They had read much and did not know how simply a person must begin. I did not know what to read to learn the fundamentals of social science; even if I went to the Public Library I did not know what book to ask for. Many of them belonged to those interesting and charming intellectuals who idealize the workers, from afar, believing that within the working class lies buried some magic force and knowledge which, at the critical moment, will manifest itself in the form of a social revolution and transform the face of the world. Those who really talked with me tried to discourage me from studying in the university, saying life and experience was of more value than books. Some found my naiveté interesting and did not wish to see it disturbed. I was indeed naive and I had no complexes. When some one of Karin's friends proposed: "Well, let's go to that anti-war mass meeting in Madison Square Garden," and others agreed, I arose at once to go, not realizing that it would be an hour before they finally reached the point of moving, sitting in the meantime and humorously discussing their inability to overcome their complexes against moving. The sign that you were one of them seemed to be some psychological complex, and it was taken for granted that I would eventually achieve one myself. In the meantime I was raw and green, awkward and ignorant, unclear and resentful, saying "statiktician" instead of "statistician," and acting at once on any suggestion.

I recall that I met a member of the I.W.W. in a book store about this time, and that we talked. He was a seaman and was dressed like a workingman. He had red hair and blue eyes. We went to the moving pictures together and then ate dinner in Childs Restaurant afterward, sitting across from each other at a white marble table, and talking until long past midnight. He knew a lot and he had been in many foreign countries. He did not talk about the working class as if it were some far and distant wonder. He was a part of it and he spoke with scorn of the intellectuals with whom I was now associating. I called him Red and he called me Marie, and we felt very natural and got along well together. The next evening he put on a new tie and came to spend the evening with us in Karin's apartment. There were a lot of people there and he called one of the women a cigarette-smoking, cocktail-drinking, pink-tea-parlor Socialist. It was all very interesting. I was very sorry when he went away and joined his ship and I never saw him again.

I read and re-read a letter lying before me. It was from my brother George. I could tell no one of its contents, for I feared that none of the people I lived with would understand. They idealized the working class, and I feared they might not understand the things that grow in poverty and ignorance. They would say my brother would have been justified had he stolen bread, when hungry, but he should not have stolen a horse. Even I, who loved him so dearly, felt this.

He had written the letter from jail. It was an appeal for help. He didn't explain why he had stolen a horse, nor did he say how or when; he did not try to excuse himself, nor did he express a word of regret. He merely wrote that he had stolen a horse, that he was in jail awaiting trial, and that he needed help.

His letter tortured me. I thought of when I last saw him—he was a little boy holding Dan by the hand on the station platform, his eyes filled with tears, watching me go away. I recalled the room when I had found the two of them with my father that early gray morning in Trinidad—and the gaping cracks in the floor filled with the dust of years. I recalled the cry of appeal in his letter when Dan had been beaten until the blood ran from his back. Since then I had not heard from him—and it had been years. What grew in his child heart, what developed in his young life through those years, I do not know. But life out there was hard and merciless and there was little chance of anything beautiful growing there. And so he grew up, without the tenderness of mother or sister, without education or training, in poverty, and from the moment he could use his childish hands he had labored for his bread. At what I did not know—but first surely at the unskilled work a child can do, then that a boy can do, and then all that an unskilled laborer can turn his hand to. What went on within his spirit, what sort of creature he would be when he became a man, no one knew or cared. Perhaps my father—yes, but he himself was a victim. When I think of my brother's life I think of stretching gray plains, without trees, with but rough clumps of prairie grass here and there.

He stole a horse. Why should he not have stolen a horse, I ask myself now. He needed it to make a living with. He was perhaps like me—filled with too much energy and too much resentment to tolerate without revolt the poverty and hopelessness of his existence.

All of this I realized later, and I realize it now. But with George's letter before me then I did not. It was a blow. With the shock fresh in my mind, I wrote him a letter. Could he not have waited, I wrote, until Beatrice had finished with her school, that I might have had enough money to help him; didn't he know I wanted to send him somewhere to study some trade or help him as I could; didn't he know that life was hard for me, too, and still I did not steal; didn't he wish for something else but the kind of life he lived there and couldn't he have the strength to work, or starve, as I had done—for a time longer? I wrote page after page, pouring out my misery and disappointment, self-righteously. What had I done to deserve this? As I wrote, somewhere I had the consciousness that it was all my fault, for I had deserted him and Dan. Again and again I wrote of my own bitterness, forgetting that he had troubles enough, sitting in jail awaiting trial for theft. And he but a boy.

Then I sent the letter, and enclosed in it all the money I had and all that I could borrow from Karin. But I did not tell her why.

The weeks passed and no reply came. If he received the money or the letter I did not know. I regretted the letter with each passing day—it was so self-righteous, so without understanding. As soon as Beatrice had finished studying, I thought, I would write him again, or try to go.

It was a few weeks later that I returned home one evening from work, and as I turned to hang up my coat, my eyes caught sight of a yellow folded telegram that had been pushed under the door. I paused, with my arms reaching upward, staring at it, for some way or other it seemed connected with George. Had he been convicted and sent to prison, I wondered. Or perhaps the telegram was for Karin. I dropped the coat and picked it up. It bore my name, I opened it, and read:

"George killed today. Am writing. Dan."

I read the telegram again when I reached the living room. They were only words there on the yellow pages, and words are nothing but words, I thought. They could not be true. Then gradually I realized that they were true.

The streets were deserted that night and the light glinted on them as I walked . . . without weeping, without thinking. The heavens were black. There were trees and the Hudson was dark and silent, flowing . . . the earth cold and damp against my body when I lay face downward in Riverside Park. Above on the hill—on Riverside Drive, were the mansions of the wealthy . . . they who live and sleep in peace and luxury . . . during the day they never work . . . their women do not know what work means. My mother was gentle, sweet; my father did not drink so much as the men up there . . . their sons go and study . . . my brothers hunger and die. My brother . . . so young and so miserable. We pay for those up there . . . we, such as my brothers and I. . . .

A few days later a letter arrived from Dan. I read it once and then burned it—for I could not again see his handwriting nor read the things he said. He was not schooled in the art of gentle expression and he wrote plainly. George had been killed while working as a day laborer digging a ditch—a sewer for a town in Oklahoma. The walls of the ditch had caved in and broken his neck. They dug him out and his mouth and eyes were filled with mud. They had buried him beside my mother and the Company he was working for had paid my father fifty dollars for his life.

The letter then continued: George got out of jail without trial because he was so young and the man from whom he stole the horse was induced to withdraw the charge. George then found work as a day laborer—just as he had worked before. He had received my letter, but had never forgiven me for writing it. I ought to be ashamed of myself for having written it when he was in jail, for I didn't know anything and I didn't have to work as he did; I lived in a fine city and could study and live well. George could not. None of them could out there.

Now he was dead. And the Company thought his life was worth fifty dollars.

I lay awake through the night that followed, trying to

forget, trying to force all thoughts from me. The noise of the city gradually died away. There was quietness broken only by an occasional automobile or passing footsteps on the pavement below. Once I wept, and then lay silent again, trying to forget the years that had passed, the moment I had left my brothers, the letter I had written; trying to forget the words of Dan telling how George had been killed—like a rat in a sewer . . . dragged out with his mouth and eyes stopped with mud . . . there was the little cemetery surrounded by crazy posts . . . the graves headed by little boards marked with the names of the dead . . . the gray plains . . . my brother Dan and my old father. No . . . no . . . I did not want to remember . . . I would rather that my memory were dead.

The months passed and America entered the war. I had been called upon to take part in the anti-war propaganda, and I did. But now I recall that I hardly knew why I did this. The thought of George had always been with me and I was glad for any activity that absorbed all my energy and thoughts when I was not working. But I was also opposed to war, even if I did not have the same knowledge of social science as did my friends.

The war had been going on for three years, and it was always being discussed. There was the danger of America entering it. President Wilson had been elected to his second term on the slogan that he kept the country out of war. I had heard Hughes speak against him, but I was against war. At the time I had been a Socialist, at least on paper, and had been one of the many Socialists who deserted the Party and voted for Wilson purely because of his anti-war slogan. I was too ignorant, too unclear about social forms and institutions to realize that Wilson or any other individual was but a tool of forces and organizations stronger than himself.

About me at that time—and it was in California—were small Socialist groups who knew little more than I did. We had often met in a little dark room to discuss the War and to study various problems and Socialist ideas. The room was over a pool room and led into a larger square room with a splintery floor; in the corner stood a sad-looking piano. In the little hall leading to it was a rack holding various Socialist or radical newspapers, tracts and pamphlets in very small print and on bad paper. The subjects treated were technical Marxist theories. Now and then some Party member would announce a study circle, and I would join it, along with some ten or twelve working men and women. I recall one such class. Our leader was an atheist, and for the entire first evening he talked steadily, unceasingly, on atheism, defining the word "belief," upon which religion rested, and the word "reason," upon which science rests. I listened, knowing that I must be educated on such subjects, but I never went again to the circle. It seemed to be pure desertion to stay away, but the man talked too long and repeated the same thing over and over again; and since he always did the same thing in public meetings, it was boring.

I joined another circle and leader gave us a little leaflet in very small print, asking us to read it carefully and then come prepared to ask questions. It was a technical Marxist subject, and I did not understand it nor did I know what questions to ask.

Other men, little dried-up fellows, would often waylay one and declaim on Single Tax. During one election campaign they drew me into their work and I spent all my spare time typing for them, hoping the election would soon be finished that I might have an excuse to desert with honor. But I learned considerable in the campaign, and was at least able to explain what unearned increment was.

Once or twice a month our Socialist Local would announce a dance and try to draw young workers into it. Twenty or thirty of us would gather in the square, dingy room with splintery floor. The Socialist lawyer of the city came, with his wife and daughter. They were very intelligent and kindly people upon whose shoulders most of the Socialist work in the town rested. The wife had baked a cake for the occasion and her daughter, a student, played a cornet. While the piano rattled away and the cornet blared, we circled about the room, trying to be gay. I danced with a middle-aged machinist and we said not a word during the dance. An elderly Single Taxer, who had come for the specific purpose of gaining converts for his ideas, was my second partner, talking Single Tax while we danced.

I attended a few such study circles and dances, but there was seldom enough interest or beauty in them to hold me. The leaders of the study circles did not know how to teach in a manner essential to such a subject. Beatrice attended one class only and never went again. I recall them as sad and dreary affairs.

The war in Europe was being followed by every person, yet I learned nothing that I should have known—why such a thing was possible; the nature of the present system in which wars are inevitable. And thus it was that when Wilson came with his anti-war slogan, I was ignorant enough to vote for him.

That had been in California. In New York I learned but little more. I always knew that the men who would be sent to the front as common soldiers to be blown to pieces would be working men; that only rich men would become officers. I learned from Karin and from the press that American financiers were loaning heavy sums to the Allied Powers, that American munition manufacturers were making vast fortunes, and that these powerful combines would never permit the Allies to be defeated. I once heard a man from India speak in an anti-war meeting, explaining that England was fighting Germany because Germany was her naval and commercial rival, threatening the routes to Indian and British control of the sea. I also had the typical American anti-English bias, based upon the history I had studied in the schools—of the American Revolutionary War, the War of 1812 and the Civil War. I knew nothing of Germany, but England had always been a vampire and a conquerer.

When the propaganda for America's entrance into the European slaughter became more violent, I was one of a group that went on a speaking tour against the war. I got leave from *The Graphic* to take a few days off. Our group, consisting of Pacifists, Socialists, and Anarchists, addressed meetings in many towns. Large gatherings had been arranged for us, for there was widespread feeling against the war. Working men stood outside a factory to hear us, and in one such gathering someone pushed me forward and told me to speak to them. For the first time I stood before a meeting of working men who listened quietly and with interest to what I had to tell them. I have often heard or read in novels how a man or woman suddenly faced with great responsibility rises to the occasion; how eloquently and magnificently they speak or act until the audience breaks into wild applause. It seems that their rise to fame begins from that moment. But I was not a character in a novel, and I stood on the fender of the automobile, looking with astonishment into the up-turned faces of working men. I had nothing to give them. Suddenly I realized how very ignorant, how very confused, I was. Uttering a few empty sentences, I stepped down. A few of our party scattered in the crowd applauded faintly to give me courage, but it did no good. Someone stepped up on the fender to take my place to eradicate as quickly as possible the impression I had made. The audience looked at me kindly but without interest. Afterward many of the men stood in groups talking, and they said they were against the war. I knew that their opinions were not based upon my speech.

When we passed through Princeton, where sons of the wealthy study, a mob of students dressed in sports costumes tried to storm our car. There was violent dissension among us about coming to a halt and meeting them, but the driver said that we were the ones who would be arrested and jailed for creating a riot and disturbing the peace.

"No, *they* are trying to start a riot," someone disagreed when the driver refused to stop.

"It does not matter—it is not they who will go to jail—where do you think you are, anyway?" I was deeply humiliated that we did not stop. I was against this war, but I was most decidedly not a Pacifist, and I felt that I could express my emotions very well on a gang of well-dressed Princeton college boys.

In Washington, Karin and I slept on the benches in the railway station because the city was jammed with tens of thousands of men and women from every part of the country opposing America's entrance into the war. We marched by the thousands before the capitol, and I vividly recall an incident that became a symbol to me. As we marched a tall, big-breasted woman in an elegant, tight-fitting, black riding costume elbowed her way through our lines directly before me. Her face was hard, tense and hateful, and she held her riding whip like a club in her hand. Her hate-filled eyes looked at me as she passed and I knew she wanted to bring her club down over my head. In her I saw a symbol of the ruling class that was forcing us into the war, making our laws, owning our land and industries, forcing us to work for them for the right to live on the earth. And as there was hate in her face, so was there no love in me for her as she passed.

Then came the time when the first khaki-clad troops marched down Fifth Avenue. I had watched them from the office window of *The Graphic*. The Book Review Editor had been exultant ever since the declaration of war. The sight of khaki-clad troops being shipped for slaughter in Europe filled him with happiness. I had wept in bitter misery. I was transferred from his department to another on the same day because of an open quarrel between us. It started when I told him of a wealthy woman, a friend of Karin's, whose brother had gone to the officers' training camp, and had then been exempted from military service on the ground that he had a wife and two children to support. He was a rich man.

"You'll not find one working man sitting here in New York in officer's uniform, with spurs on his heels to keep his feet from rolling off the desk," I had said. "They will all be rich men." After this I was transferred.

At that time Robert Hampton wrote me a patriotic letter, telling me he had enlisted. It didn't seem to matter—death was better than his life, and he perhaps knew it.

"I hope all the front ranks are filled with miserable clerks," I once remarked.

Beatrice wrote that she was doing war work. I opposed it, but she said one must do something for one's country. Whose country? I asked her—the country that would let her starve as it had our mother, become a prostitute as it had Helen, or be killed like a rat as was George.

Another letter came from my brother Dan. He was thinking of joining the army unless I could help him. I had done everything for Beatrice, but nothing for him.

"You always promised you would do something for me and George," he wrote, "but you have never done nothing. I want to learn to be a machinist. I ain't stuck on starving any longer. I work when I can find work. If you don't help me learn something, I'm going to lie about my age and join the army."

For hours that night I lay awake. Would I lose this brother also, as I had lost George? No, this must not be. He was a boy not yet eighteen. Money . . . where could I get money? My salary was not enough for Beatrice and myself and only by living with Karin could I exist. There was Helen . . . how could I ask her to draw upon her bank account when I could make money that way myself. What right had I? I could cut down a little more on food and walk to work—still that would not be sufficient. How did one approach a man, I wondered— how could I? I must go along Broadway and study the actions of the girls who did that. But everything shrank within me when I pictured myself approaching a man. What did one say to a man? Where did one go? Suppose one were arrested—or got a disease of some kind? Then I would not be able to earn any money at all. And even if I did not—if they paid me but a little money, it would not be worth while. I needed more money and I must find rich men. But where? I did not know where to go or how to find them. There must be fine-looking houses uptown where rich men went. . . . I pictured myself walking up the steps of one of them, and saying to the woman who kept it, "I've come to apply for a job as prostitute in your house,"—or something like that. . . . But one has to have very nice dresses to be taken into such a place. . . . I must try some other method of earning money.

The next day I tried to borrow money. Two girls in

the office where I worked refused my request and left me embarrassed and ashamed. Who would understand, among these well-dressed girls, if I told them of my family, of the truth. Poverty and hunger are shameful and humiliating—no one has respect for you if you are poor or hungry. Wolves attack and destroy one of their kind that is defeated, lamed or wounded—human beings so often seemed like wolves to me. For "to him that hath shall be given and from him that hath not shall be taken away."

One day I went to the chief editor of the magazine and tried to be matter-of-fact.

"Have you no relatives to apply to for money?"

"Yes, but it will take too long. I need the money at once."

"Where are your parents?"

"In Oklahoma. My father is a physician there, but it will take too long to hear from him," I lied. "Please, here is my Indian bracelet and ring. And you can keep a part of my salary each week if you do not trust me."

I looked him straight in the eye and my tone was frank and sincere. I thought it would be more difficult for him to refuse the daughter of a physician than the daughter of an unskilled working man. What he thought I do not know, but he studied me for a moment and then said:

"Keep your bracelet and ring . . . take this check for fifty dollars to the cashier and get the money."

That night I sent the money to Dan, and wrote him to try and hold out a few weeks longer. I had borrowed the money to send him; he must find work of some kind for a short time longer.

I knew it would take two or three years for Dan to learn some trade. These years for me would mean no books, no theaters, no music, nothing that I longed for. It would mean that I would have to postpone my university studies, for I could not pay the fees. But that would not matter.

An Irish girl student who came to Karin's home argued with me about all this. My life was my own, she said; I had not brought my brothers or sister into existence, nor was I ever responsible for them. If I really had a social conscience, I would go on and study and prepare myself for better work. It was useless to waste one moment of time or one cent of money on an individual. Carried to its logical conclusion, that was not only charity, but it was like spending a lifetime giving beggars a nickel. Only a new society could wipe out poverty, and I should give myself only to such a movement.

I never could quickly reply to such arguments. The ties that bound me to my brothers were very strong. I had lost George and I must not permit Dan to go also. I had deserted them when they were but children. I explained this to the Irish girl.

"You were also a child, and were not responsible," she answered.

"I was a child only in years," I insisted. "I was conscious of what I was doing, and when one is conscious, one is responsible."

The weeks passed. No word had come from Dan. I wrote to Sam, and after a month he answered, saying that Dan had received the money. He had worked on first one job and then another, but his work had not been regular. He could not always starve between jobs. At last he had enlisted and was now in a training camp. He would write me and see me if he came through New York when shipped to France.

I left the flat and walked through the streets for hours after the letter came. Dan was only eighteen. Now he was offering his life for a country that could not feed or educate him. And so I hated the city about me, hated the wealth that rested upon the bodies of working men. On Forty-second Street and Fifth Avenue I paused and watched the automobiles roll by, automobiles many of which cost more than I could earn in a lifetime. In them, reclining in comfort, sat people who had never worked a day in their lives, who would never work, who would never fight in the War.

I do not write mere words. I write of human flesh and blood. There is a hatred and a bitterness with roots in experience and conviction. Words cannot erase that experience.

I waited and watched for Dan. When columns of khaki-clad men marched through the city, I crowded to the edge of the pavement and searched their faces. It was insane that I thought I might find him. And yet I watched. The columns marched by—his face was not there. Or perhaps the mist before my eyes blinded me and I could not see him. Often the lines of brown faces and blue eyes all looked alike, all looked like him, my brother—marching, marching, marching, their feet falling in the endless tramp of death. The music they marched to was to me but the drum-beats of death, the flag they carried but a black banner at half mast. The

256

faces of my brothers marched by—thousands upon thousands of them—hungry faces, young faces, driven faces, sad faces.

I hoped. He might not be killed in France. The war might not last much longer. Perhaps by the time he finished his training it would be ended. He was so young. Not all men were killed who went. I would save my money until he returned, and then he could stay with me and we would work and study together.

Time passed. Beatrice finished school and became a teacher. I wrote to Sam, asking to be informed if they heard from Dan. Daily I returned home to see if news had come. But none came. Was he still in the training camp; had they shipped him to France by another route? The weeks passed and something within me always waited—then became fainter and fainter. It became mingled with depression. I felt that I would never see him again.

Part 7

I was reading Gorki's "Mother." For weeks I had abandoned other European and English writers, for Gorki held my entire attention. He was a discovery. I often talked with Karin about him and she explained many things I did not understand. It was not only what he wrote, she said, it was his spirit; he treasured women and the intimate tenderness between man and woman; and he expressed the yearnings for beauty in the hearts of the masses. It was his positive love of freedom that impressed me. Why he had chosen the name "Bitter" I could not understand, for he himself was not bitter. I also wondered why, out of the most miserable of conditions, he had developed such a positive attitude toward life. This was one of life's paradoxes that always troubled me. I recalled many such paradoxes: how often I had been so miserable that I felt an impulse to laugh; how George's death had so stricken me that I had been very calm and could not even weep; how someone once said that he who has never loved has never felt pain, and he who has not suffered can never know the meaning of happiness; I recalled the international slogan of the workers—"Workers of the world, unite; you have nothing to lose but your chains, and a world to gain." These contradictions were paradoxes—I have met them throughout my life and I have yet to understand them.

These months after George had been killed and Dan had gone into the army were not easy ones for me, for I had my own conscience to face. More and more I tried to readjust myself, to become absorbed in the university lectures that I now attended at night. I had left Karin and was living alone in a little furnished room. All day long I worked in the office, then when my working hours were over, hurried to the university. By the end of the day I was very tired, and it was a weary brain that tried to apply itself to study. Of my father I thought hardly at all, for once again I began building a wall against the past. To think of my mother and my brothers brought pain and depression. To think of my father or to think of Helen brought misery. And my sister had always been a stranger to me. My father—he must have been a gray-haired man keeping vigil by those lonely graves, deserted by those he had so badly loved, bitter against the woman whom he had loved in his own way but who had died as if to spite him; not understanding why he was still poor after a lifetime of hard work. But my mind built a wall of forgetfulness against him. Perhaps my spirit brooded over him; perhaps it was the memory of him and of my brothers that troubled me when I awoke from dreams to lie staring into the darkness of my little room.

Before me now lay a university degree; and beyond—well, it might be position, one day money and power. Success, written on the heart of America, was also written on mine. And to as little purpose. All that I learned in the university, much that I learned from my few friends or associates, only strengthened this tendency. Even many of the Socialists who were my acquaintances were the same. To rise to be a Socialist leader—such was the goal of many. Among them were rich and noted men and women who lectured on poverty, injustice and the suppression of the masses. They seemed to be personal friends of the great of Europe, and they spoke of the Russian Revolution as if it were their private property. As always their brilliance stupefied me. I wondered if I should ever be so learned as they—if I could ever discuss with such authority the difference between left wings and right wings. It would perhaps never be; for I was but a worker, while they had time to study theory. It was not that they were less sincere than I—they belonged to another world.

I felt deeply, reacted violently and thought little. It was easy to defeat me in an argument. I recall one such instance. It was in one of the university lectures. The professor was blonde and immaculately clad. He was also an adviser to a great international rubber concern with heavy interests in South America. He told us of the gathering of rubber in the Amazon Basin. We learned how difficult it was—and we learned also that such things as an eight-hour day would be impossible in such an industry! If such a thing were done, the price of rubber would increase so much in our country that few of us could afford even to buy a rain coat! Then he spoke of the Negroes who worked in the terrible heat along the Amazon—that they did not object to a working day from dawn to darkness. Without thinking I arose to my feet, and protested:

"I don't believe you. I think if those men work under such conditions their hours should be very short and they should be paid very much. Why do you try to tell us they don't mind it?"

"They do not mind it," he assured me with conviction. "In fact they like it. I have even seen one of them stand and take a good licking, then trot off, perfectly satisfied."

"I do not believe you! Even were it true, we should be ashamed!"

"But I have seen it, I tell you! You judge them as if they were like you or me."

"How do you know what they feel or think—what do you know of their suffering—what could you know? And do you believe that Negroes are less sensitive than we are just because they are black?"

"I have worked with them. I've seen them do things and tolerate things *we* would never tolerate. They don't feel as we do. An eight-hour day to them is an unheard-of thing; it would cut their wages in half, and they would not stand for it."

I was filled with rage, but my mind could not find replies. The picture of those black men, working in the deadening heat for unearthly hours, just for enough to keep life in their bodies, aroused ferocity within me, and I wanted to kill. That any living man or woman could demand less for another than he demanded for himself aroused not only my hatred, but my fear. When I faced such things, I saw that human beings are wolves. That frightened me and erased from my mind all hope of convincing people by argument that such things should not be. The enslaved must be strong enough to destroy such things—until then they must suffer and go to the ground. My emotions were deeply touched when I thought of those black men—big men perhaps with stooped shoulders, laboring blindly, watching the earth as they worked; perhaps some of them talked to themselves also . . . could it be that I saw my father, and perhaps my brothers, in all that was dumb and helpless before existence, all that was denied humanity, all that was defeated? . . . It was but chance that I was born white and not black; free and not slave; I believed that a truth is a truth only when it covers the generality, and not just me.

Professors could silence me then; they had figures, diagrams, maps, books. Protest was my only reply. I was learning that books and diagrams can be evil things if they deaden the mind of man and make him blind or cynical before subjection of any kind.

Then a man came into my life. A lover,—no. But it was not my fault that he was not. For I was a turmoil of vague yearnings and of confusion. He was a teacher and a wise man. A dark man with white in his hair, a man from India, ugly and severe. There was a scar down one side of his face and one eye was blind. He stood for a brief hour upon the threshold of my life, and I think he always had a touch of scorn for me. Why he concerned himself with me at all is still inexplicable. Perhaps he was lonely in exile; or perhaps my need for affection, for someone to love, for someone to take the place of a father, was strong, and when I found a person who seemed to promise this, I did not lightly release my grip. For I was as primitive as a weed.

The Indian came to lecture before the University and I thought he was the same man who had once come to the school in the West where I had taught. Sardar Ranjit Singh he was called and I came to know that he was from the North and was of a people whose faith was militant and had been built upon the bodies of martyrs; that in his own life he had but lived again the history of his people—in the struggle for the freedom of his land, in prison; and that he had once faced the gallows. When he arose in the University to speak to us, tall and lean, I almost forgot that he was ugly. There was a fugitive wistfulness in his voice and I wondered that a man so ugly could have such an appeal; that his face could be so calm—as if he had solved the secret of existence. The Professor who had introduced him had said he was a historian and would speak of Indian history.

Of what he spoke I remember little in detail—it was of his country's past, and of the present; of color and beauty, mingled with suffering and pain, and the sound of trumpets. What he said came very close to me—there was so much of pain in it; but it differed from my own life, for there was a call to struggle for a new world. His voice reached out and touched me lightly, and yet so deeply, that I bent forward and clutched the arms of my seat. He finished abruptly, his last words apparently spoken into emptiness; and still they were a challenge:

"You Americans—can you be at peace in your minds when your system, your leisure that creates culture, rests upon the enslaved bodies of others? Is this law of the jungle the law of life to you? If so, you are machines without a soul, without a purpose. I have spoken to you of the freedom for which we Indians are working; can it be that you, like England, believe in freedom only for yourselves? Your War is for democracy, you say. I doubt it—your principles do not extend to Asia, although Asia is three-fourths of the human race."

He left the platform and passed down the aisle, and the students about me arose and began leaving the hall. I arose and stepped directly in front of him.

"Pardon me—you came to a school in California where they would not let you speak. Do you remember—I gave you my address."

His smile was very polite—he had had many women approach him.

"I am afraid I do not remember . . . you see, so many schools have refused me the right to speak. I am an Indian!"

He bowed slightly and waited for me to step aside that he might pass in peace.

"You are a student here?" he asked, seeing that I would not step aside.

"I am a student. Yes. I study economics and history. You said we Americans are like machines—without a purpose; I don't know what you mean."

He looked into my face and the polite smile was

gone; he was perhaps wondering how a people could be so much of a thing that they did not even know it.

"You do not even know!" he said.

"What should one do? You see, sometimes I don't even know what to think."

"Don't know what to think!"

"Couldn't you tell me what to study . . . what to do?"

There was a peculiar expression on his face as he stood watching me, without replying. Then he took from his purse a card. "If you really wish—if you are serious—if it is India you would wish to study, I could help. Otherwise not. I am at home on Sunday afternoon if you wish to come and talk with me."

Then I stepped aside. He bowed again, raising one hand slightly toward his forehead, and passed down the aisle. Holding his card, I turned and watched him go. He walked very straight, but his shoulders stooped.

I have learned that when knowledge and love become one, a force has been created that nothing can break.

That I learned from two men—both of them Asiatics. One of them was Sardar Ranjit Singh. If there is anything else that can reconcile one to life and to annihilation in the end, I have yet to learn it. I was ignorant, and Ranjit Singh gave me knowledge. I was rough and often cynical, and he taught me that roughness was fear and cynicism defeat. He was a dangerous man. Like Cassius, he thought too much. In him I saw reflected all that I had not been, all that most of my own people were not; thoughtfulness and humanity; the passionate longing for freedom for all men combined with a love for his own land; and the use of knowledge for good ends.

I always felt humble before him—humble and very ignorant. He talked with me on that Sunday afternoon and the tea in my cup became cold. Beyond the dining room where we sat was his little library piled with books, and a desk with the afternoon sunlight falling across it. It was a small apartment, furnished in austere simplicity. I had thought that learned men were always rich and lived in fine houses, with servants. But this man had a simple house and no servants. His housework was done chiefly by the two Indian students who lived with him.

Who was I, what had my life been, where were my people, and what was I studying—his questions followed one another. I told him the truth—he was, I believe, the first person to whom I did not say that my father was a physician. He was interested in my studies—to what purpose, he asked. I did not know.

"You are studying the social history of England," he continued. "But that study is incomplete without a study of the influence of India upon English development. England's wealth began with the plunder of India. If you can get your professor's permission to study that phase of it, I will help you."

Later he again remarked: "Everyone studies the history of Europe. Why don't you study the history of Asia?"

When he asked me what I was aiming to do with my studies, and when I admitted that I had no aim, he said:

"We need teachers in India—teachers who come as

friends, not as conquerors. Since you have no family, why don't you study to come to us?"

Before the month had passed I had given up my work in the city and had begun work as his secretary. He was writing a book on America, and each morning I sat in the window in his little sitting room and typed his manuscripts. Each afternoon I spent in the university, and in the evening rushed to my new room near his home, then on to his apartment to study. There were mornings when there was no typing to do, and there were always the long evenings.

Viren and Kumar were the two Indian students who lived with him. Viren was turned twenty-two and burdened with knowledge that he felt it essential to inflict upon me. He was very dark, thin, tall and handsome, and very poor; and he was arrogant about his ability to cook. Kumar was scarcely twenty, and as shy as a girl. Perhaps it was his ugliness that made him so wistful and tender-hearted, and so very, very gentle. "Sardarji" we called Ranjit Singh, for it was a title of respect. I often wondered what would have happened had I lived so intimately with three American men. It would have been impossible. Yet here I lived as if they were my father and brothers. Perhaps that was the reason why I sank so easily in among them and felt that they belonged to me.

I came to love them, and they must have loved me in their own way, although their bearing was always a bit distant and courteous, as was that of the other men who came to their house. Only Viren broke through his dignity to quarrel with me.

"Marie!" he began one day, to my back, as I typed.

"I suppose you think you know everything about Irish history, too!"

"Yes, I do!"

"Well, that's a bit too thick! I suppose you've read everything Nietzsche ever wrote,—isn't it?"

"Oh, no! I know everything he wrote without reading him!"

"Oh! . . . You need one good hammering!" From his sprawling position on the couch one long leg came down to the floor with a bang and he was on his feet, bristling.

"Of course—if you feel able!"

Kumar rushed to my aid. "Back! You silly ass!" he cried at Viren.

Sardarji's voice back of us brought the scene to an end. "At it again! Leave the house, all three of you . . . and don't come back . . . at least for two hours! I have a right to a little rest in my own house!"

We three found ourselves contemplating the icy pavement below.

There were long, beautiful hours when Sardarji and I sat, the outlines of books I had read, before us. It was not just study from books; it was long travels through India. Living men and women, not strange names, marched before me; art and literature unfolded before my eyes. Buddha preached social revolution; great empires rose and fell; invaders came and mingled with the people, accepting their customs and thoughts. There were mountain fastnesses and strange flags and the sound of trumpets; beautiful rivers, deserts covered with a soft green fuzz in the early morning before the sun comes up. Their fragrance came to me, as did the fragrance of the jungles. There were purple hazes in the distance and the tinkle of bells as the cows came home in the evening, casting up a cloud of dust against the setting sun—"cow dust" they called the sunset; there were brilliant flowers with heavy perfumes and delicate blossoms as tender as the morning; bright *saris* of the women and the pure white costumes of the men. At night the skies were a deep purple, with the shadow of robed women on flat roofs.

The hours passed and we studied. Heavy things at times, made beautiful by the man who loved them. Reluctantly I came back to reality and saw Sardarji across from me, explaining references, comparing facts and dates, and giving new work for the next lesson. Discipline and more discipline in study, he demanded; without discipline no goal could be reached; I lacked discipline and must learn it. Strange it was that he, so ugly, made things so beautiful.

There were the two evenings a week when Hyder Ali came to teach me economics. He was a young professor, and a Mussulman; apostle of asceticism, worshiping at the feet of God Statistics. Figures and facts were holy things to him. Had he been less beautiful I could never have learned anything from him. But I studied and remembered much that he said. He was very slender, and graceful when he walked; his face was of a loveliness such as I had never seen in man or woman, and he wore a black Indian coat fastened high up about the throat that cast his face in sharp relief. His voice was as sharp as the edge of a knife and he had no time for such foolishnesses as sentiment, or love. He sat me on one side of the table, he himself took the opposite chair, and we began. He felt it necessary to crush any show of femininity in me, to build about me a row of figures that should be my armor in work for his country. I wore the armor, perhaps a bit awry, but I wore it, always leaving loopholes through which I could look at him.

Often I forgot what he was saying, for his eyes were so black and of such depths, with darker shadows beneath them. His black hair caught the light from the electric bulb above our heads, and I wondered if it felt like a bird's wing if you stroked it. When he turned his head in profile I caught my breath at the profile of his face—little wonder it was that the Indians had created art of such exquisite beauty. . . .

"You are not listening!" his merciless voice would cut in, pausing in the midst of a translation.

"I . . . I am sorry. . . . I was just thinking of something else. Please say it again."

"Unless you listen and make notes we can go no further! You can not keep these things in your head!"

I listened hard, and stared at the book before him along which his long slender finger roamed, pausing as he paused to explain. It was difficult to look at him and to think at the same time. Even his finger was beautiful, long and slender like that of a woman. Long after I have forgotten the dates and figures he made me learn, long after I have forgotten the canal systems of India, the systems of land tenure of the past, the present, and perhaps the future, I shall remember his eyes and his hair, and the long slender forefinger traveling across the page.

Many Indians came to Ranjit Singh's house and they dissected everything between earth and heaven. There was a pale youth named Talvar Singh who wore a white turban. His black eyes burned as they turned from one speaker to another; but for his eyes, he expressed no emotion, and he often sat with his hands under him, rocking slowly back and forth. The rocking paused for a second when someone said something he had not heard before, and he seemed to be considering it. Then it began again. He was a student and often came with a man named Juan Diaz, an Eurasian—half Hindu, half Portuguese, a Christian by religion.

Juan Diaz was fairer than the others, but his hair was also so black that the light caught in it. A cynical smile was often about his lips and he was so tall that when he walked he stooped just a bit. He believed in the sincerity of few men and of no woman, and his speech was filled with cynical and irritating remarks.

Christianity, Islam, Hinduism, Sikhism, met and warred in Sardarji's house; the women of the West and the women of the East were dissected, limb from limb; Socialism, Communism, Anarchism and Democracy each had its defender; God was worshiped and He was denied existence; asceticism was defended to the death by Hyder Ali,—and Juan Diaz replied that "the cat, having eaten seven hundred mice, has gone on a pilgrimage to Mecca." I objected to this attack upon a man who to me seemed little less than a God, but Juan turned to me and said that a pea in an empty gourd makes a loud clatter! As if meeting some argument in advance, he informed me that his revolutionary sentiments did not extend to women. He seemed to regard me and my ideas as a standing insult to himself.

The War was always before our eyes in that house, and I came to see it through the eyes of men from Asia—eyes that watched and were cynical about the phrases of democracy. Sad eyes, eyes filled with despair at times. I do not remember one that believed in the phrases of either side. Through them I came to know how men, intelligent and revolutionary, can suffer under subjection. I thought I had known what bitterness was, but when with them I realized that I did not know the meaning of the word. When I left them and returned to my room at night I often lay staring into the darkness, wondering why it could not be my lot to help destroy slavery. There was no light—I was too young, too ignorant, too weak. And I was but one.

As the Indians sat and talked in Sardarji's dining room week after week, I listened to their conversation filled with references to their own history and literature, with those thousands of proverbs and allusions that form a basis of racial consciousness. Their extensive study and their learning impressed me deeply. Only to Sardarji later did I dare ask for explanations of their allusions or statements. In our early morning walks he talked with me and explained. And our conversations led us to discuss every phase of Indian life, and every phase of American life, including my own.

Sardarji had brought his Indian habits with him to America. In the summer he arose at five, in the winter a little later. I met him at the entrance to Central Park and we walked before breakfast. There were spring and summer mornings when the grass was wet with dew and the leaves above our heads glistened with moisture.

"Work without result or reward," I once protested to him. "How can you say that? It is impossible—too difficult."

"You speak of coming to us as a teacher, and you object to difficult things! What do you think you are coming to? Our movement is a very hard and cruel one. Slavery brings the fruits of slavery—poverty, ignorance, superstition, disease, misery. Not beautiful or romantic things as you think, but hateful, ugly things. Do not come to us expecting anything but that, or you will be disappointed and turn against us."

"No! I will not turn against you. But I do hate poverty and ignorance and superstition."

"Then help us remove them."

"But one wants to see the result of one's work."

"Then stay in America and work only for money. You will get so much per week or so much per month. You are very American and you have a cheap and superficial view of life—the idea of profit."

"What would you have me do—work hopelessly?"

"No. It is true, we need a demand for results—it is necessary in India. But if the thing you work for is great enough and true enough, to work for its achievement is reward enough, even if it does not succeed, even if you are poor and remain poor."

"I think you mean you don't expect to see your country free. Yours is a philosophy of despair."

"Oh, no! Had I worshiped success, I would have despaired and abandoned my work long ago. As it is, I long for achievement, and I work for it, but even if I fail—still I know I am right. Marie—that is the only basis for work of any kind, and it is the only basis for life. Do you not see that you work for a lifetime and in the end get nothing for it except death? How can you, in the face of that, speak of rewards, or choose anything but what is fundamental and true, and work for it, even if it does not succeed?"

"I am human, Sardarji, and I am young. I want something out of life. Only the rich and comfortable or the very, very old can hold such ideas as yours."

"I am not old—I have perhaps as many years ahead of me as you have, even with your youth. So it is not old age that leads me to think these things. Then the rich—they are too destroyed by comfort and security to know what I mean. In the process of becoming rich they have killed not only others, but themselves."

"You have had enough to eat all your life, Sardarji, and that is the reason you speak of spiritual things."

"I have not always had enough to eat. I also once faced a moment which seemed to mean death, and when one has faced that, one knows what values are. It is trite to say it, but this is one of the reasons why I, like you, look to the working class to create a new world. You see, it can afford to think and dream and create; it has nothing to lose by doing so; it has no fear, no money, no petty possessions to cling to and stumble over. It can see clearly into the future, unimpeded by the possessions that other classes cling to."

We had paused before a huge bowlder in the Park and above our heads were the broad spreading limbs of a tree, dripping with dew. His voice continued, a touch of wistfulness in it.

"I often hope that women, also, will work for freedom for all people. They should know, like the working class, and like all Asia, what subjection means. But I fear . . ."

"Oh, I don't think women have a vision broader than men! It all depends upon the individual and the class they come from."

There was another morning when we walked and I remember he told me of a drama by Rostand that he had seen. "It was very interesting," he said. "There is a line in it that says there must be in the heart a faith so faithful that it comes back even after it has been slain . . . do you like that? . . . I also."

There were other mornings when he almost forgot my presence, and talked as if I were a part of the air about us. Once as he sat resting on a bowlder for a few minutes, he said:

"I see ordinary men rise to positions of power in your country. I see them, forced to carry responsibilities, develop into men of thought and influence. Then I always think of my own people—how the ablest and most creative of them must step back before mediocre Englishmen who come to rule and ruin us! Drain our country, from one generation to the other—to fill their own pockets and the pockets of their countrymen,— while we sink deeper into poverty and ignorance."

The passion in his voice left me speechless. To say "I am sorry" would have sounded like a tin rattle on a mountain top. His face looked very thin and ugly, and the scar down one cheek was like a dark, badly-healed wound. I felt helpless, nor could I touch him in sympathy. He continued:

"You do not know what it means to love the very soil of your country. I—I am a patriot. Marie—sometimes—I fear that I may never return; sometimes in the middle of the night when I am awakened by my old heart trouble, I wonder if my end has come. Then I have but one desire—one passion—to step on the soil of my country, to kiss it before I die. Can you understand that?"

As he spoke his hand had reached down and gathered up a handful of black earth.

"Love my country, Sardarji—do you mean the soil? Yes, I love that. I love the mountains of the West. And I love the deserts. But what most people mean by country is the government and the powerful men who rule it. No. I do not love them. But the earth—yes. This is our earth. Or—it must one day be."

"What do you mean?"

"I mean all of us who work and live and suffer. It must belong to all—not just to individuals."

"If you were in exile, and all this country here where you live were ruled by a foreign, armed power, would you love it and work for its freedom?"

"Yes,—of course. But I would not want to work just to put it in the hands of a few rich men or groups who would make the rest of us work for them and live in poverty—and call it 'our' country. Today this is not our country, but their country. We are permitted to live only so long as we submit to them."

His voice came slowly. "When I think of India, I

don't think of classes. I think of the land, of the suffering people, of the place where I was born, of the sweet language, our history . . . everything."

"If you were a peasant, you would think also of the landlord; and if you were a worker, you would think also of your boss."

"You are perhaps right . . . you see, I myself am a landlord. Or was. But my lands have been confiscated by the government because of my political activities."

"You are a funny land-owner. We don't have such here."

Sardarji sighed heavily as he slowly lifted himself from the stone. To talk to me was at times like talking to a person he had never seen before—we found no point of contact. To him I was a raw, impulsive, inexperienced girl. I was but a brief incident in his life. His life had been long and his work was intense. And I? To work for the freedom of a subjected country, to feel the full weight of such a movement upon your shoulders as did he—no, I could not understand the meaning of that.

There were times when Ranjit Singh doubted my ability to help the movement he was in. He tried to discourage me, to turn me back from the road he himself was following. It was too hard for a girl—anyway, for a white girl, he said.

"I have no fear!" I replied defiantly.

"It is all the same where you work, or in what, provided the work is for liberty and provided you know what you are doing," he urged.

"Surely your cause is a good one!"

277

"To me it is—holy."

"And it is also a part of the workers' struggle for freedom, isn't it—and do I not want to help in that?"

"Yes, it is that. But I doubt if you have the strength or the endurance to hold out. You are very American."

"Do not always hold that against me, Sardarji!"

"Marie—listen once and for all to me; if you enter our movement, you cannot play with it in the spirit of adventure for a few months. This is a life's work, and it is dangerous. To work in it requires knowledge and the ability to suffer for a principle—which means you must know what the principle is. In this movement one is hunted like an animal, and you never feel safe."

"Sardarji—why do you try to drive me away? If you and those other countrymen of yours can endure such things, I can also. I have known little else than suffering. It is true I don't know very much about your movement, but I can study, and then later I can come to India. If—it may not be—Dan really does not come back . . . if he comes it may take a few years longer."

With one hand he caressed my hair, gently, saying, "You are a good girl!" And then we laughed.

The months passed, and it was Ranjit Singh, a man from Asia, a man of the colored race, who taught me the most valuable things I have yet learned. He worked with me although I was raw and ignorant of many things. I was not an interesting person to associate with. And yet he worked with me and taught me, filling my life with meaning. He introduced me to the movement for freedom of his people and showed me that it was not only an historic movement of itself, but that it was a part of an international struggle for emancipation—

that it was one of the chief pillars in this struggle. It was not a distant movement. Because I loved him as I might have loved my father, I learned more than I could have learned from any other source.

Happiness, like almost everything else, was also transient with me.

Sardarji came. The winter of the following year had hardly begun, and he was gone. It was but circumstance that he had noticed me as he passed. It was perhaps but circumstance that I had responded; and it was but chance that he was a wise man who did not exploit my affection, but used it for my own good.

It was a misfortune that I was too ignorant, too undeveloped to grasp the meaning of all he might have taught me—and all that I might have taught others. Through him I touched for the first time a movement of unwavering principle and beauty—the struggle of a continent to be free. I could not, and perhaps still do not, grasp its full significance. Had I been otherwise I might have spoken in words so deep, so true, so convincing, that even the people of my country, with their worship of external things, might have listened; have listened and seen that difference of race, color and creed are as shadows on the face of a stream, each lending a beauty of its own; that subjection of any kind and in any place is beneath the dignity of man, and that the highest joy is to fight by the side of those who for any reason of their own making or ours, are unable to develop to full human stature. I might have shown that the movements of peoples to be free, to build a society upon other than a slave foundation, are not only materialistic, but the greatest ethical manifestations that mankind has experienced. I might have shown that life itself is the one glorious, eternal experience, and that there is no place here on this spinning ball of earth and stone for anything but freedom. For we reach scarce a hundred before we take our place by the side of those whom we have directly or indirectly injured, enslaved, or killed.

One understands these things faintly—even if one is not learned enough to express them—as I am not. Or—is it but egoism that I wish I might have been able to do this, instead of knowing that the emancipation of a people can come only by the great masses organizing and fighting for it.

"Study," Sardarji constantly enjoined me. "Study, for there is a difference between the mere physical reaction to misery that has been your life, and the year-in-and-year-out following of a clear line of thought and action."

Once he said to me: "Make conviction the basis of your action. Do not let your affection for me influence you. For I am like the wind,—old, and must one day die."

I replied: "I have always loved the wind; it was always my companion." He did not understand.

I continued: "I often think knowledge without love is useless—of course I do not mean just personal love. I mean the love for great and beautiful ideas."

"You are right. I have met many people here in the West. Take the Socialists, for instance. Many of them are narrow-visioned. When we Indians speak of the freedom of India, they say we are nationalists. I have had English Socialists tell me that they do not intend to turn the Indian working class over to the upper classes of India to exploit. That reasoning but hides imperialism, more deadly than that which exists today, for it wears the garb of ethics. For they cannot rule our country, even if they call themselves Socialists, without the machinery of imperialism. Sometimes I think the struggle is not just a struggle against the Capitalist system, but of all Asia against the western world.

"But there is Russia," I protested.

"That is the one exception. And it is at least half Asiatic."

"No, race has nothing to do with it. It is nothing but a new world order being born. That order is neither eastern or western."

Now, Sardarji, this man who had been a friend, a father, a teacher, was gone. The train that carried him to San Francisco rolled away one early morning and Kumar and I wept. Viren stood with his head high, too learned to cry. Juan Diaz had raised his hands to his forehead in farewell, and I had seen Sardarji respond and pause to look into his face—as if doubting something. It was one of those glances that one does not forget. Hyder Ali stood apart and his thin, beautiful face was sad. He spoke with Sardarji in low tones, then embraced him quickly and stepped back. Turning, he walked quickly past me. As he passed I glanced down and saw that the bottom of his trouser legs was worn into shreds, and the heels of his old shoes had almost disappeared.

On that day I moved downtown again, and began my work through the day and my university studies at night. The room where I now lived was tiny, with a fireplace at one end. The only light came from a gas jet in the center. There was a small window in the door, and a window high up, opening into another room, through which the ventilation came. It was good enough, I said; I could pay university fees, buy books and still save a little money. What did it matter that it was little more than a closet in the wall; I would be there only at night.

The city became lonely and cold again. The intense and regulated life of Sardarji's house was gone. And gone also was the circle of men who studied always and discussed with interest everything from new kitchen machinery to new forms of society. About me now during the day were girls and boys who chewed gum and told of the "swell time" they had had the night before. "Oh, Boy!" they would exclaim, summing up their deepest emotions. At times I dropped in on Karin and her circle of friends; at other times I spent an evening listening to acquaintances pigeon-hole everybody and everything according to the latest ideas in the revolution, in the social drama, in psychoanalysis.

The *Graphic* office, where I again worked was patriotic, and to speak against the War was to run the risk of arrest. With one word of criticism some girl would brace her hand on her hip, and say, "If you don't like this country, why don't you go back to the one you came from?"

Once I replied: "The one I came from! My people were so American that this was their country before any white men came here."

"Then you ought to go to jail!" she informed me, and looked about to catch the smiles of admiration bestowed upon her for her brilliancy.

From the office I again went directly to the evening university classes. There was a precious hour or two with Hyder Ali in his miserable little room. On Saturday afternoons he sat with glowing eyes and taught me the importance and beauty of facts and figures. There were rare Sunday mornings when Viren, Kumar and I met and explored every nook and corner of Central Park. Sometimes Juan Diaz hailed me on Fifth Avenue, invited me to a cup of tea and asked if I still believed in the freedom of women. His smile showed what "free women" meant to him.

"You do not believe in love?" he jeered.

"It is good for those who have nothing else to do."

"Less sentimental women than you have said that and repented."

There was a Sunday morning in deep winter when a soft knock came on my door and, opening it, I found Talvar Singh standing there, bundled up to the eyes. He entered, removed his coat and stated his business with startling abruptness.

"You know I am a revolutionary, isn't it?" he began. "Well, I have come about that. I have tried to get a book published, but all publishers refuse because it is war time and the book is for the freedom of my country."

"You have written a book!"

"Oh, no—not I! Two of my friends—they are not in this country. You can help me."

"How?"

"You are an American, isn't it? You can have it done by a printer and he will not be afraid, because, you see, *your* skin is not brown."

He explained further and showed the manuscript to me.

"But you will never say a word to anyone? Good—you promise? And you will tell nobody that you do such things for me—no one? Good!"

He had remained to talk further of it, and had then left.

The next day, meeting Viren in the university, I remarked casually:

". . . this Talvar Singh—is he only a student, Viren?"

"Why do you ask?"

"Oh, I wonder about all Indians now—I think they all must be revolutionaries in their hearts."

"In their *hearts!* He's more than in his *heart!* He has been sent here by a revolutionary organization in India!"

"Oh-h-h!"

"But it's a dead secret! Dead!"

"I understand. What does he do?"

"No man knows what another man is doing and no one asks. We suspect everyone who asks questions about things that do not concern them."

"I'm sorry. Talvar seemed such a boy to me."

"Boy! He's old enough for what he has been sent to do. He's old enough to have read Schopenhauer and Nietzsche!" Viren worshiped Schopenhauer and Nietzsche.

The following Sunday the same soft knock came on

my door again and Talvar Singh entered, his turban very white in the dull light of my room. I had success to announce—a printer had been found and the book would be published. Each Sunday he came for weeks and when the book was finished we sent copies to all officials and noted men and women.

One evening, upon returning late from the university, I found him waiting. He had built a fire in the fireplace and stood watching it. When I entered he turned.

"What is wrong?" I exclaimed.

He had to go away, he said; if he stayed he would be arrested. British spies were following all Indians. Some-one had entered his room while he was away the day before, and had searched it. His eyes saw everything—it was just as in India.

"I wish to leave some addresses with you—they are of our men in various countries. I cannot have them with me."

He drew from his pocket a purse and from it took out a thin sheet of paper. I glanced at it and saw that there were names and addresses. I recalled the things I had read of the Russian revolutionary movement; there had also been Mazzini before that, with his "whispering gallery" from London to Italy. There had been the American revolutionaries with their own whispering gallery from America to France. Here was I, standing face to face with another such movement.

"Can you trust me with such things?" I asked, looking at the thin sheets of paper in my hand.

"Yes. And you must keep them. Suppose I should be killed. Or arrested like the others? If this happens we need someone to do things for us. Or, I might just disappear—our men often do, and we never find them again."

I studied him. He was young, yet speaking as if "disappearing" were a thing that had to be reckoned with at all times. Was this what Sardarji had meant? The memory of my brothers returned to me—they should have lived as did this man. But they were working men and could never take their noses from the earth. Talvar was not a working man. He had studied and had chosen freely and consciously this way that might even mean death. It seemed to me very beautiful to live and work like that.

"Keep it," Talvar was urging, nodding at the paper. "You are an American. You may one day be able to help us very much. The British cannot touch you. You will never tell of them—it matters not what happens."

"No, I will never tell of them—depend upon me."

We then took my black soft leather notebook, with the double back, and steamed open the inside cover. Between the two layers we placed the thin sheets of addresses of Indians in India and various parts of the world. Then we very carefully sealed the covers together again.

"No one has the right to have these except these men," Talvar then said, and he gave me the names of two men whom I knew. He himself would be leaving within two days—until then he was at a new address. I wrote his address, and the new address of Viren, which he gave me, in my little address book.

When he reached the door to go he turned with a

smile, raised his folded hands to his forehead and gave the Indian revolutionary greeting: *"Bande Mataram!"*—Hail, Motherland. He waited for a second to see my response, and with a smile I awkwardly returned his farewell.

He was gone and I stood staring at the black notebook. The whole incident had been so simple, and yet before me lay the names of men whose lives were in my hands. This realization grew upon me as I stood, and then it appalled me, filling me with fear. I wished to return them to Talvar—but he was gone and I might not see him again. I sat down to think it out. It was not pleasant—in fact it was a most miserable responsibility. I felt that I knew so little and was so little prepared to undertake such a responsibility. But perhaps Talvar was right . . . as an American I would remain unmolested. Could I refuse to help these men who asked me for help, these men who were so kind to me, who were so learned and who were fighting for the freedom of their country? It was such a little thing they were asking of me—to protect certain sheets of paper in case they were arrested. They were subjected, they were colored, they were alone and unprotected in the United States . . . they had come asking for help . . . they were the countrymen of Sardarji—perhaps his co-workers. I recalled that once I had deserted my little brothers who needed my help and protection. I had been selfish and in my drive to save myself had sacrificed them.

Then I took the notebook in my hand and decided that I would not again desert anyone who trusted and needed me. To me the Indians became a symbol of my duty and responsibility. They took the place of my father, of my brother who was dead and of the brother of whose destiny I was as yet uncertain.

It was two days after Talvar's visit to my room that I again stood by my table, the black notebook before me, and a newspaper in my hand. I never let the notebook from my hands now. It contained Spanish and history noted from university lectures and I always carried it under my arm.

Attracted by the headlines, I had bought the newspaper upon leaving *The Graphic* office. Talvar had been arrested and his name was blazoned across the afternoon press. Taking the black notebook under my arm and collecting a few things that I needed, I started off for my evening university lectures. I would most certainly find Viren, for he attended some of the night lectures. Waiting before the room where I knew he would come, I waited until I saw him down the corridor.

"Have you read it?" I asked him as we hurried to meet.

"We must be careful. These *heramzades* are everywhere!" He used a Hindi curse word to indicate English spies.

I protested. "They've no right—this is America and we can protest if they bother us."

He laughed. "Protest . . . and get arrested yourself! No, when you fight with a cobra, you must use a long stick!"

I attended one lecture, without hearing a word. I would go home, cook something for my dinner, and try to study there . . . it was useless to sit through lectures and hear nothing. Halting on my way home I bought a small sack of wood, then hurried on and ascended the stairs to my room. I opened the door and then halted in fear—someone was standing by my fireplace! The sack of wood clattered to the floor at my feet and the man turned his face to me. It was Talvar Singh—he had removed his turban and his hair was cut.

"For heaven's sake!"

He was calm, but his black eyes seemed blacker, and deeper. "I got away from them when they took me into the subway . . . you must help me . . . if I go to Viren they will arrest him . . . you are an American."

Talvar picked up the sack of wood, closed and locked the door, and pushed me into a chair. He told me of his arrest and later of his escape.

"A number of our men have been arrested . . . why and how I do not know," he concluded. "America is carrying out England's orders to arrest us."

"What can I do?"

"I do not know. Perhaps you can help me across the frontier. You have friends, isn't it . . . they can tell me how to get away."

"Yes . . . I have friends. I will go to them and ask."

"If you can help, come and tell me or leave a note. I will go now to a friend uptown—here is the address. You can come there. You will know my friend; he is a short man and old. Please . . . tell no person that I have been here—no person."

I wrote the address in my address book beneath the name he had given me two days before.

Then we both went out. He turned to the right and I to the left.

It was nearing eleven that night when I reached the uptown address he had given me. A little old man opened the door.

"Who are you?" he inquired.

I told him.

"What do you want?"

"Talvar Singh."

"He has gone out and is not yet back."

"Then I will write a note." I wrote the note, including in it all that I had learned from friends. Then sealed it and gave it to the little old man.

Again on the streets I felt more at ease. Talvar would, if he followed my note, leave the city that night and be in a place of safety before the week had passed.

Reaching the door of my room, I saw through the smoke-glass window that there was a light—the gas jet had been lighted. Perhaps Talvar Singh had again come to me. Pushing the door open suddenly, I stood on the threshold and looked in.

Juan Diaz was sitting before my table, wrapped in his big coat, reading from a book.

"*A-ré!*" I exclaimed, using an Indian exclamation. "How did you come here?"

"Your landlady let me in. I have been waiting an hour."

"So!"

"What is this—has Talvar Singh been here?"

"Talvar Singh!" I gasped. "What a question to ask! Don't you know he was arrested two days ago?"

He stared directly into my eyes.

"Your landlady said a man had been here this evening and she thought it was Talvar."

"What nonsense! A friend called and she must have made a mistake."

His eyes had narrowed just a bit as he watched.

"Why this secrecy? You know I am also a revolutionary. Your landlady told me he wore a cap instead of a turban. And that you went out together!"

"Nonsense, I tell you! A friend called and we went to the university together. I have just returned. How on earth could Talvar Singh be here when he is in jail! . . . But now I am very tired from my work and I have not eaten. I will build a fire and cook something."

He still stood watching me.

"Sit down," I said, "I will make a cup of tea for you."

He smiled, removed his great coat and sat down.

"Do you always eat so late?"

"Yes. I never have time before. There is that miserable office all day, then I have to run to get to the university."

After lighting the gas plate under the kettle, I knelt before the tiny fireplace and began to rebuild the fire. Juan Diaz sat in a chair close to my back, bending forward with the light of the fire on his face. My mind was on Talvar Singh and I wondered why this man had now come here. Why did I remember Sardarji's expression as he bade him farewell!

"What has brought you here?" I asked over my shoulder.

"You, of course!"

"Strange—so late at night as this!"

"Yes, I am leaving the city and called to see you first."

". . . That is good of you, considering your opinion of women."

"I . . . I haven't the same opinion of you as of many others."

"Perhaps worse."

"Oh, no—quite the contrary." His voice was pleasant when he laughed and he reached out and tapped me lightly on the shoulder. I felt him at my back; I had always been able to feel him in a room. There was always a trace of some scent about him. . . . It was perhaps true that he was going away—that was why he had come. . . . Talvar had told me all men were being arrested.

"Where are you going?" I asked, turning slightly and resting back on my heels. Then I forgot the question, for the firelight had caught his glistening belt buckle and my eyes became fastened upon it. Where had I sat just like this before and seen that belt buckle! Above was his face, so strangely familiar, the high forehead, the broad shoulders, bent forward. There was the faint trace of scent about him—or was it from the pine knots in the fire?

"Your belt buckle—it is silver, inlaid with green and red, isn't it? Or is it the firelight?" Some memory was haunting me.

He was bending very close.

"Are you interested even in my belt buckle?"

I sat staring back and up at him, hearing my jeering voice reply:

"I am not interested in *anything* about you!"

But something had weakened within me even as I jeered, and I was confused.

His voice was close to my ear and it was saying, "Are you quite certain you are not interested?" His hands closed softly, firmly, on my shoulders, and then slid gently down along my arm and caught my hands in a warm, trembling grip. With a quick, impulsive movement he drew me back until my head rested against him, and his lips closed upon mine.

"Why do you lie to me?" he whispered. "Why? Marie . . . tell me the truth . . . was Talvar here?"

I jerked. "No . . . let me go!"

Arising, he drew me firmly to my feet, holding me still in a vice-like grip from the back.

"Marie . . . tell me."

"Let me go, Juan! Do you hear?" I jerked in blind fear, for I liked him and a yearning in my blood, long suppressed in shame, had begun to struggle with my mind. It grasped at the words that followed:

"Marie . . . dear . . . you love me, don't you? Marie dear!" The lips were very hot.

"Juan!" I struggled to free myself and tears choked my throat. The chair back of him overturned and clattered to the floor. "Juan . . . please . . . let me go. . . ." But his arms were unyielding and his hands held both mine in a hot and trembling clasp. When I felt the trembling a blind panic seized me and something closed in upon my throat. Quickly he whirled me into his arms and his big shoulders crushed me. "Don't!" My voice was choking. "Don't . . . you see . . ." My mind could no longer think. . . . I struggled, gasping for breath, about my waist a cold, fearful trembling, so cold it froze me. The room became a whirring, blurred image, then clear, then whirring. Terror . . . the shadow of dark, outspread wings of a bird, swooping . . . he was carrying me in his arms . . . his lips were hot as fire . . . and his body had hurled itself upon me.

He was moving about the room, and the gleam from the firelight caught in his black hair. I turned my face to the wall. He sat down beside me and shook my shoulder, gently.

"Why do you cry like that, Marie? . . . Come . . . I will go."

"Go!"

"Of course, don't you want me to go?" There was a shade of triumph in his voice, a hint of a smile.

"I cannot live through this night . . . I am afraid."

"Come, come! Do not weep so!"

"Now I understand why you came here!"

"No, no! I swear to you. I came to say good-by. But you jeered at me . . . and you lied about Talvar Singh."

"I did not lie about Talvar Singh!"

The minutes ticked themselves off.

"Forgive me," he entreated, throwing one arm across me. "Forgive me, Marie . . . to think . . . you . . . forgive me. Promise me you will forget it. That you will tell no one."

"Forget it! Tell no one! Why should I not tell. . . . I am not ashamed."

He arose and walked away. His voice came across at me.

"You must not. It would ruin me in my work . . . you know how our men regard such things as this. Do you hear?"

"I hear only too well."

I arose to my feet and stood facing the fireplace, my back to him.

He began again. "You will let me help you . . . this miserable room . . . you must have a better one."

"I want no help from you!"

"I see no reason why I should not help. . . . I have more money than you."

"Do you want to make a prostitute of me? I feel like one already."

"What! I merely want to help as a comrade."

"Then you could have offered it before . . . and even then I would have refused."

He paced the room uneasily, pausing for a moment in the corner and I heard him turn off the gas in the gas-plate. Then he returned and halted by the table back of me.

"I came to see you before I left. And I wanted to warn you in case you had helped Talvar Singh in any way. When I heard he had been here, I waited until you came home."

"Why do you keep saying Talvar Singh has been here!"

He was again silent, as if thinking, then began.

"You have no right to be so bitter . . . to try to make me responsible for all this. Remember the things you said and did. You asked me to stay—I am not a fool!

And your fight against me was a bit of a sham, you know. You are a strong woman, but you suddenly become weak—why was that? You could have screamed—why did you suddenly lose your voice!"

His words sank deep and bitter within me. For, dominated by a feeling of shame, I believed them. I could not face him, could not be entirely honest and open about such things—it was too shocking, too shameful; I was not entirely conscious of their truth. I was too poisoned with shame and dishonesty about sex to face any situation clearly. It was very easy to make me feel guilty, for I believed I was guilty because of desire that had so often tormented me. Now before him and his violence I could not face responsibility to any degree, even when his words were partly true. No decent woman feels sex desire, no decent woman faces responsibility for it, I thought! Such had been my mode of thought for years. It was more comfortable, more respectable, to think of myself as completely innocent, to think of myself as irresponsible. And even to commit injustice against men.

Now, with distance lying between me and that night, I see that this thing could never have happened without either my conscious or my unconscious consent; that had there been no unconscious response in me to the masculinity in him, he would have left my room as calmly as he came. Had I been twelve years of age, I might have been overpowered; but I was more than twice that. Desire had burdened my spirit through the months and years, and I suppressed and hated it. Then this man came with perfume and light in his hair and a many-colored belt-buckle that caught the light from the grate. He was very animal. Such a man divines things in women—in jeering words, in the glance of an eye, the gesture of a hand, the meaning that lies in silence. But I was too dishonest to admit that I was even a passive participant.

"It is a lie! It is beastly of you!"

He stood watching me, smiling faintly, as if wondering at the duplicity and hypocrisy of women.

"You always boast of being a free woman . . . now you act like an innocent little girl instead of a woman."

"I suppose I should laugh—as you do . . . because you attacked me!"

"I am not laughing! But you know yourself that you always jeer at me. What right have you to throw a challenge and then blame me for taking it up?"

"Keep out of my way if you don't like jeers. Please go now and leave me in peace. I am sick—sick of life and you. I do not wish to live!"

"Marie . . . I am sorry . . . don't cry. I will go. Don't you understand . . . all I ask of you is that you should never tell this to anyone."

"If I am to blame, why do you fear?"

"Fear—I do not fear. I only do not want such things to interfere with my work." Then there was a long silence between us.

"Very well. I promise to tell no one."

"No one?"

"No living soul. I promise."

"Why do you look like that . . . Marie . . . I will stay a few days longer."

"Thanks! I am quite able to look after myself. Well . . . are you not going?"

Bitterness was in my heart and voice. He picked up his coat and, without a word, was gone. Nor did he look back. His feet descended the steps, halted for a second, as if hesitating, then continued. With a rush I was against the door, trying to suppress the hard sobs that could not be smothered. These things that could not be recalled even when both wished it, when both regret it . . . it is not fair! The outside door opened and closed softly. No . . . no. . . . I could not be alone. . . . I would die if left alone with my thoughts. I stumbled down the stairs, out onto the street . . . started to call, but stopped. He was passing down the street, the arc-lights casting his dark figure in relief against the snow; his shoulders stooped as he walked, the broad hat was pulled down over the eyes.

I turned and stumbled blindly up the stairs again. In the center of my room lay a letter . . . it must have fallen from his coat. I picked it up mechanically . . . it was addressed to some woman, with Juan's return address on the back. I turned and dropped it on the table. But . . . on the table lay . . . money! A fifty-dollar note! I stared at it. So he had eased his conscience . . . he had paid, as he would pay a prostitute! Stupefied, I dropped the note beside the letter he had left, then threw myself on the bed and buried my head in the pillow to forget. Perhaps I would awaken soon and find it but a dream . . . dreams happen so quickly, but seem to last forever.

No, it would not go . . . it was not a dream! The fire

died and it was cold. It must be late . . . very late. The
hours dragged so . . . the gas jet flickered in the center
of the room. I arose, turned out the flame, then turned
the gas on again . . . now it could run and perhaps when
the morning came I would be so deeply asleep that it
would not matter what the future held.

"She was a little fool for leaving the gas jet open!"
my landlady's voice came from somewhere. "If the
window had not 'a' been open, she would 'a' been dead
by now . . . laying there . . . clothes on . . . chair up-
set. . . ."

The voice trailed off. A nauseating taste of gas was in
my mouth and nose, and I saw afar off the outlines of a
strange room, particularly hard, and two deep voices
were talking. A woman in a white apron and cap was
bending over me and there seemed to be a jeer on her
face. "Back!" she ordered as I tried to lift myself, and I
hated her because I obeyed, and because the world into
which I was being borne was so hard and brutal. I had
been away at some place where existence was a rhythmical clicking, a waiting and waiting for something to
happen. Now it had happened and I had been sent down
here on this earth as an experiment for someone . . .
someone was making an experiment on me and laughing
when I shrank back . . . someone was standing somewhere, watching and laughing and jeering . . . why did
they jeer so . . . at the nausea . . . that was a part of the
experiment also . . . why was it so white and hard above
me . . . it had been strangely pleasant before . . . but
such a painful waiting and a clicking that never ceased

... someone was experimenting on me to see what I would do ... a jab here ... joy and pain ... laughter ... someone was sending me back onto this earth to suffer again.

For three days I lay in the hospital. When the doctor came with the same question, "Now! Now! How are we this morning?" I turned to the wall and waited for him to leave.

To be alone. . . . George should have been with me always. Sardarji had gone away. . . . I did not know enough to help him. It seemed that I had always been alone. And these men, my new brothers—do brothers act as did Juan Diaz?

Why should I be alone always. . . . Helen had said . . . "What are you saving yourself for anyway?" The words throbbed through my mind. How I hated myself for weeping before Juan Diaz ... fool that I was ... over a mere physical thing ... such a humiliation! Why could I not have acted as he did ... laughed and paid him some money? There was that letter to a woman—perhaps someone like me; perhaps there were many such. That he had laughed and called me responsible ... why had they brought me back to this earth?

Laughter. . . . I also would laugh. They who are experimenting on me shall see how I can laugh ... how I could laugh ... why should I suffer because of a purely physical thing. To men I would say:

"Come! Come! I am going now. But perhaps I can help you with a little money!" Then I would leave money on the table, and go away!

A knock sounded on my door at seven in the morning. It was the day after I had returned to my room from the hospital. I listened wearily as the knock came the second time. It might be Talvar . . . no, he was gone . . . and he knocked softly.

I arose wearily and opened the door. Outside, directly blocking the doorway stood, not Talvar Singh, but a short, thick man in a black bowler hat cocked sideways down over one eye. His jaw was heavy and the expression on his face was so brutal that my heart almost ceased beating in fear. Instinctively I stepped back to slam the door. But the man thrust one heavy boot between the door and the frame, forcing it open, and, to my terror, entered.

"You've got to come with me," he announced, taking a metal badge from his pocket and showing it. A detective!

"I . . . I . . . I can't. I'm sick. I'm not dressed. I've not had my breakfast."

"You've got to come with me or I'll take you. I'll wait outside till you dress." I stood, confused by the shock, as he closed the door behind him.

"Ain't you ready yet?" his voice bawled after a few minutes.

"Just a minute more."

I thought of the black notebook—no, I dared not take it with me.

"Whatcher doin'? It's long enough!" He threw open the door and stood glaring in at me. "Come out!" I reached for my hat and jacket, and he stood aside to let me pass, then grasped my arm and led me down the stairs. I hardly felt his heavy fingers dig into the flesh of my arm. For I had suddenly remembered two names, Talvar and Viren, in the address book in my purse.

In the subway I opened my purse to take out the address book. The detective's little, round, hard eyes followed every movement, suspiciously, and in fear I closed it again. Nervously I clicked it open and shut, open and shut . . . then began to count my money over and over again—one dollar and sixty-five cents, one dollar and seventy-five, one dollar and . . . The detective became bored watching and turned to stare at the people entering at a downtown station . . . to him they seemed suspicious people; some of them, anyway, ought to be arrested on general principles. I quickly opened the address book, ripped out the page with the two addresses, and as the man turned his hard little eyes on me again, I shoved the page in my mouth, chewed it to a pulp, and swallowed it.

"Uh-huh!!" the detective grunted, his eyes becoming smaller and harder still.

Leaving the subway, he grasped my arm again and pushed me toward a skyscraper facing Broadway. We ascended by elevator and he shoved me before him into a little waiting room high up on one of the top floors. The little room was gray from light that entered through a transom over the door. We waited for hours. Other prisoners were brought in, accompanied by bull-necked detectives, and they also sat waiting. The silence of the dim little room was broken only by a prisoner tapping the floor with his foot, and a buzzing fly bouncing against the ceiling. In fear, in terror, I sat and waited.

An inner door at last opened and I was led down an inner hall and into a long room. In the farther corner of the room a hard-faced, dried-up little man, with very thin lips, sat behind a desk. Back of him on the wall hung a huge map of the United States. On the other side of the room against the wall was a table surrounded by three or four chairs. I sat in a chair before the little man's desk.

I gave my name, address, parentage, nationality. No, I was not of German birth, nor were my parents. Very, very certain. My father was of Indian descent, my mother an old American also. Indians from India? No, American Indians. Did I know any Indians from India? My voice was low as I answered—I knew no Indians from India except an elderly Indian professor the year before and a few students who came to his house. I had not seen them for months. Yes, I was quite certain that I knew no Indians now. Not a Talvar Singh by chance? A what, I asked, my heart drumming in my ears. The man repeated the question ironically.

"No." The man looked at me, smiling cynically.

Other men entered, sat down and listened. One would occasionally ask a question. In the corner was a red-faced man, much like a stuffed sausage. His hands were jammed deep into his trouser pockets. He interrupted the man behind the desk with a question, and I turned quickly and in fear—he had spoken with a pronounced English accent. I sat staring at him. He was a big man, with black hair, somewhat Jewish in appearance . . . perhaps one of those English spies whom Viren had said were everywhere having Indians arrested. Since then I have learned that he was really one of the chief spies in the CID, the secret service department, of Bengal, India. His accent and his presence filled me with deeper fear. So this was what Sardarji had meant when he said this movement was a dangerous one. How should one meet such a situation—I had never been arrested before, never been before the police or secret service. What did people do in such a situation—was it true that the secret service tortured people—I had heard and read such stories in the press for months. Fear gripped me tighter when I looked about at the men. How unknowing, how unclear, how inexperienced!

Other men entered, bearing everything from my room—my books, my clothing, even my soiled laundry. I watched them, speechless. They made a little pile of the books—in horror I saw the black notebook among them. My first impulse was to walk over to the table and take it, never to let them take it from me, to fight and tear them to pieces if they tried. But I saw the men all about—it was many floors before I could reach the ground floor. Then I recalled that when one is arrested one has the right to have a lawyer.

"I demand the right to see a lawyer," I said, standing up.

The men smiled at each other. The examiner smiled as he replied, "Oh, this is just a little examination, Miss Rogers—you are not arrested."

"By what right do you bring my books and clothing here?"

The men smiled again and again the examiner spoke: "Just to see what kind of person you are."

"I demand a lawyer!"

"You've no right to demand *anything!*"

I was a prisoner. And then the examination began:

"Miss Rogers: do you smoke?" No answer. "Do you curse?—here is a letter in which you use the word 'damn' rather freely." He was reading through my private letters—they had been stealing my mail! "To what church do you belong? Oh—you are not a Christian? Then do you believe in God? No! What do you mean, young woman! What *is* your religion—are you a *yogi?*"

"I have no religion—except to help people who work for freedom."

The men exchanged glances. "I thought so!" the examiner exclaimed, cynically, and his lips compressed into a thin, hard line.

He picked up a card—it was the old photograph of an Indian that Viren had given me—of a man who had been in prison for many years. Above it was written the words: "Bande Mataram"—Hindi for "Hail, Motherland."

"Who's your friend Bande Mataram?" the examiner asked, suspiciously.

I did not reply. My eyes kept traveling to the pile of books where the notebook lay—where the lives of men lay.

"Here is a letter . . . how does it come in your possession?"

I glanced up and saw . . . the letter Juan Diaz had dropped in my room that night! It had been on the table . . . Could it be that they had been to my house while I was in the hospital . . . yes, that was it . . . it had not been there the night before.

"I do not know how it came there."

The examiner dangled a fifty-dollar note in his hand. "Is this money yours? It was lying by the letter! So you know no Indians!" He shook the letter and fifty-dollar bill before my eyes.

"I know no Indians!" How choked my voice sounded!

"There is more to this," a voice remarked hurriedly and I glanced up to see another man standing close to my shoulder. The examiner had approached me and now he bent down.

"You have been in the hospital, Miss Rogers . . . from gas it seems. Two Indians called to see you the night before. Do you remember now?"

"I do not know what you are talking about."

He was angry.

"I will help your memory further—one of them was Juan Diaz. Now do you remember? Your landlady has told us everything. Why was the chair overturned in your room and why were you lying fully dressed?"

I half arose to my feet . . . that night . . . the over-turned chair . . . the struggle, the money . . . responsibility . . . gas . . . the endless night and the clicking that never stopped. . . .

The examiner bent close, watching me intently.

"Leave me alone, you! Leave me alone! I am tired!" I cried.

"Why did you try to kill yourself?" He grasped my arm. What were they going to do with me . . . a cry arose to my lips . . . but before it was uttered a memory returned: it was of an early morning, and Sardarji and I had paused near a great bowlder in Central Park; the branch of a tree, its leaves glistening with dew, hung over us. I had slipped and nearly fallen, and Sardarji had reached out and grasped me just where this man was now grasping me; a twinge had passed down my arm just as now. He had released me and we sat down for a time to rest and talk ... what was it he had said ... that the movement he was in was not beautiful, but dangerous ... that I was not strong enough and did not know enough to devote my life seriously to it ... he once spoke about a drama, saying " 'there must be in the heart a faith so faithful that it returns even after it has been slain.' " ...

I glanced about the room—at the well-fed men, at the Englishman in the corner, at the thin-lipped examiner, and then at the black notebook on the table. I sat down again. The examiner and two men were standing near me now.

"That's it, just take your time and talk," one of them said.

I looked up. "Leave me in peace. I will have nothing to do with you."

"Young woman—this is wartime and it is dangerous to play with the United States!"

"The United States! Well, I'm as much a part of the United States as you are—and more than that sausage in the corner with his English accent!"

"It will not go easier with you if you are fresh! I know you think you are being a grand person, protecting these yellow dogs you have been running around with."

"Yellow dogs!"

"Asiatics—you know what I mean!"

"What Asiatics?"

He pressed a button and a man from an inner office appeared.

"Arrest this man at once," he announced, and gave the man a paper from his desk. I listened, fearfully, wondering of whom they spoke . . . Talvar . . . Viren . . . Sardarji. . . .

"Here is a letter you wrote to Talvar Singh a few days ago telling him how to escape from the country! You knew he was a fugitive from justice! Your duty as a citizen was to notify the police. Where is this man?"

Their question showed that Talvar had not yet been arrested. I watched the Englishman in the corner—my duty as a citizen indeed!

"I don't know what you are talking about," I replied.

"You are lying! We have no intention to fool about with a German spy!"

"Who are you calling a German spy, you! You dirty English spies, you!"

The men arose to their feet, and the examiner, red as if I had struck him, shouted: "We will arrest Sardar Ranjit Singh at once!"

I sprang up.

Then I saw the men exchange hasty glances—I caught myself and watched.

"So-o-o! You *do* know Indians then!"

"I told you I knew an old Indian last year, but had not seen him for months. It was he. He is an old man and a scholar—why should you bother him?"

"You lived in his house?"

"I lived next door and worked for him."

"Did he—*also*—give you money—for your *services?*"

"Don't judge him by yourselves!"

The examiner snorted in reply.

"And this . . . Talvar Singh . . . what was your relationship with *him*?"

Silence.

"Come, speak to us . . . quite openly . . . you can say any old thing to us . . . you can't shock us; we're all married men."

All the men were standing up, watching. Married men—I couldn't shock them! So! Perhaps married men *are* more rotten than other men—I don't know. I turned my back and walked to the window. . . .What if they found those addresses! Outside the sun was shining and the hum of the city came softly.

"Miss Rogers," one of the married men was saying to my back, "we know more of your personal life than you suspect. We will keep it out of the press if you tell us the truth about these Indians."

They made me feel sick! If I were only out on the street where things were clean! There were long dark shadows on the buildings opposite the window.

"Miss Rogers, you are an American woman. Yours is a silly attempt to pose as a martyr. If you tell us the truth you can walk out of here a free woman in ten minutes."

The sun on the building opposite was very soft and the shadows crept just a tiny bit.

"Of course we know of the addresses you swallowed on your way down here."

Little good it did them to know I had swallowed addresses! These married men!

"Very well, madam, we will give you time to think it

over . . . perhaps by tomorrow you will have changed your mind!"

I glanced around. They had called two men in from the outside hall—red, thick-necked men, bull-necked. One crossed over, grasped me by the arm. I was cold with terror, but it was useless to resist. They dragged me down to the street and put me into a closed automobile. We drove for an interminable time. Then the door swung open and I was dragged out. Above stretched a bridge . . . we were down on the East River, under the bridge, and they were forcing me into a building with bars across the windows. "Federal prisoner," one of them paused to say to a man sitting behind a desk. Then I was thrust into a room in the back where a big policewoman searched me, her big hands clawing into my flesh when I resisted.

When I had dressed again, the woman unlocked a thick steel door and put me into a cold cement corridor. An inner barred door was unlocked and I was pushed into a tiny cell. The bundle of keys at her belt clanged and sent a shock through me as they struck the iron bars. Then the door closed with a resounding clang and I was alone.

The cell floor was of cement, the walls were of steel, the door was of thick steel bars. A bench, made of crossed pieces of flat steel, served as a bed. There was no blanket or covering of any kind. In the corner was a broken toilet; the water had spilled over onto the floor and lay in a thin sheet of ice.

I measured the cell . . . four steps long, and just wide enough to brace myself against the walls with my outstretched arms. Through the barred door came the cold creeping sense of the short, cement corridor, at the end a barred window admitting a patch of light. I listened . . . a faint tapping came from above somewhere . . . far away amid the rumbling on the bridge. Someone was hammering . . . on steel it must be . . . perhaps a workman on the bridge. What had he done to gain the right to freedom . . . sitting up there high in the air like a bird! The hours wore on and darkness crept upon me—like an enemy. What did other people do when they were locked up . . . If I only knew! I sat down on the iron bed . . . The cold from the steel penetrated my clothing and I arose. I walked to keep warm . . . four steps, turn, four steps back . . . what was that walking down the darkening corridor! I stopped and listened . . . it stopped and listened! I walked . . . it walked! I sat on the bed again . . . such ideas must not enter my head. I shivered and arose. What had they done with Sardarji and with Talvar Singh? Suppose they found the black notebook . . . the men would be killed . . . the Indians would always think I had been responsible. The thought tortured me. Suppose I should be left in here always! If I could only climb out, or just squeeze through the bars . . . if I could only reach the window in the corridor and send a note to Talvar Singh . . . no, he was not at that address! How could I get out . . . how could I get that notebook . . . surely there must be some way of meeting a situation like this . . . maybe I could get out . . . the roof above me was of steel and it was fastened down tight, even when I stood on the iron bed and pushed up with all my might. The space between the bars of the door only admitted my arm . . . hairpins twisted together and thrust in the lock would not turn it!

I walked . . . down the dark, silent corridor something else began walking! I stopped . . . it stopped! From afar came the tapping. Perhaps the man would hear—he was a working man and would help me. I called aloud . . . down the corridor my voice echoed and re-echoed, crowding back in through the door and shouting in my ears.

I lay trembling on the cold bars of the bed and closed my eyes . . . perhaps my body would warm the steel. The night wore on. How shivering cold it was . . . would the dawn never come! What would tomorrow bring? Suppose they found the notebook . . . and the men were killed and their comrades would think I had betrayed them! . . . A black notebook took form in my mind until it seemed my head itself was a black notebook.

The dawn came crawling, slowly. It was like a friend. Sardarji would have heard of my arrest and would help me. But now my head ached and my hips were tired and cold and stiff. Hours passed . . . the patch of light down the corridor became lighter and lighter. After a long time the rattle of keys sounded, the policewoman opened the door, and behind her stood two detectives.

We went without a word. We sat once more in that little dusky waitingroom on Broadway, then once more through the inner corridor into the examination room. The lean, hard-faced man sat behind the desk and other men were in the room. The clock pointed to two—it was afternoon. I glanced at the table where my books lay—the black notebook was among them.

"Well, Miss Rogers, what have you to say to us now?"

"To say? The cell is freezing cold and the toilet has broken and the water spilled over the floor; there is no covering and there is no food or water. You know that."

"You should have thought of that before! What have you to say about these men you have been mixed up with? What about this letter you wrote . . . where is this Talvar Singh?"

"I do not know what you are talking about!"

"Perhaps you know that Ranjit Singh . . ."—I listened intently—". . . that Ranjit Singh has said in San Francisco that he knows little of you except that you are a silly little girl with high-flown ideas about leadership. . . ."

The examiner had a peculiar expression about his mouth. I always read truth by the mouth.

"You are a liar!" I exclaimed impulsively. "Ranjit Singh has said nothing of the kind, and you know it!"

The man became very angry. "You have a brother in the army, and it will not go easy with him when his officers learn that he has a sister who is a spy."

You ought to be ashamed of yourself! You know I'm not a spy and you know, if you know anything, that I've not seen my brother for years and don't know where he is now—he may even be dead—fighting for democracy!"

"We'll find that out soon enough!"

"Leave my brother alone . . . he's only a boy . . . and he may be dead . . . he was hungry or he never could have been driven into the army."

He sneered at me:

"Your friend Karin—your former sister-in-law, if you

313

can remember your marriages—has been arrested. She has told us things about your private life; they won't sound well in print. . . . We know these Asiatics always take advantage of women."

"You always judge them by yourself!"

"To whom do you think you are speaking, young lady?"

"You told me yesterday you had been a Senator and were now a Dollar-a-Year man . . . that means you are a rich man."

"Your freshness gets you nowhere!"

I studied the map hanging on the wall behind the desk; there was Denver . . . Helen lived there and she had never seen an Asiatic, perhaps . . . only white men . . . patriotic men. . . .

"You have a friend Loretta who has lived with a man for ten years without being married to him! . . . and even has an illegitimate child . . . you have other such *friends?*"

My ears listened, but my eyes were on the map . . . down there was western Oklahoma . . . there were three lonely graves there now . . . my father was becoming old . . . his hair must be very white now and his shoulders more stooped. . . .

"Your university professors say the things you have written have had a seditious tendency."

. . . that dark spot on the map on the other wall must be France . . . if I could only see more closely; Dan had perhaps been shipped there and killed . . . for democracy. . . .

"Juan Diaz . . . where is he? Unless you answer we

charge you with helping another fugitive from justice ... do you know what that means in wartime?"

... San Francisco there before me on the wall ... it was always gray-green with fog. Juan Diaz was to sail from there to Japan; I wondered if he had left. ...

They took me back to the jail under the bridge and when the detective put me through the cell door, I turned and reached out to him ... surely he was human ... surely he would help! As I reached out, he leaped back, as if protecting himself, then with both hands violently pushed me through the door and clanged it behind me. We two stood looking into each other's eyes; my throat was tight as if someone were choking me; his eyes were like the eyes of an animal ... brute unconsciousness.

"Strange," my voice was saying to him, "you are like an animal—not yet human ... do you know we both live but a few days ... I have done nothing to hurt you ... Who do you ..."

He drew away from the iron gate as if I were an insane person. He was afraid. I was left alone again.

Far away, high in the air, came the tapping. If they would only give me water! I did not wish food ... there was no hunger in me, with this fear, this weariness, this pain in my head. There was ice on the floor ... it was dirty ... one could not eat that. Perhaps tomorrow the detective would stop somewhere and give me water.

I walked ... ghostly footsteps paced the corridor. The tapping came again from afar. I buried my head in my arms to forget. My throat and stomach burned ... my head one terrible pain. Silence. ... Thirst. Thoughts

. . . a black notebook, with the names of men . . . Did Sardarji say those things—he also? Yes, it might be—but what did he mean about leadership? What would they do with me in the end . . . the notebook . . . Sardarji had warned me. . . . Juan Diaz, where was he—even he would have helped me if he knew—he was more human than these men. Faces! George with his mouth and eyes filled with mud . . . Dan, a boy of eighteen, in danger because of me . . . or dead in France . . . Helen . . . my mother as she lay dying, her eyes large and glistening. Suppose they found the addresses of the men . . . I sprang up. I could not endure all this . . . alone in this dark silence. Terror! A shrill scream fled down the corridor like a frightened animal, turned and came rushing back upon me. I crouched, covering my ears, and waited. Silence . . . darkness . . . thoughts . . . the notebook and dead men. . . .

An eternity passed. A gray haze crept over the corridor, a faint patch of light. Then the office on Broadway and lean-faced man—the men whom nothing could shock because they were married. The examiner watched me and exchanged glances with the men about the room. I glanced at my books,—the black leather of the notebook was visible. I drew a deep breath.

"Well, are you able to talk this morning?"

"Do not send me back there . . . there is water on the floor, but there is none to drink. I am sick and freezing."

A cough came tearing through my lungs. The night had been freezing cold.

316

The lean-faced man became very kind. "I feel very sorry for you . . . I have a daughter just your age and I feel as if you were my daughter. If you will answer my questions you can go free in a few minutes."

The liar! A daughter perhaps who had never worked in her life . . . such people do not know what work is . . . a "Dollar-a-Year" man, he called himself—that meant he must be very rich. *I* his daughter!

He argued gently, and when silence was his only response, he left the room. It was warm and comfortable . . . if only my mouth and throat were not so parched . . . perhaps if they thought I did not care they would stop all this—I would pretend I was not thirsty. I glanced about . . . no, no one had left water in the room. I leaned back in the comfortable chair . . . my eyes closed.

The door was opened and someone was bending over me. A broad face red, thick. "Are you . . . a . . . German . . . spy?" The voice was cold and commanding.

I thought with difficulty—the heavy face there, the horrible breath in my face.

"No."

His mouth and eyes were very cruel. I wondered if he would strike, and just when; but it didn't seem to matter much.

"Tell me the truth, you street-walker you!" His heavy hands clawed into my shoulders and a pain shot down one side of my body. I was being shaken violently and my head struck the back of the chair. "Tell me the truth, you!" the voice commanded again.

"I have done nothing to you . . . why do you do this to me? . . . Let me go . . . what right have you to touch me, you! . . . Damn you, let me go!"

"Tell me the truth!" His jaw was thrust outward as he shouted, holding me by the shoulders.

"I've told you the truth . . . you know it too . . . let me go! I've done nothing to hurt you . . . no, I'm not a a a spy . . . if I were I would not be so poor,—I'd be here in the Secret Service!"

He slammed me back in the chair again. "You dirty, lying, little slut! You've lied from the minute you came in here!"

"Beasts! . . . your profession is lying and sneaking . . . when I get out I'll tell what you're doing to me now—I'll publish it everywhere!"

"We'll see about that, my young lady!"

Burning rage was in my brain, and no fear. The man turned away and left the room. I sank back, trembling, exhausted . . . nervous tears shamed me . . . perhaps it was all a dream, a nightmare of some kind. . . .

They took me back to that cell. I heard nothing or thought nothing . . . The dry burning in my throat and stomach, the dull pain in my shoulder and head. Silence. Darkness. Thoughts. Sardarji's face. The black note-book . . . Juan's face, laughing and accusing . . . the gas . . . George . . . my father . . . Talvar . . . cold. Silence. The cough. The fear of tomorrow.

The policewoman heard me scream and shake the cell door violently. She came and looked in.

"What are you screaming for?"

"Give me water!" I reached through the bars and touched her arm.

"I've no right."

"Then stay with me."

"It is too cold."

"Then leave the door open that I may see you."

"The air here would freeze me too."

"Do not go away—I shall go crazy . . . the silence and darkness and the cold . . . the thirst burns . . . please!"

She went away, leaving her office door slightly ajar. The warm couch was so warm in there, the lovely brown desk glinted in the light, the soft armchair looked restful.

After a few minutes she returned, followed by a blue-uniformed policeman.

"Look at her eyes," she was saying to him, "and her hair!"

The policeman stared at me through the bars. He had a good-natured Irish face. I took a chance.

"Please listen . . . you are Irish. I am in here for helping Indians who are trying to get their freedom from England. You are Irish and you understand. I am sick and cold. Give me some water."

He and the policewoman returned to her office and stood talking. Then she disappeared and the policeman returned to me.

"What do you want?"

"Water."

"Wouldn't a cup of coffee do better? It's just between you and me—see?"

319

"Yes, it is just between you and me—you needn't be afraid."

He left as the policewoman returned, two dirty old comforts over her arm. She unlocked the cell door and gave them to me. "I'll have to take them early in the morning, though," she cautioned. "We're doin' what we've no right to do."

"I'll keep quiet," I promised, and touched her arm.

The policeman returned, carrying a cup of steaming coffee. I drank it. It filled me with nausea and I had to lie down. I was faint and filled with a deeper thirst. But they had left and I could not call them back. I crawled between the dirty comforts and tried to sleep.

Once more the Broadway office. A tall, handsome young man in officer's uniform, and with spurs on his spotless boots, was alone in the room, sitting in the sunny window gazing at the street below. I stood near the door, near the table where my books lay. My eyes ran down the little pile of books—no, it was not here—some of the books had been taken away, and with them the black notebook. Once more I studied them closely—perhaps I was too sick and dizzy to see clearly; down the pile, then back again, down and back, over the table, then back again. The black notebook was gone!

"What are you looking at?" the man in the window asked.

Unsteadily I turned to him, half stupefied.

"What are you going to do with my books? Why do you keep my books here—who gave you the right to take my books!!"

I wanted to ask for the notebook, but dared not.

Perhaps they would not find the names—if they did I would learn by their questions. And then it would always be said that I had betrayed the names. There was no excuse for asking for the notebook—one does not read Spanish in jail.

I coughed continuously and my head was heavy with pain.

"Come into the sun," the officer invited. "Look at the street below."

I stood near him in the sun. "I ride," he began. "Do you? ... Come, finish this silly business here and come out for a ride with me. It will be only a few minutes ... tell this gang what they want to know. I believe you and I could get along well together."

He caught at my sleeve, pulling at it gently and teasingly. "Come, Marie! ... You will let me call you that? A dinner to forget this, and then a long ride through the Park. Or, if you don't feel like it, there's my little old gasoline go-cart ... you just lie back and look at the scenery."

I was very tired and my body ached. Could he mean what he was saying? I remembered that I had not washed for three days ... that my hair was uncombed ... my suit disheveled ... how could a handsome young officer make such a proposal to me? His voice continued, close to me, and it was pleasant there in the sunshine. I did not know ... perhaps it was a trick ... I did not know.

"Give me some water first," I said, testing him.

"Then you'll talk to them and finish it, won't you?"

"I'll ... think it over ... give me water first."

"Aw, finish it and then get all the water you want . . . come!"

He bent over and argued, gently, teasingly, almost lovingly, and the warmth of his vigorous body reached me. His eyes were a gray blue and he was very handsome. His whole manner and body spoke of comfort, of good care. Beneath his smooth chin was a military collar, fastened tight about the throat—khaki . . . khaki . . . Dan wore a khaki uniform too. They had perhaps killed him by now . . . and other boys just like him. The khaki-clad arm reached out and lightly touched my shoulder. I shrank back.

"Leave me alone, you!"

"I'm telling you the truth!"

"Then give me some water! No, you won't! Yesterday a man shook me and hurt my shoulder and my head. You are all a gang of murderers . . . you've killed my brothers . . . you're trying to kill me . . . you are all British spies!"

I stumbled into a chair and buried my head in my arms and wept bitterly. The man left the room.

Back in the cell. The thirst burned. Again silence, again the darkness, again the faces of those I had loved . . . again the black notebook with its pages opened, the back ripped open, the names of men being cabled to India, to other parts of the world . . . the men I had never seen and would never see . . . the men whose sole crime was that they were fighting for the freedom of their people . . . the men of swift and beautiful thought and of gentle ways . . . who had trusted me . . .

who would think I had betrayed them. I sat on the iron slats, huddled in the dirty comforts, and hid my head against my knees. I must be quiet . . . for tomorrow.

The minutes ticked off, then came the turning of a key in the lock and the Irish policeman stood there with hot coffee, smiling! He took two huge chunks of bread, with hot sausages, from his pocket.

"I guess a hot dog won't hurt you," he smiled through the bars. The woman unlocked the door and I went out into the corridor. I ate and held to the arm of the policeman, longing to ask him if he thought they had found the names of the men in the notebook, but not daring.

The next day before the examiner in Broadway. The notebook had not been returned to the table. The examiner began:

"Now, Miss Rogers, I ask you but one question, and then you can go free. Explain that letter you wrote to Talvar Singh."

My brain was just a bit faint and dizzy. I feared to talk. I might say something to help this crowd . . . the cough racked my body. Yet . . . why did they ask only that one question . . . just that one? Why not . . . why not the address of Talvar Singh? I needed time.

"Just let me think and rest for a moment. . . . I am cold."

"Yes," he said gently, "just take your time. I heard that yesterday you asked for water and no one gave it to you . . . criminal of them!" He walked quickly into another room and called to someone, and in a few moments a girl entered and set a cup of hot tea before me. A thin cup . . . with red Japanese figures on it. Japanese . . . Japan . . . Juan Diaz in Japan!

"Drink the tea!" the examiner urged kindly.

"The cup is . . . ugly . . . hateful!"

He regarded me strangely and said nothing. I sank back in the chair and closed my eyes. If only I knew why they didn't ask for the address of Talvar Singh. . . . Oh, yes . . . they must have arrested him . . . that was it! So! They were being kind now because of that! When they had brought me here today they had not brought me through the little waiting room outside, but by another door . . . now why was that . . . why had they avoided that room . . . yes . . . Talvar Singh was perhaps in that little room where I had always had to sit! The thought tortured me . . . it might just be! I turned to the examiner.

"If you don't mind, I'd like to go to the ladies' room for a second, please."

"Certainly, certainly!" He called two women stenographers, and they started down the inner corridor with me. They turned out of the door leading into the main corridor outside. Just ahead of me was the door of that dusky little waiting room where prisoners were kept . . . just a step . . . a mistake I could say. Quickly I stepped forward and threw open the door. . . .

There, across the room, against the wall, sat Talvar Singh between two detectives! He glanced up quickly . . . . I saw his eyelids quiver the briefest of a second, then he gazed at me coldly, as if at a stranger, and his eyes dropped to the floor again, as if unseeing. The detectives looked sharply from him to me. Then someone jerked me savagely from the back and I was forcibly shoved into the examination room again.

"Now we have had enough from you!" the examiner shouted, and I saw how all pretense of kindness, of humanity, had vanished. He left the room for a moment and stationed a detective by me. I picked up a paper to read. The detective struck it from my hand.

The examiner returned.

"There's the woman!" he exclaimed, nodding at me, and two detectives stepped forward and placed their hands on me.

They hurried me through the streets, not a word was spoken, and then they thrust me through the door of a building further downtown. Around the long room into which we at last came, a row of men were perched . . . newspaper reporters I later learned. I heard other steps behind me, and a faint click of steel. I turned. Talvar Singh, with a bloody gash down one pale cheek, was entering, between two detectives. His black eyes were burning coals, his lips were thin and white, and on his arms were steel handcuffs. Quick, uncontrolled anger rushed with a wave of fierce heat through my head and face. I rushed forward and tore at the handcuffs, unthinking. A detective grasped me from the back and I felt the twinge in my shoulder again.

The voice of Talvar Singh came through the struggle: "Take your hands off her!" A pair of huge hands whirled me, and I caught the flash of Talvar Singh's steel-bound hands swing above his head, then descend with all the weight of his frail body upon the detective who held me.

"Stand back!" a voice shouted, and in horror I saw the gun of a detective pointing at Talvar Singh.

Talvar's face was as if frozen, and the wound was bleeding in the quivering cheek. Men grasped him and dragged him across the room. Hands forced me forward before a white-haired official sitting at the end of the room, who had arisen at the excitement. He now resumed his seat. His old face was trembling as he turned to me.

"Have you no love for your country?" he exclaimed passionately. "Don't you want to help us expose this terrible plot against your country?"

The cold passion did not leave me.

"You are a white woman! I give you a last chance before signing this indictment against you; if it is signed you will come to trial and it is certain you will be sent to prison. I ask you—will you help your country?"

Silence.

Across the table Talvar Singh was watching, the wound in his face bleeding, his black eyes glistening. My eyes traveled from the gash in his face to the steel handcuffs. They told me I was a white woman! So was my mother who lay under the earth . . . so was Helen . . . so were all the Helens and the mothers of my class! My country! *Their* country!

"Think of your country!" the official again cried.

"*You* are not my country!"

"What do you mean? . . . What do you mean?"

326

"I have done nothing wrong . . . you are indicting me because I help men who are trying to get their freedom—as America once got its freedom!"

"These men are German spies!"

"No—no more than Benjamin Franklin was a *French* spy."

"I had never hoped to live to see an American woman betray her country!"

"Who are you to say that! It is you who are the betrayers! English agents all of you!"

The old man was speechless. With an angry, nervous flourish he bent down and signed the paper before him. His pale old face was trembling with emotion as he arose, turned as if to say something to me, then walked out of the room without a word. I watched him go. No anger was in me now. It merely seemed so strange that the gulf can be so deep between people—as between me and that old man. My countryman—no, a stranger to me; these people my countrymen? No, strange creatures that I did not understand.

"*Bahin!*" Talvar Singh's voice came, and I turned to him. His eyes were warm and black, his dark, boyish face glowing. Two heavy detective hands descended upon his shoulders.

"What is that . . . What did you say there?"

"Leave him alone," I cried. "*Bahin* means sister!"

The Tombs jail—called so by some man of grim humor. And the name has clung. Its sullen gray walls loom within ten minutes of Wall Street. It is the shadow of Wall Street, for it is the detaining place for those who are poor and commit crimes because they are poor. It is sullen and cynical. Savage. A monument of the savagery within man. Men and women pass into it—slouching, defeated, debased. Inside, the odor of carbolic acid penetrates everything and a gray twilight clings like fog to everything. Inside the women's prison is a cell-block, three stories high, surrounded by a wide corridor, and this corridor by a blank stone wall rearing upward. At the top of the wall is a row of little windows. In this jail women sit for weeks or months awaiting the trial that condemns them to servitude in one or another prison of the State, or to the freedom that sends them back into a world that is as pitiless as the prison. As they wait, some weep; some sit for hours in that dull, hopeless misery compared with which death would be a relief; some wait in sickening fear; some in sneaking bravado.

I was one of the endless stream that passed in and out of the Tombs gates. It is good that I did. It is good that we should each know how others suffer; and if we have already known, that we should not forget; that we be forced to the level of the most miserable of men before we judge, and that we experience in our hearts again and again the suffering of the dispossessed.

I was sick. When I walked, or as I lay, I thought of all the things that had been used to torture me: Dan—if he was still alive ... Sardarji ... Karin ... Loretta. Then there was the black notebook. When I sat on the cot with its straw mattress and its coarse black blankets, and the darkness came creeping upon me, I thought of all this. Since that night Juan Diaz had come to my room, years instead of days seemed to have elapsed. Sometimes I arose from my cot at night and stood grasping the bars of the gate-like door, staring into the dark corridor. Fantasies swarmed in my brain—fantasies of my creeping out of the jail, down Broadway, up the flights of stairs into the rooms of the Secret Service, finding the notebook, hiding it in the front of my dress, and then just as magically finding my way to the street again.

Then I would come to consciousness and find myself holding the bars of the door and would shake it violently. The matron would come, heavy-footed and heavy-witted, and ask me what I meant, acting like that in the middle of the night? I would stare at her through the bars, answering nothing. My thoughts, my beliefs, had failed me! I turned and beat my fists against the wall; a dull echo was the only response. I attacked the bars of the door, believing that the intensity of my thought could break them.

When the morning came I was very sick. During the following weeks I lay between the coarse black blankets in the narrow cell. At last came days when I arose and paced the long, broad corridor that ran like a lane before my steel-barred door. Women, old and young, paced with me or sat along the low rough benches, their faces deadened by hopelessness: prostitutes, murderesses, thieves; first offenders and old-timers. All were poor. Most were ignorant, some were debased, and they poisoned the air with their vulgarity.

They were physical women—as I had once been physical. But now I had some measure of thought, some measure of belief in the power of ideas; in this only did

I differ from them. When the world, with its eating and sleeping, its dancing and singing, its colors and laughter, was taken from these women, they were without understanding or resistance. It was easy to make beasts of such women. They had nothing to support themselves with.

It was because I, like them, did not know what my fate would be—whether a few months, or long years—that I knew what prison did to them. The prison officials did not know, the prison investigators did not know, the judges did not know. For imprisonment does more to the mind, to the spirit, than to the body. It deadens and debases. When such women are treated like animals, they act like animals. The second time it is done does not matter—the first time kills. . . .

But one woman of the upper classes came among us—a college girl in black silk and jet, charged with grand larceny. Fifteen hundred dollars worth of goods, stolen. Two days later she was released without trial. Influence of her family saw to that. The young Negro girl who took her cell was sentenced the next week to the workhouse for petty larceny—for stealing a pair of green silk stockings! She was poor and black. . . .

One morning a worn-out old Irish prostitute, pockmarked and with a voice like a foghorn, stood by my bed and asked:

"What are you doin' in this here hotel?"

"You wouldn't understand if I told you," I replied.

She sank onto the rough stool near me, her hands relaxed across her old protruding stomach; she sat staring at the bars like a wounded animal. Then her voice, hoarse and low, came across to me:

"I could 'a' understood once; I was purty once."

In her eyes lay memories of days when she was young and sweet, a slender girl dancing on the green in Ireland,—those days before she came to America as a servant girl. She had been poor, and ignorant. But for the grace—not of God, but of the wildness and selfishness within me—I would have been like her. She had undoubtedly been docile and very lovely, and she was still a devout Catholic. All the things that men praise in women had been hers.

The priest, once making his rounds, opened my door, came in and sat down on the rough stool. We talked. I did not like priests. In the end he said:

"It is women like you who land in prison—you women who believe in study instead of in a home or children."

I arose on my elbow and looked outside at the old Irish-woman sitting at a 45-degree angle against the radiator in the corridor, singing an unmentionable barroom melody.

"Look at old Nellie out there. She was a very womanly woman, I am sure. She was a Catholic like you, and she was sweet and gentle, believing undoubtedly in a home and children. Why don't you say such things as you say to me, to women like that? They have not studied."

"You are an educated woman!" he replied.

"Yes, I am an educated woman—so educated that one day I will help destroy the prisons you Christians build to ruin our race."

"You are also a Socialist?"

"Yes, but a bit more than that." . . .

There was an old forger—fat and blonde, who sat and talked with me. In the locket in her purse was the photograph of a young man—a man whom she had loved and worked for through many years, forged for, sneaked for and gone to prison for. She wept bitterly when he did not come the day they sentenced her to seven years at hard labor. For all women have love in their hearts.

"Maybe he didn't know I was up for trial today," she said, hiding her face from the truth.

I lied with deep sincerity: "Yes, that is it. He did not know you were up for trial today... How could he know . . . it is not in the papers."

There was a young girl of seventeen, an unmarried mother with her baby in her arms. Their eyes were clear and very, very blue, and their skins as delicate as the silken petals of a flower. They looked so much alike that they seemed an inseparable part of each other. Alice was her name and she gave no other. She was innocent of life and very stubborn. She sat by me and her baby crawled all over me, gurgling in delight until we forgot that we were in a cell. Driven out by her family because of her illegitimate child, Alice had at last stolen fifty dollars to feed herself and her baby. She refused to give the name of her parents or the man she loved—she would not bring further disgrace upon them.

"If he knew," she said, referring to the father of her child, "then he would *never* marry me."

A woman laughed.

"Listen to the angel—she thinks he'll marry her! Why, kid, don't you know if he'd 'a' wanted to marry you, he'd 'a' married you before now? Chances are that before he's through, there won't be a kid in the city he can slap without fearin' it's his own!"

Alice was sent to the reformatory for three years, and I knew that at the end of that time she would not care about disgracing her parents. . . .

There was a girl just twenty, with red hair and a very lovely face. She was also an unmarried mother and had been arrested for forging a check to pay the hospital where her twin babies were suffering from whooping-cough. I was in the corridor on the day the news came of the death of both children. Two women prisoners half carried the girl up the steel steps to her cell on an upper tier. Her hair was a soft glow against the grayness, her face as white as death, and as they carried her, her head fell back limply against the shoulder of one of them. No tears were in her eyes, but hard sobs were wrung from her. The women prisoners and the women officials alike stood staring upward in silence, their faces filled with pity.

"Oh . . . the God damned dogs!" came from one of the women prisoners.

The red-haired girl was sentenced to three years hard labor for forgery. They said she did not seem to hear the judge when he spoke, nor did she seem to care. Her white face was stunned, and she did not look back at us when they took her away. . . .

Six months passed and I watched them come and go, the unfortunate, the miserable, the debased. All of them were poor.

The War had come to an end and I found myself free even without trial. Depressed by the spirit of the jail, my mind filled with the eyes of women who, from behind the great iron gates, had watched me go out of their lives, I walked along the street and watched the crowds of free people flow past. I felt that I should scream: "Stop! Think! Listen to the things I have learned and left behind!" They would have hurried faster, perhaps, had I done so, believing me to be insane. Behind towered the dark gray walls of the Tombs—the people did not even see it!

Viren and Kumar met me at the jail door. Without waiting for me to speak, they told me of the fate of their other countrymen. Viren had been arrested, imprisoned for a few days, and released. Talvar Singh and Hyder Ali were both in jail. Twenty other Indians had been arrested, tried and sent to prison. Now they were all held for deportation to India—deportation would mean death.

"And Sardarji?"

"Of course he is free—he left the country. Juan Diaz also disappeared."

Without the ability to control myself, I began to weep nervously. The hurrying people in the streets, the noise and jostling of the crowd, this news, all tore at my heart.

We took a street-car and went to Viren's room, high up on the top floor of a building. It was bare of furniture except for a soldier's cot, a small bureau of drawers and a gas plate and some cooking vessels in the corner. I lay down on the cot and from one of the drawers he drew out the newspaper reports of my arrest. One of them read:

"American woman arrested with swarthy Hindu in

house on 122nd Street!" Reading further I caught the words: "The Rogers woman was dressed in modest brown but had a fanatical look in her eye. She attacked the detectives when they brought her Hindu lover into the courtroom. Asked if she were not willing to help her country she replied scornfully that she was not. Asked about her other Hindu lovers, she refused to talk. Asked if she had subscribed to the deadly oath found in her possession, she maintained a stony silence. . . .

"When arrested her Hindu lover had vials of poison in his pockets. As he was led from the courtroom he shouted a secret password to the Rogers woman, who responded with the same word! The couple belong to a secret band of Indian anarchists who have been plotting with the Kaiser and with Trotzky against the Government of the United States!"

Kumar waited until I had finished, then said: "It is a bloody account, isn't it?" But I had begun to weep senselessly again.

"Marie! Marie!" he kept repeating, frightened at my tears. Viren walked to the window and kicked the wall repeatedly.

The next day we went to the office of Mr. Gilbert, a councilor-at-law whom they had retained and who had secured my release. When he came to greet me I saw a heavily-built, lion-headed man, somewhere beyond fifty, his hair sprinkled with white—a type of man that is fast disappearing—a man of the West who fought for the traditions of the days when America was young and believed in freedom for all men; a man of composed, quiet manner, with blue-gray eyes beneath bushy eyebrows; a firm handshake. With him this case was not a matter of money—he smiled a bit when we spoke to him about his fees. He was one of those rare men who stand and fight for the principles they once learned were precious; a man holding the fort, hoping a new generation would arise, filled with the spirit of the days when he was young—and when America was young. All his knowledge and power—and he had both—were used to defend men and women whom he believed to be fighting the good fight.

"They didn't arrest you; they kidnapped you," he told me. "Your arrest was illegal and we will let them know it—we will get back everything they took from you."

I thought of Sardarji as he spoke. The two men were very different. Yet the spirit that lay back of their words seemed to spring from the same source. Except that this man, standing upon power and security, was calmer, more confident, less heavily burdened. It seemed strange to meet such an American—a man whom I placed at once in the upper classes, although he perhaps was once a barefoot farm boy. Before him I felt very humble and unknowing; his steady gray eyes, his few words. For I was restless, nervous, uncontrolled, hasty and unformed in word and judgment and action; and now always on the verge of weeping. But through it all I saw respect and kindness in his eyes and manner, and this made me humbler still. Respect for me? Or was it pity? I was suspicious—but grateful.

"Do not worry," he comforted me. "They will not deport these men. This was once a land of asylum—we will see why it cannot remain so."

"Your brother has been here," my lawyer said,

gently, after a pause in our conversation. "I think I should tell you that." Then he continued.

I listened, hardly understanding. Dan had been shipped to France nearly six months before, and he passed through New York City a week or two after I was put in the Tombs. The boy had searched for me, going from one address to another. He ended at the Tombs, where he argued with the Warden. No one could see me without written permission from the Prosecuting Attorney. Dan went to him. The Attorney saw him—a boy in soldier's uniform, and when he learned who he was, he called the examiner from the Secret Service. Of what they said, Mr. Gilbert knew but little, except that they told him I was a German spy, that I "had been living with Hindus" and that a soldier in uniform should give up such a sister if he was a patriot.

"He was a very simple boy," my lawyer said. "Yes—his eyes were blue and his hair black; he was half a child. But nothing they said against you made any impression upon him."

He was refused permission to see me. He went back and forth from the Prosecuting Attorney to the Warden of the Tombs, arguing and pleading. He stood before the Tombs for hours, in line before the visitors' gate, arguing with the guard. He wandered the streets, looking for my friends, asking them to help; they took him to my lawyer. But the authorities not only refused—they threatened him if he continued.

I heard the story in silence, following my brother through the streets, and seeing him standing for hours before the Tombs, arguing in his simple, unsophisticated way with men whose profession was cunning and cruelty. He had asked my lawyer what I looked like, what my voice sounded like when I spoke, and how I lived. Other people were permitted to see me, he said—why not he? Then they shipped him to France. The months had passed without a line coming from him. I thought he would have written me had he been alive. It seemed they might have spared him this before sending him out to die.

The winter passed and the spring came. Mr. Gilbert brought Hyder Ali and Talvar Singh from prison. I told them of the black notebook. They did not believe the names in the book had been found—we would have heard of it; we could only wait and see if Mr. Gilbert's plan to demand all my books and papers back succeeded.

My home was now an apartment, shared with a young Jewish girl who was my friend, a girl with brown eyes and masses of brown hair. She was a student and a writer of verse. She had never worked for her living and did not know what it meant. Florence was her name. She was a friend who loved, but did not understand me. To her, life was a place of verse, music, literature, love. She protested at my manner of life: "Why pin yourself to a cross?"

Then as the weeks passed Mr. Gilbert fought in the courts in defense of the Indian exiles, trying to force their release from prison and prevent their deportation to India. He brought a case against the branch of the Secret Service that had kidnapped me, and forced them to return everything they had illegally taken from me. There came a day when he and I went to the Broadway office, with the court order in our hands, and again I faced the lean-faced examiner—the man whom nothing could shock because he was married. Faced with the court order, he ordered everything to be returned to me. A few things were brought out. He said he had nothing else. I searched them through—the leather notebook was not there. Of it I had told not even Mr. Gilbert. I insisted upon other books being returned to me.

After a time they returned with more books and papers, and among them I saw the black notebook. Trying not to appear too hurried or nervous, I said that was all. Mr. Gilbert arranged the books to be sent to the taxi below, but I picked up some of the papers and the notebook and carried them. Quickly I got into the taxi, leaving him to arrange about the books. Opening the notebook, I stared, not believing my eyes; for it had not been touched. Still not believing, I took a penknife from my purse and hastily cut down the inside cover. The soft thin sheets lay inside. Unbelieving, I ran my finger over them—they were exactly as Talvar had left them! Telling Mr. Gilbert that I would see him the next day, I directed the taxi driver to go as quickly as possible to where I would find Talvar.

When I had come from jail, I could find no work. My name had been in the press and that was not a recommendation for a position. *The Graphic* had offered to take me back, but the position open was the old one with the Englishman in charge of the book reviews. I looked further for work. Urged by Mr. Gilbert, I had written and published my first short stories, based upon the women I had met in jail. The stories appeared in various magazines and I was paid for them. After reading some of them, an American woman came to see me. She was the head of the birth control movement.

"I know nothing of India, or what you have done," she informed me, "but I believe America needs women who have backbones. We have few. Will you come and work on my magazine?"

Then I worked on her magazine for many weeks. I learned much of her work while there, much of the poverty-stricken women from the East Side who came asking for help to prevent them from having more children. Once two men came and tried to induce me to give them such information, telling me very sad stories about their large families. I had not been in the hands of the Secret Service for nothing and now I knew them when they came. One could be arrested for giving this simplest of information, and our offices were haunted by these spies trying to catch a human victim.

My new American woman friend hoped to win me from the Indian work and bring me into hers. It was impossible. Someone has said that one loves most where one has suffered. That may be true. But I do not know if I suffered more in jail than I had suffered in my childhood and girlhood. I remember little but suffering in my life. The Indian work was the first thing I had ever suffered for out of principle, from choice. It was not just living, just reacting to life—it was expression. It gave me a sense of self-respect, of dignity, that nothing else had ever given me.

When my office work was now done, I went directly to a little office that Talvar and Viren had established to carry on their work. Viren had half-day work; Talvar could find nothing to do. He wrote much and sold some of his articles. We three shared what we earned, and that was not much. Both Talvar and I had to report to the police every other day, and he was never without his shadow. He even came to know the spy whose business it was to follow him, and sometimes they walked and talked together. The spy was a nice young man, Talvar said; he was out of a job and had to do what he was doing. There were times when he took his girl to the theater or on an excursion, and then asked Talvar later what he did during that time so that he could give a report. Talvar told him he was working as usual—writing for the press in defense of his countrymen in prison; the articles were in the press. The spy reported accordingly.

During this time I met many liberals. They were teachers, writers, lecturers. I remember them as one long lecture on what I should do or not do, what I should have done or not have done while under arrest. I should have worn a service star and have been proud that my brother gave his life for democracy! I should have bowed my head and got out of it the best way I could. One woman, with whom I discussed the threatened deportation of the Indians, put me through an examination to find out if I was sexually interested in any Indian. Only when she found that I was not was she willing to help the Indians. One man held me to be nothing but a fanatic; I should study for many years and learn to reason without emotion, he said. One man who posed as a psychoanalyst after having read a few books, came upon me in a club library one day, and standing in the door observing me for some time, finally asked:

"Why do you always frown? Why is your face so drawn?"

I did not reply. I should think anyone would know why I was not well after my jail experience.

"What I think is wrong with you," he continued, is that you are in love with your father."

I stared at him. He sat down and talked in this strain for a time until I arose and left the room. He spoke to my departing back: "You can't get away from it by running away—it is in your unconscious."

I stood in the midst of them, confused and unhappy. They all wanted to change me from the ground up. They were all kind and meant it for my good, but had I followed their advice I would have advanced in a dozen different directions at one time. I was too stubborn to change, they said. I know they carry the key to personal happiness—for they can adjust their brains and actions to any situation.

One day Karin, who was preparing to go to Denmark for a year, brought a young man and his wife to the office where I worked. The young man was a reporter on *The Call*, the leading New York Socialist daily. He talked at length with me and it was through his efforts that I became a reporter on the same newspaper.

I was the only woman on *The Call*. It was with great fear that I began the work, with the eyes of the whole staff upon me. The city editor was a French-American, a thin, pale-faced man who had formerly been a European correspondent for one of the great New York dailies, but who had been discharged because of his opinions. He worked with great intensity, and his tongue was like a lash. He was embittered against women and his own unhappy love was later to lead to his suicide. His remarks about women were sufficient to make me hate him, and yet from the moment he talked with me about my first assignment I liked him. His caustic remarks when I turned in my first story made no impression upon me—they seemed not to be meant for me. I felt depressed and miserable that I could not even report on an Irish mass meeting, but I knew he was right in saying I knew nothing about writing a news story. I stood miserably before him, watching his white tense face and bitter mouth—then he told me to come with him. He left his table and sat down at my typewriter, and for one hour re-worked my story, paragraph by paragraph, teaching me what he was doing, and why. In the weeks that followed he did the same thing over and over again, with unwearying patience. He was especially harsh in his criticism of my work, but his harshness was so impersonal that it never hurt me.

There were times when I told him that he was a slave driver when he heaped me with assignments that seemed beyond my strength. He gave me everything in connection with India or China. Then special work in connection with the Russians who were deported because they were Communists. Later the trials of two of the four men tried for treason for the foundation of the American Communist Party. One of these men was an Irish labor leader, and daily I sat in the courtroom, taking the testimony in shorthand and writing my stories upon this evidence. The city editor was very exacting, for our paper ran the risk of suppression. Each morning in the courtroom I saw *The Call* in the hands of the judge. When the prisoner was finally convicted, and was to be sent to Sing Sing prison, I inquired until I learned on which train he was to be taken. Without informing the city editor, I waited at the Grand Central Station, boarded a train on a chance of finding him, and waited until we were well under way. Then I went through all the cars until I found, in the end of the smoker, the Irish labor leader sitting between two armed detectives.

I sat at a distance for a time, watching. The two detectives were obviously Irish, and they were engaged in conversation with their prisoner. Taking a chance that I would be put off the train, I approached them. I knew the Irish leader and he knew me. In astonishment he watched me approach. Speaking directly to the detectives I said I was a friend of their prisoner and wished to accompany him to Sing Sing.

"It will be a long time before I see him again," I said, knowing they would think I was his beloved. One smiled slightly and said something to the other. The prisoner saw the situation and said, "Yes, ten years is a long time not to see her again—can't you let her sit here by me?" There was discussion and argument and at last they agreed that I could go to Sing Sing with their prisoner.

We sat talking of Ireland and the Irish labor movement until we reached the town where he was to be taken to Sing Sing prison. The detectives took him to the high road beyond the village, then told him he could walk slowly with me in front. Arm in arm we walked while the two detectives followed some distance behind me, deeply engrossed in conversation. The labor leader bent his tall shoulders down and talked with me. Walking with my shoulder hid before his, I took in shorthand his final message to the workers in Ireland and to the American working class. We reached Sing Sing. They thought I was his beloved, and they permitted me to see him weighed, his height and thumb-prints taken, his name and history registered. Then they led him through great iron gates down a long corridor. I stood with my face pressed against the bars and watched his big form disappear. Through the tears that blinded me I saw him raise his hand in final greeting before they led him out of sight. Then I went outside the walls of Sing Sing, sat on the earth by the road-side and wrote my story of his sentence, his imprisonment and his final message.

It was nearing midnight when I again stood before my city editor. The *Call* was the official organ of the Socialist Party. The final message of the Communist leader contained a criticism of the Party, and yet we published the story.

I was no longer a member of the Party at this time. The echo of the Russian Revolution had reached me, as it had so many of the Party. There had been a split into the left wing and the right wing, but I had joined neither. The entire ideology of the right wing made no appeal to me, for it had no vitality, no strength; step by step progress seemed to me short-sighted. And I did not join the left wing because many of its leaders were those brilliant intellectuals who had formerly so aroused my resentment. They were *leaders* and I had no use for leaders. I didn't want to be led by them. Nor could I believe that the Russian Revolution was their private property. They were fighting dramatically and with conviction, and they were undoubtedly right in their opinions. But I did not wish to be led by them, to permit them to tell me what to think or do. It was at about this time that I met many members of the I.W.W., heard them speak, talked with them, and that I became a member of their organization. Its ideology and its form seemed more natural to me than that of any other organization. It most certainly came closer to expressing my own manner of life and thought. The one thing in the Socialist Party that had seemed to me so utterly useless, so unspeakably futile, was voting. But although I joined the I.W.W., I took no active part in it, then or later. I continued my work as usual on *The Call*.

My work was very heavy. There was the time when the Communist prisoners were sent to Dannemora prison near the Canadian border. It was the worst prison in the State, to which serious criminals were sent; it was noted for its medieval conditions. There was an insane asylum next to it—often prisoners had to be transferred to it.

The city editor told me to get into Dannemora prison by some means and investigate conditions. I used Irish political connections in New York to get letters to the warden, and with some fear set out. It was not known that I represented a newspaper. My letters said that I was a university student studying criminology. I arrived in the little town near the Canadian border at nightfall. The gray stone walls of the prison reared above the town. Beyond lay the insane asylum. One of my letters was to an Irish guard in the prison, and to him I went. Unsuspecting, he gave me a room in his house, and for hours that evening we walked about the prison walls, around the insane asylum, and talked of his twenty years of service there.

I was a bit fearful when, the next morning, he introduced me to the warden of the prison. This man read my letters of introduction and was very glad to show a student of criminology his institution. He conducted me through the prison—down the long, low stone corridors, with their double rows of narrow, low, stone cells. He took me to the cells where prisoners were in isolation. I stood in silence before the cells and once heard a movement behind the bars, the shuffling of a foot, the breathing of some captured human being. I thought the warden must have heard my heart beating when he told me that one of the "Bolshevik" prisoners was in there, lying on the straw, being fed on bread and water. For a long time I stood listening, my brain whirling, as I had once stood when arrested, thinking there must be some way of meeting this situation. My eyes traveled over the iron door, up and down, the heavy lock—at my back stood the warden, armed. I had the impulse to call out to the prisoner, to tell him that a comrade was just outside.

Then the warden led me down the corridors of the old prison cell, dank and dripping with moisture. Here prisoners condemned to death once awaited their fate, and it was said they still did so. It was true, the warden said. In one cell was a bed of straw, with a tin plate on which lay a piece of dry bread. Someone had been there recently.

Then I was introduced to the electric chair, no longer in use there. "Try it," they said. I shrank back, then forced myself to ascend it and sit down. My arms lay along the broad, straight arms. The guards, laughing at the university student of criminology having a lark like this, strapped down my arms and my legs. They shoved the steel head-piece down over my head, telling me that a wet sponge was always put in first. I was almost speechless with horror, but I sat in the death chair that I might experience to a tiny degree some of the wonders experienced by the less fortunate of this earth.

Then they led me to watch the prisoners brought in from the mills where they worked. The lines of them, walking one behind the other, passed me by, going to their cells. Some were boys—they could not have been more than sixteen or seventeen. I studied their faces, these products of our civilization, and my heart was like lead. Down one line I saw a tall, gray-haired prisoner approaching. The face was pale and drawn, the eyes on the floor. I shrank back in the shadow of the stairs that the Irish labor leader might not see me. I waited and watched for the other prisoners, for I knew all their faces. Two more passed. One was in isolation. That night I did not sleep. The guard sat on his front porch and related tales of prisoners he had known. I heard nothing he said.

The next day I asked the warden if I might not interview some of the prisoners. He did not like it. I was interested in some of the younger ones, I said, and would like to see one or two of the politicals. He stood watching me for a time. Then he asked me to return the next morning, for this day it was impossible.

The day passed and the next morning I stood before the warden again. My heart shrank as I saw his face.

"If you were a man," he announced, "I would hammer hell out of you and then kick you out of this town. You are a woman—leave this prison and leave this town at once."

Later I learned he had telephoned all over New York City to learn who I was. I went by the next train to New York and wrote the story of Dannemora that lost me my Irish politician friends but that caused mass meetings to be held. Eventually the prisoners were removed from Dannemora.

I did other similar work. One day a working man came into the office to tell us of garbage barges lying along the East River. I was sent out on the story. I found from twelve to fifteen long barges, loaded with uncovered garbage from the city, lying near the shore of the river, to be tugged out to sea. They had been there for days. The swarms of flies from them entered the miserable tenements of the workers, lighting on the faces of sleeping babies, on the furniture and on the food. Babies had died and I visited the homes of three families where children were sick or had died. Everywhere crowds of protesting women met me. Men showed me petitions, signed by thousands of names, which they had taken to the City Hall, only to be refused admittance to the Mayor. I took the petitions with me and interviewed the men who had been turned away from the City Hall. The clerks who had received them insisted that the barges were not dangerous, for they had been sprinkled with disinfectant. One man bitterly said:

"We get the garbage from the rich houses; they keep it under our noses; if it was the Hudson River, with

Riverside Drive above, they would tug the barges out to sea."

I went with the petitions to the City Hall and there was told that there had been some men there with what they called petitions about barges. And I learned that the barges could not possibly be tugged out to sea for a few days longer—because the great international yacht races were going on outside the harbor! When the yacht races, participated in by the rich of America and the Continent, were finished, the barges would be tugged to sea and dumped!

We published the story. The thing that prevented us from being called Socialist liars and agitators was that the next day the great capitalist press was forced to investigate and publish the same story. Then the barges were moved. But the babies who had died did not return to life, and it was only by accident that the incident came to public notice.

When Florence left the city for a vacation, she rented her room in our apartment to a manicurist. This girl's name was Margaret. She was pretty, with red hair and a lovely skin. She had a most elegant wardrobe. She arose late, and she and I often had our coffee together in the kitchen. She had been a manicurist in a barber shop in New York City for about three years, she told me. Before that she lived up-State and had been married. She ran away from her husband because, as she explained, "he chased me around the room with a knife because he said . . . he said I had been . . . well . . . doing it with other men."

She manicured the nails of gentlemen, she said, and I

saw she had no respect for women. Her talk concerned itself with her quarrels with the head barber and with her conversations with "gentlemen" clients. One morning she said:

"Of course I would never dream of telling my gentleman friend—he's a traveling salesman for cigars you know—but today a gentleman looked at me and said it's a shame for a pretty girl like you to wear a cotton blouse."

"What did you answer?"

"I told him I was always willin' to accept silk."

She wouldn't dream of letting a gentleman know she was cheap, though, she continued. Gentlemen had a habit of thinking they could get a girl cheap, but if a girl had the right taste and knew how to wear her clothes, gentlemen never made a mistake like that. A nice girl, she said, would never let a man fool around with her because he didn't respect her afterward. She spoke mysteriously of some girl friend who went out with gentlemen, but only if they gave her a present of twenty-five dollars or more—of course she didn't mean to say she *did* anything for it. Sometimes suspecting that I had heard a man's voice from her room the night before when I came home, she would tell me that her gentleman friend was again in the city, but she thought I wouldn't mind if he sat up late talking with her, because I was a Socialist and she had heard that Socialists believed in worse than that—even free love.

"I suppose you don't earn much money just by working for a newspaper, but if I was you I'd eat once a day until I bought myself a nice silk dress, you'd look like a million dollars if you got your hair marcelled and wore a nice dress. Now when I came to New York I used to wear cotton stockings, but now I wear silk and no gentleman would think of having anything but respect for me and they ask me to swell restaurants where they spend a lot of money. If you look cheap they treat you cheap."

She asked me what a Menshevik was and I told her. She remarked: "Well, as for Bolsheviks or Mensheviks, I suppose they'd treat a girl just about like other gentlemen."

Florence returned in a month. Margaret refused to pay her rent, saying she had no money. We put her out by the simple method of standing her things in the hall, and what she said to us would have been a surprise to her gentlemen friends. Florence and I regarded each other in amazement.

"Such women will get along well in life," she finally remarked. "Who knows—perhaps she will marry a banker."

I held two unopened letters in my hand. One bore a Danish postmark; it was from Karin, trying as usual to induce me to visit her. She had gone to Denmark a short while before.

The other letter was from New Mexico and had been written by an unschooled hand. I had seen the writing but once before and could not forget it—it was when my brother Dan wrote me of George's death. Unable to believe that it could be he, I tore the letter open. It began "Dear Sis"; I turned the thick pages over to find the end—"With love, from Dan."

I had thought of him as dead. When Mr. Gilbert had

told me of his vain attempt to see me before they shipped him to France, I had been almost convinced. Months had passed since then, and not a line had come from him. The letter he now wrote was the story of his life since he had tried to see me in New York City. He was not versed in expressing his feelings, but I saw how miserable he had been. As I read I contrasted his actions with my own when my brother George was in jail. Dan had asked no questions and had been impressed by nothing the authorities had said against me. I had written George a self-righteous, accusing letter.

The letter went on to tell of the War. Dan had been at the front from the time he landed in France. He had been in some of the most disastrous battles. He wrote not one word about democracy, glory or patriotism. He wrote, instead, of marching and fighting for his life in water and mud up to his hips—and the water and mud were mixed with the blood of his comrades; of the steady downpour of rain; of men torn to pieces before his eyes, of their screams; of days without rest, always face to face with death. He wrote of his hopelessness and horror as he marched on where driven, without knowing why and without knowing where. He could not forget what he had seen, and now he awoke from dreams at night, again living through the War. It was only by chance that he was not killed, for all about him men fell—his friends; perhaps as hopeless and as unknowing as he.

He had at first been with the Occupation Army in Coblenz and later had been shipped back to America by way of New Orleans. He was one of those soldiers who had been given land in New Mexico—dry desert land, without any possibility of water, without a penny to bring water or to develop it—a stone thrown to a man who needed bread. He had nothing but his bare hands to work a desert.

When he was shipped back, they put him in the Reserves—to be called to fight when the ruling class again felt its interests in danger.

Dan's letter closed: "I've decided to stay out here with Dad and work with him and Sam. I don't know how you stand on the War, but I don't think you are for it or you wouldn't 'a' been in jail. But I can tell you this—when the next war comes, I don't fight. They can stand me up against a wall and shoot me, but I won't go."

The *Call* was a morning paper and we worked at night. We left the office after midnight and went to a near-by restaurant for dinner. There we often sat talking for hours. My comrades were young men ardently believing in what they were doing. Except for two, who had been discharged from great dailies because of their opinions, the others were from the working class. From them I learned very much.

I often reached home around four or five in the morning, but before noon of the next day was at work in the little Indian office where Talvar and Viren worked. We were carrying on a campaign for the release of the Indian prisoners who were to be deported to India. This would mean their death, and we worked untiringly.

My Socialist friends could not understand why I worked with the Indians. I was from the working class, they said, and I should devote myself to it. Did I not, I asked—as much as they? It was only that I did not stop there. The Indians, they replied, were nationalists, and were interested in a purely nationalist revolution. One of them answered my arguments by saying: "Yes, India is suffering from many lice—the English are only a part of the lice. The Indian people must shake off not only the English, but also the Indian capitalists and feudal landlords who only hope to step into the shoes of the present rulers."

"Is that any reason they should not try to get the British out?" It was not, he said, but I should be clear about it.

"Good—then let us take it for granted that I am clear about them. Despite that I shall continue working with them."

"Only a nut can work for such a distant thing, and with such people," he exclaimed.

"I do not see that the idea is distant. Nor do I care what these people are like—I am not working for individuals. I am working for the idea of liberty ... for myself also because this is the way I find happiness and expression. It may be that I am a 'nut,'—every person who works for an idea that is not right under his nose and from which he gets no money is perhaps a nut."

"There is enough for you to do right here in your own country!" he continued.

"I have no country ... my countrymen are the men and women who work against oppression—it does not matter who or where they are. With them I feel at home—we understand each other. Others are foreign to me." We stood for a time, thinking, then I continued in my justification: "Even from your viewpoint I am doing things for this country—the workers know nothing of India; I can teach them the little I know . . . it is good for them to know it."

The last was all he could understand. It was all that most of my associates could understand. They were always driving me on the defensive. Why was I in the Indian movement? It may be that they were right and it was not normal that I went deeper and deeper into this movement, making it more and more the center of my thought and devotion. Driven on the defensive by my friends, I talked much with my Indian friends those days, and each day tried to convince my comrades that without the freedom of Asiatic peoples, the European or American workers could not gain their emancipation; that one of the chief pillars of world capitalism was to be found in the subjection of Asiatic peoples. Above my desk I hung a map showing India as the strategic base from which China, the Near and Middle East, and a part of Africa, were dominated. I also explained to them that Russia was almost as distant as India, and yet their eyes were always following the Russian Revolution. There would one day be a revolution in India, I said, and they would then be ignorant of the conditions there.

They brought me face to face with many bitter truths—with the attitude of most upper-class Indians toward women, sex and the working class. The Americans were just as primitive, I replied; the American, like the Indian, regarded a woman as a physical being who became "ruined" by sex experience, whereas men became *men* by the same experience. The Indians regarded the working class as congenitally inferior; the American thought that any man worth anything would "work himself up," and that if he did not, it was his own fault; he did not stop to consider that to "work yourself up" you had to stand on somebody's back, and somebody had to be kept in subjection for this purpose.

I read and talked and argued. Yet I worked with and clung to the Indians. Why? Forced to find answers, I was driven more and more to study Indian history and conditions, and more to analyze my own motives. But I could not tell my American friends one bond that held me to the Indians— the bond of love. They would have smiled, for they would have seen only sex love. And yet it was not sex love. Throughout my life I had needed and longed for the warmth of human affection. I had always instinctively drawn closer to people, searching for warmth, tenderness, affection. Most men saw in this nothing but a physical appeal. I was seldom insulted by their proposals, for it seemed that it was my fault that they were made.

Among the Indians I found much that I was seeking—a warmth, an intimate closeness that was not just sex, a gentleness. Sardarji personified this. In this I rested. Had I been really mature, and had Sardarji been less wise than he was, the course of my life might have been otherwise—and I perhaps would have remembered him only as I remembered other men. But he was a wise and a good man and did not misunderstand my need of love and of a place to rest my spirit. The bond of love, of gratitude, of affection, that held me to him swept beyond him to his people and his movement. This bond has endured the strain of class, of political and of intellectual differences. I write now from the perspective of years; my way in this movement has not been without pain, depression, disappointment; there are unhappy things in it as in every movement. And yet its colossal significance in the struggle for human emancipation has held my mind captive, as the idealism and warmth of the men within it has held my heart captive.

Few people understood this. I always felt like a besieged city, standing in the midst of friends and comrades who demanded an explanation of my interest and activity. At worst they considered me insane; at best neurotic. The more sophisticated took it for granted that I was in love with some Indian and was living secretly with him. They, at least, left me in peace, tactfully avoiding questions. They thought that I might be engaged in Italian or Russian or Patagonian activities some months later—and from the same motives. I found rest from all these people when I went amongst the Indians. We often did not agree—there were heated discussions, disagreements and even quarrels—but we parted only to meet again.

Our movement in defense of the Indians advanced daily. I worked as I had never worked before. My mind, for months sick and crippled, now became like steel, and my body as tough as a weed. All the belief and passion of my being was now concentrated in this work. All hesitancy and fear of the police or of social opposition gradually left me. Together with my comrades, I was speaking and writing, and I felt that I was molding the native earth of America. In working with them I realized how American I was, how native of my soil, and how I could instinctively appeal to principles, traditions and ideas of the American people, when they could make but an intellectual appeal. *Bahin,* some of them called me, and it warmed my heart and aroused strength and determination within me. For in it was not only love, but comradeship. I loved them with the love I had been unable to give to my brothers, to my father, to my class.

I came to know another America; it was small, but living and struggling for free things, and it was fearless. Some were men and women of the working class who helped us; some Irish men and women; and I recall those few precious souls whose roots were in wealth, position and family, but who deserted them all to help us and to help imprisoned American working men. I recall them as almost a distinct physical type: tall, cultivated men and women who had never known a day of hunger, who had studied and traveled and created, and who were regarded by their families as freaks or as bad-mannered and disagreeable betrayers of respectability. They were few but they were precious.

I admired these Americans. And I loved the Indians. But I could talk to no one intimately. There was a gulf between me and others—a gulf of my own making. If at any time respect was shown me, I shrank from it, feeling miserable. Even when the day came that all the Indian prisoners stood free, and I knew I had helped free them, still I shrank from any demonstration of respect from them.

They, like the Americans, had a physical standard for women. I also had these physical standards even as my mind refused them. I defied these standards, but to my friends I pretended that I did not. I led two lives—a private life and a life open to the public. Believing sex experience to be a thing of shame, a disgusting thing, and still having clandestine love affairs, I felt unworthy of the respect shown me by friends. I felt unworthy of the title "Sister," unworthy of the respect of Mr. Gilbert with his clear eyes watching me. Had all of these people known that I had love affairs, they would not have respected me. At least not the Indians.

My mind was hard and clear and I worked with steady assurance. But my heart was heavy with guilt. I did not listen to my heart. About me everywhere I saw men, and I knew what their private lives must be. Why should they be so care-free, so happy, while women must submit to other standards? At least I would not, and did not. I longed for tenderness, for love, but these I feared. When one loves, one can easily be enslaved; and I would not be enslaved. Freedom is higher than love. At least today. Perhaps one day the two will be one.

My intellectual justification of my hidden life was as reasoned as that of any business man who does likewise and whom society so highly honors. There was this difference between my life and the life of business men: I did not offer to pay the men I lived with; I saved them that humiliation. I did not try to buy their bodies; our relationship was based upon friendship, not upon purchase. That night in the hospital long ago, I had thought I would offer to pay as an insult; but when the time came, the men I knew were too kind, were too human for that. They were friends whom I respected.

It began with a newspaper man who worked with me. He was a healthy, blonde, humorous beast, worried by no such puritanism as mine.

"You are nervous because you are an ascetic," he laughed one day, bending over my desk. "Now I am perfectly willing to—well—you see, to offer my services."

"Accepted, my friend," I replied.

"Only remember," I continued, when he asked if I was really serious, "I am not private property; nor are you. And it must be secret."

Why I left him I do not know . . . any more than I know why I left any man after that. He was a friendly, comradely man. But because we maintained secrecy there seemed something poisonous about it; natural and beautiful things do not have to be kept secret.

I seemed unable to face myself for any long period of time, so I left him. Then later some other man friend, perhaps finding in me a person he liked or loved, or perhaps interpreting my friendliness as a wish for intimacy, would become my companion. Often I merely drifted into a situation. Then my sick spirit, so in conflict with my intellect, would revolt again. I was then, as later, often torn to pieces by this emotional conflict within myself. I could not reach a conclusion one way or another, could find no clearness or peace. I was physically mature now, but the impulses that came with maturity shamed me; I have the atmosphere of America, the unnatural, Puritanical attitude, to thank for this. Against this shame stood my intellect, knowing my life was my own; knowing the standards about me

were hypocritical. But I was too active, without philo-
sophical introspection, to spend hours analyzing my life
and my difficulties. I reacted instead of thinking and
analyzing. My reactions vented themselves upon the
men I knew. There was one man who loved me and with
whom I lived.

"Marry?" I exclaimed to him one late night as we
walked along a dark street toward my home. "No, I
would not marry. I have no desire to submit to the life
that most women live—darning socks, cooking, cleaning,
depending upon a man for my living,—in other words,
just existing."

"I did not ask you to consider such an existence. You
are a cruel woman, Marie, to think in such terms."

"You are a cruel man to talk of marriage. There are
plenty of women who want nothing else—go to them;
leave me in peace."

In his misery he once said he would end it all. I
replied:

"So you are trying to *force* me to marry you? Get
out . . . it will save you from further pain. I hate a man I
have to be cruel to."

He had become very pale. We never met again after
that. Perhaps he met a woman who had more respect for
marriage than I had. But when he was gone I did not
sleep that night for thinking of him and his drawn face.
Yet why should I feel badly, I asked myself over and
over again—so many men did worse than that to women.
The world was filled with women who weep, enslaved
by the institution of marriage and by their love for men.

There was one man who wept and I still smile. He was
a writer, and I knew he would use the pain of our

parting to write this scene into a story. So I sat and watched him weep, observing him with critical curiosity. He did it well. And he liked it—it was romantic, beautiful. He spoke of everlasting memories and worked himself up into quite a state. He was a very handsome man, with gray eyes and lovely brown hair and he himself appeared as the hero in all his love stories. I had a quiet affection for his boyishness.

"Don't weep so," I comforted him. "Just think—I have given you a new idea for a story."

"You will come back to me again," he assured me, repeating the same words that at least three men had said to me before. For the man who believes himself resistible is a rare creature.

I was cynical, and so I answered: "Oh, yes, I may come back, for you are very charming. But still don't hold your breath till I do."

I thought that I was fairly well insured against marriage because I had lived with a number of men. No man would marry me after that! Of course women married men who have led an independent sex life before—but men didn't marry women who have. It gave me much comfort that I would not find it easy to marry even if I fell in love and wished a child. For I feared that I might one day love a man enough to wish to be always with him, to tolerate everything. My present life fairly well eliminated that disaster.

How strange that I should have been lonely and fearful and—how very empty it sounds—innocent through it all. Is there anyone who will believe that a woman can live with many men and still feel innocent and inexperienced through it all! Yet I did—and if I wished to evade the truth I might have started before writing what I have written. I wonder now why I felt so. It seems to me that I felt untouched by sex experience because I did not love. Love is the force that leaves its ineradicable trace upon the spirit. The men I knew were friendly and gentle persons. If they had another side to their nature, I did not experience it. I really believed them to be high-minded, clean, good men. My experience with them was not so much a physical experience as a human adventure. They taught me very much of their work and intellectual interests, and I have learned more from such experiences than I have from books. Then gradually I began to trace a common thread that ran through each of them: they were all grown-up little boys, and I could never think of them apart from their childhood and boyhood. They often told me stories of the earlier years of their life; and in such stories I came to understand them as men. I was a mother nature and most men felt this. This was not only the basis for my intellectual work, but it was the basis of my personal relationships. It seems to me now that had this part of my nature been permitted to develop, instead of being poisoned, I would have loved life more than I do now—and sometimes I love it very much—and I would have been very happy and very creative. For these emotions, together with intelligence, comradeship and friendship, can make the happiest of lives.

But as it was, I came into constant conflict with the standards that had been ground into my soul. I searched for peace, for harmony, and found none; for there was no peace in my heart. I searched for rest and found none, though there were many to give me a resting place. In the early hours of morning, leaving my work, I often passed through lonely streets. Sometimes I heard the voice of a woman weeping. "She is perhaps a married woman," I thought, hurrying on, her voice haunting me. "Why do women weep so. . . . I cannot endure the weeping of women!"

I would reach home, and across the darkness of her room Florence would call sleepily: "It is late. You work too hard . . . this is no life you are living. I suppose you will get up at eight in the morning—or will it be seven?"

"It may be six, you!"

"What sin are you trying to wipe off your conscience that you work like a mad woman?" she asked. "You are like the Christians flaying themselves for sin."

"Sin? I have never sinned—I am not a Christian!"

And I bundled my pagan body into bed and slept.

The morning came and she stood by my bedside. When she soothed my forehead with a gentle hand I complained:

"Let me sleep."

"Get up and work, and expiate your sin!" she replied.

Sometimes at night she stood by my bed in silence and looked down at me.

"Don't be sentimental . . . go to sleep!" I exclaimed.

"I think if you found a man friend and lived with him, you would be happier and not live such an insane life," she protested.

"Do you, now!"

Once she stood and the light became tangled in her hair. Her eyes were soft and dark, and she quoted lines of Kabir about a wild swan that flew from lake to lake and built a nest in none. I hoped it was a female swan, I exclaimed . . . the males have considered this their prerogative for too long.

Once she said: "I love you as I have loved no other friend."

"Love is for weaklings," I glibly answered, and a twinge of pain crossed her face. "You are the type of girl who will some day fall in love and get married, become a housewife, and stay with your husband out of habit."

"Well," she retorted, "you are just the kind who will fall in love one day and be simply finished off! I will get my own way with life, for I don't value men enough to think that they are worth fighting against all the time. Just wait until you fall in love!"

I laughed hilariously. "You write too many lyrical poems."

"You are afraid even of the word love—we fear things only when we are weak before them."

In the autumn I fled to the Adirondacks. The city editor at first protested. But at last he agreed that I was working badly of late. Why, he asked. Because he was a slave-driver, I told him. He traced the grain of the wood in the table before him, as he always did when talking with me.

"That's not the reason you are writing in the style of a sob-sister these days," he declared. We quarreled about the word "sob-sister," but at last he told me to take my salary for the week and clear out, but to return prepared to work in my old style.

Viren and Talvar could not understand why I was going alone. Like most Indians, they were social animals who needed people about them. I wanted to be alone, to try and come to some decision about my personal life. I had a vague idea that if I walked alone in the mountains for many days, I would feel better and could plan my life and actions in the future. There was not one soul to whom I could talk. It was difficult enough to have to face myself. What could anyone say to me—do this or don't do it! I could say that myself, and still it made no difference. I was given to merely avoiding a disagreeable thought or memory, to pushing it back into the darkness of my mind and hammering it into unconsciousness.

As I tramped through the Adirondacks that late autumn, all was unclear. To forget seemed the best and easiest way. I was leading a crazy existence—asceticism, then a sex life, then asceticism again. The future— perhaps a senseless continuation. I was tired, weary of the conflict. Asceticism gave no rest. Sex gave no rest. There was my public life—a good life. There were Americans who respected me and whom I honored; there were the Indians who loved and respected me—unknowing. Why should those two not be enough—why should my body be so tortured, my spirit so heavily burdened? . . . Then back to the city again, as weary as I had left it.

Viren met me on Fifth Avenue one afternoon a few days later and asked me to his room. There was to be a conference—men were coming from many countries to discuss their future program. We climbed the flight of stairs to Viren's bare room on the top floor. He had brought in some camp chairs and two or three men had already arrived. An elderly man arose to meet me.

He clicked his heels together and introduced himself as the Germans do: "Hussain Ali Khan." He turned to another man and introduced him: "Comrade Feroz Chand—from Paris," and we bowed. Other men began to arrive and we greeted. Then I heard a familiar voice in the back and I turned quickly. There stood Juan Diaz, with his stooping shoulders and mocking face, watching me curiously as he talked with Feroz Chand. A nervousness tugged at my heart as he walked toward me and extended his hand.

"You look none the worse for wear!" he laughed.

"Why should I? Did you expect to find me in sackcloth and ashes?"

His laugh died at the sarcasm in my voice and we stood watching each other's eyes. Before either spoke a quick light step entered the room, a voice shouted at the room in a happy greeting, and I turned to see an Indian trying to embrace two or three men at once. The others gathered around him, then separated, and I saw the man turn toward me. He was thin, with a light brown skin, and his hair was black and very glossy. His eyes, shaded by heavy eyebrows, made me think of a black Indian night when the stars hang from an intensely purple heaven. Over the eyes was an intangible veil of sadness—how could a man with such an intense face have sad eyes! He was perhaps in his early thirties.

The man stepped toward me with a very quick movement, his speech was swift and his voice deep. "You are Marie? I know . . . yes, yes, that I see . . . I have been told!"

He held both my hands, without any ceremony, and was looking down into my face, and my whole being responded to his youthful energy. His lips were smiling as he spoke, but his eyes were not—they were black, intense eyes, searching my face without gentleness or kindness, as if trying to read my mind and my heart. I was meeting another Indian who studied all people and all things with the hope of finding help for his country.

"You are . . ."

"I am Anand Manvekar."

"Oh, yes! You have come from Delhi! You have been in prison throughout the War! I know you, you see! How did you leave the country?"

"There are ways!" His lips smiled, his eyes studied. "And I also know you. Viren has told me."

His fingers were still closed over mine; they were tender and yet unyielding—long, tough and tender. They did not harmonize with his face, nor with such a record as his. For, before his imprisonment, his tongue and pen had cut their way through the wall of lies about his country. I had expected to see a weakened man, an older man. But he was young, and his manner was of an experienced, poised, self-mastered man. His movements and his speech were as quick as light.

The evening passed, and at last Anand and I were sitting together on the camp cot in the corner. The room with its moving figures seemed far removed. This man was the only reality. I had listened to his voice all evening—to his defense or criticism of Gandhi, who had appeared upon the horizon of India; to his description of the Amritsar massacre; to his discussion of world events; to the things he said about women—his revolution extended to women—without the freedom of women the world could never advance; my ears caught every word he uttered. He attacked the opinions of Juan Diaz and I listened, hardly believing that a man existed who could hold such views. Then he had come and sat by me and we had talked. I had dropped my purse and he picked it up and sat twirling it in his hand. Something quivered within me as I saw that, and a traitorous question fled like a frightened animal through my mind—I wondered if he were married! A silly, sarcastic scoff at my own imbecility followed fast on the heels of the thought . . . then something akin to jealousy sent a hot wave through my face when it occurred to me that no such man could have remained unmarried in India. I bent over and took my purse from his hands. He gave it up, but his fingers touched mine and lingered for the briefest moment. Something quivered within me again, and, frightened, I glanced up into his face. His eyes were watching me, and his face was very earnest!

"Pardon!" he had exclaimed . . . but his eyes did not beg pardon.

I arose to go . . . he was an Indian, and this thing would never do. He arose with me. We paused in the window, watching the sea of roofs beyond and the sky above, talking of everything that came to our minds.

"Strange we agree so well when we come from the two ends of the world," he said, and I turned to look at the men in the room. . . . Juan Diaz was standing under the light in the center of the room, and his eyes caught mine.

"I will go over and talk with Viren," I told myself. But I did not go. Anand was still talking with me and I was still watching his face and the sky, and listening, knowing that I was treading dangerous ground, and yet unable to get away ...

It was one evening a week later that he walked with me to Florence's home. She had not yet returned from her trip to California, and the apartment was deserted. Anand had talked without reserve to me. We reached the door and he said:

"If you are not going to bed immediately we can gossip a little longer." And we entered the apartment.

He was asking me of my life.

"It is strange that you should work with us," he said.

"Strange—why so? I think it natural. I was tired of hunger and poverty and loneliness. I want friendship, understanding, and a resting place."

"You will not find any rest in our work!"

"No—but I find the warmth and the feeling of closeness that gives me rest. Then the sheer greatness of your movement holds me—you all work without compromise, and you work without hope of immediate success. I hear and read so much about your countrymen giving their entire lives in this work, being shot or hanged, still believing passionately in what they are doing. The movement is sometimes terrifying in its greatness."

"But do you not, as a woman—and as a human being—desire love?"

"I do not know if there is such a thing as what I consider love. I have searched—no, I do not want love! There is sex, to be sure, but the thing I call love does not exist."

"What is that?"

"Understanding, tolerance, freedom—all combined."

"You are wrong—love exists; but it is beyond those things."

We stood in the center of the little workroom of Florence, talking. Now I jerked at the hook of my cloak, and he reached to lift it from my shoulders. His hands touched my neck, gently, and involuntarily my eyes glanced back and up into his face. He bent forward slightly and his face was solemn with earnestness, very pale against the black hair. We stood looking at each other for an endless time . . . the cloak sank to the floor softly about our feet and I heard his voice, gentle and earnest, saying . . .

"Dear . . . you must believe in love. . . . I think I have always expected to find you. . . ." His arms turned me until I faced him and his face came very close to mine. "Can't you love me . . . I understand all things . . . dear, here is your rest. . . ."

His arms were about me. I struggled within myself, but my body was weak. A lightness had swept through me and loosened the leaden weights that had seemed bound to my feet. A feeling, as if I could sweep the stars, lightly, tenderly, obsessed me and fought against the fear that held me. The lightness prevailed, and under the touch of his hands I felt the walls of protection that I had built to guard my soul for so many years begin to crumble into dust.

"I am afraid . . . let me think . . . you do not know."

"Know what?" he laughed softly.

"You do not know who or what I am."

"Nor you me . . . but I love you . . . that is enough."

"No . . . no . . . I cannot!"

372

But his lips took the words from my mouth and I was silenced.

Anand and I were married within a week. There seemed no question about it; it just was. I wired Florence that we were living in the apartment until she returned. Her reply read: "I told you so!"

The earth had suddenly become a very beautiful place to live on, and people were good. Even Juan Diaz I felt to be a good man and I was very friendly with him when we met again. The habitual cynicism of his face had now taken on new lines—he seemed to be sneering at us . . . perhaps I read sneers in the smiles of everyone. For I was married again, and sometimes I remembered what marriage meant—a beastly relationship. Most of the time I forgot, for I loved Anand, and he explained away all objections and reactions that arose in my mind.

I felt kindly to all people and I often wondered if one could not stand before British officials in India, explain to them just how it is that we live in this one brief and precious hour called Life; and that it is not in keeping with the nobility of existence to keep other human beings in subjection; surely I could creep right down under their hearts and find that one spot of universal human consciousness, and convince them.

"No, no," laughed Anand, "don't let love destroy your reasoning capacity!"

"Perhaps love is stronger than intellect."

"It may be—but use it on people who have human traits. We are not dealing with human beings when we deal with the British Empire, but a system of iron and steel."

"Well—I see you sitting down and talking with all kinds of people; yesterday in the Club you were trying to convince a man who is on the Stock Exchange that he makes his money by wrong means."

"Oh, yes, if someone comes my way I say what I think."

"Love is not only a personal thing, I sometimes believe," I told him. "It is like thought—it sweeps in every direction and affects the actions of people."

"Yes. But it must be combined with other things. Do you remember what you told me—of your first night in the Tombs, when you discovered your thoughts could not break steel bars?"

"But Gandhi believes in the power of love!"

"Yes, it may be that we Indians will be forced to evolve a new weapon of struggle—we have no guns, so we must use something else. But much in Gandhi's philosophy is like the philosophy of Jesus Christ—it is despair. He preaches personal perfection because he is appalled with the terrifying political difficulties. He is trying to combine the two, but throughout his political life he has preached personal, instead of social and political, perfection. He is unclear socially and knows nothing of economics. He was trained in British constitutional law, and that is always a poison that works in the system of Indian leaders. A terrible poison, emasculating them, causing them to betray our people time and again for the sake of British phrases."

"But Gandhi is doing more than any revolutionary has ever done for India!"

"Yes. That makes him all the more dangerous—if he

should waver at a decisive moment. I fear. The movement is just in the beginning, but he has tremendous power even now. I think he is of more importance to the world than to us ... he is the synthesis of an international tendency ... and as such he loses his distinctive lines as an Indian."

The glorious days of work, study, endless discussion, passed, colored by the beauty of love. I feared our great happiness at times; surely such a blending of all things in two human beings cannot endure for all time.

"Marie," he said one day to me, lifting my chin in his hand and resting it there, "you told me once that you had searched for love—and found sex. I think you meant that. Tell me ... there have been other men in your life, haven't there?"

"Yes," and I looked into the eyes that I thought understood all things.

"How many?"

"Please, Anand," and I felt my eyelids quiver ... "please do not ask me such a question. That is too personal—you had nothing to do with my life then. Only love me and believe in my love.... I have loved no one but you. I ... I am not a bad ... woman."

"Bad?" he caught strangely at the suggestion. "Bad? I have said nothing about bad!"

A flicker passed over his face—the slightest of shadows. I believed in my own heart that I was an evil woman, as I had been bad as a child. It was perhaps because I believed it that Anand caught the thought from me.

"I will not question you further, dear. I ask but one

375

question and then stop: I hope that not one of those men were my countrymen . . . were they?"

My mind caught the one word—he *hoped*. Beneath his heavy brows were the eyes, black and tender, filled with love and an everpresent wistfulness, watching me. He *hoped!*

The mind often works as quickly as light. And mine did. A picture formed in my mind, a picture of my entire life with its pain and uncertainty, the hunting for things that were beyond me. It was a hunger. I had a shrinking, fearing attitude toward sex expression, an evasion, a shame. And I took it for granted that others had it also—that Anand had it. For the briefest of a second the memory of Juan Diaz came to me—I evaded it, thrust it back into forgetfulness, and I caught at the memory of the promise I had given. That secret belonged to dead years.

I stood facing Anand, watching his face, wondering what sort of man he was. Was he different from me, different because of his race with its peculiar development? It had been but a second since he had asked his question, since he had said he *hoped*. And then I answered him: "No, not one man was a countryman of yours."

"I am glad," he said, and I saw that he was.

"Why?"

"Because I would not want to be in the presence of any man who had known you like that. . . . I mean one of my countrymen. Such things must be kept from our movement . . . you know our comrades and what they think of such women. Our work is difficult enough as it is without having any such things confusing it. Don't misunderstand—I believe in the personal freedom of women—you know that—but our comrades do not. They are like most men everywhere."

"I don't see why you would not wish to be in the room with such a man, Anand. Why do you feel like that? The men I have known have been clean and intelligent men. You see . . . here you are a man. . . . I know you are not a boy and that you have not waited until you met me to live, to love. I do not think I should object to knowing any woman you have loved, or lived with . . . such a woman must be a fine person, for you are a fine person. After all, what are men or women of the past to you or to me? We love each other . . . we two stand alone, together."

"Yes, we two love each other . . . we stand alone together; but I am human; I am glad that no man in our movement has come into your life, in that intimate way."

"Your attitude makes me feel very guilty . . . as if I had sinned!"

"Sin! Your idea of sin, as of good or bad, is purely Christian. I do not have such primitive conceptions. I only know what is—what is social or anti-social."

"I don't know if you do or not! . . . Do you regard a woman who has lived an independent sex life, as I have done, as anti-social?"

"No. That is purely a private, individual matter, if you have injured nobody."

"Then why should you care if . . ."

"I care only for political reasons! So many western

women have nothing but an erotic interest in Indians. I have not married such a woman, and I don't want such things used against us politically."

Even as he spoke so well, so reasonably, I watched him and doubted. I did not believe that race had anything to do with man's primitive attitude toward woman as a purely physical being. And because I myself was poisoned with the belief that sex expression was sin, a fear took possession of me. It grew from that moment, at times mounting to terror. Juan Diaz was always in my mind. And Anand sensed my uneasiness, my fear; for we were very close to each other, and he was as subtle as light. Words meant less to him than manner, facial expression, a glance, a movement of the hand.

"I do not like Juan Diaz," he once remarked to me.

"Why?"

"Because of the way he looked at you."

I became watchful of Anand and myself—and he saw it. Sometimes his eyes followed me as if I were a stranger, searching for something he could not quite understand. Then I became afraid, unreasoningly afraid. Once I introduced him to an American man friend, and he was hostile to the man.

"Why did you act like that?" I asked him later.

"Is this one of the men you lived with?"

"No. Why?"

"I do not wish to meet any such man."

"You told me before that it was only about your own countrymen you felt that way."

He turned upon me with a sudden fierceness: "Do you dare infer that I am jealous!"

We stared at each other, strangers. I knew that he was

jealous; he knew that I knew it. But he was a man who could not face weakness within himself. He hated weak and unjust emotions. He, like me, could not face himself.

There was a night when I awoke to find him bending over me, watching. I stared, speechless, at his strange, drawn face.

"Tell me what men said to you," he asked.

"What—what men?"

"The men you lived with!"

Trembling from the shock and from fright, I arose and switched on the light, then stood across the room staring at him. With an effort he drew his hand down across his face, senselessly, miserably, and then without a word turned and left the room, closing the door behind him. I lay through the night, trembling. When the day came and we faced each other again, he did not mention the incident. I feared to mention it. For he hated such a thing in himself so much that he would not even recall and discuss it. I know now that he and I did not know each other, could not understand each other, and that understanding is the basis of love.

But despite the differences that arose between us, to me he was all that love means, all that comradeship seemed to mean in work and in life, all that friendship means; all that is gentle in the human heart. So he was to me. I sought in him all that my life had been empty of. There seemed no barriers between us . . . except those within my own spirit; except those within his . . . except when some man friend advanced to meet me . . . except when Juan Diaz faced me in hostility. Except!

There were nights when I lay in my bed, watching the

sky through the window, black and studded with stars. What is most valuable in life, I contemplated? There were many things—freedom of men and women to love and live their lives in a way that brings them happiness; a really great work such as ours, or such as that of the working class—they were parts of the same struggle for freedom of the oppressed. I longed for another thing— an all-pervading understanding and tolerance. Surely Anand and I could work these out together. Or could I? I seemed to know so little tolerance—of myself or others. Understanding? I understood so little. What I longed for was that Anand should understand my life, with all its actions and reactions, its mistakes and achievements, its stupidities, its unreasonableness.

In the silence of those nights I considered what Anand meant to me. I knew that if a child should ever stir within my body, he alone should be its father. It meant that when my time came to pass into annihilation, I should wish his arms to be about me, his swift voice the last thing I heard on earth, his touch my last conscious memory—even though the years divide us and a sea of tears be washed between us. That was my love for him.

One late afternoon when I reported to the city editor of the *Call*, he said:

"Twice this week you say you can't do an assignment!" Before us lay a large volume, a report of a strike, and I had been asked to write a story of its contents, choose the most important sections for publication. I had sat for hours before the book, reading one line over and over again. Beyond the pages was Anand's face, his eyes, his voice.

The city editor was out of patience. "Take the book with you and return in two days with the story." But it took me five days to do it. When it did appear, Anand asked:

"Why do you write under your own name? It is cheap—nothing but cheap American ego."

"They put my name there."

"Tell them to take it off. It is cheap and American."

I argued with him, but contempt took the place of his dislike. Cut to the heart by his manner and words I left the house and walked alone through the streets. I did not care for my name—it was that I had been called cheap and American—as if I could help that. That evening I asked the city editor to take my name off future articles. He refused. Anand watched each day and saw my name. His silence was unbearable. Again I insisted that my name be taken from articles, and at last the city editor agreed, saying: "It is perhaps just as well—the sort of things you are writing!"

There was no joy in my work those days. I had hated to have my name taken off my articles—not because of ego. To do this thing because of personal pressure instead of conviction humiliated me. All force, all vitality, was now going from my work. I was unhappy, miserable, at times bitter, and I felt ashamed before my comrades. There were long silences between Anand and me now. I never knew just what point in him I might touch that would bring discord. Often my heart was too filled with misery to speak. Once he asked:

"Why do you so often remain silent?"

I looked at him in misery, not answering. He again asked the question and I answered: "I do not know."

"What are you thinking of?"

"Nothing."

"That is not true! Why do you try to keep things from me? You always seem to have some secret."

We were in a restaurant, but suddenly I wept with unrestrained bitterness and misery. It was a scandal, and with a white, drawn face he paid the bill and we left.

There were times at home when I whirled to find Anand standing at my back, laughing, creeping up to throw his arms about me as a surprise. But I could never forget unhappiness or pain—it tinged my entire life. Feeling him behind me, I would whirl in terror. He drew back before my face.

"What is wrong!"

"Please, dear, do not come upon me like that—I am afraid!"

"Afraid! Afraid of what?"

"Of . . . oh, Anand, I am afraid of you!"

"Of *me!* Why of me?"

"I don't know. I'm afraid of everything . . . afraid that you will strike me from the back! . . . when I don't know."

"*Marie!*"

"Forgive me, Anand. . . . I don't know why . . . it is insane."

"Strike you! Forgive you! Where did you ever get such ideas. . . . Marie, what have you *done* that makes you fear or say such things?" He stood watching me as if I were a stranger, and I saw that he thought I knew, but was lying. What does one lie about most . . . about erotic matters . . . he thought I was lying about that—he was doubting my love of him! Yet I did not doubt his love for me because he had loved other women. Surely love recognizes love, I thought, surely he would instinctively know that I loved him above everything else! How could he doubt me?

More and more I determined to protect our love. My eyes passed over a room when we entered. Who was there? And Anand's ever-watchful eyes caught my glance! He said nothing. Our love endured, fighting its way, at times forgetful of other things, overcoming all things. There were times when I saw that his eyes held limitless trust, limitless love; and then I felt humble. That he, with his intellect, his experience, his life, should love me—no, it seemed impossible at times. I recalled his tenderness for all suffering things that constantly revealed itself to me in strange places and at unusual times, and this tenderness awoke in my heart a deep and passionate sense of protection—as if he were my child. This man my husband, my comrade, my friend—no, it seemed a dream at times. And yet a dream that was reality and that I was determined to keep.

When I think of that Indian Conference, I think of the eternal paradox of life. To me comes the memory of many women who have loved, suffered and remained true to the one man who did not love or remain true to them; to me comes the memory of a man who betrayed many good women for the sake of the one woman who detested and was cruel to him. I think of the great loves

that seem to have been great because they were hopeless; of the pain that is constant companion to joy; of
the night that follows the day; of love and hate that are
separated by less than a hair's breadth. And I think of
annihilation that irrevocably follows creation. But above
all I see that I have had to pay with my life's love for
the one experience for which I was least responsible.

The conference had proceeded for days. Juan Diaz sat
across the room from me and his eyes were not friendly.
Why I did not understand; now I see that it must have
been because I, a woman, was going my own way, as
was he, and to him that seemed indecent. He was one of
those who believe that sex experience enriches the lives
of men, but ruins that of women.

My clash with him came at the end of the conference.
To the eyes of the other men present, it was an
impersonal thing; to Juan Diaz and me it was not. Back
of each word uttered by him lay a cynicism and a threat
that was hateful. Once I caught Anand's eyes travel
from him to me, questioningly, and something within
me quivered. He would find out—he was subtle enough
to find out anything!

"I am opposed to point four advanced here," I said,
rising and speaking against a resolution advanced by
Juan Diaz. Anand, listening, followed, and supported
my objections. When he had finished Juan Diaz sprang
to his feet.

"I object to foreigners influencing our movement.
Not only am I opposed to foreigners, but I object to
women and to wives influencing our members."

I was on my feet livid with rage. "Foreigners! You do
not object to foreigners who help save the lives of your

men! Wives! Don't you insult me, Juan Diaz! I am not here as a wife, but as a comrade and a co-worker, and I demand to be treated as such!"

Anand was also angry: "We speak of no wives here, Comrade Diaz; nor foreigners. I have been in our movement for years, and this is the first time any one has had the unmitigated audacity to suggest that I cannot think for myself. I oppose resolution four, as do other comrades here who are *not* married to Comrade Rogers. Unless you, Diaz, apologize for this insult, I withdraw from the conference. I make this demand not as a husband, but as a revolutionary."

"I also," came from Viren in the corner.

"I also," sounded the voice of Hyder Ali as he arose.

Anand and Viren also arose to leave the room and I prepared to follow. A man stood before the door to bar the way.

"Manvekar! If you go the conference is broken up! You are the only one directly from home!"

"It is Diaz or it is I . . . as you wish."

"I see no reason why I should go," replied Juan Diaz. "Women are always the cause of trouble. Let women be kept out of our work."

"Remain, Anand, if you wish—I will go. It is more important than I am."

"What . . . after this insult! Friends,"—and he turned to the room—"unless you expel that man, I leave."

Beyond his shoulder I saw Juan Diaz watching me. All the men had arisen. Juan had bent over and was talking to Hussain Ali Khan, and Khan's face was shocked. Another man, fair-skinned and round-faced, a business man who had come, stepped over to listen also.

Then Anand, Viren, Hyder Ali and I left the conference, and we heard the confusion of scraping feet and chairs that followed as we descended the stairs.

It was late that evening when I heard Anand answer a ring at our door. I did not go out to see who it was. Anand returned to his room and then left the house, evidently in company with someone who had called for him. Over an hour passed and then heavy footsteps ascended the stairs and paused at our door. No, that was not Anand, for when he came, he came running, as if hurrying to reach me. The steps now pausing at our door were as heavy as iron. Still . . . the key turned in the lock! The heavy feet approached my door, tore it open, and Anand stood upon the threshold. With a spring I was on my feet, my heart a dead oppressing weight. Anand's face was ashen gray.

"Anand! . . . what has happened?"

He stood as if transfixed, looking at me, hope and despair mingled in one, the wistfulness heavy over the eyes.

"Marie—did you ever love Juan Diaz?"

"No!"

"Then what is this I hear . . . is it true . . . was there ever anything between you two . . . some time ago?"

My heart had surely stopped beating. I could not believe this . . . it came from some unknown region. This man I loved stood there with a face as cold as death, speaking to me in a voice that pleaded passionately for a denial. I gazed into his face, hoping he would read my heart and understand without words . . . surely explanations were not necessary!

"Answer me, Marie . . . yes, or no!"

"I cannot answer yes or no."

"Then it is true! Now I understand your attitude these days!"

"You must hear me."

"I do not want to hear you . . . after this!"

"I appeal to you in the name of our love. . . ."

"Don't speak of our love again!"

"Then I demand as a comrade, as a human being!"

He stood waiting, and in a few words I told. . . .

". . . and he took a pledge from me that I would never tell because it would injure him in his work . . . now he has come and told you to hurt me and to destroy our life together."

"It was not *he* who told . . . that would not have been so bad, but it was Hussain Ali Khan. He appealed to me not to listen to you, but to stand by them as a countryman. That you oppose Juan Diaz because you loved him and he would not marry you . . . that you are a woman with a loose character!"

His voice came from afar, as if from a void, and so did my voice answer:

"And you . . . what did you reply?"

"I said I did not believe . . . that even were it true it would make no difference in my decision."

"I thank you."

"But while he spoke I believed him . . . your attitude made me. While he spoke I knew I would have to return to the conference or have them ruin us both."

"Anand! I will go before the conference, before all the men, and tell my version of the story. I will lay my so-called 'loose character' before men everywhere and prove that human being for human being I am as good as the best man that walks!"

"Good . . . there you are again . . . it is that that I hate! And you would stand before a body of men and tell such things! Don't you know that not one of those men would believe you or would respect you even if they believed, even if you were in the right and Juan Diaz in the wrong? For he is a man and you a woman."

"Is this the sort of men I am working with!"

"Yes! They are no better than other men—except that they are a bit more honest, more frank, and they don't pose as liberal or modern in such things! As American men pose."

"You mean Juan Diaz shall have the right to lie. . . ."

"I could not live if I thought of you standing before those men. You do not know men . . . you must say nothing . . . perhaps they will have enough respect for me and my work to let it go no further . . . especially if I return and work with them!"

"What! *Your* work! Anand, I will not depend upon your work, your name, or your reputation, nor my position as your wife, to defend myself from *any* man! I will stand upon the right that is due me as a human being!"

"I will defend you. . . . I know how . . . you do not know men!"

"I will defend myself!"

"If you do, you, with your ideas, will only injure yourself—and me—more. I have suffered enough through you!"

"Suffered enough through me . . . what do you mean, Anand!"

"You have treated me as an enemy, not as a friend. You have acted as if I were an ordinary, stupid Christian husband to whom you had to lie! It is dirty! I can never forget this thing. You have always been hiding things from me!"

"Hiding things—that is not true! I kept a promise to a man I knew long before I met you. And even had I told you of him, as I told you of the other men friends . . ."

"Friends—you call them *that!*"

"Yes, other men *friends*—you would not have understood, as you now say. I told you of them—but you have not acted right!"

"Why did you lie to me . . . why did you leave me unprotected before such a rascal as Juan Diaz? Can't you realize what it meant to me to hear this from a strange man—unable to reply about my own wife!"

"Anand, can't you understand—I did not tell you because of two things: my promise to him; and my love for you. I feared to lose your love, the one dear thing in my life, apart from our work."

"I would tell you anything, for I know no difference between you and me. I have no secrets from you. Now that I know you have lied, how do I know but that you have lied about everyone else . . . that perhaps all the other men are my countrymen also . . . that I am sitting in their presence each day, and any time I take an independent stand, one of them may arise and try to break me because of you!"

Then I saw that the suspicion had entered deep,—the suspicion that had its origin in Juan Diaz. My tongue was dumb. All hope and trust had gone from him. He stood like a tortured animal. Neither of us spoke.

Through that silence my mind traveled back to that little room with Juan Diaz sitting in the firelight back of me. The months followed, the bitterness, the cynicism, the distrust of love and the negation of life that had blended with the poison already in my blood . . . then my brief hour of happiness . . . and now. . . .

Then I knew that I hated!

"You seem to think it is all my fault!" I protested to Anand. "As if Juan Diaz were all right, but I all wrong."

"What I think of him could best be said with a gun, except that it would always be said that I had done it for personal reasons. What I say to you is bitter because I love you."

He turned and went to his room. The hours wore on. I opened his door and entered. He lay in bed, curled up, his head buried deeply in the covers, as if trying to sink into oblivion. I stood silently and watched his dark outline. Then I bent and touched his shoulder. He crouched more deeply into the covers, as if my touch gave pain. The shadow of dark outspread wings of some bird swept across my memory . . . somewhere, far away. I would make him understand . . . this could not be! I dropped on my knees by his bedside and buried my head in the pillow, for I could not speak. The silence enfolded us. An eternity passed, then a hand stroked my hair tenderly and his voice, heavy with pain, was saying to me, "Go to bed, dear. It is late. . . . I should not be so harsh. . . . I have also made mistakes . . . leave me a bit longer."

That was all.

I arose and went to my room. The night wore on and

I watched the strip of heavens from my window. Then a heavy sleep fell upon me.

I dreamed:

I stood contemplating a bowl in my outstretched hand . . . a beautifully shaped flower bowl, curved gently, broad and low, and about it was painted a wreath of flowers as delicate as all the art of ancient China. So beautiful and delicate it was that I held it far from me to see it shimmer as a ray of sunlight fell upon it. As I stood wondering at its beauty, a crack crawled down the side, to the bottom, up and around to the top again, and the broken fragment rolled over and lay on my palm. I had not broken the bowl . . . nobody had broken it . . . but it was broken, irrevocably broken by something I knew not what.

Despair hung over me. I turned and awoke. It was very dark. I arose on one elbow and listened. No sound came from Anand's room. The silence of death hung over everything . . . worse than death . . . the silence of despair.

I knew that I must either do better work or resign from my position on the newspaper. My writing was lifeless, dead. When I entered the editorial room now, I was greeted by silence and the men with whom I worked did not look up. Often I did not report at all. Desperately I considered my condition. What kind of work could I do if I gave up this—should I go back to taking down the thoughts of some man, then spend the day typing them? Should I have to sit at home, a wife, a housewife, doing nothing but the work I hated—a female at last? Desperately I cast about me, then worked harder than ever. If the time ever came that I had to depend upon another for my bread, I would not wish to live.

One late night I came home from the office and found Anand working at his desk. I stood near him and watched . . . the light was upon his black hair, and I saw that there was gray about the temples now.

He turned to me: "Some of our friends . . . our Indian friends, have asked me to meet them tomorrow for dinner."

"Will Juan Diaz be there?"

"Yes . . . stop it, Marie! You must come! I have talked and it is all settled now!"

"Settled . . . how?"

"They have promised me the story shall go no further . . . and we return to the conference . . . They have enough respect for me to keep their promise."

"So this is what you call settling it! Respect for you! What about me?"

"This is the best way . . . you must come."

"You expect them to keep their promise, don't you? Yes, of course . . . then why don't you understand that I should have kept my promise to Juan Diaz?"

It was difficult to give up the fight. Then I glanced at his face and my eyes rested again on his temples. He had understood why I had lied to him . . . had surrendered, still unbelieving . . . his mind opposing his emotions. There was something indefinable about him, in the abandon of his love for me . . . why could I not find love enough? If he could go on, why should I not also?

He had surrendered . . . why could I not? . . . I owed him something in return.

"I shall go, Anand, but I go in hatred."

"Yes, you seem to treasure hatreds and revenge. That I do not understand about you. I want you to come and forget all that has happened, to show them that this makes no difference between you and me! Men need this lesson."

"No difference between us! . . . I shall laugh in a moment!"

When we entered the restaurant next day a number of men sat about a table. They did not see us approach. One was pounding the table and I caught the words:

". . . . are we revolutionaries or are we cave-men?"

They saw us then and the conversation suddenly ceased.

Anand talked as if nothing had happened, and once he reached over and lay his hand gently upon mine. Perhaps he was right . . . my way was often wrong. . . . I must trust. To Juan Diaz he was explaining something, and Juan was listening, his eyes turned to the table, the others listening in silence. But my eyes were on Anand's hands. They were long, thin, strong hands, and now they were nervous and grasping as he spoke . . . moving ceaselessly, tearing at the napkin, at the tablecloth. His hands were never nervous before! I glanced up and my eyes rested on his whitening temples.

When we were ready to leave, Anand was still talking, and his hands were still nervous. We reached the pavement and all greeted each other and started homeward. Anand and Juan stood apart, talking. I joined them and the three of us stood face to face. Although Anand's hand reached over and closed over mine, I could not stop my words:

"Juan Diaz! Why did you break your word—the word you asked me to keep? Why have you used it as a political weapon against us? Hasn't Anand done enough to deserve your respect? Haven't I?"

His face was cynical as he answered, smilingly:

"I had no intention of hurting Manvekar. . . . I merely happened to be talking to a personal friend and it slipped out."

The smile on his lips was the smile of a liar.

"Just slipped out! You boasted of something you asked me to keep a secret. *Your* version of the story— God alone knows what it is. It is dishonorable!"

"Why so noble! The thing is passed, and as I was telling Manvekar, I am deucedly sorry."

"Past . . . sorry! Those things mean nothing."

I watched the long gray street that stretched to meet the darkness. Then Anand's voice reached me. . . . I would rather have been stricken deaf:

"You have promised, Juan! If you have any respect for me, say nothing of this—deny the story."

Respect for him! Taking promises! His hands nervously twitching. I watched the taller man, with the thin, long, cynical face, and wondered why I had so little courage that I did not strangle him to death where he stood. If he were only not part Indian . . . if he were only not in this movement!

Anand and I were alone. He walked heavily now. Whenever I looked at him I saw the graying hair. I tried to sleep that night. Hours passed and no sleep came.

Then through the darkness came a sound . . . a strange sound. Noiselessly I raised myself on my elbow and listened into the darkness . . . listened towards Anand's room. Yes, it was sobbing! I sprang from bed and, in my bare feet, ran through the darkness and dropped beside his bed. His eyes were wet. With the tears streaming down my face I gathered his head into my arms and crushed him against my heart. He tried to push me away: I held him savagely, fiercely. "They shall not, Anand! They shall not!"

He lay quietly. Then his voice came, as heavy as the night.

"I feel crippled, dear. I am bound hand and foot . . . I have never feared any man before, in private or in public . . . now I shall always fear when some man stands up to reply to me . . . always."

It ran through my head over and over again. Anything was better than that . . . even a lifetime of loneliness was better. I had loved for a day . . . surely no one can ask more from life.

"Then you must leave me, Anand. Say anything to explain . . . put all the blame on me. Say you left me because of this. They will respect you then. Your work is more than I am."

"I cannot go. I seem to have waited for your coming for years. My life would be empty without you now. Even were it otherwise, I would remain, out of principle."

I crept into his arm and lay against his heart. With its steady throbbing against my cheek I dropped into a disturbed slumber.

I dreamed:

I stood on the outer verge of the world. The earth lay back and below me. I was suspended in the air by my own weight. About me was the universe—deep blue, shot through with gray. Unchanging, never-ending. Before me, above me, below me, stretched nothing but this color. This was Infinity, I thought.

Then I stood gazing slightly upward, and from out the vastness tear drops were falling. They fell just before my face, a row of large, dark, gray drops, and by their side, a row of small rose-hued drops. I listened . . . they fell into nothingness below me, without a sound . . . there was nothing to make a sound. I neither heard them come nor go. How slowly and endlessly they fell!

The large gray drops were tears of pain, I recalled with unquestioning finality, and the small rose-hued ones that came so slowly were tears of joy.

Above me stretched Infinity, soundless, unbounded in immensity. A dim humming came . . . the dim, never-ceasing humming of the cosmic universe. The uncomprehending vastness of it filled my being.

I turned restlessly and awoke. Infinity hung over my spirit. A heavy despair tugged at me. Anand's heart was throbbing against my temple.

Anand was writing at his desk. I placed before him an article I had written for the magazine his comrades had decided to publish. IIc read it through and I stood looking at his hair—the white was clearly visible in the black. Before another month had passed it might be white! My eyes would not leave his head. Once more I recalled that little room with Juan Diaz sitting in the firelight back of me—the following months, my cynicism, my misery.

"It is not a good article," he began. "Permit me, dear—you ought to stop writing, at least for a time. You are doing unspeakable work. And then it would be better for other reasons."

"Which reasons?"

"What you write will have no influence—men will only say your ideas are an attempt to justify your own life."

"What are you doing to me!" I cried.

"What have you already done to me?" he exclaimed in reply, springing up.

Hot words passed between us again. In the end I surrendered, then went to my room and wept.

That night I dreamed:

That a large white hand was outstretched before me, palm upward, and about it was blackness blacker than the blackest night. The hand turned slowly, immutably, and the back became hidden in blackness, the palm gleaming in a bright light. Turning still, the palm vanished in darkness, the back becoming light again. Turning, endlessly turning. As it turned I heard a great throbbing hum-m-m . . . hum-m-m . . . hum-m-m. . . . With each throb the white palm appeared and then vanished, appeared, vanished, appeared, vanished. I watched in fascination, with the knowledge that I was gazing on life and death, life and eternity. The white shining palm was life that flashed for a second from blackness. The blackness was eternity.

Life and death . . . life and death . . . life and death
. . . throbbed through my consciousness.

I awoke with a cry. Despair again held me prisoner.

Anand stood before me in the doorway.

"Dearest, two of our comrades want to borrow some
money from us for a month. They are leaving for
Europe at once . . . they will return the money from
there. I have some money with me . . . have you any
here at home?"

I looked up. My eyes clung to his whitening hair. He
did not like to ask about the money . . . so I gave it
quickly and without question.

"Ask them to come in."

"They are below . . . they say they have no time to
come up."

He was soon back.

"By the way—who was it?" I asked.

He turned his gray face to me, and mentioned—Juan
Diaz, and Hussain Ali Khan, the man who had come to
Anand that night.

"Anand . . . it is blackmail!"

"What would you have done?"

"Kicked them out!"

He looked at me resentfully. "Well, I cannot permit
such personal feelings to play a part in my work!"

"They have no right to come here after what they
have done to us! They could borrow money from
someone else."

"Your methods would make them talk all over
Europe and India about you—you will hear your story
in the bazaars of India when we go there!"

"Then I will tell the truth!"

"Who would listen or believe? ... Their story will travel quicker—by word of mouth. When you tell yours, no one will listen. Lies always travel more quickly than truth. I assure you—you must let this miserable story be buried—hushed up."

Anger, defeat, exhausted me. I wished to stand on a housetop and tell the truth as it was, instead of being caught in a trap like this. An acid bitterness ate into me; to think that a miserable sex story was causing such misery—not to Juan Diaz at all, but to Anand and me! I stood speechless with anger, facing Anand. But when my eyes saw the white about his temples, and his face drawn in misery, my anger gave way to pain. Guilt and confusion, unreasoning emotions swept through me, leaving me exhausted.

That night I lay awake for hours, watching the patch of black sky and the stars through my window. The solution of the problem came to me—to leave Anand; to go away and not return. But I put the thought from me—there must be some other way out. To go away—no one would suffer except me, for men do not relate the sexual histories of each other unless in boasting; it is only of women that they are so physiological. That I should be judged as a pure piece of flesh galled me. If this went on, my life would be poisoned. Yet, if I left Anand, I might have to give up this work also; and this work was as precious to me as was Anand. The two were one.

That night I dreamed:

I stood in that little room and the firelight was shining on a face. Someone was sitting before the fire. I looked closer, more closely. No, it was not he . . . it was . . . the face of Death . . . and Death was a gigantic woman with the face of my dead mother! But with the stooping shoulders of . . . that man! The cheeks were bloated as if from the grave, the mouth parted . . awful.

Death turned its head and the horrible mouth smiled . . . no word was spoken. The smile was a challenge to my fear. Slowly I approached to answer the challenge . . . bent down in horror . . . and kissed Death on first one cheek and then the other.

I stood straight again. But Death smiled once more . . . once more the challenge to my cowardice. I closed my eyes to hide the horrible face, then stooped . . . and kissed the mouth of Death!

I screamed—and awoke.

The night was heavy about me. Flinging back the covers I sprang up, flung open my door and rushed across the cold floor into Anand's room. He lay with head buried deep in the covering as if trying to shut out even dreams. He was sleeping heavily. I bent and touched his shoulder . . . his shoulder shrank from my touch, even in his sleep.

"Anand! Anand!" I shook him in panic. "Anand, I cannot endure it!"

He awoke with a start. I threw myself face downward on his pillow and lay trembling.

I was ill. My head was dull, my heart cramped. A hand seemed to be choking me. The ceiling swayed above me. For weeks I had been ill; had then arisen, returned to work and again had gone to bed. It began when I suddenly fell to the floor and, without moving, lay through an eternity. Speech left me. All control of my body or of my will vanished. My mind floated endlessly through space. I had recovered and returned to work again; had become again ill, and had again recovered. Now I was in bed again, and would soon be up again. I saw no end to this torture.

"I suppose you think it my fault," Anand said, white and miserable, when he spoke of my illness.

I turned my face to the wall and did not answer. I did not know whose fault it was—or if it was the fault of anyone. It just was. What the illness was I did not know—but it filled me with ungovernable terror. Insanity—could it be that! Anand nursed me—tenderly, tirelessly. He called doctors. They could find nothing wrong. Hysterical, perhaps, one suggested; these modern women seemed to find nervous trouble most attractive.

"I want a rest; I want peace," I said to Anand.

"What do you mean?"

"I wish to go away."

"Without me—or with me?"

"Without you. I have a friend . . . listen, Anand. . . . I have a friend in Denmark. She has often invited me to come to her. Maybe I will be better there."

"You wish to go without me! You find peace with others, but not with me!"

I wept in misery.

And yet my mind clung to this hope. Or—perhaps—I would go away and never return. He, Anand and I were destroying each other. Circumstances were destroying us. Our love—my illness was destroying us. Anand clung to me desperately. . . . I could not stay . . . It would mean insanity or . . . death.

Again one night I dreamed:

It was again that little room with the firelight glinting on the walls and . . . on a prostrate figure on the floor. I was bending over the figure and in my hand was the little pearl-handled dagger I had carried with me through all the years. The firelight caught the silver knob at the end. I touched the big shoulder of the figure and it rolled of its own weight onto its back. The firelight touched its face . . . yes . . . it was he, Juan Diaz . . . as handsome in death as in life. I glanced at the dagger in my hand . . . it was bloody. An unspeakable misery, a burden of disaster, filled my heart.

I sat on the couch . . . that couch . . . and talked with the cold gray body at my feet. "Your shoulders stoop," I told it senselessly, "and that belt buckle has been stolen."

My voice filled the room. The face of the dead man smiled and answered: "Give me back the clothes I bought you!"

I awoke with a scream. Anand came through the darkness to me and I clung to him in trembling horror.

"What was it, dear . . . What was it?"

"I dreamed . . . I dreamed . . . why, Anand, I have forgotten!"

I wept in misery against him.

Then I fell into a heavy slumber again. Suddenly out of the night, or out of the depths of my own heart, came the clear, distinct words: "Count . . . the . . . years!" My eyes opened and I lay staring and listening in terror into the darkness, listening to the voice that seemed to be the voice of destiny. "Count ... the ... years!" What did that mean! The years of my life, the years of Anand's life, the misery of these years, the years that were passing us by.

Hours passed before I slept again—could this be the beginning of insanity? Anand's hair was turning white. . . . "Count the years." What years! . . . What years! What years! The years of poverty, of loneliness, the years of the bleak future—with Anand, or . . . *without* Anand? Without the man I loved. If I remained with him—his life ruined, politically and personally. The years! I counted them that night. And I decided. When I made the final decision that would deprive me of the love I had longed for and fought for and lied for, that would perhaps even deprive me of all hope of work in the movement I loved, it seemed that I had decided to give up life itself. But then I fell into the first dreamless sleep for months.

It was late the next morning when a gentle hand shook my shoulder and Anand's voice was saying:

"Wake up, dear—listen to what has happened—wake up, Marie! Do you feel any better? Listen to me—I have news. Here, take your coffee."

Slowly I returned to consciousness. "Thank you for making coffee."

His hands caressed my hair and I wished he would sit far from me until I had told him my decision.

"Dearest, I have serious news!" His hands passed through my hair. Perhaps, after all, I had had but terrible dreams. The daylight is very matter-of-fact. I would wait before deciding.

"A new man has arrived from India, over Japan. He

403

accuses Juan Diaz of being a spy." Anand's voice came down to me. Speechlessly I listened.

"A spy all these years. He was in India during the War. No revolutionary could have gone there and come away again. Yet he traveled everywhere in safety."

His voice continued, now bitter—"He perhaps had you arrested."

I recalled the hospital before my arrest . . . then the night before that . . . Juan coming to ask about Talvar Singh—I had thought it was because he could not endure to have a woman know something he did not know. I recalled the Secret Service and the things the examiners had asked me—then Sardarji's strange expression as he said good-by.

Anand's voice went on: "Just think what he has done to us, and what he will do in the future. Now that we know, he will openly boast of his relationship with you—he will do it to ruin me."

For a long time I lay and for a long time Anand's voice was silent. I arose, slipped into my dressing-gown, and stood holding to a chair.

"Well, Anand, he will not use it against you, for I will not give him the opportunity. I am going away. I can endure our life no longer. Men do not use such a weapon against a man—they use it only against a woman. Juan can hurt you only through me. He cannot hurt me—for I shall refuse to be hurt."

"What do you mean—going away . . . !"

"I am going away and not coming back—or you must go. We are no longer happy. I am sick and my work has been ruined. My newspaper has been helping me through my illness, but they can't help me forever. I'm going to resign and go away."

"Going away—where are you going!"

"To Karin, in Denmark—ever since she went there she has urged me to come for a time. I am going."

"You cannot! You said you loved me!"

"Love, yes. But look at you—look at me. There is no trust or understanding between us—and without these there is no love. We are both too miserable. I cannot go further."

"We have been happy."

"It has cost too much—those few moments."

"We can change. . . ."

"Change the story of Juan Diaz? It will always be a political weapon against you. I prefer to be alone after this—"

"And our love—and the children we wish?" His voice was bitter.

I closed my eyes and cried: "Do not make me suffer any more! I hate life. . . . I hate love!"

With a spasmodic movement he covered his face with his hands. "You hate life—you did not hate it when I met you!"

It was not that I hated love, but that I hated life, that so horrified him. Then I saw that his love for me was greater than himself. We stood for a long time without speaking. Then he said:

"You know our men will not work with you after this."

"If it must be so—it must be. . . . I must stand alone. . . ."

"And I will have been but another man in your life!"

"Anand!"

"I am sorry I said that. . . . I am unhappy . . . you have made me unhappy, miserable, bitter. . . ."

"It will always be like this. Please go—or I shall go." I felt lifeless, incapable of thought or feeling, as I said that.

"Good God, are you trying to kill me, Marie!"

"I am trying to save you—go at once or I shall go."

I heard him strike against a chair as he turned to leave my room. Locking the door behind him, I turned and threw myself face downward across the bed. There was a long silence from his room. Then my mind followed him as his steps moved about—to his trunk and back again. It was a long time; he left the house and then returned with someone—the trunk was dragged out. His steps approached my door—silence as he listened. His feet stumbled toward the corridor, the door closed, and he descended the stairs. The outside door clanged shut. Silence. Emptiness. Hours passed. The coffee beside my bed was long since cold. I was cold and numb. Slowly, with difficulty, I arose and began to pack. Out of this house—out of this country. . . .

Afterword

This is a novel about the profound destructiveness of not-knowing—of ignorance caused by poverty and isolation. It is also a novel of education. Its protagonist learns to live in the world of the literate, the self-possessed, those with choices. But like many who have made such a journey into knowing, she is haunted by her past, and it shapes her perceptions and actions. As a young child in the dirt-poor Missouri farming country of the 1890s, Marie Rogers is confronted brutally and violently with the stark truth about gender relations and social class in the culture of the frontier. Her only recourse is flight from each exploitative situation. Not until her late teens does she acquire the analytic power of mind to move from gut reaction to the beginnings of conscious understanding of working-class womanhood in the United States. Later her education broadens: She questions her U. S. identity, not just on its own terms, but as it appears to non-western people of color, a perspective the importance of which we are only beginning to realize in the 1980s. But living on the borders between the unknowing silence of the working classes and the glib articulateness of leftist circles, Marie is nowhere at home.

More than any novel I have ever read, this novel demonstrates a painful irony: that the economic and social forces that cause deprivation irreparably maim the heart and the mind even as they strenghten the will to change the world for others. Marie Rogers lives out her life struggling to act as a whole person—to give and receive love in a relationship of equality and to work against oppression—despite the image that inhabits her imagination, the image of the endless horizon where gray sea and sky meet, the image of meaninglessness and despair. Ultimately, she finds meaning and purposefulness in political work, but she remains without intimate companionship, her love relationships poisoned by her uncompromising commitment to sexual equality in a society unable to tolerate it.

First published in 1929 (and reprinted in 1935 with an introduction by Malcolm Cowley), *Daughter of Earth*'s return to print in 1973 with an afterword by Paul Lauter was a consequence of the rebirth of women's activism, and, with it, the founding of The Feminist Press. Among the first Feminist Press reprints of "lost" literature by women and quickly a classic, *Daughter of Earth* compares remarkably well with the best of the recent feminist novels written out of the compulsion to understand women's situation; it is also prescient in anticipating the questions raised and the answers given in the new anthropological, psychological, and economic scholarship about women. But, like that scholarship, *Daughter of Earth* looks backward as well, less to a literary tradition than to the radical feminist ideas on "the Woman Question" of the first decade of the 1900s. Smedley knew and corresponded with, for example, the anarchist revolutionary Emma Goldman, and shares in part the analysis presented in

Goldman's essays that women are made "compulsory vessels" in marriage *and* in prostitution; that marriage is "an insurance pact" or protection agreement of a different order than love; and that personal relations are not separate from the social structure, but mirror it.[1] Schooled in feminism as well as in European Marxist and psychoanalytic practice, and recognizing the contradictions among these perspectives, Smedley used each theory for its explanatory and therapeutic power, but embraced none as a credo.

As a literary work too *Daughter of Earth* is unusually interesting. Placed beside the best-known novels reflecting U. S. life in the World War I period—*The Great Gatsby, The Sun Also Rises, Main Street, The Sound and the Fury,* or even *Death Comes for the Archbishop*—it forces us to redefine our notions of realism. If Fitzgerald chronicled the underside of the jazz age, Hemingway expatriate decadence, Sinclair Lewis the narrow materialism of the midwestern United States, Faulkner his own emblematically incestuous southern family, and Cather the harshness of the southwestern desert, each of these did so with an attention to language and form that blunts the representation of the darker realities. "Her rude pastorals have an expansive nobility," says one critic in praise of Cather.[2] Poverty, ignorance, and class exploitation are never noble in Smedley's drab shacks beyond the tracks or in the Rockefeller-owned mining camps of the West, nor is landscape in any way responsive or nourishing. Indeed, in a haunting image (discussed below), an inexplicable crack crawls down, up, and around a delicately painted Chinese bowl marring its once perfect form. If Hemingway's or Cather's novels are like the bowl, Smedley's art is the crack.

While Smedley's realism distinguishes *Daughter of Earth* from the central tradition of U. S. literature, her work does belong within a literary genre. The themes she treats—class conflict, the strait jacket of gender expectation, liberated sexual relations, the pain of childbearing, the search for work, the development of revolutionary politics—appear in the novels of her immediate contemporaries, the leftist women writers of the twenties and thirties. Indeed, Fielding Burke's *Call Home the Heart* (1932), Josephine Herbst's *Rope of Gold* (1939), and Tess Slesinger's *The Unpossessed* (1934), three novels recently published in the The Feminist Press's Novels of the Thirties series, explore these themes. But even among her sisters in this special circle, Smedley presents the most radical and daring "reading" of childbearing: It must not happen. While other novelists present pregnancy, childbirth, and childbearing as inevitable dilemmas complicating the lives of their protagonists and exposing the sex/gender system, Smedley's protagonist aborts two pregnancies. Babies with their dependency arouse her horror, not her longing to nurture. Living in a world where women support children alone, she recognizes that only unencumbered might she seek work and demand equality in love. (The only comparable protagonist is Zora Neale Hurston's Janie in *Their Eyes Were Watching God*, but Hurston, unlike Smedley, never makes a statement about the barrier children raise to heterosexual equality. Janie inexplicably has sex but no children, a lacuna that has troubled readers.)

If thematically *Daughter of Earth* defies convention even among the works of feminist authors, it does so also in its structure. The novel appears to move from mythic to novelistic to autobiographical form roughly in accordance with the movement from childhood to young womanhood to adulthood, and this movement, while psychologically realistic, throws the reader off balance. Convention suggests that the tone and level of narrative detail should remain consistent, but they do not. Regarded in retrospect, people and events of early childhood stand out not for their narrative continuities, but for their enormous proportion—the grandmother as powerful as "an invading army," a barn-raising, the family's tent swept away by a flooding river, the sounds of physical violence. The middle years are presented more sequentially, and despite their particular twists, conform to novelistic conventions of growing up: departure from home, work, romance, education. The final chapters, in contrast, again defy formula, and present so unique a set of circumstances as to resemble a memoir. There are excursions into political analysis, details of meetings, questions from judicial proceedings, office disputes, the pedestrian trials of urban poverty, all told by a narrator on the way to becoming a journalist. These stylistically disparate sections are in part linked by repeated images from the protagonist's unconscious world depicted in standard psychoanalytic language—dreams, symbols such as fire, the horizon, and darkness. Indeed, one fascination of the book is the degree to which it asserts that the painful distortions wrought by gender and class oppression manifest themselves in a troubled sexuality, persisting from the earliest memories of childhood into adulthood. *Daughter of Earth* is a book of unique emotional and political frankness, more likely to change its readers' lives than their aesthetic theories.

I discuss below the novel's themes, then provide briefly an account of Agnes Smedley's work as a teacher, journalist, and revolutionary in the socialist circles of San Francisco, New York, and Berlin; as an observer of the Russian Revolution; as an activist in India's nationalist revolutionary movement; and, most significantly, as a participant-observer of the Chinese Revolution. Smedley was one of a handful of westerners who lived in China for most of the period between 1928 and 1941.

"The weeping of women who are wives—what is more bitter?"

Perhaps most powerful and fundamental in the education of Marie Rogers, the name Agnes Smedley gives her fictional self, is the emotional lesson she learned early in childhood: Love expressed in sex enslaves and humiliates married women. It is the toll men exact for giving economic protection to their wives. This perception punctuates the book like the refrain in a sad folk song: "The weeping of women who are wives—what is more bitter?" Sleeping in the same room as her parents, Marie is filled with "terror and revulsion" at the sounds from their bed; she learns as well that male animals cost more than female animals, that her father pays to bring a huge black stallion briefly to the field where the other horses run loose, that her father can beat her mother and desert her because she refuses to tell him how she will vote, and that he can beat her sister and threaten her aunt on a suspicion that they are "carryin' on with men" (34). But the incident that reveals most viscerally the political economy of marriage to the young Marie occurs in the family of a newly married couple to whom she is hired out as a maid. After lying around the house, the wife, Gladys, wants to return to work, but her husband sees his ability to support her as a symbol of his manhood; she is his possession to keep idle at home. Once she is "expectin'," their fights grow more bitter. The following exchange strips bare the marriage contract. "'Give me back the clothes I bought you,' he bellowed at her one day. 'Damn it, kid, you know I love you!' she begged through her tears—for now she could not go back to work even if she wished"(66).

This revelation, that women become powerless as wives and mothers, that they must produce care in exchange for food and clothes, that they must take orders and obey as a condition of the contract, forms for Marie, although at this early stage she is yet unaware of it, the kernel of her politics. For the same domination she hates in marriage she comes to hate in class relations, in party politics, in western and Japanese imperialism; but first she must experience—a key word for this novel—woman's struggle to live independently. Like most women, her guides in this endeavor are few (two), and both have their independence still in relation to men. The mythic figure of her great-aunt dominates Marie's imagination—the tall, strong tyrant with the body and mind of a man, the woman who not only controlled her children's love affairs but took a lover as well. But it is Marie's beloved aunt Helen, a prostitute, who teaches Marie the depths of society's hypocrisy about women. Despised and abused by Marie's father, Helen turns the tables on marriage, and exposes the inequalities in the institution. Helen is, in a sense, her own husband; she receives money herself, buys her own clothes, has "nice things," as she calls them (64). But although Helen can order a man out of her house and has more rights over her body than most women, to Marie she still lives out women's destiny in service to men. When she loses her sexual attractiveness, she loses her livelihood. Encountering her again as an older woman, now working in a factory, and learning to shake dice, Marie feels the awfulness of her brief existence: "Such useless pain . . . so useless . . . so useless" (218).

Among the strongest feminist scenes in literature, a series of events seal Marie's pact with herself to avoid the misery of women who are wives. On three separate occasions after her mother dies, Marie chooses to leave her drunken, brutal father and young, vulnerable brothers alone rather than assume responsibility for their care (133, 148, 185). Here the refusal to serve, obey, and care for anyone—family, father, brothers— comes to the severest test, and one about which many readers of this book have felt profoundly ambivalent. How are we to understand a passage in which the protagonist reasons that her family is no more to her than any other people; who says, "so deeply did I love them that I even forgot them . . ." (149); who chooses to study rather than to protect and care for; who separates from a comrade and husband because he orders her, weak from an abortion, to "sit up" on a city bus; who becomes a wanderer with the world for her home and the wind for her companion (211)? For a woman, such choices are a form of heroism, uncompromising

414

decisions never to allow love and servitude to be linked, and yet these are choices that repel. May women not love and care for without losing their autonomy? If the first two sections of the novel prepare us to believe that women must reject marriage and the economic dependency it brings, the final third of the novel reintroduces the quest for love. Indeed, the intellectual and emotional task that Marie Rogers sets for herself might be characterized as an attempt to resolve the contradiction between love and autonomy, the theme of much of women's recent fiction.

"When knowledge and love become one, a force has been created that nothing can break."

In the final section of the novel, the form and texture change in a way that has been disconcerting to some readers. The gripping drama of Marie's extraordinary coming-of-age among the gamblers, cowboys, miners, adventurers, and wanderers of the West might have ended with her marriage to Knut, the man who agrees to be her equal and companion. But instead, at chapter six the novel enters a new phase. If earlier Marie's teacher has been experience and her own sharp wit, now books and the critique of ideas draw her into a world which can both explain her experience and connect it with that of working people the world over. She comes slowly into history; her intellectual awakening coincides with the First World War, the growth and repression of the Communist and Socialist movements, and the Indian nationalist movement of which she becomes a part. No longer is her landscape the western desert and mountains, or even the college campus, but rather an unusual one for fiction—the New York offices of small magazines, the apartments where political meetings are held. Her subject is no longer the weeping of wives—personal stories—but economics, social history, and philosophy. And her primary realtionships are not with family and lovers, but with teachers and revolutionaries.

We have come to expect in literature by women that daily work and learning will provide a backdrop for the great subject of the novel—relationships. In the second section of *Daughter of Earth,* by contrast, work and learning dominate while lovers come and go in the backround (350). The novel enters its most obviously autobiographical phase; it is of a particular place and moment. That readers should on occasion call this section of the novel dull underscores how accustomed we are to novels of private lives, how little, particularly for our heroines, we expect a novel to chronicle the preparation for public life—the life Marie assumes here in the Indian movement and as a socialist writer, and later the life Smedley lives as a journalist and political activist. The question then of the final chapters concerns Marie's choice of the Indian movement as an intellectual and spiritual home, and the tragic irony of the event that poisons her final attempt to fuse knowledge and love, work and personal intimacy.

While Marie's first encounter with an Indian is in a sense by chance—he comes to speak at her school in the West—her attraction to him has a kind of compelling logic. A member of a subjected race, judged and humiliated for his color as well as for his ideas, he is nonetheless willing to speak out for freedom. In his isolation, he illustrates the difficulties of the life Marie is choosing for herself. A woman who has given up her family, who has divorced a companion on principle because he has once spoken to her as a wife, who steels herself against tenderness and weakness, is as much an exile in the United States as is the Hindu. She sees in him her own loneliness, her asceticism, but she does not yet understand the compelling ideas that motivate him, "the use of knowledge for good [social] ends" (256). Indeed, from her first meeting with the Scandinavians, Knut and Karin, she begins the process of intellectual development. Seeing a play with them, she is suddenly aware of the existence of abstract "ideas"; these differ from the knowledge born of experience or factual knowledge from books. "Independent thought" can be "manufactured" in the course of conversation (183). Later, in New York, she castigates herself for her inability to argue, to muster facts, figures, and diagrams, and is enraged by the power of her opponents. Under the tutelage of her gentle though demanding teacher, the Indian Sardar Ranjit Singh, however, she embraces disciplined study and begins to understand its power. Challenged to question U. S. ethnocentrism, she comes to understand, for example, how incomplete is a social history of Britain without the study of India's influence (257). Finally, through Ranjit Singh's eyes, Marie sees her own country and herself, and experiences for the first time discipline and risk for a purpose beyond her own survival. Tested time and again by the Indians—you are too "American," this movement is not an adventure, you will be hunted like an animal—Marie gains physical and intellectual power concentrating "belief and passion" in her work. And she experiences for the first time the bond of love—fatherly, comradely love that suits her because, unlike romance, it liberates rather than enslaves.

That the novel ends in the bitterness and despair of failed romance returns us full circle to the weeping of women who are wives, and this time, it is Marie who weeps. Smedley, the novelist, shapes *Daughter of Earth* to makes its final episode the parting of Marie and her Indian second husband, Anand. Marie weeps because neither she nor Anand can endure the censure of their Indian comrades, critical of Marie because *she* was raped prior to marriage by one of Anand's countrymen. Indeed, the failed search for love frames the book which begins and ends with Marie's recuperative exile from the United States. I take this to mean that despite the broad sociohistorical canvas on which it is painted, unlike many working-class novels, this one gives full weight to personal psychological need, to the power with which the unconscious shapes our destinies. The ending then provides an ironic commentary on the uses of knowledge and underscores the split between intellect and emotion, the former quality there to be honed and disciplined, the latter out of Marie's control like the horse—"white, lathering, mad" (178)—that gallops off in the moonlight. There is a terrible poignancy in the lines below which declare that one may use language for understanding—write novels, for example—but words cannot remake the past or heal the scars resulting from what one has lived through:

I do not write mere words. I write of human flesh and blood. There is hatred and a bitterness with roots in experience and conviction. Words cannot erase that experience. (246)

"Where I am not, there is happiness."

If a circular structure binds the story together as a narration, it is bound aesthetically by recurrent images which, presented as the language of the unconscious by the retrospective narrative voice, provide a second story to complement the first. There are the actual events of Marie's life, and there are the psychological mechanisms she uses to endure those events and survive. If, as she tells us, after leaving her father and brothers, after divorcing her comrade-husband, Knut, after her brother George is killed digging a ditch for a sewer, and at other points, she "draw[s] that veil of suppression and forgetfulness" (210) or she wishes her memory "dead" (236), now, to write the novel, she must draw back the veil again. Indeed, the novel itself is the process of remembering. And that memory comes back triggered by recurrent images.

Marie's mother and her family, for example, are icons of dejection associated with the gaping cracks in the floor (65, 148), the earth that swallows up its own. The quality of her own freedom, and, with it, loneliness, exist in the haunting domestic image of the world as a "home" and the wind as a "companion." And in the terrifying scene in which she is raped, Juan Diaz appears in the image of a great swooping bird pf prey, the same bird that appears over the gray sea in the opening lines, and that might be contrasted with the small gray bird that sings harmlessly in the dawn. But there is one image of terrible power which occurs late in the book and comes to symbolize, as Marie has said earlier, the "bitter harvest that a harsh and distorted society had sown within [her]" (193), the harvest that destroys her love relations. She dreams:

> I stood contemplating a bowl in my outstretched hand . . . a beautifully shaped flower bowl, curved gently, broad and low, and about it was painted a wreath of flowers as delicate as all the art of ancient China. So beautiful and delicate it was that I held it far from me to see it shimmer as a ray of sunlight fell upon it. As I stood wondering at its beauty, a crack crawled down the side, to the bottom, up and around to the top again, and the broken fragment rolled over and lay on my palm. I had not broken the bowl . . . nobody had broken it . . . but it was broken, irrevocably broken by something I knew not what. (376)

Here is the magic and the tragedy of *Daughter of Earth*. The bowl recalls the opening pages of the novel: "I belong to those who do not die for beauty," the narrator tells us, "I belong to those who die for other causes—exhausted by poverty, victims of wealth and power, fighters in a great cause. . . . Our struggle is of the earth" (4). While the dream suggests Marie's recognition that she will never experience love—the perfect beauty of the bowl— it suggests as well that the crack is in the nature of things, not in her own control. Because she is strong and of the earth, however, the despair for lost beauty will not prevail.

"Work that is limitless in its scope and significance, is not this enough to weigh against love?"

In the autobiographical first chapters of *Battle Hymn of China* written some decade-and-a-half after *Daughter of Earth,* Smedley asserts that friendship, not sex, is the chief bond between men and women. Echoing one theme of *Daughter of Earth,* she declares marriage "at its best an economic investment; at its worst, a relic of human slavery." Comprehending that no society has solved this problem, she reveals that she will dedicate herself to the non-western world where "people were struggling with the rudest forces of nature to build a new world of their own choosing." The account of her personal life, the narrative that underlies *Daughter of Earth,* ends in 1928 as Smedley's train passes into the Soviet Union, the first socialist country. Before the "rough-hewn" customs station on the Polish border stands a Red Army guard, "silent and watchful, facing the Western world." "In such a position," Smedley muses, "had once stood the men who had founded my own country." Smedley will dedicate the rest of her life to fighting for a great cause alongside people who do not wish to repeat the mistakes of the United States. And she will write always with a special sensitivity to the plight of women everywhere, and with an insistence on women's need for economic independence.

As if the years covered in *Daughter of Earth* are not enough, when one contemplates the courage and the contribution of the decades Smedley spent in China and the Soviet Union, one is astounded. I can only suggest here in the briefest outline the life that was Agnes Smedley's.[3] Book I of *Battle Hymn of China* recounts the years chronicled in *Daughter of Earth* with small variation: The years after her mother's death were spent in "semi-vagabondage" (her word); then Smedley attended Tempe Normal School (now Arizona State University) from 1911 to 1912 and there met the Swedes Ernest and Thorburg Brundin. Ernest became her first husband; brother and sister remained her lifelong friends. Smedley spent the years 1917–20 in New York as a night student at New York University, writing for the socialist paper *The Call* and for Margaret Sanger's *Birth Control Review*. As in the novel, she was arrested as a spy because of her association with Indian nationalists and spent six months in prison in the Tombs where she wrote her first short pieces, *Cell Mates*. (Because the British were U. S. allies in the First World War, anyone working against the British—to free India from Britain—was considered a traitor.) However, when she was released from prison, she did not, as in the novel, resume her work in New York; rather she shipped out as a stewardess for Europe with a vague notion of joining Indian exiles in Berlin. The tragic relation with the revolutionary leader Virendranath Chattopadhyaya, Anand in *Daughter of Earth*, actually took place there.

More important, however, than location is Smedley's emotional state. In the novel she conflates the impact of prison and the failed relationship; in actuality, the prison term leads her to flee from the country where her brothers had lived "like animals without protection or education," where she saw middle-class men and women completing school, starting careers with protection and guidance while she slaved by day and strove by night "for some kind of meager education . . . and a shabby hall bedroom." Several years later, the end of her relation with Viren forces her to turn her unhappiness upon herself. Smedley writes of this period, "The circumstances of my youth, combined with the endless difficulties of my life with Virendranath in Germany, drove me to the verge of insanity . . . once I attempted suicide."[4] After two years of psychoanalysis with an associate of Freud's (a woman), and with the writing of *Daughter of Earth,* Smedley regained her equilibrium, but, the MacKinnons (see note 3) tell us, "Smedley would never again join a political organization nor become emotionally dependent on a man."

With the exception of trips to the Soviet Union to rest and regain her health, and to New York to seek, unsuccessfully, a writing job, Smedley lived in China from 1928 to 1941. While she contributed much to the Chinese revolution as an organizer and field worker for the Chinese Red Cross, and as a nurse in the Red Army, her unique contribution was as a journalist with an independent voice and an unwavering sympathy for the peasants and workers who, like her brothers and sisters, were of the earth. During her first five years in China, Smedley lived in Shanghai and reported for the *Frankfurter Zeitung,* the *Manchester Guardian,* the *Nation,* the *New Republic,* the *New Masses,* and other U. S. journals. One of the few westerners to understand and seek to explain the complex events sweeping China—the Kuomintang's persecution of Communists, the Japanese imperialist threat, the brutal exploitation of factory workers—Smedley wrote always with her eyes fixed on the daily lives of workers and peasants, and particularly on the footbound and large-footed women.

In 1936, Smedley moved to the Communist capital, Yenan, and using her power as a reporter, urged westerners to see China and the revolution for themselves. Later she marched from Yenan with the Red Army; she reported on that struggle in *China Fights Back: An American Woman with the Eighth Route Army* (1938). After Hankow fell to the Japanese in 1938,[5] Smedley began her most intense and dangerous reportorial mission—several years marching with the Communist-led new Fourth Army. This story is told in her book of war reportage, *Battle Hymn of China* (1943). A section of this book recounting Smedley's desire to adopt a Chinese boy assigned by the army to care for her appeared in a collection edited by Ernest Hemingway, *Men at War*. In 1940, her health again failing, Smedley left the army, flew over the Japanese lines to Hong Kong, and returned to her estranged family in San Diego. Through the forties, Smedley continued to write and lecture about China in the United States, to enjoy the many and varied friendships that grew from her years in China with reporters such as Edgar Snow and Jack Belden, and to form relationships with writers such as Katherine Anne Porter and Carson McCullers. Although independent of party affiliation all her life—and sometimes criticized for it—during the political scares of the late forties Smedley was accused in a U. S. Army report of having been a Soviet spy since the thirties. Unable to find anyone who would risk hiring her, she could not support herself, and, with news of the Communist victory in China in 1949, she set out to return there. While awaiting a visa in London, she became ill, and on May 6, 1950, she died during an operation for ulcers, at the age of fifty-eight.

Only in China was her death an occasion for public mourning. There her lifelong friends, the writers Ting-Ling and Mao Tun, contributed lead articles about her in the daily papers. The MacKinnons report that in 1960 Chou En-lai opened his first interview in twenty years with Edgar Snow by saluting Agnes Smedley and Franklin Roosevelt. And much more recently, Florence Howe, Director of The Feminist Press, recounts in her afterword to *Portraits of Chinese Women in Revolution* that, going through customs in China in 1975 with books from The Feminist Press including *Daughter of Earth,* she was stopped by a Chinese official who seemed dismayed by the many volumes. As Howe attempted to describe Smedley as a friend of China and the biographer of Chu Teh, a floor sweeper popped up from behind a counter. His description of "Aganessa Schmedaleya" allayed all suspicion; smiling, the official asked, "You are a teacher?" "Yes," Howe replied, "I teach about Aganessa Schmedaleya." While the resurgence of the women's movement, an active Left, and the opening of China have increased interest in Smedley in the United States, unfortunately it is still unlikely that a U.S. airport could produce a worker who knew *Daughter of Earth.*

NANCY HOFFMAN
University of Massachusetts/Boston

Notes

1. Key Goldman essays are "The Tragedy of Woman's Emancipation," "Marriage and Love," and "The Traffic in Women" from Emma Goldman, *Red Emma Speaks: Selected Writing and Speeches*, compiled and edited by Alix Kates Shulman (New York: Vintage Books, 1972).

2. Mark Schorer, *The Literature of America: Twentieth Century* (New York: McGraw-Hill Book Company, 1970).

3. For many of the details in the following pages, I am indebted to Jan MacKinnon's and Steve MacKinnon's reconstruction of Smedley's biography which forms the introduction to their collection of Smedley's short pieces, *Portraits of Chinese Women in Revolution* (Old Westbury, NY: The Feminist Press, 1976). Smedley's literary estate is in China, uncatalogued and unavailable to the public.

4. Agnes Smedley, *Battle Hymn of China* (New York: Alfred A. Knopf, 1943), 17–18.

5. See Andre Malraux, *Man's Fate* (New York: Random House, 1961) for another account.

Books and Pamphlets by Agnes Smedley

India and the Next War. Amritsar, 1928.

Daughter of Earth. New York: Coward-McCann, Inc., 1929. Reprinted in a shortened version with an introduction by Malcolm Cowley, New York: Coward-McCann, Inc., 1935.

Chinese Destinies: Sketches of Present-Day China. New York: The Vanguard Press, 1933.

China's Red Army Marches. New York: The Vanguard Press, 1934. Also published as *Red Flood Over China.* Moscow and Leningrad: Co-operative Publishing Society of Foreign Workers in the U.S.S.R., 1934.

China Fights Back, An American Woman with the Eighth Route Army. New York: The Vanguard Press, 1938.

Stories of the Wounded; An Appeal for Orthopaedic Centres of the Chinese Red Cross. Hong Kong: Newspaper Enterprises, 1941.

Battle Hymn of China. New York: Alfred A. Knopf, 1943.

The Great Road; The Life and Times of Chu Teh. New York: Monthly Review Press, 1956.

REDISCOVERED CLASSICS OF AMERICAN WOMEN'S FICTION
from The Feminist Press at The City University of New York

Brown Girl, Brownstones (1959), by Paule Marshall. $10.95 paper.

Call Home the Heart (1932), by Fielding Burke. $9.95 paper.

Daddy Was a Number Runner (1970), by Louise Meriwether. $10.95 paper.

Daughter of Earth (1929), by Agnes Smedley. $14.95 paper.

Doctor Zay (1882), by Elizabeth Stuart Phelps. $8.95 paper.

Fettered for Life (1874), by Lillie Devereux Blake. $18.95 paper, $45.00 cloth.

Guardian Angel and Other Stories (1932), by Margery Latimer. $8.95 paper.

I Love Myself When I Am Laughing: A Zora Neale Hurston Reader, edited by Alice Walker. $14.95 paper.

Life in the Iron Mills and Other Stories (1861), by Rebecca Harding Davis. $10.95 paper.

The Living Is Easy (1948), by Dorothy West. $14.95 paper.

Not So Quiet . . . Stepdaughters of War (1930), by Helen Zenna Smith. $11.95 paper, $35.00 cloth.

Now in November (1934), by Josephine W. Johnson. $10.95 paper, $29.95 cloth.

Quest (1922), by Helen R. Hull. $11.95 paper.

This Child's Gonna Live (1969), by Sarah E. Wright. $10.95 paper.

The Unpossessed (1934), by Tess Slesinger. $16.95 paper.

Unpunished: A Mystery (1929), by Charlotte Perkins Gilman. $10.95 paper, $18.95 jacketed hardcover.

Weeds (1923), by Edith Summers Kelley. $15.95 paper.

The Wide, Wide World (1850), by Susan Warner. $19.95 paper, $35.00 cloth.

The Yellow Wall-Paper (1892), by Charlotte Perkins Gilman. $5.95 paper.

To receive a free catalog of The Feminist Press's 150 titles, call or write The Feminist Press at The City University of New York, Wingate Hall/City College, New York, NY 10031; phone: (212) 650-8966; fax: (212) 650-8869. Feminist Press books are available at bookstores, or can be ordered directly. Send check or money order (in U.S. dollars drawn on a U.S. bank) payable to The Feminist Press. Please add $4.00 shipping and handling for the first book and $1.00 for each additional book. VISA, Mastercard, and American Express are accepted for telephone orders. Prices subject to change.